Scott Crawford, born in Fleet, Hants, the second son of an army family, attended Liverpool College in his early days, with attendance severely limited by health problems. During those months, his uncle, a dour Scot, with great patience taught him to read and write, and stimulated his imagination with Greek legends that, as a school inspector, he had compiled for children.

As his health steadily improved, Scott resumed his education at St Edward's School, Oxford. Upon leaving, he joined the Royal Engineers and qualified as an electrical and mechanical engineer at the School of Military Engineering. Subsequently, in civilian life, he became a consulting engineer.

As a result of his uncle's tutelage, books became his constant companion and refuge, particularly during frequent long and tedious flights to all parts of the world. In this, he is indebted to those authors who, by their craft, welcomed him into their own world of make-believe and emotion, and he hopes that his first novel will offer his readers quiet moments of enjoyment and, yes, although only a novel, stimulating controversy.

THE KA OF ISIS

THE KA OF ISIS

Scott Crawford

ATHENA PRESS
LONDON

THE KA OF ISIS
Copyright © Scott Crawford 2006

ISBN 1 84401 669 2

First Published 2006 by
ATHENA PRESS
Queen's House, 2 Holly Road
Twickenham TW1 4EG
United Kingdom

Printed for Athena Press

This book was conceived from the experiences of a large number of overseas visits, lasting for periods of between one and three years, to such places as Palestine, Jordan Valley, the Dead Sea, Aqabah, Egypt and Mexico.

The impressions of those visits have been fixed like a series of snapshots in my mind, but until the present time I had no intention to incorporate them into a framework for writing a novel.

Please remember this is fiction and does not pretend to be anything else.

For Charlotte, in recognition of her support and contributions.

Contents

Foreword

In my office I have a bejewelled statue of Isis which influences or commands my thoughts, which are now concentrated on the myths and fancies passed up through the ages by three hundred and forty-five generations of Egyptian high priests, in order to explain the origin of the Gods who they believed founded their religion.

Generally, most ancient myths have been established by some incident, the story around which becomes embellished over time. In this case, the myth of the children of the Sun (Ra or Atum) founding the Egyptian religion and, after death, returning to the stars, or, in the case of Osiris, ruling over the Kingdom of the Dead, was possibly, at that time, acceptable fantasy. However, I suggest that the myth of Osiris, Isis, Seth and Nephthys was based on the arrival of an immigrant family, whose culture, knowledge and size made them appear like Gods to the locals, and doubtless that acceptance was encouraged.

This particular cult was probably initiated by the early deaths of Osiris and Seth and then the priests developed the story to suit and embellish their religion, to the amusement of the Atlans, who possibly manipulated it to subjugate the natives.

Having read the Egyptian story of their Gods in numerous books, it seemed sensible for me to construct a story explaining a possible reason for the arrival of the immigrants in Egypt. There is no pretence that any of my reconstruction is based on firm facts, but rather on selected information that is well known to those interested in the period. Hopefully, the general approach will generate thought and discussion amongst my readers, and stir interest in the period between 5500 and 3500 BC. Hopefully, it will also relate to events during that period with regard to the Mayan Prophecy concerning the termination of their civilization.

To begin with, it was necessary to find a country that had a substantial land mass ("Solon suggested a land mass larger than Asia minor"), and a cataclysm that could have killed or dispersed a large population. The flooding of the continental shelf round Sumatra and

Indonesia at the close of the Little Ice Age in 5500 BC seemed to be a reasonable choice for the Atlantis of myth or the "Atlan" of my story.

Assuming the floods recorded in both the Bible and the Mesopotamian *Gilgamesh Epic* occurred in approximately 5500 BC, apparently the same date as the Black Sea flood, then it is also reasonable to consider that prior to that time there existed a race of giants – see Genesis 6:4. However, as the average height of the natives in the Middle East around that time was about 1.4 metres, the presence of a race of people averaging 2.2 metres in height would surely qualify as giants. Today we would refer to them simply as "tall", and only remarkable when they played basketball.

For my story, the population of that ideal community is assumed to have been sufficiently strong and stable over the previous six thousand years; necessary in order for them to prevent attacks from their neighbours who lived inland in the mountainous areas. Until the approach of the expected cataclysm they had been prosperous and lived in peace, with an abhorrence of technical development for which they had no requirement in a land of plenty.

Evidence from the ancient history of the Indian continent suggested to Atlan that excessive technical development inevitably led to conflict; the conduct of their society was formulated to prevent that direction of development.

In Mexico the Maya historical records refer to a number of civilizations proceeding up to the present and assert that each one was preceded by a cataclysm, and, according to *Breaking the Maya Code* by Michael D Coe, it is alleged they calculated a date for their present civilization to end as 23 December, 2012, a period of 5,126 years from the time when the Maya calendar was initiated in 3114 BC! But I am not aware of any evidence that links the start of their calendar with the occurrence of their previous cataclysm. In fact, it is more likely that it would have taken many generations for the few survivors to re-establish an effective community, with the essential social structure capable of devoting time to matters of this nature. In addition, it would be necessary to rebuild their centres of astronomy to calculate a final date for the next occurrence to that degree of accuracy.

If we accept that the forecasted cataclysm is based on a number of cataclysms occurring at fixed intervals, it is reasonable to assume they were caused by astronomical incidents that, by their nature, could provide a precise date when a large asteroid might pass the earth's orbit sufficiently close to cause catastrophic conditions.

It might be that their calculation, together with their astronomical expertise, calendar and form of writing were obtained from the Olmecs who, judging from their sculptures, appear to be Negroid and of the African Continent.

Recently, the earliest known date of Maya presence in Izapa, Mexico, has been extended to 1200 BC and the Olmecs were also in that area at that time. This link with Africa may also provide a connection with Egypt and could explain the similarity of the alignment and base dimensions of the Pyramid of the Sun at Teotihuacán outside Mexico City, and the Cheops Pyramid on the east bank of the Nile in Egypt. In accepting this assumption it seems reasonable to connect the Mayan Prophecy to the Ethiopians in Africa as well as the Egyptians.

Ethiopia, the country in which Isis and Thoth sought refuge from the wrath of Seth, was known at that time as Punt, the Divine Land of Legend. For reference purposes I called it Ethiopia. For our story we have assumed a relationship between Punt, Cush and the Olmecs.

My choice of 5500 BC, the time of the Small Ice Age, has a number of incidents that reinforces my selection of that date as a suitable one to adopt for my story. For example:

Jericho (Ariha) in 8000 BC had a population of three thousand living in enclosed settlements, the occupants existing by cultivating the land. In 7000 BC they started to manufacture pottery. In 5500 BC the area was abandoned and remained so for the next five hundred years.

Studying a space photograph of the area from Aqabah on the Gulf to Lake Tiberius, the line of the strike-slip fault stands out and suggests that, like the flooding of the Black Sea during a period of earthquakes and associated plate movements, there could have been flooding of the Dead Sea via the Gulf of Aqabah. The flood could have been finally curtailed either by the fast current displacing the sand banks at the entrance to the Gulf and depositing them in an area of velocity pressure exchange some one hundred kilometres north of Aqabah, or by plate movements in the area – or both. It is interesting to note that fresh water can be obtained just below the surface of the sand on the seashore at Aqabah. When digging deep wells two metres in diameter one kilometre north of Aqabah, the fresh water aquifer level was similar to sea level. But there was no evidence of rocks at that level – only the presence of Sheba's gold (disappointingly, small particles of iron pyrites).

The depth of seawater off Aqabah is some two hundred metres on the east side of the Gulf and this increases intermittently down its length to depths of one thousand metres plus. At the present time the land is below sea level for some fifty kilometres south of the Dead Sea.

The main problem with my proposal in the book is to determine how the land was lifted above sea level from Aqabah, before rising slowly for one hundred kilometres, then descending rapidly down the Wadi el Jeib. Was it a plate movement due to the earthquakes occurring at the time of the destruction of Sodom and Gomorrah circa 1900 BC?

If we accept that before the Little Ice Age the sea level was approximately twenty to thirty metres below present levels, then the Gulf of Suez would have been a series of sand banks and shallows that would not have encouraged trading by that sea route. Taking this into account, my story (which is fiction) selects Quseir as the trading post with the shortest route to the Nile.

The selection of Sumatra – apart from considerations of its massive landmass at that period – was based on the position of the North Equatorial current and Indian counter-current. This feature would have facilitated trading with the African mainland and also the provision of easy access to the Red Sea and the Persian Gulf.

The fact that the area around Qena on the Nile has evidence of Dynasty One and Dynasty Zero occupation, together with the sudden arrival of a writing system, tends to support my assessment of events. For that reason I selected Quseir as the entry into Egypt for the Asian group fleeing the impending cataclysm, on the basis it was the shortest possible route to the Nile.

At that time, prior to the flood, the surface area of the Red Sea was possibly twenty per cent less than it is today. Also the width of the straits between Aden and Eritrea would have been reduced by approximately fifty per cent making the straits not much more than ten kilometres wide – less than the Straits of Gibraltar (known in antiquity as The Pillars of Hercules) which were apparently taken as the gateway to Atlantis by Plato, and frequently been quoted by others as a fixed point in that fable.

The landing point of the Mesopotamian group at Bashi on the north-east side of the Persian Gulf was selected by taking into account the sea level prior to the cold snap in 6000 BC which, it is believed, produced the largest flood within the previous five and a half million years.

When considering Seth's flight from Kou Senjaq in the Zagros Mountains to the Mediterranean coast, it was difficult to determine how much damage might have been caused by the cataclysm and the effect on the local farming communities. Certainly the Northern Triangle had been heavily populated between 10000 BC and 4000 BC. By 8000 BC fruit and grain were being harvested over that period, but it was difficult to determine what occurred between the Tigris and the Euphrates around 5500 BC.

However, for the story it is assumed that the main damage from the cataclysm was suffered just below the Equator in the Southern Hemisphere. The effect was reduced as the results of that devastation entered into the Northern Hemisphere, accompanied by earthquakes and plate movements.

Should you consider the story you are about to read is completely untenable, then kindly refer to Isis! For my part it is a flight of fancy in an attempt to make my story preferable to the original myths, and hopefully to reject the mistaken ideas some people hold firmly as regards aliens, multiple gods, and technically adept Atlantians.

Please note the transporter in the story did *not* belong to the Atlan people; they bought it a long time ago from another community.

With regards to measurements in the book, it seemed appropriate to use the Egyptian forms of measurement for the period of 5500 BC, and these are as follows:

- 1 standard cubit = 46 cm = 0.46 m (Royal cubit = 52.4 cm not used in this book)
- 1 khet = 100 sq cubits
- 1 itru = 5000 cubits = 2300 m = 2.3 km
- 6 spans = 1 cubit; 1 span = 7.7 cm
- 24 digits (fingers) = 1 cubit = 1.92 cm (28 to Royal cubit)
- 10 kites = 1 deben; 10 debens = 1 sep
- Liquid – cubic cubit = 0.14 cubic m or 37 US gallons

List of Ancient Characters

RERA, Sun God

RAIE, President of Atlan, High Lord

OSIRIS, High Lord, Leader of Egyptian Expedition

ISIS, High Lord, Member of the High Council

SETH, High Lord, Leader of the Mesopotamian Expedition

THOTH, High Priest

LEDA, Personal Attendant to Isis, later Hathor

BAKH, Captain of the *Sea Owl*

BATA, Sailing Master of the *Sea Owl*

HEKT, Lookout of the *Sea Owl*

TETI, Captain of the *Sothis*

ZESI, Pirate and Giant

AMLE, Captain of the *Sea Eagle*

JELR, Captain of the *Sea Fury*

AWELIN, Astronomer

AESTAD, Lord of Sea Trading

ZON, Controller, Trading Centre, Quseir

TESH, Assistant to Controller, Quseir

SHIVA, Companion of Seth

ENKI, Companion of Seth

HETI, Companion of Seth

SHEHA, King of Ethiopia

List of Characters

RICHARD MCKAY (RICKY), Expedition Sponsor and Leader

YAX NIXTE, Leading Maya and Archaeologist

MARIA MARTINEZ, Double Agent

DUNCAN MCNISH, Hale University

KIRK FREHIER, Retired Lecturer on Archaeology

CAPTAIN JAMES GRENAVEAR, RN, Disposals

JOHN GODDARD, Neighbour and Ricky's friend

PTAH SANI, Last of the Giants

JAMES WHITE (BLANCO), RN Retd., Ship Selection and Captain

JAMES FOLEY, Attaché, Indonesia

RASHID, Ship's Chandler, Jakarta, Indonesia

VERNON DRINMEAD, Archaeologist, Opposition

MOHAMMED ISMAIL, Indonesian member of the Expedition

DAVID CARTWRIGHT, Financial Director

LIEUTENANT AMIN ADOUD, Indonesian Navy

SUSAN SLADE, Secretary

MUSTAFA HASSID, Egyptian Minister for Ancient Archaeology

ABDEL HASSID, joined in Cairo, Student Archaeologist

LIEUTENANT ASHRIF SADAR, Parachute Regiment, Egyptian Army

KINUW NIXTE, Ka of Maria Martinez

WAK TUYUE, Senior Maya Member of the Opposition; adopts Sax Kinuw and becomes President

SAX KINUW, marries Richard McKay

POPUL YIPJAY, Senior Maya Member of the Opposition; becomes Minister of Defence

ALACRAN, Commander of the Maya Resistance; known as the Scorpion

AUISPAS, Commander of the Maya Resistance; known as the Wasp

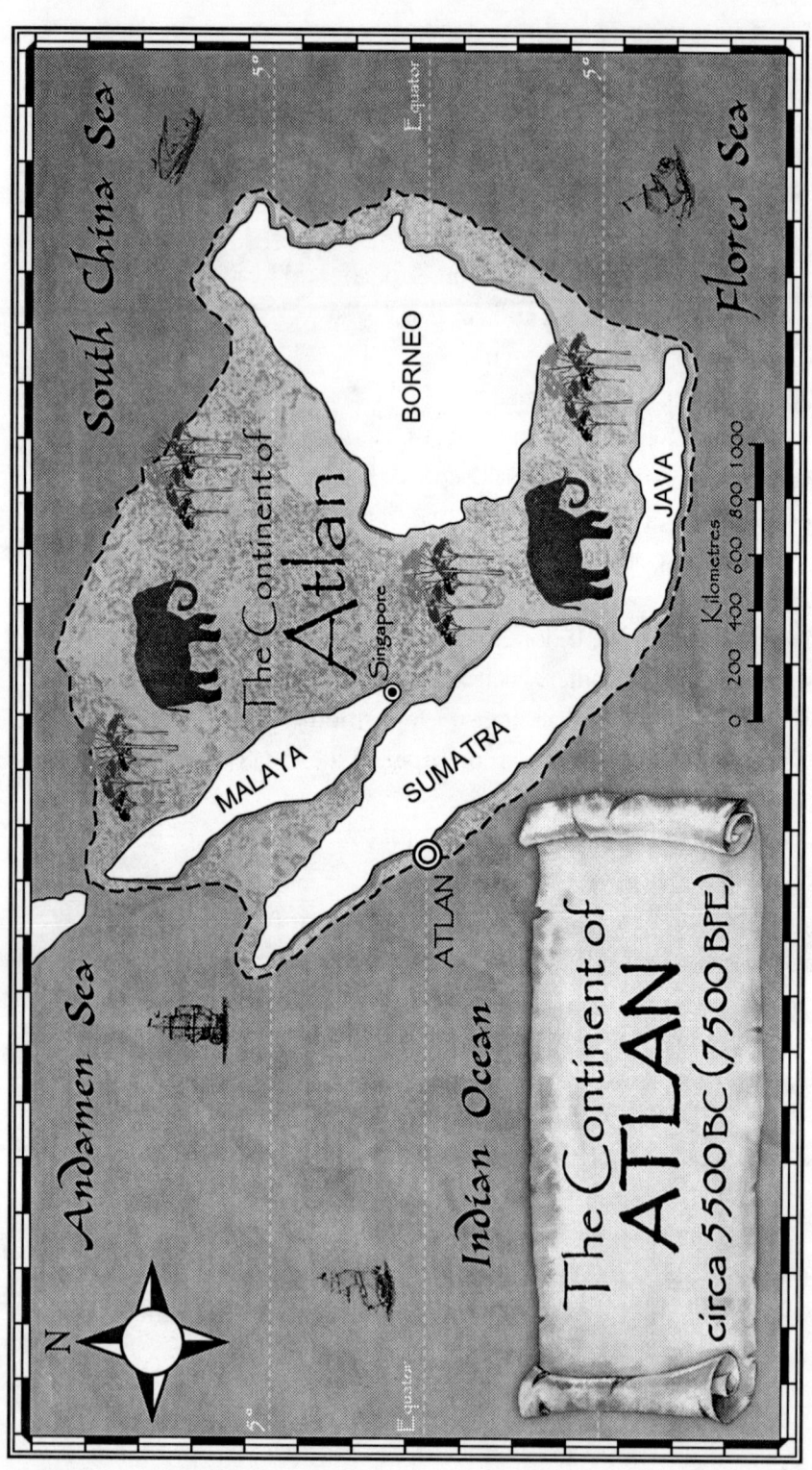

The Continent of
ATLAN
circa 5500 BC (7500 BPE)

The Council

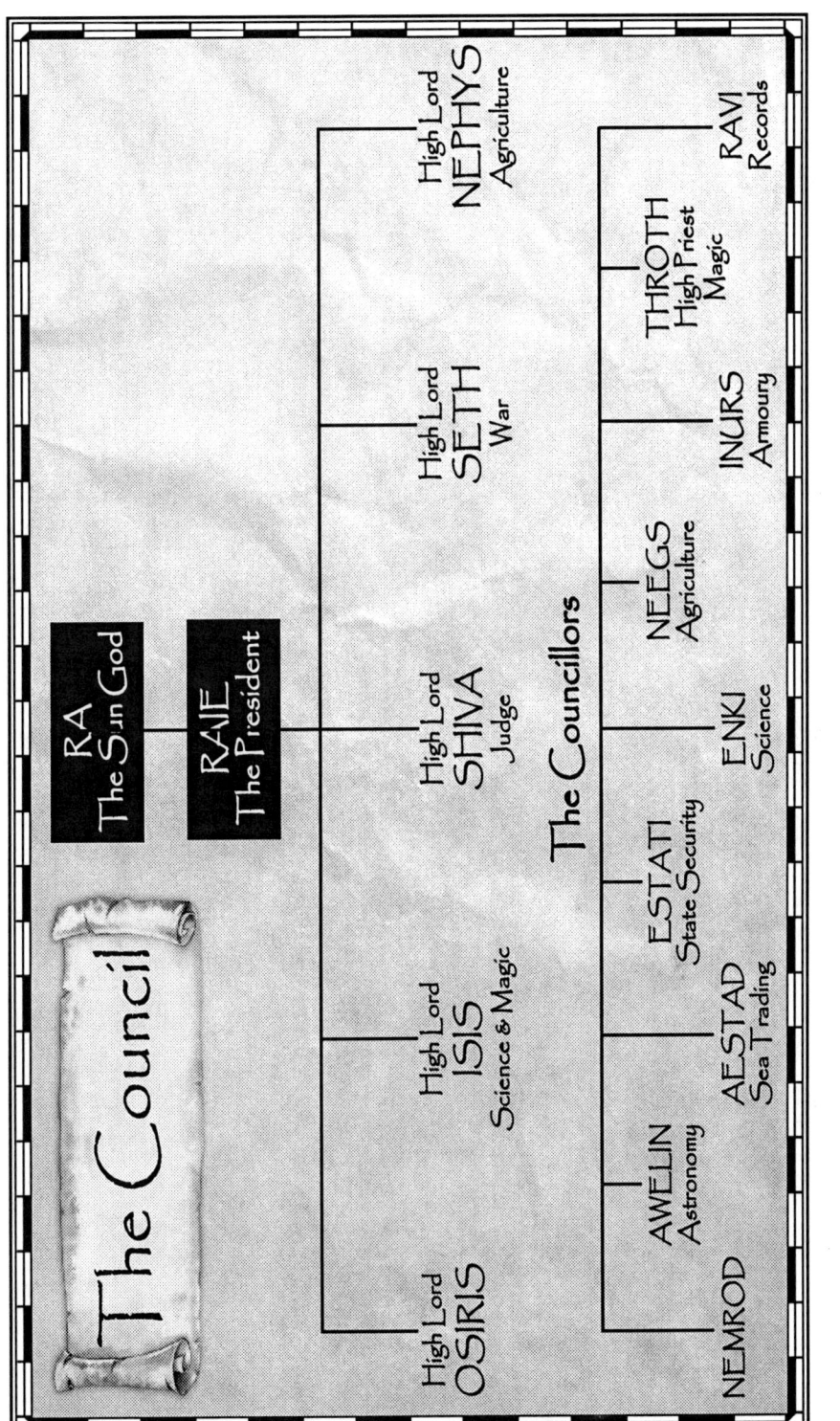

RA
The Sun God

RAJE
The President

High Lord
OSIRIS

High Lord
ISIS
Science & Magic

High Lord
SHIVA
Judge

High Lord
SETH
War

High Lord
NEPHYS
Agriculture

The Councillors

NEMROD

AWELIN
Astronomy

AESTAD
Sea Trading

ESTATI
State Security

ENKI
Science

NEEGS
Agriculture

INURS
Armoury

THROTH
High Priest
Magic

RAVI
Records

Escape from Atlan

5500 BC

> There were giants in the earth in those days; and also after that, when the sons of God came in unto the daughters of men, and they bare children to them, the same became mighty men which were of old, men of renown.
>
> Gen. 6:4 (King James Version)

The light and warmth of the sun slowly disappeared over the vast blue horizon, and the moon raised her pale head to help dispel the night's dark clasp on the world of her children below.

As the last droplets of the sun's rays caressed the sea's surface, the blues and greens of the bay rejoiced in their coming and danced like glittering diamonds in the slowly darkening space above. But, however beautiful this sight was to her companion, nothing could compare to the earthbound star standing close to him. Looking across the bay, watching the water run over on the silver sand, the eyes of the High Lord Isis were full of tears.

Standing at his side, five and a half cubits tall and perfectly proportioned, her long raven black hair set ashine by the last rays of the evening sun now enhanced her high forehead. No longer restricted by the heavy golden bejewelled clasps, flung aside on the warm rich earth, her hair flowed free in the thyme-scented wind, which washed over her like the waves on the shore below.

Her eyes, a light sparkling green, were outlined, as was the fashion, with kohl to emphasise her Asian origin; and against her cream complexion, she looked as dramatic as the world around her.

Clad in a diaphanous white robe, embroidered with the constellation of Orion's Belt in diamonds and emeralds, a white-skin girdle accentuated her hips. Delicately decorating her feet were soft doeskin sandals, encrusted with precious stones on the cross-straps.

At twenty-seven years of age, she was still considered young by her people, who in general lived for at least eight hundred years.

Thoth was standing behind her, guarding her precious moment of freedom with determination. At thirty-eight he was already a High Priest of the Sun God and a Wise Magician. Not handsome and less than four and a quarter cubits tall, his contemporaries regarded him almost as a dwarf. Only by superior intelligence did he achieve general acceptance as an important Councillor, and from that position became her honoured friend.

By birth, Isis was a High Lord. The close friendship was unusual but in spite of this social division, he remained devoted to her and considered himself her protector.

The two of them gazed down on the massive harbour block walls built by the Ancients some eleven thousand years ago, its deep-water entry into the city warehouses and shipyards; constructed to maintain and protect its merchant ships, which ceaselessly traded throughout the known world.

The pure white quartz-chipped roofs of the houses picked up the colours of the sunset, and beyond these the public buildings with their gold and silver cladding dazzled the eye. This exemplified the wealth of the state, accumulated over the past six thousand years from their mines, which had consistently produced gold, silver, copper and tin in substantial quantities.

Isis turned to Thoth, using her familiar name for him. "Zu, it is all so beautiful, and I feel heartbroken to realise that our peaceful society, having existed for five and a half thousand years since the cataclysmic termination of the previous civilization, must be lost when the Prophecy is fulfilled."

"I believe it is inevitable, as all the signs are there – the recent increase in sea levels, the unpredictable changes in climate, shortage of food, shipping losses due to storms and icebergs across the trading routes. As a result, for the first time in memory the general population is becoming frightened and restless."

"Zu, I have been informed that the Lord Protector Raie has convened a meeting for tomorrow morning."

"Where?"

"In the Great Hall of his official residence."

"Why on earth did he choose that location?"

"Those massive granite blocks are practically impregnable."

Thoth shook his head. "We have seen granite blocks fall down before."

"You forget, Zu, the blocks are held together with silver bronze ties; this building has survived all the cataclysms – why not another?"

Thoth chuckled. "Doubtless he has that in mind!" He paused. "At least our recent expedition in the northern mountain range may strengthen the Council's belief in the existence of the previous civilization."

"Zu, I hope it will, but at least half the Council has always dismissed that possibility, and Seth's group will ignore, or discount, any evidence we produce at the meeting."

"Yes, but what a once in a lifetime experience, to establish our link to an earlier civilization, previously dismissed as a myth."

"Anyway, we will know the answer tomorrow!"

After standing a while in comfortable companionship, drinking in the overpowering view, Isis, slowly turning from the city, said, 'Zu, do you remember that brilliant autumn morning when we set out from camp on the trip into the high mountain range to prospect for minerals? When the air was so clear and crisp as we followed that gurgling stream up the mountain?" she added hesitantly.

Thoth smiled to himself, still looking over the vast city, and replied, with a sense of humour in his voice, "Of course, my Lord. It was such a wonderful time... I can remember every detail," he murmured, as he turned his face towards the endless, shadowy mountains. He, like his Lord, was remembering the vibrant scent of the mountain flowers, the strong wash of the wind as they climbed upwards into the heights, everything...

The light breeze, accompanied by the joyful sounds of birds in the lush undergrowth, was enriched by a continual whisper of the stream as it gurgled and trickled happily over a series of small cascades. Despite the heavy packs, loads of tools and maps, and the long trek up the slope to reach the rock face, the small party had enjoyed every precious moment of freedom away from the suffocating responsibilities of work and life in the city of Atlan.

As they steadily covered the distance, Zu turned to Isis.

"The other day I was fascinated watching urgent works being carried out in the Atlan shipyards, where two of the cargo ships being built for Osiris are nearing completion. I wondered if he had mentioned them to you, in particular whether the work is in any way connected with the Prophecy?"

"Zu, he told me that with the Prophecy in mind, partitions are being fitted in the second cargo hold of both ships to carry passengers. In addition, they are enclosing the stems in a copper tin composite to reinforce the bows, and this essential precaution will provide some protection from ice and debris for the ships. I then realised that manufacturing the stem claddings had exhausted all available stocks of tin and copper, and that is why the High Council permitted our foray into the mountains to search for new deposits."

On reaching the rock face, they removed their packs, and after a quick glance at the site, Isis said, "Zu, it does not look too hopeful. I suggest we separate and check the rocks for a couple of hours, then return to our packs. If you look higher up on the mountain face, you will see signs of a major landslide. If you are agreeable after our brief survey here, let's make that our new site."

"While this site is both unattractive and difficult to examine, we should make a brief survey for the record. I agree the other location is far more interesting, so let's limit this search area to one and a half hours, then climb up to the landslide site."

As they expected there was nothing to be found, so picking up their packs, they started a steep climb up a goat track. Eventually the track unexpectedly came to an abrupt end and they found themselves above the landslide.

Looking down over a sheer drop, they discovered a large shelf sticking out from the rock face, and, on one side, it curved away into a deep ravine. Searching for access to the shelf, Isis noticed that at the end of the shelf nearest to them there was a very narrow goat track leading up to the path they had just traversed.

Isis, full of enthusiasm, shouted, "Zu! Come on, let's go down."

"No! It is far too dangerous."

The warning was too late as Isis was already on the way down, shouting, "Come on, Zu, I have the food and I am famished!"

When they both arrived on the shelf, a repentant Isis apologised.

"I am so sorry, Zu – that was far too dangerous; at several places I was absolutely petrified! I promise to wait in future until we have an agreed route. Am I forgiven?"

"Of course, let us forget it. There is a wonderful view from here so please produce the promised meal, and providing it is acceptable, total forgiveness is guaranteed!"

They settled down to have their midday picnic on the shelf, where, after a brief rest, they planned to study the area of broken rock face.

While the shelf was still in shadow they started by making a quick survey, and halfway along they came across a number of heavy boulders packed against the rock face, which blocked the way to the larger and more interesting side of the shelf.

"Zu, impress me with your great strength by rolling that massive boulder over the cliff to provide access to the far side."

"It's not large enough for a really impressive demonstration!"

Then, wrapping his arms around the boulder, Thoth swung it out from the cliff face, over the edge of the shelf and sent it thundering down the mountainside.

The action displaced a number of smaller boulders from above the shelf which, when the dust cleared, revealed a small opening into a deep dark space.

"Zu, this could be interesting, let us clear away the debris to enlarge the opening sufficiently to gain full access. Hopefully it might reveal evidence of previous mining or the presence of mineral deposits."

As they set about clearing away the boulders, they disturbed others sealing an entrance, which fell away and revealed a cave penetrating deep into the mountainside.

Clearing the entrance of substantial accumulations of debris, they decided that the cavern had been deliberately sealed many generations ago, and from their point of view, it was a prime site to commence their search for minerals.

"Zu, I suggest we conceal our packs a short distance in from the entrance, light our torches and explore the limits of the cave, then closely examine the rock faces on the way back."

By the light of their brightly burning torches, they walked down the cave until Zu stopped Isis.

"Have you noticed that the floor of the cave is level and while the sides of the tunnel are rough, also the ceiling has been worked at intervals to maintain a clearance above your head? I believe our ancestors undertook this work, the height of local natives seldom exceeds three and a half cubits, and would not have needed to make these clearances."

"I had noticed and I am puzzled. Substantial work indeed, but they might have had another purpose."

After walking a considerable distance, they arrived at an almost flat but rough-faced rock wall.

"Zu, this is most strange; although it appears to be a natural formation, the rock is different from the sidewalls of the cave. If you look at the junction with the cave sides there is evidence of some very skilled work. I believe this could be the concealed entrance to an ancient tomb, its weight must be massive. Have you any ideas?"

"If our ancestors were concealing a tomb, doubtless they would have left some text to identify the owner, who must have been of sufficient importance to justify the considerable construction work. However, it seems sensible to examine both the adjoining cave walls and the end wall for some sort of plaque."

Making a palm-by-palm examination of the rock face, Isis suddenly gave a shout of delight.

"Look, Zu! There is a block of ancient hieroglyphs on a smooth part of the sidewalls at eye level."

Zu commented wryly, "Making it only suitable for very tall people to read!"

Isis started to laugh, then, realising the implication, said, "Clearly the markings have been deliberately placed at that level to make it difficult for people other than our race to notice or attempt to read! Zu, what does it say?"

Zu spent a considerable time trying to interpret the meaning, and eventually found a few of the hieroglyphs similar to those in present use.

"At a rough guess they seem to be part of an instruction for opening a portal."

After further examination, with frequent interruptions from an excited Isis, Zu eventually added, "From a very rough translation the hieroglyphs seem to indicate that we should search for a small cavity in which a hand has to be inserted."

Commencing a meticulous search, Zu found a promising cavity, then, with some trepidation, inserted his hand. There was a warm feeling, but nothing happened.

By then Isis, impatient and highly excited, could not wait and thrust her hand in the opening, and gasped as it seemed to have gripped her hand for an instant. Suddenly released, surprised and somewhat nervous, she jumped back. A few seconds passed then, without any sound of machinery, the complete back wall slowly lifted until the base was flush with the tunnel roof.

The opening revealed a perfectly formed circular tunnel; the surface was smooth with the appearance of black glass, almost as if the rock had melted when it was formed.

At first it seemed that the light from their torches illuminated the entire length of the tunnel, then they realised that a number of small lights had been mounted at intervals in wall recesses, and that these had been activated as soon as the portal opened.

Astonished and to some extent frightened by the unexpected appearance of this magical source of light, and after recovering their wits, they immediately extinguished their torches to save them for their return to the cave entrance.

"Zu, who lit the lights? They certainly did not come this way!"

"We know from the hieroglyphs the entry was built by our ancestors and as the tunnel is part of their design with lights built into the wall, I do not believe we are in danger from anything human and by some magic or other the lights are linked to the portal. I feel we should enter, but with great caution."

Entering the strange tunnel, they noticed three skeletons, consisting only of decayed bones and dust, that had been carefully arranged on the tunnel floor.

"Zu, after having our attention drawn to such a stark warning, I suggest it is urgent to secure the tunnel access in the open position. Please check the instructions again for any reference to supports."

"There is nothing of that nature on the plaque, but I did notice a small circle with two horizontal lines carved in the rock face on one side of the opening."

They puzzled about the meaning of this sign, until Isis, in exasperation, said, "The lines would have to be vertical to be of any help."

Zu laughed, and pressed his hand on the sign, pretending to turn it. Suddenly a deposit of dust fell away from the circular joint surrounding the sign and the lines moved to the vertical position. They both jumped back as they heard a steady rumbling sound, followed by massive stone pillars moving up slowly on either side of the opening. Contacting the portal slab with a final thump, they locked it in position.

"Zu, the portal slab may be locked, but the magicians who constructed this tunnel will have other traps to catch the unwary. Is some malevolent spirit in control of the mechanisms? As Chief Priest and Magician, have you any knowledge of these devices that will afford us protection?"

"I have read of similar devices in the myths and legends we tell to our children but there was never any explanation on how they operated. Judging from the instructions we have so far successfully interpreted, the devices are to protect the tomb from tomb robbers. The skeletons at the entrance are from small people, so I suggest we move forward slowly, looking for further instructions."

As they walked slowly down the tunnel, Zu approached the first light unit to try to determine its mode of operation. As he approached the light, it went out, as he moved away it came on again.

Isis murmured, "This is dangerous and deadly magic."

Moving forward, they meticulously searched the tunnel walls for any indication that might warn them of a trap. They had travelled about fifty cubits down the tunnel before they came to another inscription, high up on the wall, that had a skull on one corner, and numerous hieroglyphs filling the rest of the space. Isis moved back and waited while Zu attempted to make an interpretation.

"As far as I can understand from the text, Isis, we have to locate a cavity, measuring two hands by two hands, about two cubits below the sign. Then one of us has to place a fist within that space and press it in for a distance of one hand. Only then can we continue. It also states that once the device is deactivated it cannot be reset."

It only took a few moments for Zu to locate the cavity, and when he was about to operate the mechanism, Isis, excited and feeling reassured, claimed the privilege of neutralising the trap. The operation took all her strength, but when it reached the specified depth there was a satisfying noise as the lock engaged.

"Thank you, Zu, I did enjoy that – very satisfying!"

They continued to walk slowly down the tunnel searching for warning signs, but no further traps are encountered. Finally, they reached a blank wall that appeared to be the end of the tunnel. The substantial wall constructed across the tunnel appeared to include two large access panels, flush with the wall with no apparent means of opening. Examining the wall carefully Zu found two small flat panels, at high level, on either side of the possible access.

On one corner of each flat panel was a minute drawing of a hand. Zu placed his hand on one, but this had no effect. Being unable to span the space between the two panels, shamefaced he turned to Isis.

"Are you able to stretch sufficiently to place your hands flat on both panels at the same time?"

"It is a pleasure and very gratifying to my ego!"

Isis reached across and spanned the two panels, and with a small metallic click the access panels slid to either side to reveal a clear opening into the room. Then after a small interval the room lights came on slowly until they were able to see a mass of strange equipment.

As they walked round the room, full of strange artefacts, it was abundantly clear that they came from an ancient time before their own historical records, and that these giants had apparently obtained or achieved a technically advanced culture.

"There is nothing here, Zu, that I can recognise or compare with our possessions; these things are not art as we know it, and I cannot conceive that they would adorn any home. On the other hand, from the devices we have already encountered, they will doubtless be very effective for whatever operation they were designed!"

"It will require a great deal of time to segregate and determine the use of the equipment before attempting to list the items and transporting them to Atlan. I propose, Isis, that we immediately take steps to extend the time limit on our expedition, and obtain the necessary stores to make a temporary camp in the cave."

So with this in mind, they hurried out of the cave and returned to their camp. On arrival a meal was immediately prepared for them while they concocted a message for Osiris which read as follows:

We have made an important discovery supporting our plan for Council. Essential to extend existing expedition time limit. For security reasons our extension must be kept secret. Will keep you informed. Isis.

With the message safely despatched by carrier pigeon, Thoth immediately called their porters to them and gave them instructions.

"We have made a substantial mineral find and need to extend our visit. You are to load the mules with sufficient food and blankets for seven days and to accompany us back to our temporary location. After offloading the stores and provisions, you must return to camp and wait for further instructions."

When this task had been achieved without incident, Isis and Zu were established in their temporary camp inside the cave entrance. As darkness fell, they were totally exhausted and decided on a few hours' rest before returning to the artefacts storeroom.

In the early hours of the morning, rest was abandoned and lighting a single torch, they hurried down the tunnel. The lights came on as they entered and, trying to control their natural excitement, they rushed into the storeroom.

"There is so much to see, Isis! I suggest that independently we spend an hour or so examining the larger items. Then we take a rest and discuss those items that we find the most interesting."

"I agree, but I feel the strong presence of a Ba – it is not malevolent, in fact totally unconcerned, but my instincts tell me the tomb is very important and is not far away. Perhaps we should search for it first of all?"

"That, of course, is very tempting, but these artefacts could be of major importance in saving lives if the Prophecy turns into reality, which I am certain will be the case! All the tomb could provide would be an insight into our past, but the artefacts have already established the existence of a previous civilization! The decision is yours, but I strongly advise that we concentrate on examining the artefacts and their application."

"Zu, as usual I find your arguments practical and convincing. Our finds will reinforce our submission to the Council for the urgent dispatch of two expeditions and may to some extent overcome the inevitable objections by Seth! The tomb, if it survives the cataclysm, can be left until we have fully investigated these wondrous devices. Even then, as no earthly treasures are ever left in our tombs could we justify disturbing the Ba?"

After completing their preliminary view, they sat down and discussed which artefact had the most potential. They reached immediate agreement that a large flat rectangular item of equipment had the most to offer, so they removed it to an open area outside the room for further examination.

At first sight it appeared to consist of layers of carpet but blowing the dust away revealed a close-weaved pattern of fine red-gold thread on the top surface. The top layer rested on a black surface that reflected no light. Different materials had been used on the lower layers, such as silver, copper, and an orange-coloured metal, each layer separated by thin translucent mineral sheets of mica or silicon. On top of the device, a strange helmet was connected by a fine-coloured wire loom to a box spanning all the various layers. Despite its heavy appearance, it was easy to lift and they carried it up to the shelf outside the cave entrance.

Settling down to an early breakfast, they discussed its purpose. Myths from their childhood told of magicians and their magic carpets and they wondered if this could be a similar device.

Returning to the artefact, which was now in the full daylight, they noticed it seemed to absorb sunlight. The top surface shimmered and developed a surprising vibration level that totally obscured the surface patterns.

"Zu, I am convinced that this is a transporter of some kind!"

"Assuming your assessment is correct, we must move it to a secluded spot to prevent any tests being observed."

Following the shelf round the corner, they found a suitable location in a depression in the mountain slope. Zu lifted the device, which was now surprisingly light and carried it round the shelf to the new position.

As Isis had obtained the cave entry device's acceptance, it was agreed that she should undertake the first test, Zu insisting that the experiment should be limited to a short duration. After that, they agreed to review the results before proceeding further, and as an additional safety measure, Zu attached a short length of rope around her waist.

So, with heightened excitement laced with some trepidation, she sat in the middle of the device and put on the helmet. Nothing happened.

"Zu – no response."

Zu, laughing, answered, "Well, what did you expect? A quick flight to Babylon!"

"Well, it could have done something, perhaps moved or lifted up."

Then to her astonishment, the device lifted slightly, moved a little forward, hesitated and then stopped. She jumped off quickly and they discussed what to do next.

"Well, Zu, as my Principal Magician, how do you think it should be controlled? Was it listening to our conversation when it moved?"

"My immediate reaction is that it responded to your voice, but, on reflection, I realised that in the presence of other voices or sounds round the device, control would be lost. If the helmet has some magic in it that can interpret thoughts then it seems possible that control is by reading your mind."

After setting up a sequence of tests using thought control, Isis slowly obtained control of the device that, as they progressed, appeared to be learning to interpret her commands. She soon had the device moving through the air, with Thoth anxiously holding onto the safety rope. As she became more confident, she discarded the rope, completed a circuit clear of the shelf, and landed back beside Thoth. Before he could say anything, a contrite Isis said, "Zu, I know I should have asked you first, I was so excited that I ignored the dangers. I will try to curb my impatience in future!"

"My lady, unless you curb your impatience you may not survive to enjoy the future!"

After Thoth calmed down, he insisted on accompanying Isis on all future test flights and in that way they gradually extended the flights. Becoming reasonably proficient, they concluded that this form of transport would solve the problem of carrying the artefacts to a place of safety.

Pleased with their progress they decided that next morning, at dawn, they would fly to an uninhabited site close to the city. There Thoth would leave Isis and enter the city to contact High Lord Osiris.

Osiris was a tall Giant of forty, who was to be coupled with Isis when she reached her twenty-eighth birthday, the age of consent. Both families agreed their union at her birth, in accordance with the rules of the High Lords Society.

"Zu, as soon as you meet Osiris please ask him, on my behalf, to observe complete silence regarding our activities. If he accepts, provide him with full details of our discovery. Together, you must devise a plan for storing the large quantity of artefacts in total security until the result of the High Council meeting is known. I will fly back the following day, at early dawn, to collect you from the same site."

As dawn broke the next morning they set off for Atlan City, landing at a secluded spot near the outskirts. Zu assured her that he would be waiting for her arrival at dawn the following day and set off for the city to make his contact with Osiris.

The next morning, after a delayed but otherwise uneventful flight, they met up as arranged. Arriving back at the site, they sat down to discuss their plan of operation.

"Zu, now tell me about your meeting with Osiris."

"Arriving at Osiris's compound I was subjected to a bombardment of questions by his staff; it would have come to blows if Osiris had not walked up and asked what all the fuss was about.

"After explaining that I was carrying a very important message for him from Isis, he hurried me into his private office.

"Having obtained agreement with regard to non-disclosure, I informed him about our discoveries. As you can imagine, he was delighted to hear of our successes and immediately appreciated the importance of maintaining complete silence with regard to the artefacts.

"After a lengthy discussion on various means of transporting the artefacts, Osiris decided that he would arrange for his private trading vessel, the *Sothis*, to be at anchor in a secluded bay, thirty kilometres north of the city, by the evening in six days' time. This plan requires us to transport the artefacts from the cave to the bay.

"The crew of the *Sothis* would be responsible for collecting the artefacts and loading them in a sealed hold. As the crew of the ship will have seen the artefacts, Osiris will arrange for them to remain at sea, out of sight of land for at least fifteen days. This should give us enough time to return to the city, using the *Sothis*'s small sailing dingy.

"Immediately we return to the city, he would require another meeting to determine the next move, and to fabricate a suitable cover story regarding our reasons for extending the expedition.

"So, in my opinion, the visit has been a complete success, and I hope for your approval."

"I am delighted with all the arrangements, and look forward to sailing back to Atlan City. The decision we took regarding the artefacts is clearly the right one, and the Osiris expedition is virtually assured."

They spent the next two days listing the artefacts and testing the light units, and then bringing everything up to the cave mouth. Zu tried his skill in flying the second transporter. In the beginning it was difficult for him to obtain control, but for an unknown reason suddenly everything changed and, from then on, he became adept.

Removing the last of the artefacts from the storeroom, Isis stood still and pondered.

"Zu, I am troubled and feel sure something important has been missed!"

"I have the same feeling; why are there no instructions or drawings for the operation of the artefacts? We have already encountered proof of the ancestors' ability to write instructions for the operation of portals and protection devices. If we accept that the artefacts were deliberately reserved for their descendants, instructions must have been left which we have failed to find. As we still have two days before making our rendezvous with the *Sothis*, I suggest we utilise the time to search for any concealed access in the storeroom walls leading to another space."

Isis agreed and they started a systematic and meticulous search for an access, but could find no trace of a concealed opening.

Standing back and viewing the construction of the storeroom, Isis pointed to where the black glazed tunnel walls extended deep into the rear wall.

"Zu, this kind of construction would not have been adopted if the tunnel had terminated in the storeroom, and if you agree, I propose we break a hole through the wall."

"I agree; whether or not your conclusion is valid, a little demolition with some heavy pieces of oak racking seems appropriate."

After a few heavy blows, part of the wall collapsed and they cautiously peered into a partially finished space enclosed by a continuation of the tunnel. Opening the access through the storeroom wall, they were able to enter and obtain enough light to examine the contents.

In the centre of the space stood a heavy black tripod with a large box structure on the top, fitted with a number of small control levers on one end and, on the other, a circular opening. On one side of the box they noticed a drawing of a skull, and under that a faded hieroglyph with signs too faint to interpret. Clearly this was a warning, but as no trace of drawings or documentation could be found in the room, they dared not touch the controls.

On the floor in front of the tripod lay two Giants' skeletons, and when Zu attempted a closer examination of the bones they collapsed into a pile of dust. When the air cleared it revealed a piece of metal glinting in the dust.

"Zu, I think this is the access we have been looking for. If we clear away the dust and debris over a large area sufficient to allow a giant to enter, it should reveal the extent of the slab."

Clearing away the debris immediately revealed a large metal bar inserted flush with the floor. As they continued to clear the floor, they exposed a large stone access slab.

Removing and lifting the slab turned out to be a difficult operation, so they returned to their camp at the cave entrance, collected their climbing ropes and tools for taking rock samples, and returned to the artefact room. Using their crude equipment, they managed to lift one edge of the slab and then just managed to slide it clear. This revealed a stone staircase leading down to two wooden doors, and lighting their torches, they cautiously descended.

One wooden door hung in a slightly open position, the hinges having rotted away. Removing the door and frame, they cautiously entered a small room full of rotting racking; under that debris they found a considerable number of scrolls sealed in bitumen-coated tubes.

The other door fell away when they touched it, and that revealed a heavy granite archway, sealed with substantial stone slabs, obviously the entry to a tomb. The construction was far too elaborate to attempt a non-destructive opening in the limited time available.

Collecting the scrolls they returned to the storeroom and dismantled the tripod and artefact, then carried them up to the cave entrance. After making a suitable container for the scrolls, they returned to collect them and after numerous journeys they returned for the last time to the storeroom. From there, they systematically removed the tunnel lights as they returned to the cave entrance.

Preparing a meal and resting at the cave entrance, they promised each other to return one day and explore the tomb, if the prophecy was not totally fulfilled, and if the site was still accessible.

On the day agreed with Osiris, they made an early visit to their baggage porters' campsite, and instructed them to return to Atlan. Returning to the cave, they loaded both transporters and commenced the numerous journeys, until all the artefacts had been delivered to the bay.

As promised by Osiris, the trading ship *Sothis* was gracefully swinging at anchor close in to a beach of silver sand on the last strip of blue sea, before it subtly changed to a soft and welcoming green in the shallows. It looked as pretty as a picture in the sheltering confines of the small bay, with her sails furled and hardly a ripple on the sea, and her outline mirrored on the surface.

Captain Teti of the *Sothis* rushed across the beach to greet them when they arrived with the first load. With a weather-beaten face, he was a strange mixture of strength and weakness that was impossible to quantify; clearly he was proud of his ship but something was missing in his character.

The ship was about fifty cubits long, seventeen cubits wide and classed as a broad-beamed ship. Her mainmast was fifty-two cubits high and carried a square sail between two yards. Her burden was rated at three hundred and twenty cubic cubits. In the high bow she had two foremasts linked together with booms, positioning two lantern sails. The bulwarks were heavily constructed and accommodation was under a raised deck, part of which extended over the stern. There were two rudders with their shafts entering through the overhang on either side of the stern accommodation; these were then linked by a tiller arrangement, with levers and fulcrums providing the necessary advantage.

The ocean-going trading ships were similar in construction, but their length was sixty-five cubits and the width eighteen point five cubits, the ships having a four hundred and sixty-two cubic cubit burden. In addition, they had a wickerwork basket lookout position fitted above the top mainmast yard.

All ships were constructed from teak, redwood, cedar and oak, the last depending on imports. The planks were fastened with a type of bronze nail cast from a mixture of copper and tin from local deposits, with additives to make them impervious to seawater.

The Giants of Atlan had established a workshop with over one hundred natives who were solely employed in producing large quantities of bronze nails, which were continually in demand for the trading fleet and the numerous wooden buildings close to the sea.

The crew of the *Sothis* had obviously observed the method of transport used to bring the artefacts to the beach, and as this might cause a security breach they were made to take an oath not to disclose this information. Providing Osiris's instructions were obeyed, the crew should have no opportunity of jumping ship once they left the bay.

Thoth drew Isis to one side and whispered, "I have a strong feeling that Captain Teti is weak and unreliable. I suggest that we have both the transporters loaded on the sailing craft."

"Zu, I am not impressed with the captain, yet find it difficult to condemn him, but I have learned to trust your instinct, so call Teti over and I will issue the necessary instruction to have them loaded. Please supervise the loading and securing of the transporters."

"Captain Teti, I require the two transporters loaded immediately on the sailing craft, so we can deliver them directly to Osiris."

After they were loaded, the sailing craft was provisioned and ready. After partaking a light meal with the captain, they wished him and his crew a safe journey, and immediately set sail for Atlan City.

With a calm sea and a light breeze, they made excellent progress, keeping just in sight of the shore. After finding a secluded bay to anchor in overnight, they set sail at first light, and by late afternoon Thoth suddenly observed a flurry of activity on the beach, and turned to Isis.

"A long boat is being launched from the beach with a large crew. I also observe, from the occasional flashes of reflected sunlight off metal, that they are armed. I believe that they are pirates. The only possible safety rests in our sailing out to sea, so I am changing course, but inevitably with oars and sail they will rapidly close the distance between us."

"Zu, darkness is still three hours away; while I am fully aware that pirates operate along this stretch of coast, someone must have betrayed our return plan."

"Surrendering to the pirates is not an alternative, as we both know all prisoners are killed to avoid the pirates being identified. They have been known to come this close to the city, but would have preferred to attack us before this late stage in our journey. This suggests they were informed as soon as we left the *Sothis*, and took this risk relying on their rowing speed to catch our small sailing craft and return to shore, before they could be intercepted by any Atlan harbour protection vessel."

It was clear that their change in course would only provide them with a short respite, and as they had no weapons, they were in a desperate situation. As a last resort they could escape on the transporters, but they would have to delay this escape as long as possible to avoid revealing the existence of the transporters before the Council meeting.

The pirates were steadily closing and starting to intimidate by shouting and waving weapons. As Isis and Zu started releasing the transporters and preparing to take off, they observed one of the city's fast patrol boats, propelled by sails and some forty oarsmen, appearing round the headland. Seeing their quarry standing up and waving, the pirates immediately attempted to run back to the land, but as they had followed the sailing craft out to sea, they had no chance of success.

Knowing the appalling fate that awaited them in the city if they surrendered, the pirates set fire to their boat; some committed suicide and others jumped into the sea and drowned.

Closing with their craft the patrol boat's captain hailed them. "Thank ReRa we arrived just in time! My Lord Osiris had become extremely worried about your safety after receiving disturbing intelligence. He ordered our patrol boat to sea immediately to intercept your craft and escort you both to safety. Unfortunately most of our crew were either at home or in the city so I had to call for volunteers to man our ship.

"Lord Osiris had been privately advised that the pirates had received information regarding your return. The source of the information could not be revealed, but he suggested it might have been an attempt to prevent you from attending the Council meeting, or for some unknown reason to remove you both permanently!

"My orders were specific: as soon as we had secured your safety any pirate ship encountered is to be destroyed and I am to take a few prisoners for interrogation, but unfortunately, as you can see, there are no survivors!

"Subject to your agreement I will escort you to the bay and then tow you in to your moorings."

Isis replied, "Thank you and your volunteers for your timely arrival. Now we will have no trouble reaching the bay, but would appreciate a tow to reach our moorings."

After covering the two transporters, they arranged for them to be removed to a secure location within the warehouse.

That achieved, they rushed off for a meeting with Osiris, to thank him for the timely rescue and to further their plans regarding the High Council meeting. After receiving a very warm welcome and excellent refreshment, they sat down together to discuss their joint plan that they had been developing over the last three months. They proposed expeditions for the establishment of settlements in remote locations in the known world. The first two would be in Egypt and Mesopotamia; these might be followed by two further settlements, providing there would be sufficient time before the expected cataclysm. It was agreed that Lord Osiris would deliver their plan to the President immediately for discussion at the forthcoming meeting, but for overall security reasons no mention would be made with regard to the artefacts.

On the cliff top, Isis turned to Zu. "Yes, it was a wonderful, unforgettable and exciting time. But having considered our preliminary proposals for tomorrow's meeting, and as it is growing dark, it is time to leave my favourite retreat."

Thoth turned round and said, "I have come to the conclusion that it was Seth who wanted to make it impossible for us to attend the Council meeting, and any of his plans are excessively violent. As a sensible precaution let us separate and choose different routes to our homes, avoiding unrest in the centre of the city."

Fearing for each other, the close friends parted and arrived home safely.

In accordance with the ancient tradition, the High Council had to meet in the month of Xul, and this session would last for ten days, but these were not normal times and that limit might not apply. Isis knew that as leader of Medicine and Magic, she had to attend and that it would include heads of all departments.

With the full Council assembled, the meeting was brought to order and the President, Lord Raie, welcomed the High Lords, Council members and their departmental experts. He then outlined the rules appertaining to this particular meeting, saying, "After the majority agree the plans under discussion to safeguard the continuation of our race, objectors would have to accept those conditions or be immediately exiled beyond the borders of the state.

"In view of the limited time available, our proposals must be implemented within the subsequent twenty days. All citizens not included in the proposed plans can either stay within the state, or leave with any possessions they are able to carry, to the High Mountains in the north-east."

He then invited the Chief Priest and Scientist Thoth to comment on the continual increase in sea levels.

Thanking the President and Inner Council members, Thoth replied, "There are several reasons that account in part for the increase in sea levels. To begin with, the melting of the ice sheets round the frozen lands, together with the increase in massive icebergs drifting into the warm currents, which we all know are now a serious danger to our trading fleet.

"Then there are recent gravitational field changes, not yet fully evaluated, causing sea-level depressions in local areas, displacing large volumes of water.

"Although it is impossible to forecast what the final sea level will be, based on the present rate of sea-level changes, the sea will cover our massive harbour walls within one year. All our harbour facilities will be flooded, and alternative facilities for our trading ships will have to be developed."

Lord Seth, unable to conceal his contempt for Thoth, shouted, "All of this is irresponsible nonsense, pure guesswork that is damaging our social stability. We have experienced sea-level increases before for short periods, which caused little concern. Unless you have something positive to say, you should be silent and sit down, at least make an effort to prevent your fears running away with the common sense you are believed to possess."

The crash of a gong stilled the uproar in the Council chamber and the President demanded immediate order. On behalf of the Council, the President apologised to Thoth.

The President then called for the Chief Astronomer to assess the immediate dangers.

Astronomer Awelin replied, "Let me start by reciting the ancient warning that has been passed down to us by the original survivors of the civilization destroyed five thousand seven hundred years ago, who obtained it from the survivors of the demise of the previous civilization some five and a half thousand years before that date:

Nemesis will arrive, the sky will be divided by its great mass.
Great waves will rise on the Oceans, and cover the low lands,
Mists will cover the Sea.
The Earth will tremble and mountains spew rivers of fire.
Fire will consume all that escapes the flood.
The few that survive will suffer great hardship for several generations.

"As you all know, we have reached that time—"

Seth interrupted, "It is about time we ignored these myths and folk tales. There is no evidence to support such predictions; all we have are a few monoliths and some massive building blocks, such as are seen in the harbour, which were built by our ancestors, not by any previous civilization."

Awelin, considerably put out, shouted, "What I can tell you is that our observatory has established the orbit of Nemesis, and it will pass close to the earth in two hundred and ninety days' time. That is a fact, and a very unpleasant one! How close it will come to the earth has yet to be established, but I believe the Ancients' prediction will be justified."

The President then called for the Lord of Sea Trading, Aestad, to put forward the proposal that had been devised with High Lords Osiris, Isis, and Councillor Thoth.

Lord Astead replied, "Our people, known to the other races as Giants, are the last of our kind. It is therefore essential to make immediate efforts to secure the survival of large enough groups, dispersed throughout the world, to achieve that survival.

"The proposal is that, as a first step, we send out two expeditions to our trading posts in Egypt and Mesopotamia.

"The Egyptian expedition will land at the Quseir Trading Post. Then inland to Qena on the Nile River, where they will establish a settlement close to the river, with deep shelters in the nearby hills. We have established a satisfactory relationship with the locals, mainly hunters and gatherers, who with our equipment can be rapidly trained in agriculture; this will establish our food supply.

"The Mesopotamian expedition will land at Bashi on the north-east side of the Gulf. This expedition will journey up the great rivers to the Northern Mountains where they will establish a temporary settlement, returning to the estuary on the Gulf after the ravages of the flood, if this should occur. The native population in this area are warlike and are difficult to control. This must be taken into account in equipping our ships.

"Both expeditions will consist of three trader ships. Each ship of its set will have similar loadings, so that the loss of one ship will not prevent the successful completion of their task.

"On reaching their appointed destinations all the expedition ships must be returned immediately, so that further expeditions to other locations can be undertaken. As you will appreciate, if the third and fourth expeditions are to be achieved within the remaining time, the first expedition must start without any delay.

"Before proceeding further with this proposal I ask the President to rule on its adoption and if that is favourable, put it to the vote."

Lord Raie replied, "I am prepared to put the proposal to the High Council and then to the Council members.

"The results of the proposals are as follows: "In the High Council, for – Osiris, Isis, Ptah and Wadjet; against – Seth, Nepha, Neith and Ekhbt." As they had reached an impasse, Lord Raie cast his vote for the proposal, and then called for a vote by the Council members. The results were as follows: Council members Thoth, Awelin, Neegs, Aestad, Horko, Rava and Rasn were for, while Nemrod, Estati, Enki, Inurs, Shiva and Heti were against.

The President then addressed the meeting.

"The decision to adopt the proposals has now been taken with a majority of one vote and this result can no longer be challenged. I now call for volunteers from the High Lords to lead the two expeditions. Let us first consider the Egyptian venture."

Lord Osiris stood up. "I have visited the Egyptian trading post in the past, and I feel qualified to lead that expedition and will be accompanied by Isis, as by the time we reach the Nile the coupling ceremony will be due. I considered the Mesopotamian venture but did not feel qualified to lead it, as the journey to the Northern Hills requires someone with military experience that I do not possess."

Now, the President was not a stupid man – although his position and authority was by birthright, he understood that Seth did not believe in or follow the old ways. Tradition, honour and respect are for others, not traits that belonged to Seth! Then the President turned to Seth, and, speaking in sickly sweetness, said, "Would you be prepared to lead the Mesopotamian expedition? Your father was famous for his prowess in battle, and, like him, you have become a courageous and deadly warrior with considerable experience in the field of battle. I fully appreciate that you have been against the proposals based on the prophecies from the outset, but it is my firm view that whether or not the prophecies are justified in the near future, this particular expedition would be of great value to our people."

Isis smiled to herself. *Seth you fool; you do not see how the President's honeyed words are entrapping you. That is your greatest fault, the ease with which you are charmed like a snake with a flute. You may be tall and powerful, but your mind is weak!*

Lord Seth, seduced by the President's flattery, smugly replied, "While I do not believe in the myths and fancies placed before the Council by persons who should know better, I do believe that the expedition to the Northern Mountains of Mesopotamia would provide excellent trading opportunities.

"On that basis, I consider the expedition justified, and I will lead the expedition providing that it should not last more than three years. After that time I wish to return home, and with the Council's agreement that if I am as successful as I intend to be, I have their firm promise that I will be granted Kingship over the whole of Mesopotamia."

This was then put to the vote. There were no objections, as those in favour believed in the prophecies, and the remainder supported Lord Seth!

Lord Raie smiled to himself; Seth had fallen into the trap. If the prophecies did not take place, then he would arrange for a serious accident during Seth's return journey. He was far too dangerous to the peace of Atlan to be permitted to return and gain a position of power.

The Committee then adjourned and the two expedition leaders

left to select their teams and started provisioning the ships so that they would be ready for departure within the next two days. Isis and Thoth had already warned their staff, and they immediately started to move food and baggage down to the ships selected by Osiris. By the evening of the next day, preparations were complete and departure was tentatively agreed for the following morning.

That evening, Isis made some final arrangements for departure when Leda, her personal attendant and friend, rushed in to announce that a messenger had arrived from Lord Seth.

Isis said, "Send him in, but you and your man must stay close, as I do not trust Lord Seth's motives."

The messenger was brought in carrying arms and after bowing to Isis said, "My master, Lord Seth, requires you to join his expedition immediately."

Isis replied, "That is absolutely impossible as I am already a member of the Osiris expedition."

The messenger replied, "Lord Seth is already aware of that situation, but he insists that you must accompany me to his house, where the delicate matter can be discussed privately."

Isis smiled and said, "I need a little time to consider this invitation which is totally unexpected. In fact I was just about to have a light meal before you arrived. Perhaps you would do me the honour of joining me for some food and drink before we set out."

The messenger, thinking he had been successful, and deeply honoured with the invitation, agreed. Isis called to Leda.

"Get the servants to bring a light meal for both of us together with refreshments – that special wine I had with Lord Osiris yesterday is very refreshing."

The meal was brought and placed before them. As hostess, Isis moved to the wine table and prepared two glasses; in the one for the messenger she inserted the small packet of powder provided by Leda.

Toasting his hostess he drank, then fell unconscious on the floor.

Leda rushed in. "He came with two armed escorts, my lady, they are waiting in the street below."

"Leda, take two of our best hunters and silently render the escorts unconscious, using the strongest poison-tipped darts. Move the bodies to the nearest secluded place where it is unlikely they will be discovered until morning."

It was not long before Leda returned and reported that her orders had been fulfilled and the bodies concealed.

Isis thanked Leda and said, "I have another important job for you to fulfil. I want you to go to Osiris in disguise by an indirect route – this precaution is essential in case there are any watchers en route so they will not deduce you have come from me. Get your man and one other to follow close behind you for protection. All of you must carry hidden arms.

"When you reach Osiris's house, tell his staff that you come from me and say you have an urgent message for Osiris. Do not discuss any of the recent happenings with any of his household.

"When Osiris sends for you, tell him everything that has happened this evening. Inform him that to avoid being intercepted by Seth's lackeys, I propose to leave with my staff as soon as possible, and travel in an armed group to the small leisure beach harbour to the south of Atlan. On arrival we will commandeer some suitable boats and row round to the main harbour and board *Sea Owl*. Also emphasise that I firmly believe Seth to be capable of considerable acts of evil, and that I fear for Osiris's safety.

"Seth must realise by now that something has gone wrong with his plans as his messenger has not returned. From now on, we must not underestimate any violent action he may take. If he cannot intercept our party, he will try to delay its departure, or if he is unable to do that, he might try to intercept us after we leave Atlan.

"As Osiris's home is close to the harbour I suggest he should leave immediately for the ships with an armed party, and make all necessary preparations for the ships to be towed out and sail to the centre of the bay as soon as possible.

"In conclusion, Leda, you must tell Osiris that I ask him to grant you and your escort special protection in his armed party, when he undertakes the journey to the expedition ships."

After saying goodbye to Isis and wishing her party a safe journey, a suitably disguised Leda and her escort set off to meet Osiris.

Isis then gathered her party of forty Giants, all of whom were expedition members, and explained the present situation and the reasons why she had selected the route they would follow. She then ordered them to travel fully armed, but as far as possible conceal their weapons.

When all was prepared they left silently on their journey to the leisure beach harbour by walking to the east from Atlan and then swinging south towards the small harbour and its leisure boats, intending by this means to avoid all contact with the city.

After discussions with Zu, Isis sent out scouts to either side of their party and one at the rear to warn her if there was evidence they were being followed, or if persons watching the road had observed them.

Initially they encountered no problems, but on reaching the half-way point, a scout reported that they had been spotted by a group of natives who, after seeing their party, hurried off in the direction of the city.

After considering the situation, Zu spoke to Isis.

"Assuming Seth is now being informed of our progress, I believe he would immediately offer the natives gold to intercept and delay our party. This would give him enough time to gather together sufficient Giants to take the immediate, and possibly violent action to frustrate our intentions.

"If my assumption is correct we must increase our rate of march over this last section, and be prepared for an attack just before we reach the leisure beach. As soon as we encounter a threatening native group, we must – without any hesitation – take up a battle formation and attack, to kill as many as possible and disperse the rest. To ensure success and minimise casualties, fast reaction is essential. No stopping to inspect the battlefield, but continue the rush to the boats and start the harbour crossing."

"Zu, all that is agreed."

Isis stopped the march and briefly explained the plan, and then, in a high state of excitement, they set out with everyone ready to take up the battle formation for an immediate and decisive attack.

Thoth's analysis of Seth's reaction to news from the natives was proved accurate when, on their approach to the leisure beach, the path was blocked by a mob of natives with flaming torches and weapons. They were very confident that the Giants would not fight, as they never did in Atlan, and threatening action followed by drawn-out discussions would give Lord Seth the time he needed.

Isis did not wait. "Attack and kill!"

Then, screaming like a banshee out of hell and waving her kris above her head, Isis charged forward, flanked by two Giants on either side and, followed by the blunt arrowhead of the attack formation, they impacted the native assembly as they started to fall back in terror and utter confusion.

The Giants, shouting their battle cry, cut their way into the natives, slicing with their krises through a tangled mass of the opposition who were desperately trying to escape the blades, but under the speed and furiousness of the attack the mob had insufficient time to make any defence before being completely overwhelmed.

No quarter given, those in the direct path of the Giants were slaughtered, and those on either side, who were not cut down, panicked and fled.

Without reducing their momentum, the Giants, now cheering, rushed down to the harbour and secured five large rowing boats already in the water. The boats were quickly filled with triumphant Giants, the mooring ropes cut, the oars manned and they pushed off from the land before anyone could react quickly enough to object!

After checking the boats for casualties, Zu returned to Isis. "I have no casualties to report. A large number of natives have been killed and wounded, but during the mad rush there was no time to count them!"

Heavy clouds were coursing across the sky, and apart from occasional breaks between the clouds it was pitch black. During short moonlight breaks, they were just able to establish their bearings and maintain a close formation. After rowing for about an hour, they were just able to make out the harbour entrance and change course to enter.

Isis called for complete silence in all the boats, instructed the rowers to paddle in lightly to limit the phosphorescence from the bow wave. By this means they were through the main entrance without being detected, and once inside, increased the rate of strike to avoid any attempt at interception.

Arriving alongside the *Sea Owl* they securely tethered the boats and quickly boarded.

They found that Osiris had not yet arrived, and a noisy mob was assembling on the quayside. Isis sent one of the crew up the mainmast to watch for the arrival of his party, and to inform her immediately if they appeared.

At the same time, Zu organised two parties of fully armed Giants, with drawn krises, to be ready to dash down to the quay and open up a path to the ship when the order was given for the gangways to be dropped. As soon as this had been arranged the lookout shouted, "Osiris party."

The gangplanks were dropped immediately and a path opened up towards Osiris's group. At the same time Osiris, with his warriors, forced a path towards the ship and joined up with the *Sea Owl* section.

No time was wasted and the whole of Osiris's party rushed on board, followed by the warriors. With all safely on board, the gangplanks were recovered to prevent the mob from trying to force their way on.

The next problem was to deliver the expedition members to their correct ships, and this was achieved by sending two boats with their passengers to *Sea Eagle* and the same to *Sea Fury*, both ships being docked close to the *Sea Owl*.

As all the members of the expedition and their baggage were now on board their ships, they were ready to leave harbour, but as a night departure had not been contemplated, there was only one tug available. With the quayside activity deteriorating, there was no alternative other than to leave the harbour as soon as possible.

The dock area became crowded with people and Osiris had to arrange for an armed guard to keep them back from the ships. The crowd was being continually incited by Seth's agents and were becoming angry, some shouting, "Stop the expedition!", others, "Let us join you, we want to leave the city!"

Eventually the President, with the support of the Lords and Councillors who were not included in the first expedition, addressed the mob. "These are only the first attempt to establish new bases; as soon as they are operational, those wishing to join them will have ample time to do so before the prophesied date of the cataclysm. When the expeditions have landed, our ships will return immediately in order to prepare for an additional dispersion of our population."

Some degree of calm was achieved, but they all felt the dangerous presence of Seth and his provocateurs in the background. As the mob was reforming, Osiris decided to order his ships to sea. With only one tug available, the spare rowing boats were manned with volunteers from the ships' companies, which were used to tow *Sea Eagle* and *Sea Fury* out of the harbour, *Sea Owl* being towed out by the harbour tug. As they departed they received a mix of cheers and jeers from the mob.

Osiris then instructed their captain that the immediate task was to find the trading ship *Sothis*, which should be waiting just outside the bay, out of sight of the city.

Due to the dangerous reefs surrounding the bay and the limited visibility, it was not possible to search for the *Sothis* until first light. Therefore, it was agreed that they should move out towards the centre of the bay and wait for first light before crossing the barrier reef.

Rendezvous with Sothis

5500 BC

Keeping close together in the poor visibility, the three ships moved like phantoms towards the centre of the bay, with phosphorescent bow waves and the creaking of the rigging the only sounds to betray their presence.

When the sound of the sea pounding the barrier reef became noticeable, Captain Bakh walked up to Osiris. "My Lord, it is dangerous to proceed further until dawn breaks. I suggest we all anchor here. If you agree I will contact the *Sea Eagle* and *Sea Fury* so we can anchor within hailing distance."

"Give the necessary orders – all ships to anchor immediately!"

Using his megaphone Captain Bakh contacted the other captains, calling for the sails to be furled and the anchors dropped. Then the expedition settled down to wait for dawn before risking the passage through the reef.

By this time all the members of the expedition were exhausted, but also elated after the day's activities; sleep eluded them. So Isis and Zu sat down on their baggage and discussed the day's activities.

"Zu, it has been a very exciting day. Let me have your thoughts on the general situation and what might be in store for us over the next few days."

"Lord Seth seems to have been behind all the difficulties we have experienced over the last twenty-four hours, but the only direct contact has been through the visit of his messenger and armed escort, who clearly intended to abduct you from Lord Osiris's group. Without any tangible evidence I suspect he was also concerned, or else directed the pirates' attempt to intercept us, despite all our precautions."

"Zu, like you I see Seth's hand in all that has happened to us since the day we met *Sothis* and loaded the artefacts. I believe the pirates had advance warning, but not until we left the bay, otherwise they would have been waiting for us further away from Atlan. I cannot accept that the pirates came on us by accident."

"There seem to be two possibilities: either the pirates had a spy at that time watching the activities in the secluded uninhabited bay, or else a pirate is a member of the *Sothis* crew. In the first case it would have been an extremely lucky chance to be there at that time, and he would not have known what we were loading or our destination. However, if a member of the *Sothis* crew left the ship after our departure, and somehow passed the information to the pirates, that is the most likely solution. If I am correct, then the pirates know all about the *Sothis* and its cargo, and by some means that information has reached Seth! This could explain his recent actions and would also suggest that he will pursue and attack us at the first opportunity when we are out of sight of land. The pirates, with the knowledge of its valuable cargo, will also be searching for the *Sothis*."

"As usual, Zu, your comments are an excellent analysis of our situation; if your assessment is accurate then we are all in a desperate situation. My first thought is that Osiris should be advised of our conclusions, as this will surely affect our immediate future."

"My lady, if we take that course there will be a problem, for referring to our plans having been leaked to the pirates, and eventually to Lord Seth, he will realise he was the only person privy to our movements. He might think that either we suspect his office, or that we are interfering with his position as expedition leader. Both of us could protest and proclaim our loyalty, but as we both know, he is very sensitive to the slightest criticism."

"All right, Zu, let us keep all this to ourselves until we locate the *Sothis*. Anyway, Osiris already suspects Seth, and really under the present conditions, what can he do to change the situation?"

Feeling tired, they both went down to their separate cabins and started to arrange their belongings to provide a comfortable space for the long journey.

Isis tried to sleep but the recent experiences held sleep at bay. After the anxiety of the previous twenty-four hours – the rushing out of harbour, the possibility of pursuit, the pressing need to reach the *Sothis* to recover the artefacts – waiting for dawn before attempting the passage through the coral reefs seemed interminable.

At last, from the east there came a shaft of light, then minutes later with a rapidly brightening sky the ships were flooded with light, and the ships and their companies seemed to spring into vibrant life.

Within minutes the three ships were making ready to weigh anchor, and Osiris called over Captains Bakh, Amle, Jelr, together with Isis and Thoth, to determine the immediate action required to locate the *Sothis*. Osiris then addressed the group. "Taking into account the recent activities of both the pirates and Lord Seth, urgent contact must be made with my trading ship, the *Sothis*. Lists of artefacts must be prepared for each of our ships, to facilitate the rapid transfer of cargo and to get us underway with the minimum possible delay. Thoth, perhaps you can comment."

"Regarding locating the *Sothis*, I respectfully suggest that, as there is now adequate light, you permit me to fly out to locate the ship. If you agree, I will use lamps to signal its position to our ships. Naturally this will require our most reliable lookouts on each ship, so that my progress can be continually monitored. You will appreciate that I have never flown over the sea, and for that reason constant observation is essential for safety reasons."

Osiris, smiling, replied, "All of us undertaking this expedition expect to take calculated risks, and naturally I am concerned for any person volunteering for this particular hazard, but unfortunately, Thoth, you have the more important and urgent task of translating the scrolls, and as you are the only one qualified, you cannot be spared for this sea search. Consequently, I must reject your offer as the information to be eventually gleaned from the scrolls may increase the chances of survival of our group. Perhaps Isis would like to give us her view."

"I agree with both the method of search, and with the observations made by Osiris. Thoth, at this time, is not expendable, and certainly not until he has studied the scrolls and assessed their value to the expedition. As we are the only two experienced in flying these transporters, I consider it my duty to volunteer to undertake the search, in the manner proposed by Thoth."

"Thank you for your courage in accepting what I believe to be an extremely risky mission. Normally I would never agree to a High Lord undertaking a project such as this, but as a dedicated company we are all equally committed to the successful outcome of our venture – on that basis and putting my personal feelings to one side, I find myself unable to object.

"With regard to the dispersal of the artefacts, Thoth, this is a matter of considerable urgency. Will you please prepare a list for each of the ships detailing rough descriptions of the items to be transferred from the *Sothis*? When that task has been completed, find a location on the *Sea Owl* and, using volunteers, construct a secure enclosure where you can study the scrolls without interruption."

At this point Captain Bakh interjected, "Subject to your agreement, Osiris, I wish to have the three ships underway immediately. In my opinion we must delay the flight of the transporter until the ships have cleared the barrier reef passage, only then can the transporter be allowed to lift off the deck. There are two reasons for this: one is to reduce the distance between the transporter and our ships to a minimum in case it runs into difficulties, and the other is if it took off immediately and our ships are delayed in clearing the reef, we might easily lose contact with the transporter and that could be fatal."

Osiris, relieved, closed the meeting. "Let it be so. Order the ships to make sail immediately. In addition, from now on, all ships will arrange to have an armed party standing by for immediate action when we sight the *Sothis*. Weapons for the rest of the expedition shall be allocated now, to be distributed immediately should the captain or myself call for such action. I will reassess these arrangements after we have unloaded the *Sothis* and cleared any pursuit."

The three ships then weighed anchor and proceeded up to the barrier reef, which was clearly marked by the surf breaking on the coral reef on either side of the narrow channel. During the passage through the reef there was a constant danger that the intermittently generated spray would obscure the passage width, but fortunately Bata, the sailing master, was too experienced to be deceived by the loss of visibility, and with the *Sea Owl* in the lead, the three ships sailed safely through.

Isis, having taken her place on the transporter, took off immediately and after climbing rapidly, levelled out just above mast height. She quickly noticed that the effect of flying over the sea was more uncomfortable than flying overland, as the transporter seemed to synchronise its levels in accordance with the waves and, at times, the result was similar to being physically pulled over corrugations, all of which she found distracting, as to begin with, controlling the transporter required her undivided attention to correct the deflections, until her thoughts synchronised with the controls.

After travelling about six kilometres she located the *Sothis*. Closing with the ship she observed that it was being chased by a pirate craft. She became alarmed, as this appeared to be a much larger craft than that previously used against their sailing skiff.

Isis, appreciating that the *Sothis* was in serious danger, immediately signalled the expedition ships, which acknowledged her by flashing a light. As it was impossible to warn the *Sea Owl* about the pirates, she flew down to the *Sothis*, on the side away from the pirate craft, and tried to pass a message to the captain. This proved impossible as well as extremely dangerous, while concentrating on flying just above the sea. However, by gaining height she observed that the crew seemed to be panic-stricken and ignoring orders.

By this time it was clear that the pirates would capture the ship unless she could establish some degree of discipline on the *Sothis*, and turn it in the direction of the *Sea Owl* to reduce the time required to intercept. After gaining altitude again, she flashed the light repeatedly to the *Sea Owl* to indicate that there was a difficult situation, and then reduced height to make a very uncomfortable landing on the *Sothis*'s deck.

On board the *Sea Owl* the lookout, Hekt, reported to the captain that he had seen repeated flashing signals from the transporter, and then it had suddenly vanished.

Osiris, realising that Isis was in trouble, ordered the ships to set all sail to reach the last known position of the *Sothis*. From a rough calculation he was fully aware it could take at least half an hour to achieve an interception, that is providing it turned towards them. By comparing the time between the two sets of signals, it appeared to him that the *Sothis* was moving, but not in the right direction.

Thoth, frantic about Isis's safety, rushed up to Osiris and said, "I beg you to give me permission to take the second transporter and go to her aid."

Osiris, under pressure from the whole crew, was forced to agree, and replied, "I grant this request although it is against my judgement of the situation, but you must promise that if she is aboard the *Sothis* you will return immediately to advise us of the situation."

Thoth immediately turned to the assembled Giants.

"I require a volunteer to accompany me so that I can concentrate on flying – also, for the protection of Isis, the volunteer must be an expert in the use of a bow."

Isis's companion, Leda, rushed forward, shouting, "I claim the right to defend my mistress. I have achieved the highest archery commendations in our city's competitions. It is also my sworn duty to protect my mistress."

As there were no objections, with bow and two full quivers, she took her place behind Thoth, and they set off immediately.

Back on the *Sothis*, Isis, with her kris waving above her head, forced her way through the crew to the captain. She then addressed the crew.

"I order you all on behalf of the High Council to return to your duty. From this moment any further defiance or lack of discipline will be severely punished. Relief is on its way as our three fully armed expedition ships are racing to intercept the *Sothis*."

One of the crew, dagger in hand, pushed towards Isis shouting, "The crew are taking over the *Sothis*!"

He got no further. With a slash of her kris, Isis sent his head rolling on the deck. In a fury, waving the bloody kris in front of her, she shouted, "Who else wishes to take over the ship and join him?"

The crew were silent.

Isis turned to Captain Teti. "You will immediately lay a course to intercept the expedition ships, which are approaching in that direction. For my part I will attempt to delay the pirates, and require you to provide a brave and trusted member of your crew to accompany me. He is to bring that cooking fire bowl with him, and drop the contents on the pirate vessel when I give the order."

The captain replied, "Take my sailing master's mate; he is my brother's son. Also lend me your kris when you leave, as there may be more trouble with the crew."

As soon as the surly crew had carried out the captain's orders to change course, Isis got back on the transporter and, with Teti's nephew terrified and clasping the fire bowl for dear life, they took off. After gaining a safe height, they turned to fly over the pirates. Crossing the pirate's boat diagonally, she shouted, "Pour the red-hot charcoal over the boat!"

As the charcoal tumbled through the air it became incandescent.

As a result, panic ensued. As they stopped rowing, their craft slewed off course, with some of their crew suffering burns. But they were quick to reorganise and set about extinguishing the small number of fires.

In a further attempt to increase the delay, Isis made a second pass over their vessel, turning to her passenger who was absolutely terrified, curled up and grasping the bowl with both hands.

"Get a grip on yourself and drop that bowl on their vessel when I make the next pass over it! A hit will be rewarded! A miss will not be appreciated."

This achieved the desired effect as the heavy bowl hit the steersman who tumbled overboard, and by the time the pirates had stopped their craft to go to his aid they were too late, and helplessly they watched him being dragged under by a shark.

After making a number of passes over the pirates to disturb their reorganisation, they then flew back to the *Sothis*. The crew were still causing trouble and, flying alongside, she told Teti's nephew to warn them once again of severe retribution if they failed to obey the captain's orders. She saw that the captain and his sailing master were still at the stern of the ship, being menaced by some of the crew, but there was nothing she could do, as now she was unarmed.

She turned round and started to make her way back to the *Sea Owl*. She observed the second transporter approaching and turned the craft around to fly alongside. She was delighted to see Thoth with a fully armed Leda.

"Zu, the *Sothis* is about to be attacked by a pirate craft – delay them while I return to the *Sea Owl* to rearm and bring three warriors to support Captain Teti."

Zu shouted back, "Thank ReRa you are safe, don't worry about the pirates – Leda will delay them for you!"

After parting, Thoth changed direction and flew directly over the pirates, who had now reorganised and were closing on the *Sothis*. Thoth called to Leda.

"Take out the helmsman and then the chieftain!"

Stringing her first arrow, with a contented smile she replied, "My pleasure!"

Her first shot took the helmsman in the neck, and he fell across the steering beam. As the craft swerved off course, her second arrow missed, but the effect caused panic in the boat.

They then kept the transporter out of bow shot until the pirates started to row again, then they moved in close and shot another pirate. They repeated this tactic until the pirates became conscious of the expedition ships closing in. They were now fully aware that the only chance of survival was to close and capture the *Sothis*.

As none of the pirates were willing to take the helm, they controlled the direction of their vessel by using their oars, achieving a fair degree of steering but at the same time delaying their progress.

Down to her last two arrows that she retained for any emergency, Leda shouted to Thoth, "I no longer have sufficient arrows to delay the pirates!" Thoth acknowledged and flew the transporter back towards the *Sothis*.

At this point Isis returned with the three warriors, landing them on the stern close to the captain.

Isis then took off immediately to join Thoth and Leda and then the two transporters raced back to Osiris to obtain additional reinforcements, as the pirates, even after their losses, had between twenty-five and thirty men available to board the ship, and the crew of the *Sothis* had to be regarded as unreliable.

As the distance was rapidly reducing between the ships, they soon had the additional fighters aboard the *Sothis*. Most of the crew were still surly, but they reluctantly attended to their duties, although quite a number were clearly supporting the pirates.

At this point, Isis and Thoth decided to bring a further six of the expedition, all of them being adept with bows, to reduce the number of pirates when they tried to board, and at the same time to remove any of the *Sothis* crew who attempted to join the pirates' assault.

The reinforcements arrived at the same time as the pirates' craft was attempting to come alongside.

With the battle about to commence, Isis took command.

"I have observed two Giants among the pirates; these must not be killed but singled out and disabled with blowpipe darts. In the same way a number of the pirates are to be disabled for interrogation. The rest must be killed; this order also includes the wounded. This concession will be merciful as otherwise they would have to face interrogation. The archers are to fire at their targets in sequence, to avoid wasting arrows on identical targets.

"The defence position is restricted to the stern deck, as this is higher than the main deck and presents a difficult barrier for the pirates to cross. I have to emphasise that our position has to be defensive until the two expedition ships board simultaneously from either side of the *Sothis*. When this occurs we will change from defence to attack."

The pirates grappled the *Sothis* and screaming their hate, brandishing krises, knives and short spears, started climbing up over the bulwark onto the middle deck, and harried by accurately placed arrows, a number of the attackers were killed or wounded. Unfortunately, offsetting this reduction in their strength, five or six members of the crew joined the pirates.

Two of the archers put down their bows and, using their hunting blowpipes, incapacitated four of the native crew, and two Giants, who appeared to be leading the attack.

The pirates had taken cover on the main deck, and having captured several of the native crew, used them as cover as they advanced to the edge of the stern deck. They then slaughtered two of the crew, and threw parts of their bodies onto the stern deck.

There were two ladders which accessed the stern deck, and the pirates formed two groups to attack on both sides simultaneously. Isis ordered the archers to target both areas from well back on the stern, and the armoured warriors to wait until enough pirates had managed to reach the deck before throwing them back to the main deck.

With maniacal screams and howls the pirates surged up the ladders to be met with well-directed arrows; some took the arrows on their small shields, but a number fell back onto the lower deck.

Isis yelled, "Throw them back!"

With her kris flashing as she waved it above her head, she charged forward to lead her warriors into the pirates – half of them escaped by jumping back onto the main deck, the remainder were killed.

The pirates in desperation tried to set fire to the stern deck, but at that moment the *Sea Owl* and *Sea Eagle* grappled the *Sothis* from both sides, and with shouts of "Borders away!" Osiris led the warriors onto the main deck.

At the same time Isis shouted, "Attack!"

Outnumbered, the pirates tried to escape by jumping back into their vessel, but they were cut down and in accordance with her orders, the only survivors were those incapacitated for interrogation.

Only six of the *Sothis*'s crew were left alive and two of those lightly wounded.

Only seven of the pirates had been kept alive for interrogation.

Osiris then ordered the prisoners to be secured with manacles and shackles and confined in the chain locker to be dealt with later.

After clearing the decks of the remains of battle, he sent for his three captains, and called over Isis and Thoth. After they assembled, he greeted and congratulated everyone, then said, "We must be ready to get under sail as soon as the wind returns. Thoth, you must leave this meeting immediately to organise the transfer of the artefacts to the three expedition ships, and I must ask my captains to give you authority to organise the transfers using whatever assistance you require from their crews."

The captains agreed and Thoth left the meeting.

Osiris continued, "The interrogation of the prisoners will commence as soon as we have resolved our problems regarding the *Sothis* and the pirate vessel. If we can get the information required from the native pirates, it will not be necessary to subject the two giants to the procedure. As you know, it is against our ancient community laws to kill Giants. However, these two can no longer remain members of our society, and will have to be marooned on the next uninhabited island we encounter, providing it has enough vegetation and animals to sustain life.

"Then there is the matter of the *Sothis*. Even if we make up the reduced crew the ship is not designed for a long ocean voyage and may well founder. If we take it with us, it will be of no immediate use to the expedition and possibly a liability. As our three ships have to be sent home immediately as we arrive at our destination, the *Sothis*, if it survived both the journey and the cataclysm, could possibly be an asset if used for coastal exploration. Perhaps someone would like to comment?"

Isis spoke out.

"I was surprised at Captain Teti's reaction to his crew's behaviour and later during the pirates' attack. I find it difficult to believe he is in league with the pirates, but they may have applied pressure to prevent him from taking an active part in controlling the crew or in repelling the pirates.

"For these reasons it would seem a sensible precaution to find him other duties when we are questioning the pirates or crew. In my view the question of the *Sothis* can be restricted to four possibilities: to take it with us as an accepted liability, to sink it, or to allow Captain Teti to sail it back to the city, with a minimum of crew members. The last consideration is that the *Sothis*'s captain is a weak and pliable character who, if we take his ship with us to Egypt, would be a liability to the aims of our expedition!

"If we allow the ship to return to the city it may be intercepted by pirates, or Seth; then by interrogating the crew it would doubtless provide Seth with further details about the artefacts and our activities to date.

"While fully appreciating the feeling of sadness Lord Osiris will have if the first of his merchant ships is destroyed, it is my view that after removing valuable equipment from both the *Sothis* and the pirate vessel they should be burned and sunk!"

Osiris asked for the view of the other three captains, who replied that they favoured sinking. However, if Osiris decided to keep the *Sothis* with them, they would have no objection.

At this moment Thoth appeared and addressed the meeting.

"The artefacts have been distributed and are being safely loaded under the instruction of the sailing masters, and we can sail at your command."

Osiris ordered, "First we remove all salvageable material from both the *Sothis* and the pirates' vessel, then destroy them both by burning. After that work has been satisfactorily completed, and providing the wind picks up, we all set sail for the west. In the meantime I require the *Sea Fury* and *Sea Eagle* to send their butchers to the *Sea Owl* to take part in the interrogation."

With the ships still becalmed, the prisoners were brought out onto the main deck, and two large sloping boards were rigged with the necessary restraints to receive the prisoners to be questioned.

Osiris addressed the prisoners.

"You have all been caught in an act of piracy against what you believed to be an unarmed coastal trading ship. During your attack you murdered prisoners who were members of the *Sothis*'s crew, cutting the bodies up and throwing them at the defenders. You are all sentenced to death!

"I am prepared to give you a choice. Answer the questions that are put to you truthfully and you will receive a quick death. Fail to answer or you lie, then the information we require will be extracted under severe torture. In the unlikely event that we find you deserve a lesser punishment you will become a slave for life after receiving twenty strokes of the whip. Apart from the first to be interrogated, the remainder will be held in the anchor locker."

Osiris then selected the first pirate, who they stripped and fastened to the sloping board. They then asked him if he had anything to say before questioning began. At the same time the butchers came and stood on either side of him and showed him their knives, flails and tongs. Receiving no reply, the interrogation began with simple questions that he could answer. After that they asked, "Who is your chief and why did you search for and subsequently attack the *Sothis*?"

The pirate refused to reply.

The butchers made a fine cut across his chest and commenced skinning. He started screaming and they threw salt water over him, and they put the question to him again.

He screamed and howled in agony and said, "I do not know. I just obey my chief." The butchers removed further strips of skin and splashed salt water on the wounds.

Each time he fainted, they revived him and repeated the question. This process continued for some time with no satisfactory answers.

More drastic measures needed to be applied so they cut off his left leg and, sealing the stub with bitumen, hung it around his neck.

The interrogators revived him with more salt water. In terrible agony and realising that there could be no hope of living, in desperation he pleaded, "I am in terrible agony – for mercy's sake grant me death."

In reply, Osiris told him again, "You can have a quick death in return for the truthful answers."

At this point the pirate haltingly, between spasms of excruciating pain, answered, "A Giant came to our village and spoke to our chief... as a result of that conversation four of our craft were manned and we went out to search for the *Sothis*. When our vessel sighted the ship we sent a messenger in a small skiff to call up the others. We held back our attack to wait for their arrival.

"After being attacked from the sky and recognising Isis, we guessed the expedition ships had sailed. This was soon confirmed when we saw their mastheads on the horizon... we then started to close on the *Sothis*, expecting support from some of the crew who are members of our village. We did not expect to encounter the additional warriors from the expedition.

"I know nothing more and ask for death!"

They then cut his throat and threw his body overboard.

The second to be interrogated was one of the *Sothis*'s crew who had joined the pirates, and who, on seeing the blood, peeled skin and severed leg, fainted. When revived, he promised to answer all questions truthfully, and asked for the chance to serve as a slave. They ignored his request and then asked, "Why did you join up with the pirates?"

He answered, "My family live in the same village as the pirate chief. When he discovered I was a member of the *Sothis* crew he forced me to join the pirates. I was instructed to provide information on the *Sothis*'s cargos and on any shipping we encountered in the harbours we visited along the coast. There are several members of the crew in the pay of the pirates, so we dare not fail to keep them informed.

"After witnessing the transporters arrival and the loading of valuable cargo, we waited until Isis and Thoth departed in the skiff. Then, while someone distracted the captain and sailing master, one of our members deserted the ship to send a carrier pigeon to the pirates. Our message told of Isis and Thoth's departure in the skiff sailing from the bay to the city.

"Our messenger agreed to continue to the pirates' stronghold and give the chief our vague details about the transporters used to bring the strange artefacts to the ship. The pirate chief has an arrangement with High Lord Seth that in exchange for protection they would keep him informed of their activities, and pay him a part of their profits. So the information would have been sent to Lord Seth, although I cannot be sure."

Osiris allowed him a quick death; they killed him immediately and threw his body overboard.

The third prisoner to be interrogated was a pirate, who in his replies to questions appeared extremely truculent. Osiris ordered the questioning to be stopped and they hung the first pirate's leg round his neck, followed by strips of skin from his body being placed on his chest. He was then warned that unless he lost his aggressive manner the same tortures would be applied to him regardless of his answering any of the questions put to him.

Responding to the horror of the previous torture, he became submissive and his answers confirmed those obtained from the second prisoner.

Osiris then asked, "Did Lord Seth ever visit your village?"

The pirate replied, "He came on two occasions: the first time it was to discuss with our chief why he was only receiving such a small portion of the spoils from their captures. Our chief replied, 'I have frequently sent you substantial amounts of gold and goods seized from both shipping and raids on settlements. I regard our relationship too valuable to risk imperilling our agreement!' Lord Seth then left and returned with a Giant. Then our chief confirmed he was the Giant who had received the payments. After rigorous questioning the Giant confessed that he had taken a substantial amount for his own use.

"Lord Seth then had him stripped and bound on a spit, and seemed to enjoy torturing him. When the Giant became very weak, he ordered a slow fire to be placed under the spit and had him roasted. Some time later, when the carcass was well cooked, he cut a large slice of the meat and ate it in front of the assembled pirates.

Lord Seth then impressed on the pirate chieftain that anyone who cheated him would meet the same fate."

Osiris granted the pirate a quick death. They then cut his throat and threw the body overboard to the group of sharks waiting patiently below.

The remaining two pirates confirmed the information obtained up to this point, the first under torture, followed by a miserable death.

The second, brought in to witness the final stages of the torture, decided to answer all the questions and they granted him a quick death.

After the bodies had been thrown into the sea, they washed the deck down and Osiris sent for the two Giants, ordered their bonds to be released and instructed them to sit down on the deck and pay particular attention to what he was about to say.

"From our interrogation of the five native pirates, we have discovered the connection between Lord Seth and the pirates, and your presence during the act of piracy attempted on the *Sothis*. While we are prepared to observe the law with regard to activities against our community, we have the possibility of selecting a barren island, which in effect would give you a slow death from starvation, for which we could not be considered directly responsible.

"Should you decide to tell us, in reasonable detail, your involvement with both Seth and the native pirates, we can maroon you on a suitable island with plentiful food and water. We would also be prepared to provide you with a few tools and a sail from the *Sothis*, so you can build a substantial boat and sail to the Northern Lands. In either event you will be branded so that you can never rejoin our society."

One of the Giants was then bound and returned to the anchor cable locker. Then after giving the Giant a short time to consider, he was asked to make his statement or refuse the offer.

The Giant then spoke. "I accept your offer and will tell you all I know about this affair. I am a member of a group loyal to High Lord Seth, who wishes to change the leadership of our society.

"The first information we received on the Isis and Thoth expedition and their discoveries was obtained from the pirates, who had spies within the crew of the *Sothis*. They said their ship had been loaded with strange artefacts in a secluded bay north of the city. Isis had flown the artefacts to the beach in a magic tray called a transporter. Isis and Thoth had then taken a small sailing dingy, loaded with two transporters, to return to the city.

"The pirates had already put in hand the interception of the small sailing dingy. Seth was doubtful about the whole report and sent the two of us to ensure that Isis and Thoth were not harmed and were delivered to him. In addition we were to supervise the capture of the *Sothis*. The complete ship's cargo was to be held for Seth's disposal – providing his order was fully implemented, he promised a rich reward for the pirates. The rest you know."

Osiris, thanking the Giant, said, "While I appreciate that you carried out this plan on the instructions of Lord Seth, you did participate in an unprovoked attack on a cargo ship. Sadly, although I regard you as victims of unfortunate circumstances, the law has to be upheld. Both of you will be marooned, but with sufficient stores to ensure your wellbeing and with the tools and equipment I promised you. Thoth will provide you with a map that will help you find a safe route to the Northern Lands.

"Your safety will depend on how quickly you can construct your boat and leave the island, which is sure to be submerged if the prophecy is realised. With regard to the brand, it will only be a small mark to fulfil the law, providing you both take an oath not to try and rejoin Seth."

To this the Giant agreed, and the second Giant was then released from the anchor cable locker and they both took the oath.

After bringing the ships close together for the night, Osiris called a conference of the captains, together with Isis, Thoth and the sailing master of the *Sea Owl*. Captain Teti of the *Sothis* was not included as his position with the expedition was still under review.

Osiris opened the discussion. "Our interrogation of the pirates revealed that Lord Seth is, and has been, in league with the pirates for some time. He is clearly intent on capturing Isis and Thoth together with the artefacts, which he believes will aid him in gaining the presidency. If we assume the worst, he will now join up with the pirates and with superior numbers attempt to capture our ships."

Isis interjected. "When I flew off to find the *Sothis* I did not appreciate that, when piloting the transporter, you become so committed to maintaining direction and height you are virtually useless to undertake any other action. I should not have taken off to hunt for the *Sothis* without a passenger. I thought at the time that including one would unnecessarily risk his life, but that must never happen again, and in future it will be essential to be accompanied by an armed warrior. Could I suggest suitable applicants be selected before we have further encounters requiring the transporters."

Osiris continued. "While I hope such encounters can be avoided, plans must be made for that eventuality and I will select suitable applicants after this meeting.

"Isis has already demonstrated the delaying effect of dropping red-hot charcoal on the pirates' vessel; perhaps this approach can be improved to burn sails?

"Thoth, are there any surprises among the artefacts to aid our defence, or other means to delay an attack until we can elude them in the dark?"

"I have been studying the scrolls and have located two artefacts that can improve our navigation; one finds true south and the other measures the inclination of a star – these may be of use to the sailing master. I have only had a short time to interpret the scrolls, and have found them extremely difficult to comprehend. However, I am building up lists of equivalents with our hieroglyphs, but this is a slow process. Possibly there are items that can be used in defence of our ships, but not within the time limits we envisage with regard to Seth's activities, so we must devise some sort of fire bomb from our own resources."

Captain Amle then suggested, "Let us link two bitumen torches with a length of rope to straddle the sail when dropped from the transporter. This would have a fair chance of setting light to the sail before the crew would be able to climb up and extinguish them."

"Captain Amle, prepare a number of sets, to be ready for use by dawn. I would prefer a solution that did not involve the transporters, as these must be held in reserve until the situation becomes critical. I must also emphasise to all of you that our purpose is to delay Seth's ships, and not to destroy the Mesopotamian expedition. Any of your proposals should bear that in mind.

"As the wind is now picking up I intend to continue with full sail throughout the night. I acknowledge this is unusual, and not to our sailing master's liking, but he agrees we must distance ourselves from Seth and the pirates. The main difficulties during the night will be to maintain contact between the ships, while sailing within a safe sailing distance from each other, and conversely not straying too far away. Thoth will supply two special light units for each ship from the artefacts; these will provide a set of markers so that their position, with regard to each other, can be maintained by reliable lookouts. If the weather deteriorates and visibility becomes difficult, sail must be reduced and lookouts doubled, even if it allows Seth to close up by dawn.

"Thoth, take another look at the scrolls and see if you can devise a practical means of keeping Seth's ships at bay."

While all this was going on, Captain Teti of the *Sothis* was leaning down over the starboard bulwark examining a sea creature, possibly a giant squid sliding through the sea close to the side of the ship. Its body was about two cubits across, five cubits long, the white of the eye the size of a dinner plate and the pupil a beautiful soft brown. From the front of his body to the end of his long arms was about twelve cubits, the massive arms tapered down to diamond-shaped pads covered with large circular suckers.

Teti called over a number of the crew to view the creature, but when he pointed down to it, a thick arm reached up and dragged him down into the sea before he could utter a sound. He vanished before their eyes and after searching the sea from the masthead he did not reappear and was presumed dead.

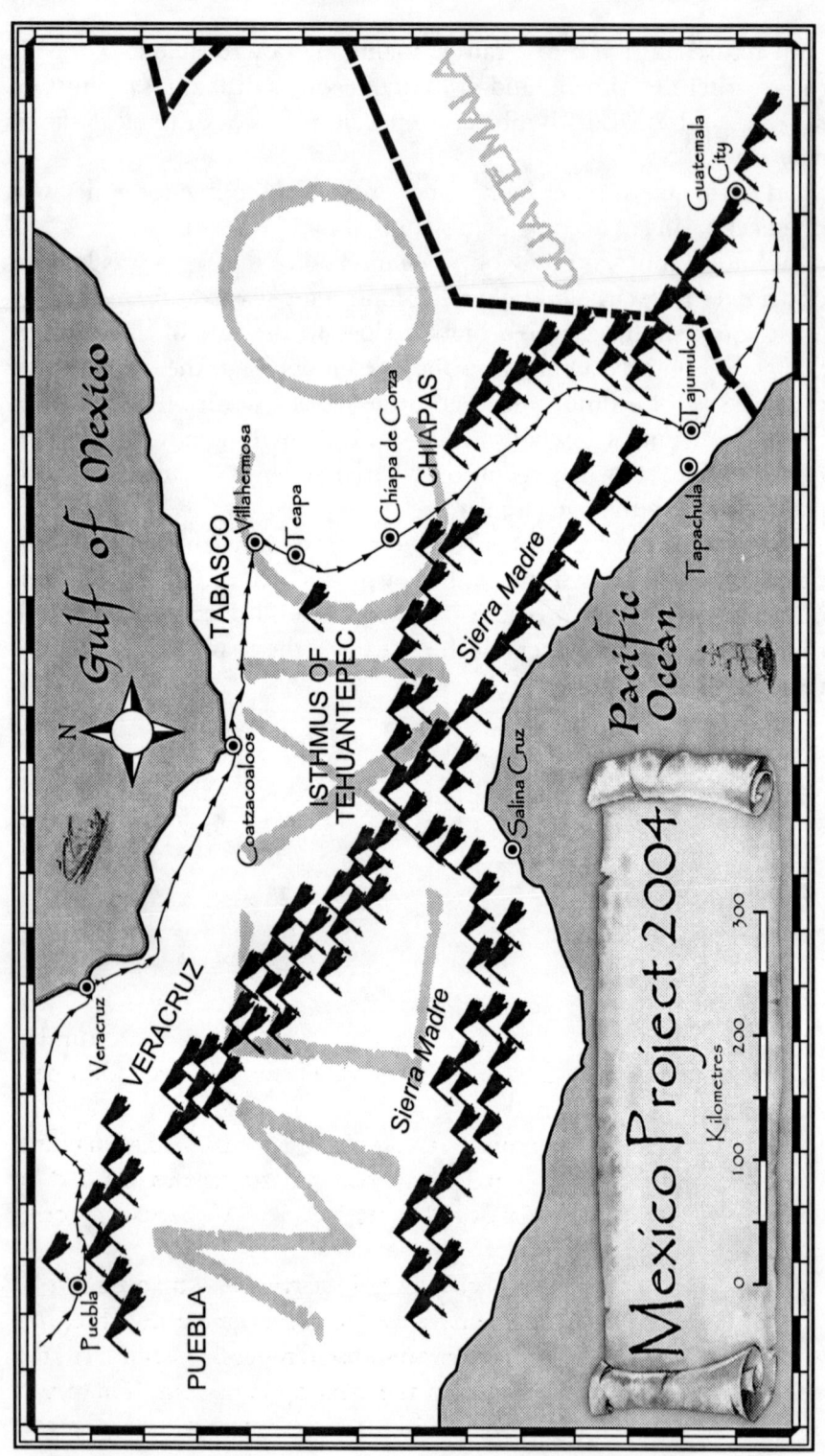

Mexico Project 2004

Mexico 2004

Richard McKay, known as Ricky to his friends, was forty years old, with dark brown hair, warm brown eyes, and a determined jaw line.

Standing at 1.83 metres – six foot – he was broad-shouldered, with a strong muscular body, appeared young for his age, and had an easy-going personality.

Ricky had gained considerable knowledge from his father who had served in the army as a bomb disposal expert. He had been injured on active service, and for the rest of his life had been surviving on a small service disability pension. Disillusioned, he warned Ricky not to join the forces, but in their many happy hours together, he passed on his accumulated knowledge for dealing with explosive devices and taught him unarmed combat techniques.

Ricky left university when he was twenty-one years old and joined a mining machinery manufacturer supplying equipment to Mexico, where he met Yax Nixte and they discovered that they had mutual interests in Mexican and Egyptian archaeology, and became firm friends.

Returning to England in his twenty-third year he married a fashion model who immediately insisted that he should change his job to obtain a better salary and improved conditions for advancement. He rather reluctantly complied, but soon regretted the move as a few months later, while he was away from home on an overseas visit, his wife ran off with a multimillionaire. Ricky was devastated, embarrassed and left blaming himself.

The company he joined was an international packaging and exporting outfit, shipping machinery to all parts of the world, and he was now their Overseas Liaison Representative, flying business class on his way to Mexico City.

Ricky was heartily sick of travelling, in particular long boring trips in aircraft, sleeping in expensive hotels in characterless box-like rooms, being entertained, attending conferences, rushing to the nearest airport then flying out to the next appointment. There was never sufficient time to travel within the country and meet the real inhabitants, but he was determined that this time it would be different!

This was Mexico and ancient archaeology had become Ricky's lifetime hobby, so consequently he had worked the visit to coincide with the annual work holidays. There had been substantial management opposition, but as he was determined, and as the management could not field any valid objections other than jealousy, they reluctantly agreed to allow him to take his annual holiday in Mexico.

Landing at Mexico City airport after a twelve-hour flight, he claimed his baggage and passed into the customs hall. Ricky was then handed the usual board that listed items that had to be declared to the customs.

The customs officer looked at the tags on his luggage. "Mr McKay, have you anything to declare?"

Ricky replied, "Absolutely nothing."

The officer gave him a peculiar look and said, "Mr McKay, is this your first visit to Mexico?"

"I was here some fifteen years ago."

"Mr McKay, I see you have not forgotten your Mexican Spanish; how long were you in this country?"

"Three years working on water extraction problems in deep mines."

"Mr McKay, what was your status, *Immigrado* or *Immigrante*?"

"*Immigrante*, but in the end nothing was finalised."

"Mr McKay, how long are you staying in our country this time?"

"Three to four weeks."

"Have you obtained accommodation?"

"Yes, I have accommodation at the Hotel Vieja."

"Welcome to Mexico, but if you wish to extend your stay, kindly inform our offices in Mexico City who will, by then, be informed of your visit."

Ricky grabbed his baggage and joined in the mad rush for a taxi.

After a short but hectic drive through the city, he arrived at the Hotel Vieja reception.

After having his booking confirmed, he asked the receptionist to arrange a visit to Teotihuacán in the morning and a flight to Vera Cruz the following day. Then congratulating himself at having completed the business arrangements, he retired to his room for a lazy bath and to open the altitude-compensating glass capsules (Tequila Reserva) so thoughtfully supplied by the management!

The next morning Ricky went to the reception desk to obtain tickets for Teotihuacán and his flight to Vera Cruz. Just before he left the desk, he was handed a letter that had been delivered to reception by a Mexican boy who refused to leave his name.

Intrigued, Ricky settled down in one of the armchairs. He was astounded to read that the message had come from an old friend who had been with him during a difficult period in the mines, some seventeen years ago. It read as follows:

Wednesday, 0530 hrs
Ricky,
Welcome to Mexico, we have missed you!
Heard you are in town, at the right place and the right time! I need to talk to you. Forget your flight to Vera Cruz; I would like to drive you down for your appointment.
I understand you have arranged to visit Teotihuacán this morning. I will be there in the underground café at 1400 hrs. Please meet me there, and everything will be explained.
Certainly for you the meeting is of the utmost importance.
I have never forgotten our firm friendship during the trials of the past, and I believe that you also treasure those memories of our many discussions regarding the link between the Mexican development and Egypt.
Until 1400.

Yax Nixte

As the tour bus crawled through the heavy traffic in Mexico City to start the fifty kilometres' drive to Teotihuacán, Ricky recalled when, accompanied by Yax, he was inspecting equipment in a deep mine; there was a substantial rockfall and they were trapped for two days. While waiting for a rescue team to break through, they had discussed the Mayan Prophecy and the possible influence of Egypt on Maya and Olmec development. Realising that they both had the same interests, it was almost inevitable that by the time the rescuers broke through, their business relationship had become a firm friendship.

Arriving at Teotihuacán, Ricky deserted the tour guide and decided to start at the south end and walk up the two-and-a-half-kilometre Way of the Dead (Processional Way) to the Pyramid of the Moon. He would stop on the way to visit the various items of interest to absorb the three hours before his appointment with Yax.

Ricky mused that the city itself was a bit of an enigma as so little was known about the people who built it, but it had been established that by AD 100 it was a going concern. Sometime after that date, there was a cultural exchange with the Maya and later an occupation by the Aztecs.

Standing on the top of the Pyramid of the Sun, he realised that by design or coincidence, it had a base size of 230 metres by 220 metres with sides oriented true north. In Egypt outside Cairo, the Khufu (Cheops) Pyramid's base is 230 metres by 230 metres and the sides oriented true north. Clearly, if a link between Egypt and Central America was to be established, it would require more tangible evidence than this.

After climbing the Pyramid of the Moon, Ricky visited the Jaguar Temple, the Temple of Quetzalcoatl and the Ball Courts. By the time he returned to the south end of the Way of the Dead, with the heat of the sun reflected off the plaza and structures, he was utterly exhausted.

At the underground café he was delighted to find Yax, and after withstanding a bear-like hug, subsided into a chair at a reserved table, which Yax had fought hard to retain.

Ricky quickly opened the conversation. "Yax, before you say anything I have a strong feeling that I have been under continual observation during my visit – this may be a figment of my imagination, but it might not be advisable to give too much detail while there are so many people around! Now to more important matters. It's wonderful to be with you again after such a long time and to tell you how delighted I was to receive your letter, but how you managed to locate me within twelve hours of my arrival in Mexico intrigues me!"

Yax laughed. "I have a friend in the airport immigration department, and a long time ago I got him to put a flag under your name and description so that if you ever visited Mexico I would be informed! Surprisingly it worked and I got all the details you provided for the customs officer.

"There is a downside to all this, not with the customs – that is covered. As you are aware, I am a native Maya and my family believe we have a trace of Olmec in our DNA. We never adopted Spanish ways and were not converted to Catholicism, so as a result we have kept our own family names.

"You will have heard of the difficulties the Maya have had in the south with the Mexican Government, and unfortunately, as I am well educated, it is inevitable that they regard me with some suspicion.

You will also be aware that I am not political and although naturally sympathetic with the plight of our people, I have refused to take part in any insurrection, fully appreciating that it could not succeed!

"Regarding being under surveillance, could anyone have read the letter I sent you? I mean, was it sealed?"

Ricky replied, "The flap was tucked in the envelope, but apart from that it was not sealed. As the note was delivered by hand, I never queried the sealing."

Yax, looking very concerned, said, "I'm afraid that you have now been associated with me. It is essential to assume we are both under surveillance at this moment either by the security services, but that is doubtful as my friends in the ministry would have warned me this morning, or alternatively by the shadowy figures who control the right-wing death squads, who, as you will know from the press, are trying to eliminate all Maya culture and Maya societies in both Mexico and Guatemala.

"In view of this possibility let us confine our discussions to pleasantries and discuss the real matters of interest in the car on the way to Vera Cruz.

"So let us have a light meal and a drink here, and then we must separate – you return to your hotel by one of the tour buses, and I will collect you from there tomorrow morning at any time convenient to you."

Ricky replied, "The refreshments are a matter of immediate attention; perhaps a Tequila Cuervo aperitif before we start, followed by tortillas would be appropriate for the occasion. With regard to tomorrow's start, let us meet at the Hotel Vieja entrance at 9 a.m. where I'll be waiting with my luggage. OK?"

So after enjoying their light meal Ricky returned to Mexico City and advised the British Embassy of his business visit to Vera Cruz, and his subsequent roving holiday in the state of Tabasco. Returning to his hotel he completed his preparations for an early start the next morning. Before going to bed he received a telephone call suggesting that he leave Mexico immediately after completing his business in Vera Cruz. No name was given and the call was abruptly cut off.

At 9 a.m. Yax arrived outside the hotel and they set off on their journey to Vera Cruz some four hundred kilometres to the east. Conversation was minimal until they cleared the appalling traffic and associated pollution in the city. Leaving the suburbs, the roads cleared and at last it became possible to hold the long-awaited discussion.

Yax started. "Knowing your interest in establishing the link between Egypt and Mexico and my own interests in that field, my vacations have been spent searching for something tangible but with little success. Now at last, by pure luck, I am confident that link has been found, and by happy coincidence you arrived in Mexico shortly after my discovery to share it with me and to use it in a manner that will benefit my people! The only drawback is that I will not be around long enough to see you succeed. I am sure you will complete the task and that my Ka will help guide you to success.

"The hard truth is… is that I am dying of cancer and the doctors have given me three months to live. Yes – before you ask, I have had a second and a third specialist's opinion and they all say the same.

"For your own protection I will not give you more details of where we are going until we leave the Vera Cruz Cordoba area, as I can assure you the people who are interested in our friendship are totally unscrupulous."

Ricky was stunned. "This news… it fills me with great sadness, and I appreciate this is a selfish attitude but you are and always have been, since our first meeting, my friend and my most valued memory of Mexico. I will welcome the support of your Ka to direct me, after we are separated by earthly time. While the security of our endeavour is in jeopardy I can understand your reluctance to reveal more details, but what about your family? Are they in danger?"

"My family was murdered by government troops during the recent uprising by the Maya and the natives in Chiapas. When I eventually found a place for their final burial, the link with Egypt was revealed to me. It is my belief that their guidance facilitated the successful outcome of my lifelong search. Last night, while interrogating the receptionist from your hotel, he revealed that the information in my letter was given to the right-wing group, so at least we know our enemy. Hotel Vieja will have to find a new receptionist to replace him now. Incidentally, he knew about your telephone call and threat, and we have the name of the caller and his card has been marked. In fact it was a busy and interesting night!"

Ricky was astounded. "You did say that you are not concerned with politics and armed insurrection but it seems you have the backing of a small army. I presume there is an answer to all this, so please tell me what you can."

"It is true that I am not interested in politics or insurrection but we do have groups set up to protect the Maya, and all the action we take is totally defensive. This policy may result in killing selected targets to protect our people, but any such action can only be taken after group approval. Before we part I will give you a list of contacts on a miniature CD; those groups will always protect you when you visit Mexico or Guatemala. This list will be written in K'iche Maya. There will be just enough information in English for you to find a reliable interpreter; he'll give you access to a mini computer. You will then insert the disc and call up the area you are in or about to visit. He will then translate the individual district contact details you have displayed, he won't make notes and no copies will be made. I suggest that when you get to the UK you make separate copies for each district and then secure the master copy in a major bank's customer deposit box."

After noticing that the car was low on fuel, Yax resumed. "Let us turn off the road and select a garage sufficiently remote from the main route that the opposition are unlikely to have covered. As the fuel level is running lower than advisable in Mexico, I suggest a drink would be very welcome."

"*That* is an excellent idea but let's make sure we can get ourselves and the car under shade from the sun as it looks exceedingly hot outside. Air conditioning would be acceptable, but it is doubtful that we'll find it off the beaten track!"

After travelling about twenty kilometres they came to an ancient garage on the approach to a small village. After topping up with fuel from a hand-operated pump they parked in the main village square bordered by small trees and shrubs, which were clearly surviving the heat with difficulty. The usual whitewashed church stood on one side of the square, and on the opposite side there was a bar with its swinging wooden half doors. It had a surprisingly clean interior, although the furniture had seen better days. Yax had a quick word with the owner, who rushed off and produced an excellent meal of enchiladas with bottles of mineral water, which he insisted would be good for Ricky's health, adding as an afterthought, "Why should the passenger drink, when the driver is by necessity reduced to water?"

"As you know I have to visit a company in Cordoba tomorrow, so I'm staying two nights at the Camino Real Hotel in Vera Cruz. The following morning I am at your disposal for ten days, and after that I have to return to the UK. If it becomes necessary to extend for a few days, that will be possible providing the Mexican authorities will grant a week's further extension; but that will require a visit to Mexico City. As to finance, I have an adequate supply of traveller's cheques and banker's cards, but are there any special items that I should obtain for our trip?"

Yax replied, "Have you got a digital camera with you with flash and suitable for recording text on a stela?"

"Yes, I have an excellent Minolta digital camera with 64 MB memory and 16 MB in reserve."

"Excellent. Will you load the 16 MB card and take plenty of innocuous photo shots tomorrow, if you can find the time? The 64 MB card can be fitted when we reach the area of operations and after use, the 16 MB card must immediately be inserted to replace it. This is a precaution in case you're stopped and the camera examined. Think about suitable places to conceal the 64 MB card. The reason for all this will become apparent later on."

The plans for their next stage having been established they drove to the Camino Real in Vera Cruz and Ricky booked in for a couple of nights and called his business contact who promised to pick him up from the hotel at 9 a.m. the next day.

That night Ricky was sitting at a corner table in the hotel restaurant with a beer and club sandwich, well away from a highly excited group of tourists standing round the bar all trying to relate their experiences at the same time. Most of the tables around the room were occupied, one of which was taken by four locals trying to play dominoes, while immersed in a haze of tobacco smoke.

Maria Martinez entered – a thirty-year-old, highly qualified, tall, beautifully proportioned Chiapas Jaguar of a woman, with long shiny black hair caressing her face as she moved purposefully towards Ricky's table.

Maria wore a light-blue cocktail dress that emphasised her form, with two small diamond clasps to set off her neckline. Her facial features were a classic mix of Euro-Asian, highlighted with the minimum of make-up and her eyes were a sparkling green. Softly spoken with just a hint of latent menace, she projected a warm and caring personality to conquer her target.

Ricky was lost even before she arrived at his table!

He was not impressed when she came up behind him and murmured softly, "Do you mind if I sit at your table, as most of the others are occupied and the remainder are too close to the bar and the pack of tourists?"

Ricky looked up, saw this smartly dressed woman, and immediately replied, "You are more than welcome, but I fear I will be poor company!"

The lady subsided smoothly into an adjoining chair.

"Would you do me a favour and ask the barman to give me a glass of red wine and a club sandwich? Charge it to my room, number twenty-seven."

Ricky went up to the bar and passed the message to the barman who promised to send the order to his table.

On his return the lady announced her name as Maria Martinez and would he please call her Maria. Her Mexican Spanish indicated she was well educated, and her jewellery and clothing indicated expensive tastes. Ricky wondered why she should risk her reputation by sitting down with a man to whom she had not been introduced, as the Spanish Mexican males would not normally allow their wives, or lady friends, to behave in such a fashion.

Maria opened the conversation. "You are English? I suspect you are in Mexico on business and not a tourist, so for you a hotel is invariably a lonely place... if it is not a rude question, can I ask how long you will be staying in this hotel?"

"Allow me to introduce myself first; name is Richard McKay – Ricky to my friends. The hotel has booked me in for two nights, so as you guessed it's a brief business visit."

A young girl then approached the table carrying the wine and sandwich and Ricky was surprised to be given a glass of red wine. He explained to the girl that the order was for a single glass. She replied that the barman had sent it to him on the house, to keep the lady company.

Maria said, "Don't worry about it – accept or he will feel insulted." So Ricky told the girl to thank the barman.

They finished their light meal and after a coffee Maria said, "Goodnight. I have enjoyed our little get together, and I hope to see you again before you leave. Perhaps tomorrow night at the same time?"

Ricky replied, "Excellent idea, looking forward to it – you must be my guest."

Soon after Maria left, Ricky returned to his room to review his papers for tomorrow's discussions at Cordoba, and turned in for the night.

The next morning all went according to plan: the meetings were cordial and with concessions on both sides, an amicable settlement was reached that was in line with his director's brief. Satisfied with the result and after a splendid lunch in the director's dining room, Ricky returned to the hotel.

After a lazy bath and change into less formal attire, he went down to the bar and obtained the same quiet table in the corner.

A short time later, a seductively dressed Maria joined him. After mutual pleasantries they ordered tequila and pulpo bits as an aperitif, followed by red wine and charcoal-braised spare ribs with salad, and to finish, they decided on coffee and mints. Happily talking about Maria's family and rural Mexico, time passed pleasantly. Ricky offered Maria a choice of liquors but she declined, saying the coffee was all she required. At that moment there was a crash at the far side of the room. As Ricky turned to see what was happening, Maria carefully slipped some white powder into his coffee, then put her hand on his shoulder and asked what all the fuss was about. The dispute stopped as suddenly as it began, and the two card players dropped back in their chairs and continued as if nothing had happened.

Ricky said, "It's just a dispute about cards and a flash of temperament."

Maria laughed. "It had me worried for a moment, but let's drink up our coffee and retreat to our rooms before we get mixed up in a riot, as I doubt it will end there." The crowd seemed to think the same and the bar rapidly emptied.

Ricky said goodnight to Maria and returned to his room. He just had time to set the alarm for the morning and go to bed before he slipped into a disturbed sleep.

Ricky imagined that Maria had slipped quietly into the room and was holding his hand; it was very comforting. Then, speaking softly to him, she said, "Ricky darling, who was that charming friend who drove you down to Vera Cruz? I'm sure I knew the wife who was killed in a terrible accident during the troubles in Chiapas."

Ricky answered, "You're quite right about his wife, and his name is Yax Nixte – we worked together many years ago. He's a very close friend and I ran into him when I landed in Mexico City."

Maria lifted his hand to her face and kissed it, then said, "Are you going to see him again? If so give him my condolences and say if he ever requires my help, he's not to hesitate to ask for it."

Maria looked so beautiful and sympathetic, so he replied, "We're meeting tomorrow morning at the hotel and then we are going on a week's trip to cover interesting archaeological sites, a subject we both enjoy."

Maria kissed him again. "You are so good, Ricky, remembering your old friends in Mexico, and I do love you. Where are you going first?"

"I don't know exactly and I agreed to leave it all up to Yax, but he said it would be very exciting."

She stroked his forehead and said, "The countryside is not very safe at this time, you should let someone know where you are at all times – have you made a suitable arrangement?"

"The British Embassy know I am at the Camino Real in Vera Cruz, and that I will advise them by telephone as soon as Yax tells me the itinerary."

Maria then said, "You have told me all I needed to know and now you get a little reward; after this I know you will always want me. My contact address in Mexico City is in your coat pocket – do you understand?"

He answered, "Yes, Maria."

She then started to gently strip off his pyjamas, and when all was removed she skilfully started to encourage him until he was fully aroused. She straddled him and with her skill extended the period of sexual pleasure. She let him rest for a while, then aroused him again, and this time it was even more pleasurable and on completion, he fell back into his disturbed sleep.

Maria opened her bag and took out two small cans of quick-drying body paint, one red, one blue. With the red paint she drew two large circles on his chest, marking the nipples with blue. His penis she painted red and the balls blue. Then, to complete the artistry, she drew a large arrow from the chest to the penis. To complete her contract she shook him awake, then lent over him and bit deep into his chest on both sides close to the nipples, muffling his screams with his socks. When he had stopped moaning she removed the gag and held him until exhausted; he fell back into a deep sleep. Then she quietly left the room, returned the key to the reception, and left the hotel in a car that had been waiting outside to pick her up.

With the alarm ringing incessantly, Ricky pulled himself out of a deep slumber. He felt too tired to get up, but the thought of Yax waiting outside the hotel at 9 a.m. forced him to sit up in bed. He was still reflecting on his turbulent dream when he saw his pyjamas neatly folded on the bedside chair and realised he was naked and – worse – the front of his body was obscenely painted. He was horrified and realised that he had been drugged. He would have to tell Yax and admit he had been a bloody fool to allow Maria the opportunity to imperil their plans.

Thank God Yax had not told him their final destination, or, for that matter, their intended direction. He had wanted to tell her everything, and if Yax had not held back that information they would now be in an impossible position.

The immediate problem was to clean up. Going into the bathroom he found the shower wasn't working. Maria obviously had friends in the hotel, or had bribed someone to obtain their assistance. Then he remembered the quarrel in the bar – it had obviously been part of her plan. Oh, he had been such a bloody fool!

There was still a small supply of water in the washbasin so he started to try and remove as much as he could from his chest. The pain was excruciating and as the clotted blood was removed he saw the deep bite marks. Fortunately he always carried an antiseptic and film-type protective plasters, so he was able to complete the necessary repair work.

He would need a solvent to remove the paint and then a shower, and as neither was available he would have to dress and cover the damage with a shirt and cravat. Another problem for Yax to help him resolve!

Glancing at his watch he realised it was 8.45 a.m. and he rushed down to the reception with his baggage to pay his bill, only to be told that his bill had been paid. He was then handed a heavily sealed note, which one of their guests had left for him. At nine o'clock he rushed out of the hotel and there was Yax just driving up. Throwing his bags into the car, he slipped in beside Yax and said, "There is much to tell; we must get out of Vera Cruz quickly. Stop the car in a safe place off the main road. I've been extremely foolish. Once we stop and I can collect my thoughts, I'll explain everything."

Yax turned off the main road and found a concealed place close to a deserted farm building. Switching off the engine, Yax turned to Ricky and said, "It sounds as if you have had a bad time, and whatever it is we'll deal with it together in friendship and as a team. Tell me about it from the beginning and I promise not to interrupt."

Ricky told him the whole story until he reached the point where the receptionist passed him a note from Maria, and then he realised that he had not read it.

Yax was intrigued. "What does it say?"

Ricky, a trifle embarrassed, opened the tightly sealed note and read out the contents.

Dear Ricky,

I just want to let you know that I was fulfilling a contract and when I took it on, I knew nothing about you or your relationship with Yax Nixte. Like you I am a professional in my field, and failure to complete a contract as ordered would, at best, lose me important clients or, at worst, could result in my receiving serious injuries. So I ask you to understand and forgive me. I have given you my address and would love you to contact me as a friend, outside my professional work.

There are two things I must tell you: firstly, the paint comes off quickly with a mixture of alcohol and washing-up liquid and secondly, do not contact the police; be reassured that if you do evidence will be provided that will result in you receiving a long jail sentence, where accidents can occur.

There is one more item of importance: search your car. There may be an explosive device fitted. Tell no one except Yax about this letter, and please destroy it immediately as my life depends on it. Tell Yax my mother is Maya; he will understand.

Ricky, I care for you, God help me.

Maria

Yax laughed. "Taking everything into account I do not believe our project has been damaged and if Maria is right, your incident – though stressful and embarrassing to say the least – may have saved our lives.

"Burn the letter immediately and while you are doing that I will start to search the inside of the car."

Ricky read the letter for a second time, then reluctantly burnt it and crushed the ashes. He knew that although it was foolish, he had felt a strong attraction to Maria when she first sat down at his table, and despite all that had happened he could not shake off that sense of loss that arises when someone you care for has gone away.

Ricky now started to search the outside of the car; lifting the bonnet he was appalled to see a sophisticated demolition installation. He yelled to Yax, "Stop what you're doing! Don't touch anything in the car and come out slowly."

Yax gasped when he looked under the bonnet. "Apparently we've been extremely fortunate! If that lot had gone up we would have been mincemeat. Maria saved our lives!"

Ricky commented, "If it failed to go up on the timer any garage attendant checking our oil would have perished. If you look near the bonnet catch, you'll notice they rigged a micro switch to initiate the charge when the bonnet was opened. After installation the bonnet was closed and the switch activated by pulling a tape away and releasing the plunger, but as you can see the tape broke when pulling it clear and the plunger remained sealed.

"To ensure that we were killed when the charge was ignited they installed a cordex loop, or a detonating cord, round the engine compartment, designed to explode and prevent the main charge from being dissipated by the bonnet flying off. By this means the main force of the charge would be directed into the passenger compartment."

"I'm afraid I cannot help you as I have very little experience of explosives other than their general use in mining. The trouble is we need this car and as I only have a little life left to lose, I'll attempt to disarm it."

Ricky laughed. "*That* is a non-starter! I would lose you *and* the car and be left with nowhere to go with the most essential part of my life in ruins. I can disarm this installation for two reasons. One is that my old firm insisted I took a month's course with ICI on the use of explosives before leaving for Mexico to work on deep mines and the other is that my father specialised in sabotage in the war. While I was growing up, at my insistence, he explained all about the various methods used. So now let's see if I have learnt my lessons well!"

"All right, Ricky, but only if you allow me to stand close to you, so that if anything happens we go together. I cannot think of a better way to die than together with my best friend, and I have no fear of disturbing you!"

"First let's find some tools – in my bag there's a pair of nail clippers – get them. Are there any tools in the car?"

"I'll search... I take it we mustn't disturb the car while doing this?"

Ricky laughed. "*That* is an understatement!"

After their search they came up with a small collection of tools including a bent screwdriver and a stiff, almost unusable, pair of pliers, but best of all, a roll of black insulating tape.

There being no point in delaying disarming the installation, Ricky started by cutting away the cortex and lifting the electrical detonator away from the primers. Then he studied the explosive pack. This consisted of a stick of gelignite surrounded by three lengths of plastic sausage skins filled with fertiliser.

At one end a primer had been joined with the gelignite in which another detonator had been inserted. There was just enough room to extract it, and with great care he withdrew it clear of the primer.

Ricky then examined all the way around the explosive pack, and there were no booby traps, so he removed it. The gelignite was still dangerous as it was sweating nitroglycerine and any knock could cause it to explode. They carried it into the deserted building where they released the ties round the wrapping, then a fire was set to slowly burn up to the explosive after they left the building; if it failed to burn, at least it would deaden the sound of any subsequent explosion.

They then returned to the car and removed the electronic control unit. That done, they searched the car for any further explosive charges and any tagging devices, but nothing was found.

After checking their clothing and luggage for electronic bugs, Yax remarked, "Have you studied those bite marks, is there anything special about them? I mean, could a tracer have been inserted under the skin? With the pain you experienced it's doubtful if you would have known at the time."

"I had not considered that possibility, but in any case, to avoid infection and remove the chip, if there is one, urgent medical attention is requires.".

Reloading the car, they then set off to Coatzacoalcos, where there was a strong Maya community some ten kilometres outside the town. There they would be protected and he could remove the paint prior to a nurse examining the wounds – embarrassing maybe, but in a hot climate essential.

They reached the small Mexican village and Yax parked outside a small bar-cum-hotel and went in, obtaining a room with adjoining bathroom. The owner's son rushed out to the village store and in a short time returned with the alcohol and washing-up liquid. Ricky took up residence in the bathroom and after an hour and a great deal of effort removed the offending paint.

Meanwhile, Yax had sent for a nurse who removed the plasters and, with Yax, examined the wounds finding, as he expected, a small object buried under the skin. The nurse, with a "Sorry, this will hurt", dug it out and cleaned the wound. After stopping the substantial bleeding, she covered it up and promised to inspect it and dress it again next morning. Yax then paid the owner's son to take the bug and leave it in a suitable place high up in a small hotel in Coatzacoalcos.

The necessary preparations having been made, they went down to the bar and enjoyed a rather basic but adequate meal. Ricky, who due to the previous energetic and drugged night, was absolutely exhausted, retired to his room. Yax, meanwhile, returned to the bar to obtain the local news and make arrangements.

Next morning the nurse, suitably shocked and intrigued, gave Ricky his antibiotic injection after cleaning and dressing the wounds, and a course of tablets to prevent any infection. After thanking her for her services and a large gratuity to ensure her silence, she left. They then relieved the guard, who had been protecting their car during the night, and set off for Chamilpa via Agua Dulce. After driving well clear of the village, Yax stopped the car, and turned to Ricky.

"Would you drive us to Chamilpa? This is essential as you may have to drive in an emergency during my end game. There is nothing difficult about it, but you must be able to jump in and drive away without thinking about the position of the controls. Also you will be driving on what is, for you, the wrong side of the road!"

"While I appreciate the main reason for this, I get the uncomfortable feeling that you'll be leaving me after we've visited the site, and you know how I feel about that. But this is your show and I won't press you too hard on that point."

Yax continued. "Getting you out of Mexico has been foremost in my mind. Returning via Mexico City is out of the question. My best plan, subject to your approval, is for you to drive to Chiapas and contact a Maya group. They will arrange for a Mexican exit stamp to be applied to your passport, and a two-week tourist's visa for Guatemala. My car will then be concealed, then they will arrange for someone to drive you to the Guatemala border, and from there to the international airport at Guatemala City to catch a London or EU flight. I have already arranged for an escort to take you to the group in Chiapas. Is this acceptable?"

"That is an excellent plan and I too had been concerned with the potential dangers of interception in Mexico City. Let's enjoy lunch in Agua Dulce and you can tell me where we're going from there."

"Ricky, pass me your camera and I'll fill up your 16 MB memory with inoffensive views of Mexico."

Their journey to Agua Dulce was pleasant with Ricky keeping his speed down, which was just as well with the tourist buses being driven by madmen in both directions. The village had a prosperous look and included several tourist restaurants. Selecting the only one that looked as if it belonged to the village, they took a table outside where they could keep a close eye on the car, and settled down to a typical Mexican meal cooked on a barbeque in the open under a shade, and while waiting, they consumed a couple of bottles of beer.

"Well, how far have we to travel from here?" said Ricky. "Have we got everything we need?"

"The answer to that is less than thirty kilometres. I have some of the equipment hidden in the site and some dark blue paper overalls in the car, and providing the entrance is as I left it, we will have enough to bring everything to a successful conclusion. The only matter holding up our visit will be the arrival of the escort at Chamilpa. After that we can complete our business in twenty-four hours. So I expect to start at 8 a.m. tomorrow, again providing our escort arrives in time."

"Let us have a coffee, relax for an hour and then drive on to Chamilpa – it looks as if the access to the village is little more than a track on the map. If that's the case, should we reserve accommodation here?"

"You're correct – there is no boarding house in the village, or at least none up to my last visit. However, there is a family who will be happy to put us up for the night, in fact I made the arrangement last night while you were catching up on sleep. After coffee, when you're ready, let us set out, as from my previous experiences the track is both difficult and time consuming."

They set out down the main road and after they had travelled a few kilometres Yax had the impression that they were being followed, so they decided to turn off on the next track leading off the road. As they approached it, Yak recognised the turning and yelled, "Ricky, keep close to the left as you turn in!"

Even then, it was difficult for Ricky to make the turn in.

Yax immediately followed up by shouting, "Get out of sight of the main road!"

As they stopped behind a screen of trees, they saw a large Mercedes saloon hurtle past.

"Ricky, I apologise for shouting, but on a previous visit to this area I spent a number of hours stuck in that ditch on the right-hand side of the turning and did not relish it happening a second time!"

Very contrite, he added, "This track joins the main road further on, in fact it is a considerable short cut, but as drivers are forced to travel slowly, it is mainly used by farm vehicles. Let's continue up to the top of the rise, as from there we can watch the road to see if they return to hunt for any turning we might have taken."

Parked out of sight of the main road on the top of the rise, they left the car. Concealed by the undergrowth, they had not long to wait when the same car raced back and swung into the turning. To their delight the car slid over to the right and ended up on its side in the ditch.

Yax chuckled. "They'll not be following us again for a considerable time. In fact it looks like a garage job. Let's continue. I doubt if these people will find us after this!"

The rest of the journey to Chamilpa was slow and uneventful, and after rejoining the main road, they only travelled a short distance before turning off to the village for a slow journey along a rutted and dust-covered track. The house where they intended to stay was in a wooded area on the edge of the Chamilpa. Yax arranged for the car to be concealed in out buildings at the back of the house.

After refreshments, and a very warm reception for Yax from the family, they settled down comfortably to await the arrival of their escort, passing the time reminiscing about the many happy times they had spent together.

Just as they were sitting down for supper, the escort joined them; a place had already been laid at the table in anticipation of his arrival. Yax then introduced Ixhem to the company, as a young lawyer who was fluent in English, and represented the Maya people in the departments of Tabasco and Chiapas.

After supper Yax and Ixhem went out for a private discussion, and Ricky went to his room to pack his belongings for an early start in the morning.

Next morning after saying goodbye to their hosts, the three of them left in the car, with Ixhem driving. The track was just passable and after ten kilometres came to an abrupt end.

The three of them set about camouflaging the car and when that merged into the scenery, Yax and Ricky put on the overalls and slung their haversacks on their shoulders. Ixhem assured Ricky he would wait for him no matter how long it took. Then Ixhem was strongly embraced by Yax as he said his goodbyes, and Ricky realised he was aware that Yax would not be returning.

As they walked away Yax said, "We are walking in a straight line to the site which is about two kilometres distance; you must leave small insignificant markers on the trees every two hundred paces to ensure that you can find your way back to Ixhem."

After a difficult walk through heavy undergrowth they came to a mound covered with thick vegetation and trees, which on first sight appeared impossible to penetrate.

Yax said, "At last we have arrived! In the past there was a large stone head carved by the Olmecs on top of this mound, but it was taken away and is now in the Museo Nacional de Antropologia in Mexico City.

"I always thought there was more to this site than that particular sculpture, but I was drawn back to this place when I was desperately looking for the final resting place for my family. It was only by a stroke of luck or divine providence that I discovered the tiny opening, which I carefully enlarged until I was just able to crawl through; the rest you can see for yourself. Please, Ricky – no photographs of the outside, and once you've left you must forget anything that can lead to its location. This is now the tomb of my wife and child and it will be my tomb. Do I have your promise?"

"Yax, you have it, I will never reveal its location and would rather die than fail you – my dearest friend, you have my solemn promise."

"Thank you, Ricky. Now, will you carefully watch how I reveal the opening so that you can close it in a similar manner when you leave. I am staying here with my family; I have been away from them for far too long. Do not feel sad for I will suffer no pain, but if I stay alive much longer the opium will no longer work. If I did not take this opportunity it would mean a long and agonising death – believe me, this is the best way and the best place for me. If you are willing I have a strong need for you to hold my hand during the last moments, to ease my passage into the other world."

Yax then started to carefully remove the rocks and their attached growth that concealed an opening barely large enough to crawl through. Before entering he turned to Ricky.

"You are now about to enter the world of at least 1500 BC or maybe a lot earlier than that." He then crawled through, dragging his haversack behind him and Ricky did the same. Looking round, Ricky saw a steeply sloping and rough tunnel through which, by stooping, it was just possible to shuffle through. Abruptly the tunnel opened out onto a wide paved platform from which a steep stone staircase led down to the base of a limestone cavern. In the glimmer of their torches a small lake was visible at one end of the cavern, fed by a tiny stream entering from one of the cavern walls. As they approached, the torchlight and the tinkling of the water into the lake made it into a mystical fairyland.

Yax beckoned Ricky to follow him and walked across the lake on a small underwater ridge of rock and on the far side appeared to vanish. Ricky, following behind, found there was a concealed entrance behind an outcrop of rock. Walking round it he passed through a portal and entered a magnificent rock tomb with a finely carved lid covering a sarcophagus. The decorations included different symbols from those used by the Maya but with the same script layout.

Yax laughed. "I can guess your thoughts and confirm it is not Maya, but although I cannot prove it, my belief is that it is Olmec. This is interesting but more important is the stela standing on the far side of the tomb!"

Ricky walked over to the large stone column and was amazed to see it was covered with Egyptian hieroglyphs. This certainly provided the connection between the Olmec and Maya cultures in Mexico with Egypt and possibly with Ethiopia. "This is marvellous! Have you been able to interpret any of it?"

"Using the only references regarding the interpretation of Egyptian hieroglyphs that are available in Mexico, I attempted to make a rough translation but with small success, although I do have an impression of its purpose. It tells of a traveller who was part Ethiopian and part Egyptian, who joined an expedition with the Olmecs. He was the last survivor of a group of his people who were killed some decades previously in a terrible accident.

"Apparently the Olmecs were good to him and in return he taught them the many skills that had been passed to the Egyptians by their gods many generations ago. As he was getting close to death, the

Olmecs decided to honour him by building a tomb for his resting place in one of their sacred underground temples. At his request they also provided him with a blank stela on which he could record his travels. When that work was complete he had nothing further to undertake and was happy to wait in the care of the Olmecs until death. There is a substantial amount of detail covering his travels in Egypt and those of his ancestors, requiring the attention of a skilled translator. I recommend that the person should be selected with great care and for security reasons bonded prior to being incorporated in your project.

"Now, take your photographs of both the stela and the sarcophagus cover, checking each as you take them and after that make a duplicate copy. While you do that I will open the grave of my family and prepare for my exit."

Ricky completed the photographs and then asked Yax to stand by the stela and sarcophagus and have his photograph taken as the Maya archaeologist who discovered the Mexican link with Egypt! He added, "In my view it is imperative that the honour of the discovery should go to you and at your bequest to the Maya nation."

Yak thanked Ricky. "You do my people and me great honour. You may have difficulties with Mexico in this regard, but I know you will stand fast against any political pressure.

"Now let me lie down on my blanket and take the last of my opium. Sit down close beside me and ease my passing with your presence. When I am dead, wrap the blanket around and lower me into the family grave, then pull the cover over the grave... Ricky! Why the tears? I am joining my family and leaving a world of pain. You will do this for me?"

"Yax, I'm selfishly crying like a child at the impending loss of a dear friend and *that's* why I can't hide the tears. Of course everything will be done as you wish, forgive my weakness. Your Ka will always be welcome in my mind, and will assuredly guide me."

"In my pocket you will find some money and papers which you can give to Ixhem for the Maya cause. He will ask questions about my death but tell him I have ordered you to keep silent on that subject."

Ricky sat down beside his friend, holding his hand and supporting his head while he took two small tablets; Ricky felt him relax and lose consciousness. Then Ricky was surrounded by the darkness and flickering shadows, only broken by the torch lighting the body on the blanket, and in his imagination he saw a woman with a young boy stretching their hands towards the body, and then with a soft sigh the spirit and soul of Yax left his body and the phantasm faded back into the darkness.

After some time sitting with the body, Ricky recovered sufficiently to test for a pulse; there was none. Then, as a last farewell to his friend to ensure that he was not being buried alive, he took his knife and cut his wrist – all was accomplished; the blood no longer flowed.

Removing the money and papers from under the overall, Ricky closed the blanket over his friend's body and lowered it into the prepared grave that held his family. After sliding the stone slab over the grave, he filled the cracks with dirt so that it became part of the floor. Saying a prayer and last farewell to his friend, Ricky collected all their possessions into the two haversacks, then slung the straps over his shoulders and left the tomb, waving a cloth to cover the footprints with dust. As he climbed up out of the cavern he had never felt so lonely in all his life.

Squeezing out of the entrance Ricky spent a long time sealing the opening securely with rocks and packed earth before replacing the top cover exactly as Yax had taught him, and standing back it looked as if the mound had never been disturbed. Ricky checked a sob and started on his way back, retrieving the markers, until he reached Ixhem who suddenly appeared in front of him. Seeing his distress, Ixhem quickly took his haversacks and put them in the car boot. Then after helping Ricky into the car, they set off for Chiapas, regaining the main road just as it was getting dark.

After a little while Ricky turned to Ixhem and said, "Yak told me to give you certain papers and cash for the Maya Cause. I do not know what it contains in detail and for security reasons I would prefer that you don't tell me. I understand that the distance to the border near Guatemala City is about five hundred kilometres, and I appreciate that the roads may be difficult, but is it possible to reach the Maya contact group near the border tonight and cross the border early tomorrow morning?"

"The Far Right Group, which has chased Yax and me across Mexico, will know from their last sighting that we are travelling towards Chiapas. If they can locate us they will use any means to delay us and prevent me from crossing the border. For this reason we cannot risk stopping at a hotel or for that matter, a restaurant. Do you agree with this or have you any other thoughts to get me safely across the border?"

"This is the plan Yax and I preferred and is the wisest course to adopt. If I get tired driving I understand you're familiar with the car and can take over. However, after Chiapa de Corzo the road is extremely difficult at night, so perhaps the best solution is for you to drive that far, and then I will drive the last three hundred and fifty kilometres. The Maya group is waiting for us, and by now they'll have solved the problems of the exit visa and the short-term visitor's visa for Guatemala."

"Thank you for that. I will take over the driving and you can check the package given to you by Yax. With the clear sky and moonlight I shouldn't lose my way! So let us change over as soon as you can find a suitable spot."

So they changed over and with very little traffic on the road good progress was made with Ricky keeping the speed below one hundred kilometres an hour and, two hours later, they passed through Teapa. The ninety-six kilometres to Chiapas seemed endless and eventually, on its outskirts, Ricky pulled in on the side of the road and asked Ixhem to take over. He suddenly realised he was desperately tired and that the activities and stress of the day had sapped his vitality.

The changeover was quickly taken and as soon as they were moving again Ricky's head fell against the side window and he was fast asleep.

Ricky woke up with a start – someone was shaking him. It was Ixhem, repeatedly saying, "Wake up, Ricky. We have arrived!"

Ricky got out of the car and collected his thoughts; it was dawn and he checked his watch… 6 a.m.

"I'm sorry, Ixhem, I didn't mean to fall asleep like that – is everything all right?"

"I have spoken to our friends and they urgently require your passport. They may need some additional money to encourage the officials concerned; have you any cash? US dollars? Or local currency? If you only have traveller's cheques, we can get those changed."

"I have two thousand pesos in local currency, traveller's cheques, and of course my bankcard. How much do you need to clear the border and take me to Guatemala City?"

Ixhem, after discussions with his friends, answered, "Fifteen hundred pesos should cover the exit visa and the Guatemala entry visa.

Regarding the journey to the airport Yax has allowed currency for that expense and has given the group his car. The group will keep the car here under cover until the search for both you and Yax has been abandoned. I suggest you cash one hundred and fifty dollars' traveller's cheques as soon as possible when you enter Guatemala, as a safety measure, and I hope you will not need them!"

"Regarding the vehicle taking me across the border – will it be driven by one of your group? If not, can you examine it for explosives? I know that this sounds paranoid but I don't underestimate the activities of the Far Right, who I suppose, having lost us, will guess we've gone down to the Chiapas border."

"We have an excellent taxi driver friend who is well known on this route. His car will be checked before you leave just to make sure all is as it should be. We know what has already happened to you and certainly do not believe you to be paranoid!

"You will be leaving in two hours' time, so as 'Our house is your house' come in for coffee and breakfast. After that, check your possessions and pack them in this suitably labelled flight bag, which you can keep. Empty the two haversacks and your own suitcase and leave them with us – anything that will identify you with Yax should be left behind."

The taxi arrived with a villainous-looking driver, who spoke some English with a broad American accent. Ricky retrieved his passport from Ixhem, which now had the Mexican exit stamp and the Guatemala entry visa. Putting the bulky flight bag on the back seat, he thanked Ixhem and said goodbye to the Mayan group. Then Ricky settled in the front seat, and, turning to the driver, said, "Let's go, non-stop to Guatemala City!"

The driver replied, "My name is Sancho and first of all we have to stop for a customs check, but not to worry, it is a formality only – everything is arranged!"

They pulled up at the customs check and two officials came over to the car and asked if he had anything to declare. Ricky said no.

The second officer opened the boot, waited a moment and closed it. They then waved Sancho through as the barrier was lifted and they drove on to the Guatemala checkpoint where they were waved through.

As they drove away, Ricky, said, "Sancho, I heard them lift the boot, then I detected a small thump just before the boot was closed. Have you got anything in the boot that they might have lifted up and put back?"

Sancho said, "Only a spare tyre, but that's fastened down – unless it's come loose. There is a side road just ahead where I can pull up and secure the tyre before it does any damage as we are travelling over uneven road surfaces."

He pulled over on the side road, got out and opened the boot. He then asked Ricky, "Is this your brown suitcase in the boot?"

"No!" Ricky yelled, as he jumped out of the car.

Sancho, being curious, started to open the catches.

Ricky yelled, "*Bomb! Throw it well away!*"

Sancho froze for a second, then hurled it towards the trees; the second catch gave way and there was a substantial explosion which threw Sancho on his back.

The car protected Ricky from the blast and, clearing his head, he ran over and helped a very dazed Sancho to his feet.

"We must get away from here immediately, you're in no state to drive." After helping Sancho into the passenger seat, he got in and drove back onto the main road as fast as possible.

Sancho was still in a daze, but he dared not take him back to the border. It was approximately two hundred kilometres to Guatemala City, and should only take about two and a half hours, so all things considered the best solution would be to drive as fast as possible within the limit, and leave him and his car at the city hospital. He planned that when they arrived there, he would remove his bags and take a cab to the airport. At the same time he hoped Sancho would have recovered sufficiently by the time they reached the hospital or that he would remain in a stupor long enough for him to leave on an airplane for Gatwick.

The rest of the drive to the Guatemala City Hospital was uncomfortable but otherwise uneventful, and Ricky parked close to the hospital entrance. Shaking Sancho gently, Ricky said, "How do you feel now, Sancho?"

His reply was a little fuzzy. "Where… where the hell am I?" Then, as an afterthought, he added, "What's happened to me?"

"After we left the border you stopped and went to the boot of your car for something. I saw you pick up a suitcase and throw it towards the trees where it exploded. You were thrown flat on your back, I couldn't find any serious injuries, but I was so worried about you that I brought you to this hospital – we're in Guatemala City. I believe you've just suffered shock. I know you've been paid for this journey but I am giving you a traveller's cheque for a hundred US dollars and one hundred and fifty pesos in cash, which should provide you with treatment if required. I am going to get a taxi so must wish you a quick recovery and a speedy return to Mexico."

Sancho said, "I'm feeling a lot better now... I will rest a little while and if I continue to improve, will make my way back to the border. Thank you for all your help. Can you leave the name on the cheque blank and I will fill in my name?"

Ricky signed the cheque and handed it to Sancho, adding, "If you take my advice, don't mention the explosion at the borders of Guatemala or Mexico, because if you do they will certainly arrest you on suspicion of being a terrorist carrying explosives. We both know it was one of the Mexican border officials who put the explosives in the car, but it will be convenient for him to put the blame on you! In fact, if questioned, tell them you didn't hear *any* explosion!"

Shaking Sancho's hand and wishing him a safe return Ricky left him outside the hospital, noting that the extra money was working wonders on his recovery. He then grabbed a taxi to the airport and two hours later his flight took off for Gatwick.

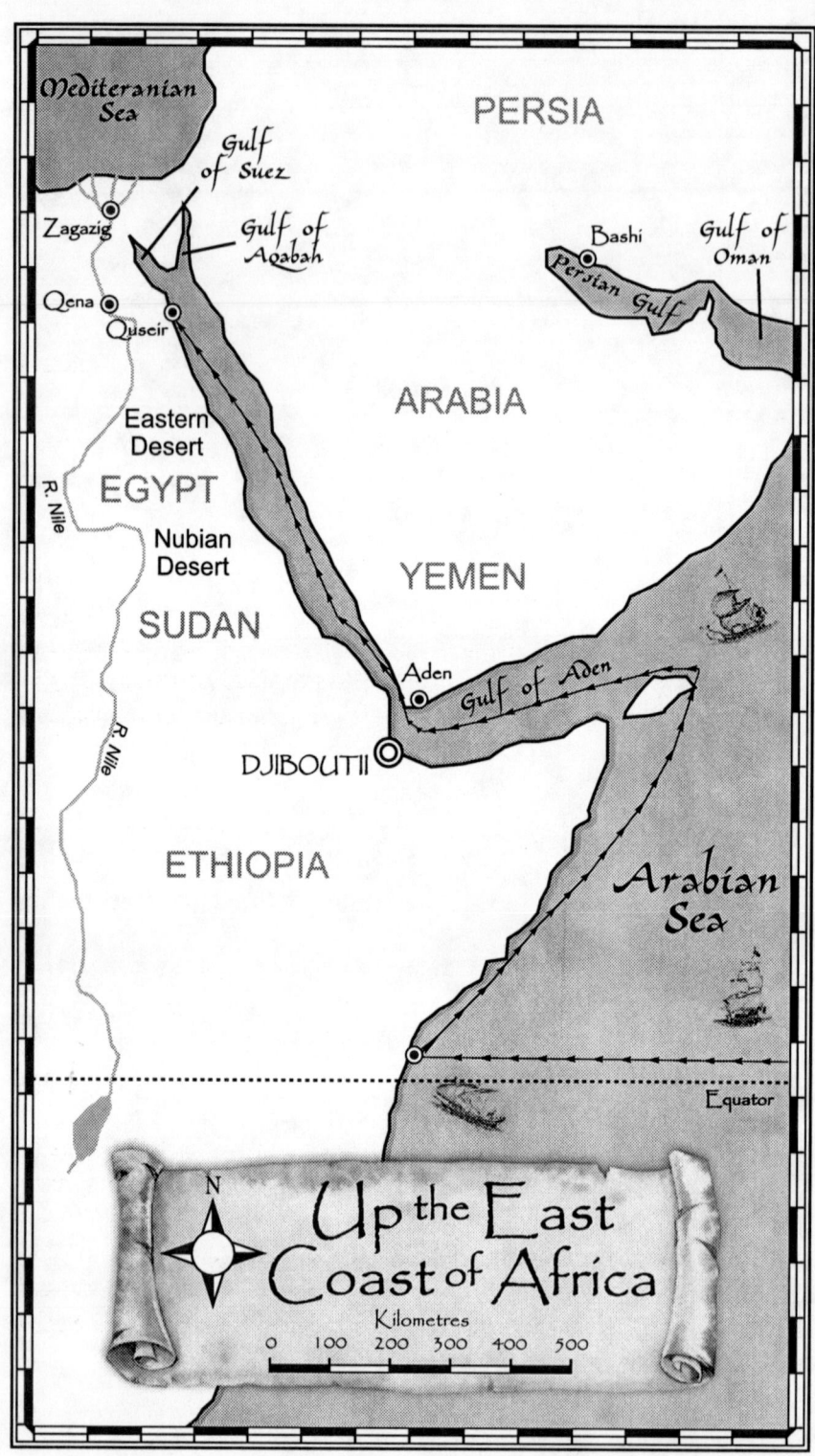

The Long Voyage

5500 BC

With the sun sliding swiftly below the horizon, darkness suddenly enveloped the ships. The lamps having been installed to mark their position and with some apprehension among the crew, they made a fair speed until, at about three in the morning, with the wind speed dropping rapidly, they were no longer under way.

In the light of their lanterns the sea looked oily and they experienced a strong and most unpleasant smell of sulphurous fumes mixed with the odour of dead fish. In addition, the crews were being distracted by a steady whistling sound, which seemed to be coming from all directions at once. Being unable to leave the area, they all settled down to an early breakfast, in preparation for whatever dangers were to be encountered at first light.

In the morning a thick mist enveloped their ship, and as the light grew stronger, Osiris called to his captain.

"Send a lookout up to the top of the mainmast to search for the masts of my other ships!"

Captain Bakh sent Seaman Hekt, who, after returning to the deck, reported, "I climbed to the very top of the mast, but even at that height the mist is still too thick to see anything."

About an hour later Hekt returned to the lookout position and hailed the sailing master to report.

"I now get occasional glimpses of the expedition mast tops – as far as I can tell they are in the correct formation, but a little further away than planned."

The sailing master ordered Seaman Hekt to stay in the lookout position, and then, with a worried look, he walked up to the captain and asked for a private word. They moved into the captain's enclosure.

"You have a problem, Bata?"

"Captain, although I have not personally experienced these conditions, I have had meetings with other sailing masters who talked about similar sea disturbances that they encountered many years ago. Based on these sailors' stories, I believe that we are in danger of a tsunami which, as you may already know, can be caused by a substantial earthquake in the sea or a volcano close to the sea exploding and breaking the walls of its crater. This can cause a major earth slide instantaneously displacing a great mass of sea water, and creating a wave of great power travelling at enormous speed across the ocean. In our condition, while we have not yet left our continental shelf, I estimate that while the wave front will be steeply sloped it is possible for our ships to survive: otherwise the master mariners would not be alive to tell the tale! But if a tsunami is met head on in shallow water the wave is slowed at the base and, by that means, reaches a great height, and there is no chance of survival.

"The sea conditions suggest that the main quake has not yet occurred; the whistling we heard last night and at times this morning is a poisonous sulphur gas escaping from the sea bed under high pressure. When the earthquake actually happens and if it is a tsunami, the speed of the wave will not provide sufficient time to make final and essential preparations.

"To ensure the safety of our ships I recommend that we immediately prepare sea anchors and place them in a position in the stern suitable for rapid deployment. At the same time we must batten down all hatches and secure all cargo, and our other two ships must do the same! As I wished to avoid panic, I thought it better to discuss this privately."

"I agree, Bata, and value your advice; the question now is how to make the necessary arrangements without revealing to the crews a very real danger, that of course may not even occur. I will consult with Lord Osiris immediately, as only he can make the arrangements to implement your recommendations for the other two ships.

"In the meantime, see if you can find the stores necessary to make our sea anchor, while keeping this matter to yourself until I have spoken to Osiris."

Bata left to attend to preparing the sea anchor, and the captain reported to Osiris and explained the situation, discussing the possible implications.

"I agree with both your comments and the recommendations made by Bata. As soon as we have sufficient visibility I will send orders to the captains of the *Sea Eagle* and *Sea Fury*, which will include the following.

"As a safety exercise, to be implemented immediately, sea anchors will be made and prepared for launching from a gantry set up in the stern, all hatches and holds shall be battened down and loose equipment in the ship secured. Sails will be reefed up, with the exception of the mainsail. In addition, safety lines should be rigged on a permanent basis to prevent any further losses from sea monsters. When all these tasks have been completed, the captains should report to me and I will inspect the results of their preparations before I consider having them cleared.

"Captain Bakh, you may implement these instructions immediately, informing the crew that although this is a general safety exercise, attention to detail is essential and the work will be carefully examined on that basis."

As the preparations were put in hand by the crew the mist started to clear and the *Sea Eagle* and *Sea Fury* had an ethereal quality as they slowly appeared through the mist.

Captain Bakh passed Osiris's message to the other two ships and work on the preparation of the sea anchors, the battening down of hatches and securing cargo, started immediately.

Sometime after midday the mist finally cleared and the masthead lookout reported, "A number of mast tops are appearing over the horizon."

As the hulls appeared, it was soon revealed that large pirate long boats, each manned with numerous oarsmen, were towing Seth's ships. Judging by their progress they would be close to his expedition ships just before dark. With his ships becalmed, Osiris realised that there was nothing he could do to resolve the situation until the wind picked up.

About two hours later, the lookout Hekt reported from the masthead.

"There is a strange band of dark cloud to the south; I am watching it growing across the horizon. In the centre there is now a red glow and round the edges frequent flashes of lightning."

Hekt paused for a few seconds then added, "The centre of the cloud has started to boil upwards. I have never seen a storm like this one." Osiris realised that even if this storm was heading in their direction, it was unlikely to reach them before the arrival of Seth and the pirates.

At about an hour before sunset Osiris called Isis and Thoth, asking them to prepare the transporters and to obtain volunteers to carry the flaming torches, and to use the bows to attack the pirates' long boats after the torches had been dropped.

He then nervously decided to wait a further quarter of an hour before launching the attack, but at that moment the lookout shouted, "There has been a tremendous explosion in the south." Then the sky steadily darkened, as if a black veil was being drawn over it, and the wind started to return.

The sailing master yelled, "Captain, turn to the south! It is as I feared – we can expect a wave."

The pirates, having observed the explosion, suddenly realised the reasons for the previous inexplicable preparations being made on Osiris's ships, and, dropping off their tow-lines, raced back towards Seth's ships.

Osiris, who was still watching Seth's ships to determine when he could delay no longer in releasing the transporters, was surprised to witness Seth's crews and their warriors showering the pirates with arrows to prevent them from boarding. Observing the battle, Osiris gave a thankful sigh of relief – Seth was no longer an immediate threat!

Seth had obviously realised that the pirates' ships would not survive the tsunami wave, and dared not allow them to board, as inevitably fearing the loss of their ships, they would attempt to take over control of at least his ship, or possibly all of his ships, and sail them back to their stronghold.

From the masthead the lookout Hekt shouted, "The sea seems to have lifted up on the horizon, accompanied by a roaring steadily growing in intensity."

Captain Bakh shouted, "Hekt! Return to main deck immediately and report to the sailing master."

"Sailing Master, deploy the sea anchor."

"All expedition personnel take cover and seal all openings. This danger will pass quickly providing sea water is kept out of the hull."

"Duty crew, fasten yourselves to the running lines. ReRa be with us all."

With the wave approaching, the sky darkening, and the roaring increasing to a mad crescendo, on the horizon the heavy clouds were glowing an angry red interspersed with lightning flashes, and the roaring became almost unbearable as the ship entered the steep slope of the long wave. Providing the sea anchor continued to hold and prevent the ship from broaching, all would be well.

The water was now streaming past the hull at a fantastic speed, when their ship approached the top of the wave; the turbulent sea crest started to break over the bow and suddenly swept the decks from stem to stern.

When the water drained off the decks they were presented with a tangle of broken rigging and the main sail hanging in shreds. Several of the duty crew, including the second helmsman, had been lost overboard and swept away.

With the sky rapidly darkening from the south, and thunderclouds approaching from the south-west, the captain called the crew, and members of the expedition, to the main deck. He then allocated urgent tasks that had to be carried out to make the ship ready to survive the gathering storm.

Calling Hekt over, the captain said, "Hekt, climb the mainmast to locate the position and conditions of our two ships. In addition try to assess the position and condition of the Mesopotamian expedition ships and return to the deck as soon as possible and report to Lord Osiris, as I will be organising repair teams."

As fine flakes of ash started to float down from the sky onto the decks. Captain Bakh spoke to Bata.

"The foremast sail must be replaced and rigging strengthened. Take down the mainsail and replace it with the spare and, as soon as possible, see what can be done about repairing the shredded mainsail. Retrieve the sea anchor, repair it if necessary, then re-install it ready for immediate redeployment. In the meantime I will examine the steering arms and swivels and find a replacement for the second helmsman."

Hekt, returning to the main deck, reported to Osiris.

"Sir, the *Sea Fury* and *Sea Eagle* have sustained similar damage to our ship and are busy undertaking repairs, and their lookouts are aware of our location. Both ships are rigging the foresail, and if we deliberately lose the wind they should close up quickly. The ships of the Mesopotamian expedition are a long way behind; they seem to be in difficulties, but it's too great a distance to make out details of the damage. There is no sign of the pirate vessels."

Osiris replied, "Return to the lookout point and repair what you can, so that it can provide sufficient cover for you to withstand the approaching storm. When all is prepared come down and report to me any changes in the other ships' positions."

The foresail and mainsail were raised just as night fell, but work continued by the light of torches; all three ships had now recovered their correct spacing and running lights were installed as before, to await the arrival of the storm.

With the waves rising and the wind swinging to the southeast, they took reefs in the main sail to reduce the danger of storm damage. The captain ordered that this restriction must apply until the original mainsail had been repaired, and once more he had a standby.

The night was black as pitch except for the occasional glimpses of the moon through gaps in the heavy cloud cover; the high air temperature and the build up of humidity tended to make any physical work exhausting.

With the waves rising and the wind building up from the southeast Captain Bakh called the sailing master.

"Bata, I fear we are in for a major storm. Have the mainsail cleated up as we cannot afford to lose it until we have the remnants of the original sail repaired sufficiently to make it reusable.

"The two fore-lantern sails must be unfurled and set in their storm position. After you have checked that all lashings and safety ropes are in position, you are to go below and get some sleep as I will expect you to relieve me an hour after first light."

The captain then called to the lookout, Hekt. "I want you to go to the lookout point above the mainmast and get in it. You have to stay there until I can have you relieved. Your main responsibility is to monitor the positions of the *Sea Eagle* and the *Sea Fury*. Shout an alarm if they are being driven too close to our ship.

"As the storm intensifies, as is inevitable, you will have considerable difficulty in communicating with the main deck – you may consider coming down to report, but I want you to stay up there unless it is a matter of life or death. Under those conditions I will send someone part of the way up to your crow's nest to obtain details from you regarding the other ships."

The wind steadily increased to storm force and came screaming through the rigging, the waves were higher than Captain Bakh had experienced during his many years at sea, and the *Sea Owl* was being thrown about as if it were a toy. Afraid that the ship might be broached, he adjusted the course to run before the storm as the high stern offered some protection to them from being pooped.

As the storm built up to full fury, the *Sea Owl* was enveloped in spray from the wind ripping off the tops of the waves and the impact of the occasional wave coming in at an angle; with the danger of broaching requiring three men to assist the helmsman, and due to the continual spray, it was impossible to determine from the deck of the *Sea Owl* the positions of the other two ships.

Captain Bakh called Teti and said, "I need a volunteer and you are lucky to be chosen; you are to be secured to the running line with a leash long enough to let you climb most of the way up the mainmast to communicate with Hekt in the lookout, you are to ask him what he has to report, make sure you fully understand his comments, then come down and report to me."

A very wet and exhausted Teti eventually staggered back to Bakh.

"Hekt told me to report that the *Sea Eagle* and *Sea Fury* are holding position; they also have reduced to fore-lantern sails. Both ships have raised their running lights to the highest possible position on the mainmast and these positions are above the sea spray. Hekt has also managed to raise the height of his lantern, with the consequence that the three ships are able to hold position.

"He also said his hair is standing on end. I did not understand what that meant but I had the impression he is terrified."

At that moment Captain Bakh became aware of a strange ghostly light enveloping the ship which seemed to emanate from the top of the foremast; it was like a brush with brilliant blue and orange bristles. Bakh rushed to the cabin and called Osiris who hurried out on deck; the discharge of light was now on the top of the mainmast.

Osiris grabbed Bakh by the shoulder and yelled, "What is it, Bakh?"

"I have never seen anything like it before, but I have heard stories from other seafarers about similar displays but I thought it was a myth. I have heard it said that it is a visible sign of ReRa guardianship over a ship."

Suddenly Osiris fell to his knees and stared up to the foremast, his face went pale and he started to shake. Bakh tried to lift him up but he seemed frozen to the deck. In anguish Bakh yelled, "What is it?"

"Can't you *see* the dreadful apparition, Bakh? Standing beside the foremast holding a great spear, wearing a grim and dreadful face with a patch over one eye, and wrapped in a swirling black cape?

"Can you not see him, Bakh?

"He tells me that the ship will be safe for this voyage only, but that in two years' time I will be with him in the stars. That I shall have a child to be called Horus who shall be the first king of all Egypt, that our expedition shall be a great success, but Atlan shall be lost for eight thousand years."

Getting slowly to his feet, he murmured, "I must go now and speak with Isis. I shall not tell her all of it, so keep what I have told you to yourself."

Holding onto the safety line and with a stricken look on his face, hunched against the wind, he started to make his way towards his accommodation.

But at that moment Bakh pointed up into the sky and shouted, "Look at that fearful ball of light streaking through the clouds!"

As he spoke the ball of light appeared to accelerate down and levelled off just above the sea, then it slowly travelled the length of the ship, weaving in and out of the rigging. Then, tearing in from out on the sea, without a sound, a second ball passed across the ship. They then left the ship together, chased each other as they accelerated and raced upwards towards the clouds, which drew back from their path. Osiris and Bakh, frozen with fear, watched as they vanished at high speed towards the star Sirius.

With the arrival of dawn and the breaks in the clouds, the full effect of the storm's fury was immediately apparent. The seas were mountainous and it seemed a miracle that the three ships had survived and maintained their positions through the night. The wind appeared to be reducing with a second thunderstorm closing on the ship, and within a short time they were enveloped in a heavy cloudburst accompanied by frequent lightning strikes that fortunately did not hit any of the ships.

The sailing master came on deck and relieved Captain Bakh.

"Captain, I am surprised to see you alive and it is a miracle that the ship survived such a pounding. Our passengers are suffering from the motion and it will take some time for them to recover! Are there any immediate tasks I must attend to?"

"Bata, I am exhausted! So I would appreciate your changing the lookout – you may need two of the crew to bring him down, as his physical condition must have deteriorated. The same may apply to the helmsmen, but at least they had room to move. Apart from that, see us safely through the next eight hours when I will return to relieve you. If there is any serious situation developing you must call me."

When the lookout Hekt was brought down he was in a poor state but insisted on reporting to Bata.

"Sir, after seeing the fires on the mastheads I was extremely fearful. It was then I saw an apparition; it was my father standing near the main spar close to me. He smiled at me and told me we would all survive the storm, and then he disappeared.

"After that I felt completely calm, as I do now, although I can barely move my limbs after the buffeting and the confined space."

Slowly the thunderstorm and heavy rain seemed to moderate the general sea conditions and these steadily improved during the day. With the improved conditions Bata noticed that the *Sea Eagle* had a considerable list to starboard and that her crew, together with expedition members, were working frantically to bail water out of the hull. As instructed he then called Osiris to the deck and explained the situation.

Osiris then sent for Captain Bakh.

"Can you run alongside to port so that we can determine the problem and lend any assistance required?"

"It is just possible, but we would have to grapple and deploy fenders, and in doing so it might cause considerable damage to both of our hulls."

"As an alternative, I suggest it would be safer to get close enough to rig a line and pass someone across to determine the immediate situation with Captain Amle, and to assess the level of assistance required. The person selected could then return and finalise their plans with you.

"As the *Sea Owl* is now in reasonable condition and in these circumstances, I propose that I should go."

"I agree, and if during those discussions you consider transferring part or all of the expedition members, or for that matter our special cargo, please start the work with my full authority, as soon as you consider it practical. Also I will support any action you and Captain Amle decide to take to save the *Sea Eagle*."

Captain Bakh then brought the *Sea Owl* close to the *Sea Eagle* and spoke to Bata.

"While I am over with the *Sea Eagle* you are responsible for the ship. Hold the *Owl* clear of the *Eagle* until I signal you to close for my return."

After a wet and difficult transfer, he met Captain Amle on the deck of the *Sea Eagle* and offered any help he required to save his ship.

Amle thanked him for coming over and outlined the situation.

"When we encountered the tsunami wave, the sea anchor was not fully deployed and we started to broach. And after recovering with some difficulty we discovered that the heavy pressure applied to the starboard side of the hull had opened the seams between the planks.

"At first there were no major leaks, but during the subsequent storm the planking distorted. Since then we have been attempting to stem the intake of seawater with our pump and by bailing out the hull. The situation is deteriorating and the crew and passengers are exhausted, and unless we take urgent action the ship will be lost."

"As the sea has calmed considerably I was considering the possibility of slinging a sail over the damaged area, but until you came over that would have been impossible with the exhausted crew."

"I agree there is no other means of stemming the inflow. I have a damaged main sheet, which will be adequate for reducing the flow, and between us we will have enough ropes to hold it in position.

"I will return to the *Sea Owl* and have ropes attached to the damaged sail we are at present repairing. These ropes will then be passed over to you, for you to attach to lead ropes, which by that time, I hope you will have managed to pass under your hull. As this work is being accomplished, I will send some of the crews from the other two ships, together with expedition volunteers to assist. You should then be able to draw the sail from the *Sea Owl* under the port side of your ship, until it covers the affected area on the starboard side. At that point, you can make fast, and release the ropes connecting you to the *Sea Owl*. Hopefully this plan will reduce the intake of water to a manageable level, and with the additional labour reduce the level of water in the hull."

"Our expedition members will assist in removing the special stores to the *Sea Owl*. When that work has been completed your passengers are to be sent over to the *Sea Owl* where they will be given temporary accommodation. After that, we will hold at our present position until all crews and passengers are rested, then Osiris will review the situation."

With the possibility of saving the ship within a reasonable time, the crews overcame their exhaustion and the plan was well executed and the leak substantially reduced. With the removal of stores and their expedition members, the list was corrected and the pressure on the sprung planking reduced to an acceptable level.

Captain Bakh reported to Osiris.

"Sir, our temporary repairs to the *Sea Eagle* can only remain effective in calm conditions, and low sailing speeds. We are attempting to improve the repair, but even then these stipulations have to be observed.

"Our immediate requirement is an island on which we can beach the ship, remove the sail and reset the planking in the usual way. Under those conditions it will not be a difficult job and should be completed in one or two days. There are numerous islands in this area, but at the moment none are visible from the ship.

"Would it be possible for a transporter to carry me up to a height sufficient to substantially extend our present horizon? There is no immediate necessity to travel more than five hundred metres from the ship, so that in the event of coming down in the sea, rescue should not be too difficult. If we fail to locate an island we can travel five or ten kilometres and then repeat this method of observation."

Osiris replied, "Your request is reasonable and should reveal the most convenient landfall. However, Isis is the only person immediately available to fly the transporter, and while I know she will agree, you are doubtless aware she has been promised to me by our two families and that I am naturally very concerned for her safety.

"If you will ensure that the flight is of short duration, and that flying is strictly limited to only above this ship, I will authorise it. Further flights will depend on separate reports from both you and Isis. Assuming you agree, the flight must be carried out as soon as possible."

As expected, Isis agreed, and the flight proceeded as planned; no islands were sighted, but cloud formations in the south-west suggested that would the best direction.

Then they sailed some four hours to reach the stipulated ten kilometres distance. Osiris authorised a further observation flight that confirmed there was an island to the south-west. With the approach of nightfall Osiris decided to wait until first light next morning to start the slow journey which, with luck, might be completed before sunset.

The next day their passage to the island was both slow and difficult, with repeated stops to tighten the ropes securing the sail. Leakage was still a problem and teams from the three ships took turns in the continual task of bailing.

By midday the sight of the island raised the crew's spirits, but by the time they reached the coral reef, which appeared to encircle the desolate-looking island, it was approaching dusk and too late to attempt to find a safe passage. Captain Bakh gave orders that the following morning two of the ship's boats were to be crewed and prepared to search for a possible opening through the barrier reef.

The next morning, with a calm sea, the boats were launched and the search began. By midday only one opening had been found, but it was too shallow for the heavily loaded ships. It was then decided that the ship's two boats should tow the *Sea Eagle* through the opening in the reef. At high tide, she would be beached and be pulled over to expose the damaged planking. The *Sea Owl* and *Sea Fury* were to remain anchored outside the reef until the repairs had been completed.

The work took three days, until a very seaworthy *Sea Eagle* rejoined the expedition and work could be started to reload her stores and return expedition members to the ship.

The two Giant prisoners could not be marooned on the island, as without water or vegetation to sustain life, it did not fulfil the terms of Osiris's promise.

Captain Bakh and Lord Osiris were discussing possible routes to the Red Sea, and the problem of leaving the two Giants on a suitable island, when Sailing Master Bata approached them.

"Sirs, there is a suitable island called Socotra at the entrance to the Gulf leading to the Red Sea. It is one hundred and sixty itru long and is inhabited mainly by goats with a few very primitive humans; it is on a volcanic ridge and may be unstable under the present conditions.

"I believe this will provide everything necessary for the Giants, and does not require a diversion as it is on our direct route to Egypt. I have studied the stars and the distance to the African coast is about 1,590 itru, followed by going north for about 783 itru along the African coast to Socotra, making a total of about 2,373 itru. With a fair wind, and assuming the best sailing conditions it could take twenty-five days, plus those days we have to stop to obtain supplies."

Captain Bakh, having considered the proposal, said, "The plan has great merit, and once we reach the African coast, in approximately sixteen days, we will be sailing to Socotra within sight of land, being carried in the south-west drift. Most important of all we would be able to obtain water and food as required." Osiris agreed, adding that it would be a bonus to have the *Sea Eagle* close to land.

On the twelfth day Osiris and Isis were discussing plans for transporting the expedition stores from the Red Sea base to the new Egyptian Nile base, and the immediate necessity of establishing a symbolic temple and its dedication to ReRa, when Thoth joined them. Osiris turned to him.

"How are you progressing with the scrolls?"

"The work has gone well and by now it is possible to translate most of the scrolls, but the technical detail provided regarding the artefacts is difficult to understand. The scrolls will require further lengthy study and detailed tests of the individual artefacts, when we arrive at our new base.

"It is interesting to read that the artefacts were not produced by the Giants, but traded for large amounts of precious metals at a strange city in the north-east of India, whose people were busy rebuilding their cities after a disastrous war. The Giants' society at that time being peace-loving, restricted their purchases to items other than the weapons used with such devastation in that conflict. The only piece of equipment that might have a wartime application is the tunnelling device, and this apparently compresses matter until it virtually vanishes. The scrolls say that although the material virtually disappears, it is still there, difficult to comprehend! In addition the scrolls warn the machine is unstable, so it should only be used for tunnelling.

"One thing is absolutely clear, that is we have neither the technical knowledge nor the equipment to replicate the artefacts. So if an item is lost or damaged it will be lost forever. They must be secured in a deep underground room with the knowledge of its location restricted to the President and priests. Even then their use must be limited to research or for the essential development work in the construction of the major Nile base buildings. The exception to this rule will be the navigation tools, which possibly can be replicated in those parts that are useful to our sailing masters."

Osiris replied, "You will have the appreciation of all our expedition members for the work you have already undertaken, and the news that our forbearers were wise in their purchases and maintaining the same opinions that the majority of us hold dear today.

"In view of your comments, that I fully support, one of our immediate tasks on reaching the new site will be to construct a safe underground store, before establishing a suitable testing programme.

"I have been discussing the bravery of Leda, in stepping into the unknown to aid Isis. I have decided that she shall become a priestess, while remaining Isis's companion. It is my wish that you will instruct her regarding both the interpretation of the scrolls and the identification of artefacts, as they become known. As a priestess she shall now be known as Hathor."

As estimated by Captain Bakh, on the sixteenth day the expedition ships reached the coast of Africa, and they then started a search along the north coast for a suitable landing place to obtain water and game to replenish their supplies, which were running low.

By the second day they found a small bay with a backdrop of mountains bare of vegetation, and a river valley with the tropical forest almost extending to the beach, with fresh water tumbling happily from a spring halfway down a small cliff face.

It all looked ideal so the three ships anchored close in and parties from each ship landed to form a camp on the beach with the intention of hunting for game the next day.

The two Giants, who had been permitted to walk on deck, approached Osiris.

"My Lord, would you permit us to go ashore, and if it looks ideal we ask you to maroon us there."

"In granting your request I will permit you to be landed at first light; if you find a suitable location you can return and I will provide you with the necessary provisions. Should you fail to return within twenty hours you may be left behind without stores!"

On the beach, after arranging guard duties, the camp settled down for the night. In the middle of the night there was a sudden scream from one of the guards, followed a moment later with screams from the second guard.

Within moments the whole camp was awake and started to grab their weapons and light torches, then more people in the camp started to howl with pain.

Isis, having seen one of the attackers, ordered everyone back to the water's edge and to stand with both feet in the water. Then with two volunteers, each with a flaming torch, she moved up into the abandoned campsite and encountered one of the creatures.

It was a large spider with golden hair on its back and when approached it stood up on its rear legs and hissed. Isis had seen similar ones, although not so big, in the forests of her homeland – it had been given the name of "Bent Spider" because of its humped back, whilst others called it "Sun Spider" because of its golden hair. If approached when standing in its defensive position, it would jump and inflict a poisonous bite sufficient to kill a small mammal, but which would only inflict intense pain to a Giant.

These spiders were also voracious hunters at night and the expedition had chosen their hunting and mating area for their camp. So surrounded by a hastily constructed ring of fire, they spent the rest of the night huddled together, comforting the injured.

When dawn broke there were no traces of the spiders. Isis, after ordering the immediate collection of fresh water for delivery to the ships, returned to the *Sea Owl* to confer with Osiris and to reconsider their plan to hunt game.

Osiris, after enjoying the humorous side of Isis's story, commented, "Fresh meat would be a most welcome change to our present diet; the incident with the spiders is no problem during the day, when they sleep in their holes or deep under rotting foliage. I have already released the two Giants as promised and they will either return to the ship tonight or decide to stay.

"However, we have not encountered any natives; after the noise generated in the camp last night they must know we are here. When the sun is higher in the sky, I will ask Thoth to take a transporter and fly over the area close to the beach. If all is well, the hunt will take place in the afternoon. As a security measure, boats will be waiting by the hunt area to take them off if there is trouble."

With the sun high in the sky, Thoth and Hathor, complete with bow, took off from the deck of the *Sea Owl*, climbed to double mast height, and started their observation flight above the forest bordering the beach.

Looking down they saw a cleared area ringed around with straw huts. In the centre of the clearing there was a large fire, over which a group of small men were roasting a large carcass. Upon observing the transporter, they all ran away into the forest.

Thinking of the hunt, Thoth flew lower down, and Hathor screamed, "Thoth! The carcass being roasted is one of the Giants!"

At that moment a spear was thrown at them, and Thoth immediately increased height. Hathor wanted to use her bow to kill some of the natives, but Thoth pointed out that even if they killed a few, this would not be an adequate reply to their dastardly behaviour, so they returned to the *Sea Owl* and reported to Osiris.

Osiris was horrified, firstly with their deaths, secondly with the impact on their Nile base, if local natives heard of this horrific treatment of Giants in a neighbouring country.

After some deliberation it was agreed that some native warriors should be savagely killed in front of their women and children, and if possible leave the impression that the Giants' God had achieved this revenge. In addition, this action must be achieved without losing a Giant.

Sparing no time, the two transporters set off with the flaming torches previously prepared for the pirates. They carefully distributed these over the thatched roofs of the village huts, which were soon burning brightly.

Down in the undergrowth bordering the beach an ambush was set up, with concealed Giants armed with blowpipes and bows with poisoned arrows. While on the beach, three ship's boats were left in charge of volunteers who would act as decoys and start to run away when the natives appeared.

The natives, incensed with the loss of most of their village, rushed through the forest and out onto the beach where they encountered heavy casualties; they tried to retire but armoured Giants closed in behind them, killing all those still left standing, with their krises and spears.

The natives who had been incapacitated by the blowpipe darts were collected up, bound and revived. Then, two at a time, they were carried high over the village, and as their bonds were cut away they were thrown off the transporter, flailing and screaming as they fell into the village.

Satisfied that enough had been done to achieve his purpose, and deciding that to go into the village would be to risk Giants' lives, Osiris recalled all the Giants back to their ships, and ordered his captains to set sail up the African coast to Socotra, the island on the Arabian Sea between Yemen and Ethiopia.

The journey up the African coast towards Socotra was uneventful, the wind and the south-west drift ensuring a fast passage.

On the eighth day of their journey, Sailing Master Bata joined Captain Bakh.

"Captain, during our previous trading journeys in this area it was too dangerous to sail between Ethiopia and Socotra. The shallow water and sandbanks made navigation extremely difficult in daytime, and almost impossible at night.

"With the recent increases in sea level it is now my view that the west passage could now be classed as an acceptable risk; going round the west of Socotra could save two days in our sailing time to Quseir. As we no longer have the problem of marooning two Giants, I wondered if you are now prepared to take the shorter route?"

"Bata, I too believe the conditions are sufficiently changed to obtain a safe passage, as long as we keep fifteen itru from the coast of Ethiopia. However, the route must be decided by Osiris who may have reasons for a short visit to the mainland of Socotra, rather than to its extensive north-western isthmus."

Osiris then joined the discussion, and when the situation had been fully explained to him, he replied, "It is my intention to obtain supplies of water and goats from the east end of Socotra, to keep us in fresh meat until we reach the Nile and to provide sufficient stock to start breeding.

"While I agree the shorter route is tempting, it is my view that obtaining these provisions is well worth the delay of adding a couple of days to our journey, and with such a small native population on the island, we should have no trouble.

"The alternative is to stop at Xiss, but this might reveal our intentions, causing delays in the Ethiopian trading village and possibly an unpleasant reception committee when we arrive at Quseir. Taking everything into consideration, we should hold to our original intention and replenish our depleted stock of provisions, avoiding any contact with the mainland of Ethiopia and Egypt until we reach Quseir."

Two uneventful days later, they arrived at a small bay on the north-east coastline of Socotra, a landing point well known to the Giants. Each ship then sent parties to replenish their water supply and to capture as many goats as possible to provide fresh meat for both the voyage and for the subsequent march from Quseir on the Red Sea to Qena on the Nile.

With the natives avoiding all contact, they rounded up sufficient goats for each ship to load its full allocation. Unfortunately, to obtain a clean water supply they had to journey inland to draw their supplies from a mountain spring that cascaded down until it finally discharged into the bay. As the stream was frequented by herds of goats it was too polluted to be of any use below the source, so all members from the expedition who were not employed capturing goats had to carry the supplies back to the ships.

Apart from this unwelcome task after so many days at sea, they managed to accomplish the replenishment within the day and in the evening retired to their ships exhausted.

The following day as they were weighing anchor prior to leaving the bay, they were disturbed by the repeated and heavy rumbling of earth tremors coming from the western end of the isthmus.

Osiris called over to Captain Bakh, "I wonder what the effect will be in the straits between the Gulf of Aden and the Red Sea, when we reach it in about eight days' time, that is, if these strong tremors end in a major earthquake and land slip?"

"The same question occurred to me and I have just been discussing it with Bata. If there are signs that another tsunami situation is about to occur, we would have to seek shelter on the Ethiopian side of the gulf. This would be out of the direct line of any high wave from Socotra, due to the protection afforded by the sheltered bays on that side of the straits."

"If we are caught in the straits, which are only five itru wide, we could not survive. Once through the straits into the Red Sea, we must keep to the Arabian side behind some large islands, relying on the diffraction of the wave front until the danger has passed. In addition we must prepare for a higher wave than we experienced on the previous occasion.

"Under these conditions, when we reach Quseir, the expedition must unload immediately and move to high ground. The three ships must leave us and sail for Atlan by a different route, utilising the south-west and north-east monsoon drift to ensure a quick passage out of the area."

I estimate the sailing time to reach the straits will be about nine days and from there to Quseir a further twelve days, always providing we have reasonable wind conditions."

Osiris agreed and sent orders to the other captains to undertake the full range of preparations previously applied to safeguard their ships, this order to be effective immediately and not relaxed until they were well clear of the straits.

Osiris went on to say, "It is clear that the next nine days are critical and we must make the best speed possible; we cannot wait for anyone who is unable to keep up until we are well past the straits, and everyone must be made aware of this decision. Bakh, kindly inform the other captains."

During the first eight days both the weather and the sailing conditions were perfect, but during that period they were all apprehensive that they were enjoying a calm before a rather deadly storm.

Approaching the straits the sky rapidly darkened in the south, and the decision had to be taken whether to risk a direct run through the straits, or to anchor in a sheltered bay in the entrance to the Gulf of Aden straits, which would offer some protection.

Osiris called to Thoth. "Can you take the transporter up to a safe height to get a better view of the weather conditions?"

"I will do this immediately, but my problem is that I do not know what level can be regarded as a safe height. I have noticed that as the transporter gets higher there is a strong tendency to drift to the west. To compensate for this factor it will be necessary to fly east towards Yemen, then climb until the drifting gets pronounced, observe the activity in the south, then return to the ship."

He left immediately and all seemed to go well, but on returning he was visibly shaken and reported to Osiris immediately.

"Sir, the darkened sky in the south is more extensive, but despite this fact I recommend an immediate attempt to clear the straits, as it appears from observing the movement of a large ship, that there is a fast current running through the straits.

"If you accept this proposal, it might be appropriate to let *Sea Eagle* lead, as her hull is still weak despite the excellent repair."

Osiris called to Captain Bakh, "My decision is that we leave immediately, making a fast passage through the straits, *Sea Eagle* to lead, and *Sea Owl* following with *Sea Fury*. Inform the other captains and warn them to expect a fast current running through the straits."

Thoth continued, "During the flight I had a severe problem when taking the transporter to a great height, as its drift to the west seemed to accelerate as height increased. I only managed to return to the ship by a steep descent. I believe it would be extremely dangerous to make another attempt at that height."

With all sails set and *Sea Eagle* leading, they started a headlong rush to the straits, where with any luck, they would arrive late next morning.

They still had enough sea room to sail through the night under full canvas.

When dawn broke they found themselves right in the middle of the approach to the straits' entrance, six hours ahead of schedule! They had failed to appreciate that the strong current would be encountered so far back in the Gulf of Aden.

The ships were now in a following sea with waves building up as they reached the narrowest part of the passage through the straits. Once again all passengers were battened down under hatches, companionways sealed off, and extra crew being assigned to the steering gear. The waves were not high enough to overrun their high stern, but the ships lifted to every wave and it was difficult to keep them from broaching.

The impact of the waves on the hull, the pitching and rolling and the high wind from the south, generated so much spray they found it extremely difficult to keep the correct station between the ships. At one point in the straits the *Sea Owl* had to deploy her sea anchor to fall back, when she nearly overran the *Sea Eagle*.

At last the straits started to open out and the expedition headed towards the Arabian shore on a long reach.

In the early morning of the third day they stopped under the lee of the Farasan Isthmus to maintain rigging. Having almost completed their work, they were disturbed by a roaring sound steadily growing in intensity from the south.

Suddenly there appeared a square wave racing up the centre of the Red Sea. As it passed, the sea level began rising on either side, flooding large sections of the low land bordering the existing shore line. The Farasan Isthmus then became the Farasan Islands.

All the expedition ships were unharmed in their sheltered position, but as Isis then remarked, the trading post at Quseir must be experiencing considerable difficulties.

Osiris immediately ordered the ships to complete their work on the rigging, and sail within four hours. With sea conditions deteriorating rapidly in the Red Sea area, it was essential to sail immediately in the hope of rescuing the trading post staff and then achieving a rapid turnaround of the ships after they reached Quseir.

Sailing at times through shoals of dead and dying fish and with variable wind conditions, the journey to Quseir took fourteen days. On the first day of their journey the fish were a welcome supplement to goat's meat, but from then on the smell was appalling!

They were relieved to see that something was left of Quseir as they approached in the early morning. The main harbour structure had vanished together with the majority of the trading post buildings, but the staff were huddled up near the water's edge, and had taken refuge under some dilapidated palm trees, which provided the only shelter available under the heavy tropical rainstorm, which greeted the expedition on their arrival.

Using the ship's boats to take soundings, they anchored as close to the shore as possible. Then from the debris of the buildings and a local timber store, they constructed rafts to offload their wares. While this work was proceeding satisfactorily, Osiris greeted the trading post Giants and their families, who were invited to join the expedition. This they immediately accepted, there being no feasible alternative.

Osiris then called a conference with the usual members, including the three ships' captains and the trading post Giants to discuss the method of transporting their supplies to Qena on the Nile.

Osiris then turned to the Giant responsible for the trading post and said, "I want you to address the gathering and advise on the method of communicating with the natives, and what method could be used to transport our goods from here to Qena."

The elder of the two Giants stood up and addressed the meeting. "My name is Zon, my assistant's name is Tesh, and we have been in charge of the trading post for the last fifteen years. During this long period, and until very recently, we had established excellent relations with the natives, but a few months ago the old chief died, and he has been replaced by a young hothead.

"Recently the new Chieftain came down to our trading post with armed warriors and threatened us, stating that unless we moved into his village he would drive us out. Furthermore he would take over the trading post, and we would only be allowed to work through him. Since then, natives who are well disposed to us, warned us that the Chieftain had decided that sooner or later we would be eliminated.

"In the past we have employed his villagers to move trading goods to the interior, but that facility has also been withdrawn. The arrangement of natives living together is unusual, normally they work in family groups hunting and clearing an area around their temporary homes of vegetables and fruit before moving on. This village group now subsist by sending out raiding parties, and charging tax on the products that any tradesmen are carrying when passing through what the Chieftain regards as his area. So taking into account our present situation, you can imagine how happy we are to see the arrival of your company!"

After a short period of discussion, Osiris asked Zon, "Is there any way we can send a message to the Chieftain, and is it likely he will be aware of our arrival?"

"It is doubtful if he is sufficiently intelligent to understand a written message; however, we can send a messenger who is unaware of your arrival to the Chieftain as he might be severely interrogated. I have such a man who is due back this afternoon from a visit to his family who live far inland. Tesh should be able to intercept him before he reaches the harbour and instruct him to convey your message to the native village.

"I do not believe the Chief will know of your arrival, as his village is two itru inland and hidden in a valley, but we cannot be sure."

Osiris then told Zon to send Tesh with the following message. "Tell them 'My trading post has been destroyed by the flood and I am now prepared to rebuild in your village, providing you give me your personal guarantee of safety for my staff and myself.

"'To recompense you for the land I require in your village, I am prepared to give you three bars of gold as payment. If this is not sufficient or you are not prepared to give the guarantee, we have decided to leave in a small boat early tomorrow morning and abandon the trading post which will not be renewed.

"'Assuming you are prepared to discuss a suitable arrangement with us tonight, I have prepared a feast for you and your bodyguard.' OK?

"Zon, will you agree to send Tesh immediately, and, Tesh, you must return as quickly as possible when the messenger is on his way to the native village, so that our final preparations can be put in hand."

Then turning to Bakh: "Finish unloading and leave within three hours. If this is impossible sail out of sight and return in two days' time."

When Tesh returned it was just past midday, and he reported to Osiris.

"I had no difficulty in intercepting the messenger who was well ahead of schedule; he accepted my message with some astonishment. I then convinced him that due to the Chieftain's threats, their withholding of assistance with the transportation of trade goods would prevent the trading post from operating. If this situation cannot be resolved then, regretfully, we will have no alternative other than to leave at sunrise the next day."

By the time the ships had left Quseir, preparations for the visit of the Chieftain were well in hand. A table had been prepared in a clearing outside the trading post and obstacles had been inserted in the approaches so that the natives could only reach the table from the old track. All the expedition members had now been armed and concealed, leaving Zon and Tesh with their native helpers to kill one of the goats, cook it and await the guests.

Isis, in her full council robes, and Thoth, were now concealed a little way from the feast area with their transporter and two armoured Giants dressed to look as terrifying as possible.

Two parties armed with bows and blowpipes were located on either side of the clearing, with orders to incapacitate the Chieftain and his body guards immediately upon a signal given by Osiris. Everything had been prepared for their reception; now it was only necessary to await their arrival.

Just as it was growing dark, a loud singing and a banging of shields could be heard coming from the direction of the track. A short time later round a bend in the track leading into the clearing, ten plumed native warriors appeared, followed by a wooden framework carried by eight slaves on which an ornate throne was mounted. Sitting with his legs crossed on a thick cushion was a young obese Chieftain with a sardonic grin on his face.

A further group of ten warriors stopped at the entrance to the clearing, when the main group reached the table.

The Chieftain gave the order for the throne to be brought up to the table, then his slaves lowered it down to the ground and backing away, prostrated themselves in a token of humility.

The Chieftain then started to scream abuse at Zon and Tesh, ordering his bodyguard to pick up the table and throw the food at the Giants' feet. Not satisfied with that demonstration, he ordered the two Giants to kneel down before him and bow their heads in submission to acknowledge that he was now their Chief.

The Giants did not move, and he then ordered his bodyguard to force them to the ground. As the bodyguards approached the two Giants, Osiris gave the signal and well-placed arrows shot the four guards while the blowpipes incapacitated the Chieftain with several well-placed darts.

Zon stepped forward and shouted in the local dialect, "Our Goddess is coming!" and threw himself flat on the ground. Hearing the signal, Isis, with her two guards sitting behind her, took off on the transporter and, standing up with her large headdress with the sun and horns insignia to cover the helmet, flew slowly over the treetops into the clearing, stopping just above head height. The Chief's bodyguards froze with fear at the apparition. Time passed; still no one moved until one of the natives, more in panic than in design, started to lift his spear, and immediately Isis raised her arm and pointed one finger at him. As previously arranged he was immediately hit by a number of darts in the neck, and just had time to drop his spear and clutch at his neck before falling insensible to the ground.

Zon stood up, bowed to Isis, and told the natives to return to their village at once, before the Goddess took vengeance on all of them. Their Chief would be returned to the village clearing early next morning after ReRa had judged his soul.

They were all frozen with fear and failing to move, and Isis slowly started to raise her arm a second time with outstretched finger towards them. Seeing this, they turned and ran.

Osiris told three of his warriors to follow but to remain concealed, ensuring that the natives had cleared the area and were, in fact, returning to their village.

The three Giants soon returned to inform him that the natives were all running for the village as if the Prince of Darkness himself was behind them with all his demons.

Three of the native bodyguard were badly wounded and these were killed immediately. The remaining two natives would recover and, together with their Chief, would be returned to the village just after dawn, so that the village could witness their struggling and screams as they plummeted down to earth from high in the sky.

The next morning the Chieftain and the two luckless natives made the spectacular return to the village from the sky, landing in the centre of the clearing. The natives who had been waiting for the return of their Chieftain, were horrified as they watched them screaming as they tumbled down, their bodies exploding as they struck the hard ground.

Having observed the general consternation this demonstration caused, Thoth returned to the expedition's camp, joining Osiris and Isis who discussed the next phase of their operation.

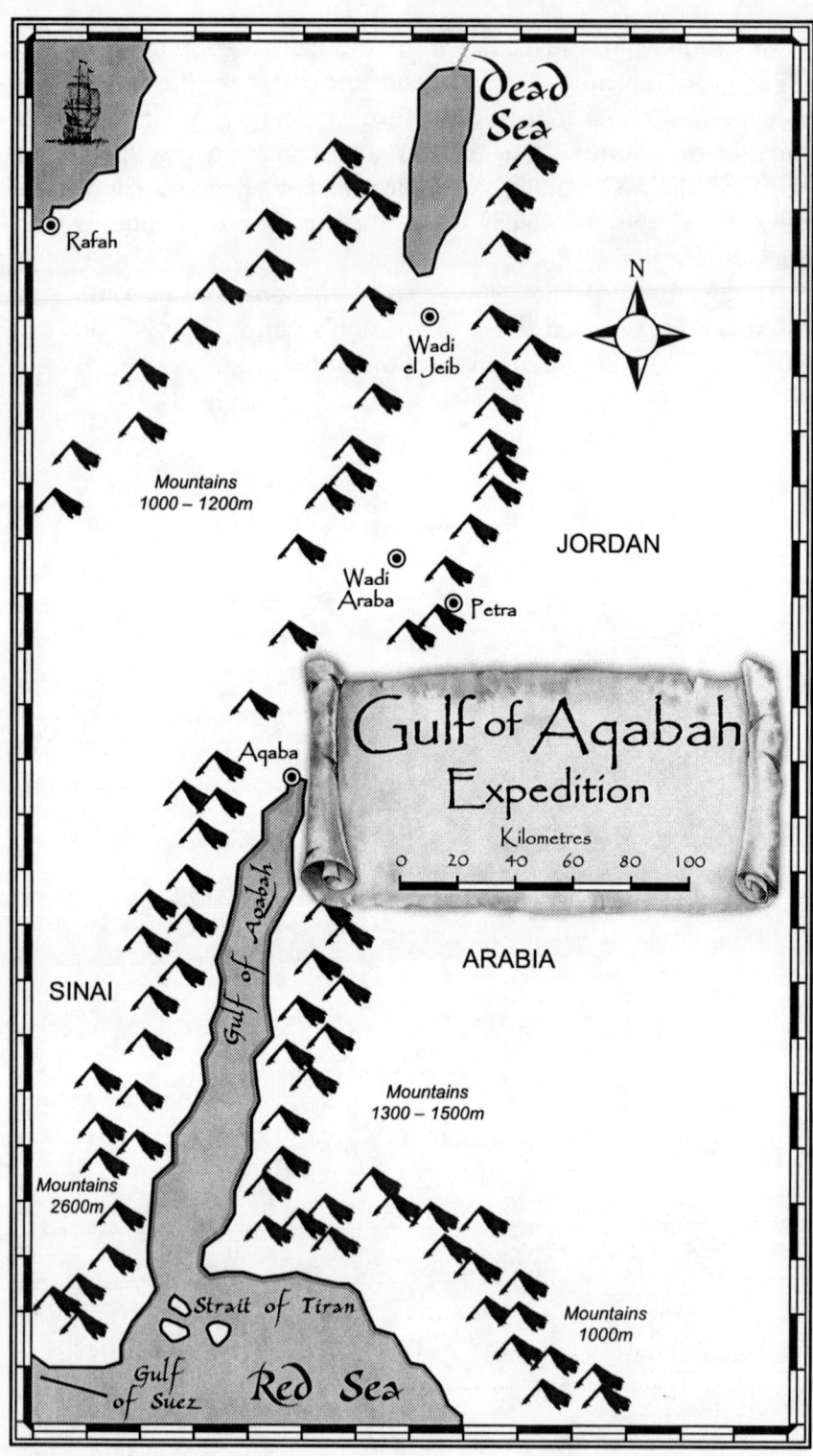

Quseir and Qena

5500 BC

Osiris welcomed Thoth's return, and after expressing his delight at the satisfactory completion of the operation, detailed the next moves.

"We now require porters to carry our stores and personal possessions the seventy-four itru to Qena on the Nile. It is estimated that this journey will take about seventeen days. I believe the natives will now be attentive to any orders they receive from Isis. To take advantage of this situation Thoth and two warriors will deliver Zon close to the native village. Zon and the two warriors will enter the edge of the village and call for the Headman.

"When he arrives he will be informed that on the orders of the Goddess Isis his village will provide, by the next sunrise, the necessary numbers of porters to carry our stores up to the Nile at Qena. The porters will have to provide sufficient food for the three-week journey.

"He will also inform them that the Goddess will build a great village on the Nile, to rule the whole of Egypt. Porters loyal to the Goddess will be able to help in that task, which initially will be difficult, but will in the end offer great rewards. Zon, you must impress on the occupants of the native village that failure to accept orders from the Goddess can only be followed by severe punishment.

"Only Zon, Tesh, the two giant bodyguards, and the essential native staff will accompany the porters carrying the stores. All the remaining Quseir natives will be left behind to recover any stores when the flood retreats, and they may then follow up to the Nile in two to three weeks' time.

"Thoth will monitor the progress of the porters once a day, and the expedition will remain half a day's march behind them. We have just sufficient food to feed the expedition for two weeks, but on the march there will be adequate time to send hunters out to supplement supplies. Expedition members will carry the artefacts. The expedition will also remain concealed, except for the two bodyguards already seen by the natives."

The Giants then spent the rest of the day laying out the stores to be taken by the porters, and erected a temporary shelter for Zon and Tesh to spend the night and welcome the porters the next morning. They then withdrew with the local natives to a camp in a nearby wadi that was concealed by overhanging vegetation.

The next morning the porters arrived and the new Headman of the village bowed to Zon and said, "The Elders of the village have had a meeting and it has been decided to ask the Goddess for permission for all their families to move to the Nile and serve the Goddess."

Zon called over one of the Giants' bodyguards and told him of the Headman's request and asked him to send the message to the Goddess. He departed immediately, and the Headman was told to wait for the answer.

In a short time the bodyguard returned and informed Zon that an interview had been granted and that the Headman would now be escorted to the Goddess.

Zol told the Headman to accompany Tesh and the two bodyguards to meet the Goddess, warning him to show great respect by bowing low when she appeared.

The Headman was then taken to a nearby clearing and, flanked by the two bodyguards, told to wait, with Tesh standing a little way in front of the group to translate. Suddenly over the treetops Isis appeared, standing on the transporter in full regalia, and slowly descended to head height above the ground. The Headman threw himself to the ground.

After a suitable pause, Isis told him to rise and then said, "Your request has been granted, but I must warn you that my decision requires the total loyalty of all those who wished to serve me at Qena. I also stipulate that the dependants are not to follow for three weeks. This will allow everyone who wishes to come to have sufficient time to prepare, and that every morning at sunrise, they should make a small prayer for forgiveness for the evils they had committed in the past, for by this means I shall know of your loyalty and good intentions for your future behaviour."

The Headman bowed and thanked the Goddess and bowed again, as she slowly rose above the treetops and returned the way she had come. Tesh with the Headman and the bodyguard then returned to the camp.

The Headman called the porters together, saying, "Rejoice! The

Goddess has agreed that your wives and families would be permitted to follow in three weeks' time."

Then with yells of joy they lifted up the stores and started their trek to Qena.

At first light the expedition started to close their distance with the porters to half a day's trek, and Thoth flew ahead and came back to report that the porters had made excellent progress as they had covered five itru. This required the expedition to attempt six itru over the next three days. This part of the journey was exhausting for the Giants as they were still feeling the effects of the long sea journey, and with the artefacts and provisions, their loads were not much lighter than those of the porters.

The expedition found some compensation in that the track was well used and dry, although it was all uphill for the first few days of the trek and there was thick undergrowth on either side that served to keep the larger animals away from the column.

After ten days the porters had covered forty-three itru and were in advance of schedule, until their column was suddenly halted at a broken rope bridge that should have spanned a deep ravine. It was clear that the ropes securing the end of the bridge to its anchors on the far bank had broken, and the complete bridge was now hanging down into the depths of the ravine, completely preventing all further progress.

Zol ordered the porters to make four long ropes from forest vines capable of spanning the complete ravine, and while this work was in hand he laid out a white sheet on the ground, telling the porters that he was about to pray to the Goddess for her help.

Thoth, on his morning flight, saw the signal and having seen the broken bridge, returned and reported to Osiris and Isis. After considering the problem Osiris turned to Isis.

"You have an impish grin on your face... have you something special in mind?"

"My proposal is that this could form the basis of another miracle. When the porters have completed the four ropes of sufficient length to span the ravine, they must be instructed to leave them at the entrance to the bridge. Then they are to be escorted half an itru from the bridge to a clearing to say prayers to the Goddess, asking for help in crossing the ravine. While they are so diverted, the two transporters can land six Giants on the far side of the crossing. Then the ropes can be retrieved from the other side and delivered to the Giants who would secure one end. Then Thoth and a Giant can take a rope with a pulley arrangement fitted, down to the broken end of the bridge and secure it. The operation can then be repeated until all the four ends are secured to the bridge.

"Flying back up to the top of the ravine, they can then haul the bridge up as far as possible. To achieve the second stage of the lift, they can, one by one, take the ends of the ropes, connect them to the main lifting ropes and as close to the bridge as possible obtain a two to one advantage and then pass them round tree trunks to secure them. Then the bridge will be in a satisfactory condition for the porters to make the permanent repair.

"The Giants' party will then return to the expedition camp, leaving one of Isis's bodyguards to go to the porters and tell them their prayers have been answered. The consequences of this will assuredly result in the establishment of another miracle!

"While all this is going on, the Giants should be sending out hunting parties to obtain enough meat to last us the rest of the journey to Qena."

Osiris laughed, saying, "Isis, assuredly you are the miracle. It is an excellent plan – we must waste no more time and adopt it immediately!"

The results were even better than expected: the porters, returning from their prayers, found the bridge re-established and after making further permanent connections, they knelt down and gave thanks to the Goddess, then picking up their loads, moved off, singing songs of praise to her, and continued the trek in great heart.

With the journey now covering gentle downhill slopes joined by long level stretches on well-worn paths, the porters made a steady four and three quarters itru daily. As a result, by the afternoon of the sixth day after leaving the bridge, they had their first sight of the Nile curling in towards them, then swinging across their front.

In the background of the Nile, the hills were magnified by the temperature difference across the Nile Valley into the small mountains, with the lush green vegetation making it an exciting view of their future home. Across the river in the far distance, Thoth could see hills of some eight hundred cubits high that might provide a remote and safe depository for the artefacts.

As the area around the native village of Qena on the east side of the Nile was heavily polluted and totally unsuitable for the development of their first city, Thoth and Hathor made a quick flight across the Nile to survey the west bank. There they found a good site for their new home, on a level limestone bed a hundred cubits above the Nile flood level.

Establishing rest areas for the expedition and porters, Osiris called a meeting with all members of the expedition, and when they had assembled he opened the meeting.

"I have decided we must build our city on the uninhabited west side of the Nile, and we must move across with all our stores and the porters. Thoth, have you any ideas on how this can be best achieved with the minimum delay?"

"From my brief survey of the west bank I noticed a substantial forest of tall trees on the east side of the river about seven itru to the south of our camp. I propose we immediately hire some native labour, and request volunteers from the expedition to take them there and establish a logging camp. On arrival they will immediately start to cut down the tallest trees, reducing them to bare trunks and form large rafts that they will float down to us. This will enable us to cross the Nile. The work will continue at the logging camp until we have an adequate supply of building material to commence construction of the temple and of the accommodation."

Zon stood up and addressed Osiris.

"I will volunteer to hire labour from the village and establish the logging camp. Tesh will come with me as we are both able to converse with the natives. We require two more volunteers from the expedition to guide the rafts down to our camp."

"Thank you, Zon, this matter must be urgently resolved; the first rafts should reach us within three days, so that must be your target. The first consignment of rafts will be used to cross the Nile, so I suggest you set out immediately!"

Osiris then turned to Isis. "Is there any urgent work that should be undertaken immediately?"

"There are two pressing problems that are required before we can make the river crossing, and these are the manufacture of strong ropes, and the preparation of offset landing places on either side of the river to take advantage of the current. I can take responsibility for organising the work on the crossing, and Thoth will make the essential calculations. Then there is the manufacture of ropes, that will be required to reduce the effect of the current. This is a job for the porters and must be undertaken by them without delay!"

"I agree, Isis, but as soon as the first crossing is made, construction of the first Egyptian temple must be started."

Two days later the first batch of rafts arrived at the curve of the Nile near Qena, and the expedition and their porters were safely rafted across to the west bank over the next two days. While crossings were proceeding, Osiris had flown across the Nile with Isis to mark out the temple site that would be dedicated to ReRa celebrating the safe arrival of the expedition, and around the site he marked out a large enclosure in which the administration buildings and Giants' accommodation would be established.

The Giants that had brought the rafts to Qena returned to the wooded area to supervise logging and to raft the next consignments to the new west bank site.

After this preparatory work had been satisfactorily completed, Thoth explained to Zon that he required a number of native working parties – one group to construct counterbalanced beams to lift water from the Nile up to the level of irrigation ditches, the other to clear areas of the dense undergrowth bordering the river to establish large fields, then prepare the ground and plant the seeds that the Giants had brought from their homeland.

The annual inundation of the Nile had recently occurred, and with two hundred and ten days remaining before the date mentioned in the Prophecies, it was possible to obtain two harvests that would secure their food supply.

In the meantime fish traps and hunting parties were to be sent out to provide for the immediate food demands for both the Giants and the natives.

After the passage of two months all was going according to plan, and Isis and Thoth set out to select a suitable place in the nearby hills to store the artefacts. After a lengthy search on both sides of the river, they found a ledge on a remote site with an entry into a small cave, inaccessible except by air, some eight hundred and thirty cubits above the level of the Nile, and the rock was limestone – ideal for tunnelling.

Isis and Thoth then returned to camp and obtained the tunnel-forming device together with its operating scrolls and transported them to the proposed site. Together they set up the device and after referring to the scrolls and reviewing the operating procedure, they nervously prepared to operate it for the first time.

"Zu, from the warning of the skeletons in front of the device in the Atlan cave, and the signs on the side of the machine, we can only stand directly behind it when it is operating. So I will stand directly behind you when you operate the levers and then we both move well back to observe what happens."

With some trepidation Thoth pulled the levers in the correct sequence, then he quickly joined Isis, standing as far back on the ledge as possible.

"Zu, there is no noise, light or flames, in fact nothing seems to be happening – altogether very disappointing! Just like our first test on the transporter... are you sure you operated the levers in the correct sequence?"

"Regarding the technical readings I am not sure of their meaning, but the sequence of operation is clear and in that respect my translation is accurate! But I will check the scrolls again to see if I have missed an instruction."

Thoth referred to the scroll again but there was no help from that source.

Returning to switch the machinery off and abandon the effort for the day, they noticed that there was a new tunnel and it was already ten cubits deep.

"Zu, where has the debris gone, has it removed cubic cubits of rock?"

"I recall that the scroll referred to there being no debris, but added it is still there! This is beyond my comprehension so let us agree it is a special magic and just accept it! But it must still be *somewhere!*"

When the tunnel reached twenty cubits in depth progress became very slow, so they switched the machine off and moved the device within a cubit of the end of the tunnel, and started again. After repeating the operation ten times they had a tunnel length of some two hundred cubits. It was now getting dark and Thoth turned to Isis.

"It is too dark to continue with safety. I think it is important for you to return to Osiris and tell him of our progress. I will stay with the machine overnight so that I can make an early start tomorrow. Try to return as soon as possible in the morning as it is not particularly safe to continue alone without transport!"

When Isis arrived back at camp Osiris was far from pleased with their arrangement, but relented when she informed him they should complete the work the following day.

Early next morning she rejoined Thoth and they continued to extend the tunnel. All was going well until about midday, when they heard a heavy fall of rock and the tunnel started to fill with dust. Stopping the machine immediately they waited for a few minutes to let the dust clear, then slowly walked down the tunnel until near the end, where the floor of the tunnel had fallen away, and it became clear they had penetrated a natural limestone cavern. The pile of debris that had dropped down from the tunnel floor formed a ramp that allowed them to enter the cavern. Slowly feeling their way down the unstable ramp with their lights reflecting off the massive stalactites and stalagmites, it looked like Fairy Land.

Penetrating deeper into the cavern they came across a track formed when a long line of stalactite groups had been removed, and they noted that although replacement stalactites had reached substantial lengths, the difference in length with the neighbouring originals suggested that the path must have been cleared thousands of years previously. Even so it was still possible to walk down the path, and they eventually came to a junction. One path led straight on, but Isis, without any hesitation, walked down the short path that led a short distance towards the cavern wall.

There was a portal in the wall with a high-level inscription in hieroglyphs, identical to that over the entrance to the artefacts' store encountered during their homeland expedition. Isis stretched her arms out and touched the two plates and reluctantly the door opened a little way. Eventually, with the help of a strong push from Thoth, it opened fully to reveal a massive limestone sarcophagus.

On the walls there were extensive hieroglyphs, using the same signs as those used to inscribe the scrolls. Then Thoth, using the knowledge previously gained, interpreted the meaning of the signs to Isis:

Before the Tomb of my King and Great Lord Osiris, whose Ka has now joined his immortal brothers in the infinite mantel of the Universe, I, the Chief Priest and Magician of the first Atlan expedition to the Great River in the Land of Egypt, record that this expedition was assembled to ensure the survival of our race at the time of the cataclysm, forecast by the Prophecy and now fulfilled by enveloping the southern hemisphere of the known world.

I record with sadness that the great trials we overcame in our journey to the Nile ended during the cataclysm with the complete annihilation of all but four of our expedition members.

This I record so that any of our race, who have survived the cataclysm and find these records, may benefit from the knowledge of our misfortunes."

Thoth then turned to Isis and said, "As you can see he goes into great detail – he mentions the Prophecy by their astronomers of destruction of Atlan by fire, earthquakes, great winds and massive waves.

"But, unfortunately, the Council, after lengthy discussions, rejected the Prophecy as an old wives' tale!

"It records how the High Lord Osiris at his own cost assembled an expedition to ensure the continuation of their race. Fortunately he had at that time completed two trading ships, the largest in the known world, in which he lodged one hundred expedition members. During their journey to the west they lost one ship and that reduced his expedition members to fifty. When they reached the straits between the Gulf of Aden and the Red Sea, their ship was wrecked and they lost a further thirty Giants. Of the one hundred that started, only fifteen eventually reached the Great River.

"There were only sixty days left until the time of the Prophecy, so they sought a safe place in which to shelter. They discovered a small cave that was an entrance to a great limestone cavern. Then disaster struck once more, when a falling stalactite killed Osiris. The remaining Giants worked without rest to build the tomb and the sarcophagus. When this was achieved, ten Giants went out to find food and after they left, a major earthquake occurred and sealed the only entrance to our cave."

Zu concluded, "Thu and his three companions were trapped and, after dedicating their lives to ReRa, left us this record. Presumably they all died in the cavern and we may still find their bodies."

Isis commented, "It is immediately apparent that these Giants are our ancestors, who date from the time of the artefacts. The family name of Osiris is certainly significant, as is Thu's rank of High Priest and Magician!

"Later we will require a full translation of the text, but the immediate problem is to open the blocked entrance; this must be completed today, so let us bring down the equipment from our tunnel and either clear the debris from the blocked opening, or open a new entrance on one side.

"After this we must return to our new home and advise Osiris of our discovery, and organise a small team of Giants with stonework skills to form a strong portal and counterbalanced door, all to be designed to appear like the normal hillside."

With the machinery in position the blocked entrance was quickly opened, and they then set about concealing the re-established opening.

Returning the tunnel-forming machine to the tomb, they clambered up through the cavern into the tunnel and onto the mountain shelf, boarded the transporter and set off to return to camp.

After their arrival Osiris called a meeting of all the expedition members and when they had assembled, he addressed them.

"Working on a storage facility for the artefacts we have discovered a cavern that was last inhabited by our ancestors, and this fully substantiates the cataclysmic destruction of our previous civilization. They left a clear warning for us, requiring us to make provisions for survival well before the prophesied date. We must not rely on one shelter, and all shelters must have two exits. As soon as conditions deteriorate all female Giants are to be confined to quarters, as they alone hold the key to our survival as a race.

"We will build two shelters close to the temple – this work must begin at once. Also all members must now have a specific task and Thoth will record the extent of those tasks. There will of course be other tasks, but those recorded must have first priority. Thoth, your immediate task will be the construction of a large reservoir in the enclosure to catch and contain the run off from the three streams that flow down the hillside."

Progress exceeded anticipation as the weeks went by; the first harvest was bountiful, and the livestock flourished, secure from predators in the lush vegetation, and purchases from the villagers on the east side of the Nile increased stock levels. Osiris estimated that there should be sufficient time to obtain a second harvest, but demanded that adequate preparations must be made in case the prophesied date was earlier than expected.

The weather conditions were perfect for growing crops in the very fertile Nile soil which had been deposited on its banks during the times of the inundation. The natives, having seen the results of channelling the water to the fields with the use of the counterbalanced buckets, were now extending their fields and making these devices for their own use.

After discussions with other expedition members, Osiris sent for Zon and asked him to take the following message to the Headman of the porters.

"The Goddess Isis informs them that, in about two months time, we expect very severe storms. To protect their people they should prepare underground shelters in the side of the hills close to their fields, no shelter should house more than fifteen persons, and they should be prepared immediately."

The days passed quickly, the weather was perfect and hunting expeditions brought in several lions and a great number of springbuck, and the second harvest was brought in with great celebration.

One morning everything had a strange stillness, the animals in the enclosures huddled together, and occasionally an animal would rush against the enclosure barriers until it became exhausted and fell to the ground, shivering and bleating pathetically.

The forests and grasslands now appeared devoid of wild animals and the birds had disappeared. With all these significant signs suggesting the fulfilment of the Prophecy, Osiris ordered all the female members of the expedition to go to, and remain in, their designated shelters, and for all expedition members to spend their nights in the shelters.

This situation lasted for two days, then a black mantle of cloud rushed across the southern skyline, illuminated on the underside by a bright orange glow as if the air was on fire. The earth started to tremble and everyone ran to their shelters. Thoth took Osiris to the tomb shelter, as he wished to be with his ancestor and Isis, in case he did not survive.

They woke up in the middle of the night to a thunderous roar starting from the south which seemed to rush towards them, the cavern appeared to spin round in circles and this terror was amplified by the crashing of stalactites as they smashed down upon the cavern floor. The roaring continued but started to reduce as it changed direction to the north-east.

Earthquakes, followed by aftershocks, continued for the next two days and it was clearly too dangerous to venture out. When all sounds had vanished for half a day, they decided to venture outside.

They discovered the new portal had survived the earthquake but when they managed to open it a little way, the outside had been blocked by a massive landslide.

After making a close examination of the blockage they abandoned that route, and reverted to the original tunnel they had cut from the ledge. This path was also heavily damaged where they had previously broken through from the tunnel to the cavern, but after a further day's work they were able to reach the ledge that had been reduced in size and undermined by rockfalls. Then using the two transporters they managed to carry the twenty Giants down to a level area, to wait transportation to the temple.

Arriving at the expedition site, the temple was still standing, but the rest of the site was unrecognisable: the high wind had torn the palm trees out of the ground, and the savannahs bordering the Nile had been flattened with numerous dead animals lying on the vast mass of debris.

The animals in the enclosure were lost, and nothing remained of that area apart from a few upright fence posts. The village of Qena on the other side of the Nile had been levelled and even at that distance it was easy to observe a considerable number of swollen and decomposing animals lying out in the open.

After giving thanks in the temple to ReRa, they began their search for the remainder of the expedition in the three underground shelters. Due to the numerous landslides these were extremely difficult to locate, and they knew that time was running out for their occupants who would be slowly suffocating.

With everyone working on the first refuge, they managed to break through the rubble to let light and air into the space. The occupants were very weak, but with the air supply secured, there was no time to open up the access, if the occupants of the other shelters were to be saved from suffocation. With a promise to return as quickly as possible, they moved off to locate the access to the second refuge.

When they arrived in the vicinity of the next shelter they could hear the occupants working to open the exit, and by working frantically towards them, they broke through and helped them out, all of who were suffering from partial suffocation and were unable to help.

They found the third refuge concealed under a major landslip which required the clearance of boulders before the exit would be visible, then they returned to the first refuge and using the few remaining fence posts as levers, managed to extract the heavy boulders and release the occupants. These Giants were now in better condition having had some air supply through fractures in the enclosing rocks and were able to help.

Returning to the third refuge they started the exhausting work of removing the heavy debris to locate the refuge entrance. After about four hours of backbreaking work, they located part of the entrance, and after clearing the rock and rubble they managed to dismantle the wooden door. Unfortunately this did not provide access as the roof had collapsed and a substantial quantity of large rocks and rubble barred their path.

Attempting to move the rocks further caused falls to occur and the situation became extremely dangerous for the rescuers.

Isis stopped the work. "Further work on this collapsed exit is futile – we will now return to the outside and burrow down past the roof fall. Form two teams until we break through then we will all concentrate on enlarging the opening sufficiently to extract the occupants."

With the teams working in shifts to achieve the maximum rate of clearance, they soon broke through on one side of the tunnel. The occupants were all huddled up at one end of the shelter then, one by one, they were carefully carried out to the temple for revival.

By morning Osiris reviewed the situation.

"Nine of our expedition members from the third shelter have revived, but sadly six had died overnight and are to be buried immediately in a temporary grave within the temple grounds. A proper tomb will be constructed later when the general situation has improved.

"It is now a question of finding sufficient natives alive to form teams to release the rest of their people from their individual shelters."

Osiris turned to Thoth. "Drive a deep cave into the rock of the nearest hillside to provide a place for a mass burial, the rest of the expedition are to go to the native encampment and search for the living."

After the Giants had opened up two of the shelters they found half of the porters had died. After reassuring the living that the storm and earthquake were over, they were soon at work rescuing the survivors and laying out the dead for a mass internment, to be held by the Goddess as soon as the deep cave was ready to receive the bodies.

Thoth and Hathor made a quick flight over Qena, and they found the situation to be worse than they had envisaged, as without preparation they had been totally exposed to the appalling storm, and survival had been impossible. The task of clearing the site would be beyond the diminished strength of the porters, and decomposition of the bodies of humans and animals was already far advanced. The area was immediately designated as out of bounds for both the expedition and natives.

The weather was getting colder, with a strong wind from the

north being drawn down to the southern hemisphere. With frequent heavy rain, everyone set to, building shelters, re-establishing the enclosure, and cremating the dead animals. All this essential survival work they managed to achieve in the first week.

Work now began to clean up the existing fields, replacing the counterbalanced water-lifting devices and, after clearing the debris-strewn savannahs, preparing additional fields. In addition, the original irrigation scheme required extending to allow for the growing population, and to attract any surviving natives to increase the workforce.

Using the transporters, Thoth managed to locate a large number of natives who were starting to descend from the hills where they had been sheltering. On his return Thoth sought out Zon.

"Take a small party with you and go out and meet the natives I have seen coming down from the hills. Promise them food and protection providing they join us in establishing the first city in Egypt."

Having taken care of the immediate tasks, Osiris called together Isis, Thoth and Hathor, then opened the discussion.

"Having overcome our immediate problems I think it is about time to determine the extent of the damage certainly between here and Quseir trading post. I therefore propose we take two transporters with Tesh as interpreter, to discover if anyone is left alive in that area. We must also leave a permanent message near the original trading post site, to inform any of our people where to find us. I realise there is not much hope of survivors but it does leave a possible link with our homeland if anyone has survived. Thoth, you have a problem?"

"It will take about a full day to reach the coast so the minimum time for the journey would be three days, for which we must carry sufficient provisions including water as local supplies may be contaminated."

"What do you think, Isis?"

"In my view once we reach the coast it would be better to take full advantage of the facility offered to explore to the north. Once we start the real building programme it will be difficult to find the time to undertake another trip. We must take supplies for at least two weeks. That level of supply is based on an almost certainty that there will be nothing left in the way of food, in particular fish, remembering the damage done to fish stocks after our escape through the straits!"

"Hathor, have you any matter you would like to raise?"

"Only to add that we should not presume that everything we encounter will be friendly, that is, man *or* beast."

Osiris chuckled. "Doubtless you mean woman or beast? But I do agree and we will all take arms, and a couple of quivers full for Hathor—"

Tesh disdainfully interrupted. "I must admit I am unhappy at the thought of travelling on a transporter. I am afraid of heights, and the thought of travelling any distance above the sea horrifies me. So I must ask to be excused from this expedition, that in any event, I regard as being unnecessary and far too risky."

"Everything we undertake on this expedition is on a voluntary basis and you are fully entitled to both refuse, and to express your personal opinion. This is especially true as you did not join as a volunteer, but are coerced by force of circumstances, there being no acceptable alternative.

"Therefore taking everything into account, you are excused from undertaking this journey, but I must warn you not to express those opinions outside this meeting, for if you do so, you will incur my severe displeasure."

As Zon was fully employed searching for additions to the workforce, they decided to do without an interpreter on this trip. In the event of a contact with the natives, Thoth had sufficient knowledge of the language to reach a general understanding with them.

Two days later they set off early in the morning and covered the seventy-four itru in four and a half hours. The route they took to reach the Nile was no longer the sub-tropical green wood full of wild animals and chirping birds; it was now an area of complete destruction and desolation, if anything considerably worse than the banks of the Nile.

Of the trading station and native village nothing was left, and it was absolutely impossible to determine where it had once been located.

Choosing a flat area on the Red Sea shore, they landed, rigged a temporary shelter and settled down for a light lunch. Isis, not being quite so hungry as the others, got up and walked to the shoreline. Suddenly she gave an excited shout.

"There is a large ship moving slowly, about one itru out to sea."

The three rushed out to join her.

Isis continued, "It's just like one of our sea traders – they may be looking for the trading post."

Osiris immediately added, "Let's give them a great welcome by flying out and landing on her."

Concealing the food from insects, they left their shelter and boarded the two transporters, and carefully approached the ship to avoid alarming her crew. Looking down, there was no one on deck, and the ship seemed to be sailing itself with little more than a rag for a sail. So they landed on the stern deck and grasping their weapons started a systematic search of the ship.

When they reached the captain's cabin, they found him sitting at his desk, a bundle of clothes round a decaying body. They extended their search but there was no trace of the crew.

Suddenly Thoth exclaimed, "This is the *Sea Owl* and that is all that remains of Captain Bakh. I recognise the shelter I made to study the scrolls – there is no possible doubt about it!"

Osiris interjected. "The main sail is still cleated up, all that remains of the squall sail are a few strips of canvas, which suggests the ship had been running before a storm, and the sea anchor has been lost. From the broken skull it appears that our captain has been murdered, but there is nothing we can do about it now other than bury him at sea!

"So let's be about it, and when that's done, clean the ship and recover our shelter and equipment from the shore. After that we prepare a light meal and settle down for the night. In the morning we can decide the best use of Captain Bakh's last gift to the expedition."

They completed clearing the ship of heavy debris in quick time, with all material and equipment that could not be recovered for use being thrown overboard. Cleaning two rooms to be available for sleeping was a different matter. By the time they had collected their stores from the beach, and prepared a rapidly consumed quick meal they were completely exhausted, and retired to their beds on the rough floorboards.

To begin with, sleep eluded them and with the creaking from the movement of the ship, they felt that a ghostly crew would return at any moment to walk the deck, but that fancy did not last long, as their sheer exhaustion could not delay sleep any longer.

Next morning they had a conference and Osiris called for Hathor to give her thoughts on how to proceed.

"I believe our ship to be seaworthy, the main sail is in good condition and there should be a spare foresail in the sail locker. In my view we should travel north to where the two gulfs meet. The basis of this proposal is my strong conviction that there is something very strange about the strong current travelling towards the north in the Red Sea. One would expect under these calm conditions that the current should be minor and heading south.

"Using the ship to travel the eighty-seven itru to the junction with the two gulfs and anchoring there would provide us with a firm base from which to explore both gulfs using the transporters."

Osiris then called for Thoth's view.

"There are immediate problems that we should consider. It will be extremely difficult to sail against such a strong current. If it should persist after we reach the two gulfs, we might have to abandon the ship. It would then be necessary to fly back to Quseir, stage there and return to Qena the next day. If we adopt this proposal we require additional help to sail the ship. On a long flight each transporter should be reduced to carrying three persons in reasonable comfort, therefore our reinforcements must be limited to four volunteers. To fly to Qena and pick up the volunteers must not take more than two days including the return, and we have to allow for the additional flying time required to intercept the ship, as it will be drifting all that time to the north.

"After the arrival of the reinforcements, it should only require a day and a half to reach the junction with the two gulfs. While waiting for the transporters those left behind should rig the storm foresail, but it should not be used unless required for steerage way.

"I suggest that subject to your approval, Isis and I should take the two transporters to Qena immediately to obtain the additions to our crew."

Isis commented, "I fully support the comments and proposals put forward by Hathor and Thoth. There is, however, one factor that has not been mentioned, but is of some importance. We have all observed that the level of the Red Sea has been substantially increased, flooding the land on both banks; for that reason sailing close to shorelines will be dangerous and must be avoided."

"It may now be possible for ships to penetrate further up the Gulf of Suez, and this facility might provide easier access to the Nile and should be investigated. Unfortunately, not knowing the depths over the flooded land, navigating and recording a safe path would be time-consuming and is beyond our resources at the present time.

"As mountains enclose the Gulf of Aqabah on both sides, there should be no great change in width, but the earthquake may have affected the gulf, also it could have changed the gulf's length. My proposal to investigate the Gulf of Aqabah is justified if you consider that the distances to be travelled are half that which would be mandatory to an investigation of the Gulf of Suez. This proposal depends on investigating by transporter from the ship anchored at the junction of the two gulfs."

Osiris agreed with the proposals and Thoth and Isis departed immediately for Qena.

While awaiting their return, Osiris and Hathor were kept busy fitting the foresail, and dropping the anchor, which as they were close enough to the shore, dragged the heavy weight along the bottom, reducing the effect of the current on their progress.

With the return of the transporters bringing the additional crew members, the anchor was recovered; the main sail set and taking full advantage of the current, the *Sea Owl* sailed faster than ever before. By first light the following morning they were approaching the junction of the two gulfs. They found an island close to the entrance of the Gulf of Aqabah, but when they approached to make a secure anchorage, they discovered that due to the deflection effect the current was faster than ever. Eventually, by swinging around and sailing against the current, they closed the shore and managed to get the anchor rope attached to a massive tree stump. They were then able to lower the mainsail, and rely on the foresail as a means of keeping the bow directly into the current.

Leaving the responsibility for the *Sea Owl* in the hands of the replacement crew, the two transporters – manned as before with Osiris and Isis, Thoth and Hathor – lifted off for the twelve-hour round trip to the head of the Gulf of Aqabah.

The further they travelled up the gulf above the sea, the surface became more turbulent and spray began lifting high above the crests of the waves. Approaching the head of the gulf they observed that the earthquake had recently formed a great ravine, and torrents of seawater were crashing down through the gap and swirling away into the distance.

Landing on the only reasonable flat space on the north-west side of the ravine, the noise from the cascading water was deafening. Sensible discussion under these circumstances was difficult, but as the flight had only taken five hours, they agreed that they should follow the ravine to the north for a further hour to discover the extent of the earth slip or fault line, and its point of discharge.

After the completion of the hour's travel they took the transporters to a great height and observed the Red Sea water descending in a roaring cataract down into a massive inland lake. Thoth then signalled that they must descend and return to the start of the ravine, as he had experienced problems taking the transporter to high altitude and they were already starting to build up speed to the west.

Their return to the head of the ravine was uneventful and after landing, and preparing a quick meal, Osiris said, "I propose that we return to the ship at a higher altitude to increase our flight speed. Yes, Isis, you have something to add?"

"I have had a premonition of some terrible danger which is somehow linked to your proposal – call it female intuition if you will, but I ask you, as a favour, to return at the same height we used to travel from the ship."

"I withdraw my proposal, then it would be absurd to take even the smallest risk to save time on the return journey, especially as we are well within the promised schedule."

With the thundering sound produced by the water it was pointless to hold further discussions so they set off to rejoin the *Sea Owl*. After about an hour Hathor tapped Thoth on the shoulder and pointed down, and Thoth took their transporter down followed by Isis and Osiris.

They were astounded to see the *Sea Owl* being buffeted by the waves and rushing at headlong speed towards destruction. The four crew members, who had been huddled in a corner of the deckhouse, jumped up and started shouting and waving to draw attention to their predicament.

The two transporters, matching speed with the ship and keeping close together at just above mast height, reviewed the situation. It was clear that nothing could save the ship, as once it entered the ravine it would be torn to bits by the rocks and turbulent water; their immediate problem was how to save the crew.

Isis made the only possible decision. "Osiris, as team leader you must be kept safe and it is essential you transfer to Thoth and Hathor's transporter. When that is completed I will attempt a stern-deck landing which, as you know, I have done on several occasions and consequently have the best chance of success.

"If, due to the violent pitching and the effect of the waves lifting the ship, that attempt appears too dangerous, I will instruct the crew members that I require them to climb the mast, one at a time, then crawl to the end of the main sail yard, and fasten a rope to the end. When the first man is in position, I will bring the transporter under the yard. When it is directly underneath, he must lower himself down, while I attempt to hold the transporter in position. It will be a difficult manoeuvre to maintain this position and the transfer must be executed quickly if we have any chance to make a successful recovery.

"The immediate move is for Osiris to transfer to Thoth, and I would suggest that Thoth should descend to his height below and to one side of our transporter and then Osiris can lower himself down onto your transporter, if possible avoiding contacting both transporters at the same time. If there are no objections let us proceed at once."

The transfer was completed immediately and without undue difficulty, but this was in part due to Osiris having no fear of heights, and having confidence in the transporters after flying from Qena. Unfortunately, the crew members did not have this experience, and Isis realised it might be difficult to encourage them to adopt this particular transfer procedure.

Isis dropped down alongside the ship just above deck level but was unable to match the lifting and rolling of the deck without wrecking the transporter and had to abandon that method of recovery.

Gaining some more height to clear the waves and spray, she shouted her instructions to the crew, detailing the method of recovery. While waiting for them to make their decision and send the first man up, it became clear that no one wanted to be first, so in desperation Isis pointed to one individual and shouted, "You first or I will leave."

This had the desired effect and he grabbed a rope, climbed the mast and got out on the yard and fastened the rope in position. He then waited for Isis to move into position. On the first run-in, Isis managed to reach the position but could not hold it. She then had a second attempt, holding the position just long enough for him to lower himself on the transporter, as it started to roll out of position.

Moving clear of the ship, Isis asked who would be the most likely to make the transfer. He thought one other might make the attempt, but all of them had been very frightened. Isis turned to him.

"You are to select the next individual and order him to make the attempt immediately, as there is not much time left. Also you must point out that even if they reach the end of the gulf they would all die in a maelstrom; there being no alternative, they have to make the attempt!"

She returned to the ship and he shouted her instructions to the group and then detailed the next man, who was not enthusiastic and made no attempt to hurry.

Isis ordered her passenger to point out that by delaying he was risking all their lives, and that shortly she would have to abandon the rescue attempt. This galvanised the selected crew member, and he climbed out on the yard and with the rope in his hand waited for the transporter to get into position.

As Isis slowly guided the transporter into position, the man became nervous and did not wait for it to hold position; he slid down the rope and would have fallen into the sea, but by good fortune the ship rolled and this swung him back towards the transporter and he was able to grab the hand of the first Giant rescued.

Isis gained height and drew up alongside Osiris. "After their ordeal it is too dangerous to attempt to transfer them to your transporter! The only viable alternative is to land them both at a level spot at the top of the ravine, then return and make an attempt to encourage the two remaining to attempt the transfer."

"While you do that I will go down and attempt to reassure the two remaining crew of the *Sea Owl*."

Having deposited the two Giants at the top of the ravine, Isis returned to the ship where Osiris was doing his best to encourage them to attempt the transfer, but one was frozen with fear and the other refused to abandon his friend.

Osiris shouted at him, "I order you in the name of ReRa to make the attempt, or receive the full displeasure of the God when you die, which you will surely do should you fail to attempt the transfer! Your friend will reap the same fate unless he encourages you to leave him!"

There was a tearful parting and then the third crew member climbed the mast to take his place at the end of the yard holding the rope. Osiris then continued, "I will tell you when to descend by the rope."

Isis then moved the transporter into position, but overshot it and had to make a second attempt. This time she was successful and Osiris yelled, "Drop now!"

With the transfer successfully completed, and as Isis veered away from the ship, it rolled over and broke up as it was drawn under.

The two transporters then picked up the other two survivors from the top of the ravine and, continuing their return flight, selected one of the large islands at the entrance to the Gulf of Suez to get water and any fruit they might be able to obtain from the stripped trees and bushes.

As it was getting late they decided to delay their return home until early next morning. Qena was only eighty-two itru away, by direct flight a six-hour journey as there was no necessity to go via Quseir.

Osiris then asked the crew, "What happened to make the ship break loose from its moorings?"

They all looked shamefaced, then Jizl replied, "We had nothing to do and were leaning on the rail watching the shore when we observed a large monkey playing on the bank. We decided to chase after it as we thought it would add to our provisions. Unfortunately, we lost him in the deep undergrowth, and on returning found another monkey, or the same one, biting through the anchor cable. As we appeared, it ran away. We then climbed back onboard and while searching for a replacement rope it broke, and you all know the result."

"You are not sailors and cannot be expected to realise the danger of leaving no guard on board. Also, taking into account that most animals and natives have been killed by the storm, I can to some extent understand your overconfident behaviour. This unfortunate accident has caused the death of the seventh expedition member and sadly the memory of his death will remain on your conscience, which is punishment enough.

"However, we must all agree that he lost his life believing he could save the ship before it reached the end of the gulf. That is the explanation we will give to his couple and the rest of the expedition! The actual cause will be left here on the island, and we will all swear never to discuss it again under any circumstance."

The next day they arrived back in Qena, gave thanks to ReRa and held a service dedicated to the dead member of the expedition. That done, they returned to the job of building up their community and making a start to construct the city in a manner similar to Atlan in their lost homeland.

It was also the time for the coupling ceremony for Osiris and Isis, which was carried out with great ceremony and jubilation by all the members of the expedition, with the hope that this would bring the first of many additions required to achieve the rebirth of their society.

Setting up the Expeditions

UK, 2004

After a long and boring flight Ricky was exhausted after clearing customs, and without the usual hire car to meet him, he took the Gatwick Express to Victoria. He then queued to obtain a taxi to his apartment in South Kensington, and by the time he obtained one he could have walked the distance.

The apartment was dusty and clearly had not been cleaned during his absence, but he found a note from the cleaning company lying on the hall floor, informing him that his previous cleaner had left, and would he contact them to select a new date and time for the replacement?

Apart from the mass of junk mail in the letterbox, there were two letters, clearly bills, and one envelope without a stamp, marked "Private". The handwriting on the envelope seemed familiar, and tearing the envelope open there was a card inside, and it read:

Hallo Ricky darling,
Remember me? I am a little busy at the moment, but we will meet after you have had the flat cleaned. Are bachelors always so untidy?
My love, when we make it!

Maria Martinez

PS: I did not open the safe although I was sorely tempted!

Ricky looked round the flat: all windows were closed and locked; the front door had been locked when he arrived and two bolts secured the back door – all as specified by his insurance company.

Maria's visit was a mystery; someone must have let her in! He would investigate tomorrow. Now he needed bread, milk, buns and biscuits, so grabbing his mackintosh he went out to the corner shop to obtain said provisions, As he hurried down the road to the shop, it was getting dark, drizzling and the wet streets seemed to absorb the street lighting.

From a darkened doorway a woman, dressed in black with her face obscured by her hat, approached and whispered, "Do not forget to buy a lotto ticket; the numbers will come to you."

Ricky turned towards the woman, but his foot caught on an uneven paving stone and he tripped. Recovering quickly, he looked round but the woman had gone.

After doing his shopping he went to the counter and, taking a lotto ticket, a list of numbers suddenly came into his head; he filled them in on the coupon and paid at the till.

The assistant leaned across the counter, smiling. "Did you have a good trip? Welcome home, we have all missed you. You may not know that there is a rollover prize of twenty million, and there has been a big demand for entries! Would you like some more?"

"No, thank you, and I did have a very interesting trip, but I am always glad to be home."

Ricky walked back to the flat and considered the strange occurrences. Could this possibly be Yax's Ka guiding him? If that was the case, the concept of time had no validity in the spirit world! If this was guidance from his Ka, then his promise to be with him confirmed the ultimate success of their project.

Ricky stopped this train of thought, there was no sense in debating these points; tomorrow was Saturday and by nightfall he would know the answers to this question. If by then his financial support was secured he would immediately start developing their project with full confidence in its outcome.

Early Saturday morning Ricky arranged for cleaners to come in the afternoon, then set out for the supermarket to stock up with food for the next week. On his way back he was delighted to see his neighbour, John Goddard, who was rushing up to him.

John was a tall, burly muscular county rugby flanker, with short blond hair, blue eyes and, like Loge (*Das Rheingold*, seemed appropriate!), had a mischievous disposition. Due to his appearance he was often asked what part of Scandinavia he came from! His replies were generally hilarious. Up to now the comradeship from his sport was his whole life. Work was secondary and his various attempts to obtain permanent employment were frequently terminated, generally with regret, by his employers. Alternatively John, having become disenchanted with the monotony of an uninspiring workload, would often leave his employment first, with apologies.

At this moment he was resting, infrequently scraping a tenuous living by working as an extra at a film studio.

Whenever John was feeling depressed, bored or happened to be the bearer of interesting news, he descended on Ricky for a jug and the companionship of a fellow bachelor; and Ricky always enjoyed his company.

"Ricky, you are a lucky devil! I met your lady friend a couple of days ago; she had hoped that by now you would have returned from Mexico. She was almost in tears at having missed you and asked if she could get in the flat to write a quick note. Being your key holder I let her in and stayed with her while she wrote the note, and when she finished I escorted her out and locked the front door – I hope I did the right thing. She is a lovely lady and I was most impressed."

Ricky did not know whether to be angry or laugh at her manipulation of the gullible – so he smiled at John.

"You did exactly the right thing and the note is very important. She is a wonderful person and I *am* very lucky."

With supplies laid in, and after the essential visit by the cleaners, Ricky settled down to wait for the National Lottery draw. From 5.35 p.m. the preliminaries to the draw dragged on and on. At last the numbered balls were inserted and they started to roll out the winning numbers: each time they were on the list held in his now shaking hand – four correct, five correct and at last the sixth, but he was so excited he missed the commentator announcing the number. Then they were put in order on the screen… there was no doubt about it – he had won the jackpot. But maybe there were a considerable number of winners? He would have to wait until the update later.

In a state of panic he consoled himself that no matter how many winners there were he would receive a substantial sum. Then he came to his senses; this money was not for him – it would belong to the joint project with Yax. It *did* matter! He would require every penny! So he immediately telephoned the National Lottery to make his claim.

The update came and they announced that there was a single winner who lived in South Kensington and who would receive twenty million pounds! Now the real work could proceed.

On Sunday he wrote up his report to the management covering the discussions at Cordoba, listing the items in dispute and then detailing the agreements reached. The report ended with the statement that these decisions conformed to the wishes expressed by their board of directors.

Reading the report again, Ricky considered it was one of his better efforts and felt confident it should be well received by the Director of External Services, although he had been the most difficult over him taking his annual leave in Mexico.

Director Percy Griddle was small, very important and inclined to be excessively pompous.

His office consisted of a glass enclosure on three sides and behind that a further office with en suite bathroom arranged so that he could survey the large open-plan office and enhance his somewhat inflated ego!

Ricky arrived to make his report and as he walked through the department gave a cheery hallo to his many friends. Arriving at Percy's office he said a polite, "Good morning, sir," and handed in his report.

Percy flicked through it, not bothering to read it, and said in a loud voice, "Did you enjoy your holiday in Mexico at the firm's expense? Now you come back with a trashy report with a lot of decisions you had no right to make!"

As his door was open the whole office was listening to Percy's remarks, and Ricky tried to calm him down.

"All the decisions made are those agreed by the board of directors before I left, and for your information the holiday 'expenses' have been paid from my own pocket, and in *addition* I also paid for the return journey."

Percy, furious at being proved wrong, shouted, "How *dare* you argue with me! Go back to your office and write up a proper report!"

Well, thought Ricky, if that was the way he wanted it, he'd punish him for this public outburst.

So he replied, "After your very public attack on my behaviour, you have certainly destroyed any possibility of a future for me in this company. I have no other alternative but to clear my desk and leave immediately. I will also be lodging a complaint with the Industrial Tribunal. You can rest assured that I will have a strong legal representation at that hearing. To conclude, I have never been treated like this before and have never received any letters of complaint from the company."

Percy, realising that he had overstepped the mark, said quietly, "Would you come into my private office and we can discuss your position sensibly. I am willing to forgive your overexcited remarks."

"I am afraid the damage has been done, the whole office has heard your remarks. I have no alternative but to leave immediately. I will be happy to have a witness to check that I do not take anything that belongs to the company when I clear my desk."

Leaving the office Ricky smiled to himself. Percy had chosen the wrong time for his demonstration of power over his underlings, who in the past had not been in a position to walk out of their employment. This way of leaving the company was ideal; he should get adequate compensation, and they could not require a month's notice. Percy will not be very popular with the other directors!

Not wishing to return home too quickly in case he met with inevitable attempts by the company to recover the inept personnel management by Percy, Ricky decided on a quick visit to the British Museum's Department of Egyptian Antiquities to ask whether they could recommend an expert to read ancient Egyptian hieroglyphs.

Responding to his request the receptionist replied, "I have been informed that no member of staff is immediately available to give you the required advice."

"I am fully prepared to wait for a discussion with staff experienced in hieroglyphs at their convenience. Naturally I am willing to pay, provided the work is undertaken as a bonded private matter."

This approach brought out a senior member of staff.

"I must apologise for the delay but we have to weed out enthusiasts coming for a casual chat... however, I am here now and how can I help you?"

"I have a substantial amount of hieroglyphic text which requires a highly accurate interpretation. I imagine the work will take considerable time and we will be prepared to pay a set fee with a bonus in accordance with results. We have made attempts to interpret but all we have to date is a general outline of the salient points."

His reply was guarded.

"It is not our practice to recommend outside experts as this could be seen as guaranteeing performance in the name of the British Museum. I can see two options open to you. If these texts are unique and if you are prepared to give us details of the source, and providing we judge them to be of major interest to our department, we are willing to undertake the translation. The find will be in your name and the results published by the museum. The alternative is to approach members of universities who teach hieroglyph translations, and find someone with sufficient time to devote to your work."

"Thank you for you advice which I will consider carefully; perhaps I should have told you that we would be mounting an expedition to various countries based on this text. I am sure you will appreciate it is far too early to put our information into the public domain, as that could jeopardise our plans. The project is substantial and a great deal of money is involved."

Shaking hands with the department's representative and thanking him again, Ricky left the museum. Delighted to recall that he had not been asked for his name and address, and feeling hungry, he decided on a late lunch before returning home.

When he returned, there were several telephone calls recorded on the answering machine asking him to contact the Managing Director. It was far too early to do that, he must augment the extent of his personal devastation and humiliation resulting from Percy's unwarranted attack, and in any event he had no reason to change his mind.

Now it was necessary to plan his general course of action. The first priority was to arrange for the lottery money to be lodged in the bank, and to obtain a safety deposit box. In addition he wished to discuss with the bank the question of interest rates on the majority of the capital with ease of draw down as required. That would take care of business for tomorrow, and the next day could be devoted to a quick visit to Ramshill College and a flight up to Liverpool to visit the University of Hale and their School of Archaeology, Oriental and Greek Studies, to find a suitably qualified expert to undertake the translations.

The initial discussions with the bank went well, but in view of the sum in question they would arrange an appointment with a senior adviser from head office in a week's time. In the meantime they would study the case in order to offer the best possible solutions.

The rest of the day was devoted to printing off photographs of the texts on his computer. Retaining one sample, he took the complete batch of photographs and a memory chip in a sealed package to the bank and lodged them in his safety deposit box.

The next day, postponing the visit to Ramshill, he took the early flight to Liverpool and a taxi direct to Hale University's School of

Archaeology. Walking down the hall he saw a student's notice board poster announcing a series of lectures, followed by discussions on the Maya, which were just about to start. Assuming one extra visitor would not be noticed, he joined in the scramble for seats and found one in the corner at the back of the hall.

Ricky found the lectures extremely interesting, then before starting the discussion period the presenter announced that they were privileged to have a visitor from the Maya people in Mexico, who would outline the present developments in their struggle to achieve equal status within the existing society. Then she introduced Dr Maria Martinez, which was followed by polite applause.

Ricky was thunderstruck!

Where and when did she acquire the status of "doctor"? How had she managed to be accepted by the university?

Maria was now standing behind the lectern and Ricky looked at her to check if she was really the same person. She was! And before he could look away, she had seen him and given a slight smile of recognition.

Maria gave a brief lecture on the difficulties facing the Maya in a Mexican population, that was separated between those who had close Spanish connections, and the restless Maya youth, who were becoming well educated and were reverting to their old Maya names, their previous names having been selected for them by the Evangelising Catholic Church after the Spanish Conquest of Mexico and enforced by the Conquistadors.

Ricky, had he not been an interloper, would have enjoyed asking Maria what her connection was with the Far Right, but that would keep for his next meeting with her, about which he had a confused feeling, and felt would be imminent.

Due to the crush at the back of the hall he was penned in and could not escape until the end without drawing attention to himself. Anyway, he was actually finding the discussions interesting.

Leaving the lecture theatre, he headed for the Department of Oriental and Greek Studies, and asked to speak with the principal, or senior lecturer. When asked by the secretary what subject he wished to discuss, he told her hieroglyphs. She asked him to wait and went into the principal's office. Returning she said, "The Senior Lecturer will see you now." She held the door open for him, and Ricky walked in.

Facing him was a very imposing lady, and with her back turned to him was Maria. She half turned to him.

"Let me introduce you to Mr Richard McKay, he has just returned from Mexico and his interests are in ancient archaeology and in particular the Maya."

The senior lecturer smiled and extended her hand.

"I understand you are interested in hieroglyphs, but I am afraid we have no one immediately available who is fully adept on this highly complex subject.

"If you can return tomorrow afternoon I can provide you with a list of people who might be prepared to discuss the subject with you. Where will you be staying so I can contact you to firm up a suitable time?"

"I only arrived from London this morning and intended to return tonight on the last plane. However, in view of the information you offer I will be happy to stay the night in Liverpool. Can you recommend a suitable hotel not too far away from the university?"

"There is a small hotel some two hundred metres from our main entrance – we often send visiting lecturers there. Would you like me to make a reservation for you now?"

"That would be most kind. Can I obtain an evening meal there?"

"Yes, but I suggest you leave for the shops immediately as you will doubtless wish to purchase articles for your overnight stay."

"Thank you again for your kindness and I look forward to hearing from you tomorrow. Delighted to meet you again, Dr Martinez, and I do hope to see you again before your return to Mexico."

"Goodbye, Mr McKay."

Ricky took a taxi to the shops and bought a smart suitcase and packed it with all the necessities for an overnight stay, then returned to the hotel. The university had booked him an excellent room and after a quick shower and a change of clean clothes, he went down to the dining room and selected a table in the corner, his usual preference.

A waitress came to his table. "Mr McKay, there is a note for you at reception. Shall I reserve this table for you?"

"Yes please." Ricky went to reception and obtained the note; it was short and to the point.

Ricky
    I am staying at the university tonight and cannot escape commitments. Will contact you Saturday pm at your flat, and you can take me out for dinner.
    My love, maybe we can.
    Maria

The next morning Ricky had a call from the university. Would he go to the Department of Oriental Studies at two to collect the list, and discuss hieroglyphs with two faculty members who could possibly help him?

He telephoned back immediately and accepted the appointment stating that his main interest was in Egyptian hieroglyphs, although a good knowledge of Maya forms would be helpful.

After lunch Ricky returned to the university and met the two faculty members individually. The first was clearly not suitable, but the second was more acceptable and compatible to Ricky. He decided to explain his immediate problem and the security requirements.

"During my travels I came across a stela which had Egyptian hieroglyphs cut into the surface. This I firmly believe has remained hidden for thousands of years. We have attempted a translation of selected parts, and I have a reasonable idea of its intent.

"It is our view that if we are correct this will form the basis of a major expedition to verify the text and may have implications on matters prior to 3000 BC. Such is our confidence, that we are already assembling the essential equipment. If you agree to observe complete secrecy and sign a note to that effect, I am prepared to let you see a small section of the text for translation. You can then estimate the cost to cover your immediate work. After studying your translation we can arrange a deal covering the complete text.

"If we use your translation and go public, you would be named as the person who will have made what we believe to be an extremely important translation. The principal thing to consider is that this will be challenged by archaeologists and for that reason accuracy is essential.

"Are you prepared to sign the agreement of complete secrecy, which includes a provision that only you can see the text? If you have a query regarding a symbol, which you wish to discuss with a friend, you will have to make a copy of the symbol and then obtain our approval before doing so!"

Duncan McNish hesitated. "I agree to do the first translation on that basis providing we can agree the cost."

"Then let us draw up the agreement now if you are willing, then let us have it witnessed, perhaps by the senior lecturer? Then I can show you the text. If you have a problem I will pay you for the time of our discussion and you can walk away from the project."

The secrecy agreement was signed and Ricky showed him the text sample.

Duncan looked briefly at the text then said, "I should be able to produce a satisfactory translation but I am not prepared to quote a price at this stage. However, I am willing to do it on a time and cost basis to be decided; perhaps you can propose a figure?"

"I would prefer to pay a small fee to reassure you of our intentions, say £200. That should cover your initial expenses for the time taken up by our discussions?"

"That is most kind and I can promise you a fair deal on translation costs, as I would like to be considered for membership of your expedition."

"That will depend on a number of factors besides the work on translation. Perhaps you could list what experience you have had during your life that would support your selection. You can give it to me when you present your first translation in a manner which it will be difficult for archaeologists to criticise, when eventually we publish."

Ricky said goodbye to Duncan and rushed off to the airport to get his flight to Heathrow.

The following day he went to visit Ramshill College, to find out if they had any specialists in the interpretation of Egyptian hieroglyphs. To begin with he was regarded with suspicion but after explaining that this was a business enquiry, they were more inclined to help. Ricky emphasised that he was prepared to pay any suitably qualified person for any assistance in this field. After that he was given the address of a retired member of their staff, who they thought might be interested.

From the address provided, Ricky realised that he lived fairly close to his flat. He then said to the principal lecturer, "As a great favour could you contact Karl Frehier and inform him of my enquiry? If he is free this evening I would be delighted to invite him to dinner at any first-class restaurant in Kensington he wishes to select. To firm up arrangements I will be contacting him in an hour's time. Even if he is not interested in my request for assistance in this field, I can promise him an excellent dinner."

"Mr Frehier is a dear friend and I would be pleased to offer him the opportunity of work in his specialised field."

During dinner that night Ricky opened the subject of hieroglyphs.

"Karl, I have a section of Egyptian hieroglyphs which urgently requires translation. The translation must be as accurate as possible based on current knowledge. If you accept our conditions of total secrecy, I will give you this section to translate, and will pay you in relation to the time you devote to the work. You should know this is only a portion of a substantial inscription, possibly inscribed in 2000 BC. Here is a draft of the conditions of secrecy for you to study. You have my temporary address and telephone number. Please consider this carefully and if you can agree I will give you the first section. That is once you have established your payment requirements per hour."

Once they had finished their dinner, Ricky obtained a taxi to take them to their respective homes and they parted in a happy and contented manner.

On Friday Ricky had to attend a meeting with the representative of his bank's main office, which fortunately he had postponed until after lunch. The meeting took the rest of the day and Ricky regretfully refused the suggested invitation to dinner to celebrate the agreement, as he had to go to another appointment. In fact he was desperately tired after last week's business, and his only thought was to catch up on sleep. Tomorrow was Saturday – it had its own problems; he had a lot of questions he needed to put to Maria.

On Saturday, just before lunch, Maria Martinez arrived at Ricky's front door, complete with suitcase, having just flown down from Liverpool. He asked her if she would like to go out for lunch, and this met with immediate approval.

"I'm completely famished!"

They took a minicab to an exclusive nightclub that also provided lunches at weekends. It was not crowded and they obtained a quiet table in one corner of the dining room.

As soon as they had settled, Ricky ordered drinks, and said, "Maria, I've a large number of complicated and difficult questions to ask you, mostly about my visit to Mexico and my journey to Guatemala. I have to decide whether or not you have been trying to kill me, and if so, how are we going to continue our friendship?

"I'm referring to your warning about the explosives in our car when we left Vera Cruz; we only survived that one when the booby trap failed to operate. Yax laughed at me, commenting that your note prior to the Vera Cruz incident was of great benefit to us. In addition there was the suitcase bomb put in my taxi as we cleared the Mexican customs control en route to Guatemala City. The subsequent explosion concussed the driver when he panicked during the disposal of the suitcase! I want to believe Yax's assessment, so let's discuss these happenings dispassionately and without any rancour."

Maria was a trifle disconcerted with the direct attack.

"I also have a list of questions to put to *you*, but first of all I will answer yours. Yes, I knew about the booby trap. As it was being installed the technician was distracted and I cut the tape before the micro switch and reattached it lower down, so that when the bonnet was closed the tape could be pulled away while the plunger stayed secure!

"With regard to the suitcase bomb, I was in no way concerned, and if you think about it, you will realise I was in London by that time and could not have been involved! I think your friend and key holder will confirm the date when I first arrived at your flat.

"Remember, I am Maya, and would do everything possible to protect Yax. I am glad he treated my note and our escapade in that manner. I am fairly certain that the suitcase bomb was not the work of the Far Right, there must be another explanation which I will try to obtain from Maya contacts in Chiapas—"

Ricky interrupted. "Maria, I apologise for doubting you. I now realise that you risked your life in sabotaging the booby trap, and on behalf of Yax and myself, I can only say thank you and offer you champagne as a reward!"

"Wait... now it is my turn to ask some questions, Ricky. I hear that you have left your company after a director insulted you – is that true?"

"It is remarkable how you are so well informed! Yes, it's true, and it will be expensive for the company, as I won't return."

"I know it's a rude question, but can you afford to do this?"

"Yes, I've come into some money and I'm now a man of independent means, and find the prospect exciting.

"Are you taking up archaeology? I mean, is that your reason for visiting universities?"

"Ricky, what are *you* up to? And is Yax involved in this project?"

"Maria, Yax was... *is* my partner! Now let us finish with the questions and order a first-class lunch."

The food was well-prepared and the service immaculate and they were both replete and content.

After coffee, Maria suggested they return home to relax and discuss the future. So they took a taxi to his apartment and relaxed.

Maria started the inevitable conversation. "Ricky, my main reason for coming over to England was to visit you. My visit to a dear friend in Hale University was a fallback justification for my visit, just in case you didn't feel the same attraction that I feel for you.

"Before entering into a firm relationship I must warn you that my sexual enjoyment depends on my dominating the action. Being dominated reduces my enjoyment. With this admission you will now understand how much I enjoyed our short time together in the Camino Real.

"Ricky, my instinct tells me you will enjoy being sexually dominated, and if you accept this sexual deviation from the norm, it will be you that dominates our partnership in all other matters. If you can accept this and enjoy the sexual relationship under those conditions we can have a successful life."

"Maria, I have been unable to get you out of my mind since that night in the hotel, and yes I enjoyed every second of it, and you could have achieved everything without the drug."

"In that case, Ricky, let us away to the bedroom and I will teach you what domination is all about, and after this you will never have enough of it!"

Maria entered the bedroom wearing a black pyjama suit with a glistening necklace of alternate black onyx, black tourmaline, and chrysoberyl cat's eyes. Hanging between her breasts was a five-centimetre plaque of emerald green jadeite bearing the Maya K'uh Ajaw hieroglyph (the Sun God). On her black waistband he perceived a miniature ceremonial obsidian-bladed Aztec knife with a silver handle engraved with a scorpion.

Maria slowly lifted her arm towards him until it pointed to his head, then slowly lowered it to point towards his knees, and Ricky, in a dazed state, fell to his knees before her, a surge of happiness poured through his very being – he had found his Goddess!

Maria dropped down beside him and took his face between her two hands.

"Ricky, I love so very much."

Then embracing, they set out on their journey of love, pain, and ecstasy. When sated with pleasure they lay together entwined on the bed, in their own little world far removed from the troubled one outside.

Morning came too soon and Maria had to return to Liverpool to continue her discussion at the university. In a confidential mood Ricky said, "I have to go up north to discuss the purchase of an ocean-going trawler, and possibly it might also require a visit to the Far East to compare prices."

Astounded, Maria hesitated, and then said, "What do you need an ocean-going trawler for? Is this the new archaeological project, and what does your partner Yax think about it? Incidentally, where *is* Yax?"

"Yes, we are considering an archaeological expedition; Yax has given his full approval. When I last heard from him he was staying with friends near Santa Rita in the Corozal District in Belize."

"I heard that Yax is seriously ill and unlikely to recover. Do you know about this?"

"Yes, he told me about it, and I understand he is now in remission. He has been told that if he is careful he could support our project for several years. The only drawback is that long air journeys could be fatal, so we've arranged special means of communication to maintain the essential project secrecy until we are in a position to go public."

"Have you already chosen members of the expedition?"

"Not yet! Once we have resolved the problems associated with the trawler and its special equipment, and have translated some hieroglyphs, that will be the next and possibly the most difficult stage."

"Would I be able to join the expedition? I might be able to contribute a little money."

"Possibly, but I would not allow you to contribute money. This is not a commercial business and in the end, regardless of our success, it is doubtful if we could recover enough to repay even part of our operational cost."

"If I understand you correctly, you and Yax are prepared to lose a large proportion of your money on this project! You must have a strong case for doing this… can you tell me why?"

"In detail, no, but I will say it is for the Maya and at this stage I ask you to be satisfied with that answer. You will appreciate I do not know if you are still working undercover for the Maya or with the Far Right in Mexico. You must promise me not to give either of them the slightest hint of my intentions."

"Ricky, you have my promise. That you are working for the Maya is sufficient for me. When I have resolved my problems you will be able to tell me the rest."

"Maria, I'm giving you the key of the apartment, and when I'm away you're welcome to use it as your base. If I'm here you will know I'm waiting for you! Now, I'd better take you to the airport or you will miss your plane."

When he returned he had a quick supper and sat down to list work for the next week. Tomorrow he would try to set up a meeting with the Indonesian Commercial Attaché and contact Karl Frehier to see if he had come to a decision – also Duncan McNish to see if he had made any progress over the weekend.

The next day the discussions with the Indonesians went well and he was promised that his application to undertake an archaeological search for structures in Indonesian territorial waters would receive favourable consideration, but the provision of the actual permits would take at least six months.

Karl Frehier had already signed the agreement and Ricky gave him £200 to cover immediate expenses and it was agreed that they would fix the hourly rate after spending eight hours on the first translation.

Ricky then telephoned Duncan McNish in Liverpool and asked what progress had been made. He replied, "I have not yet found the time to start the translation, but when I was about to start a senior member of the Oriental and Greek studies group noticed the hieroglyph text on my desk. He appeared to be very excited and asked where they had been found. I said I did not know but had been asked to translate them by a friend.

"He asked if my friend was a qualified archaeologist and whether the request had come from a museum. I replied that I did not have that information. He went on to say that I should not undertake translations that should be first reviewed by a known and properly qualified archaeologist. If I ignored his advice, he would ensure that the profession would challenge my work and consequently my reputation would be severely damaged.

"He then offered one possible solution – he is prepared to lend his name to the translation, which would give it the necessary status, provided my friend could inform him where the text had been found. I replied that I would speak to you about it."

Ricky was furious. "I am absolutely *horrified* that to a large extent you have breached the agreement made between us on complete secrecy. For the senior member to have become excited, he obviously read some of the text and realised it is a new find. I will come up to Liverpool immediately to discuss the situation with you, and should be at your desk at about 11 a.m."

Ricky decided to go up to Liverpool on the last flight that night, so that he could collect a solicitor the next morning to accompany him to the university; a quick telephone call and the necessary legal adviser promised to meet him at his hotel at 9.30 a.m. With everything arranged, he packed a bag and set off for the airport.

Everything went as planned and Ricky and the solicitor entered Duncan McNish's office at 11 a.m. precisely.

After introducing his legal adviser, Ricky addressed Duncan. "Would you kindly produce the text I asked you to translate? I also require your assurance that it has not been out of your possession and that no copy has been made of the text. Would you kindly sign a statement to that effect?"

Duncan produced the text and said, "I am unable to sign a statement to that effect, as someone might have made a copy without my knowledge."

"Let us get this point clear – has it left your possession?"

Duncan, turning pale, said, "No."

"Then how could anyone have made a copy?"

"I was called away from my desk for a short time; a copy could have been taken then. It was in the drawer of my desk."

"How many people know you are working on this text?"

"Duncan became nervous.

"Just the senior member." Then he quickly added, "He might have told someone else."

"In order to bring this discussion to a conclusion will you sign a statement to cover the questions and answers you have just given? This is in your interest, otherwise we will take you to court for breaking the signed agreement on secrecy. If someone else has obtained this text and makes it public, it will have been stolen from your desk and the person concerned can be charged with commercial theft."

The solicitor then drew up the necessary statement and, after much humming and hawing, Duncan signed. Ricky removed the original and told Duncan their cooperation was at an end, but the secrecy clause still stood. He could keep the advance as it covered initial expenses. Furthermore, he could not hope to be accepted for the expedition.

Just as they were leaving, the senior member rushed into the office and apologised for being late.

"I hope you've accepted my offer... it's the only way to ensure success!"

"I'm afraid that will not be possible, as the cost of the various parts of the expedition have to be tightly controlled. We only require Indians and that means no additional chiefs. Duncan will explain the situation to you.

"We are in a hurry so we must now say goodbye."

A quick taxi drive to the airport, a flight back to London, then a taxi home. Hurrying up the stairs to his apartment, he heard shouting and, turning into the corridor, saw a struggle outside his door. Rushing up, he found his neighbour, John Goddard, tackling two Fagin-like intruders who were desperately trying to leave. It was an unequal struggle that John, a two-metre-tall rugby forward, was clearly enjoying.

Ricky joined in, grabbed one of them by the back of the neck and took him into the apartment; John carried the other in and flung him down on the floor. Ricky then noticed his safe was standing beside the front door. The implication came to him immediately.

"John! There must be a car waiting outside! After we tie these villains' hands behind their backs, could you go down and investigate? If the car is still there, would you tell the driver his mates need his help to bring the old safe down to the car, as it can't be repaired in the flat."

The villains were quickly secured and John hurried down to the front of the block where a small white van was waiting with a nervous driver. John opened the driver's door and passed on the message. He then walked round the corner, and watched as the driver got out of the van and quickly walked into the apartment block.

John returned to cut off any retreat. When the driver approached Ricky's door he seemed to have second thoughts, so John gave him an encouraging pat and persuaded him to enter and join his friends.

"John, tell me what happened. I don't think we want to hear from our friends so let's put socks in their mouths to discourage them from talking."

When silence had been established John explained.

"I was passing your flat when I heard a noise of something heavy being dragged across the floor. I thought you needed some help and entered, only to be confronted by these two who rushed at me, presumably trying to escape. To begin with I managed to delay them until one of them kicked me on the shin. I was just starting to retaliate when you appeared.

Ricky then addressed the three pathetic objects. "At this stage I can't be bothered to call the police. I am prepared to hear who ordered you to attempt this burglary, and if you fail to answer we will wait until dark, then return you to your van and give you a cool swim in the Thames. Before we ask you to tell all, let's turn out your pockets to see what your intentions would have been had you found anyone in the flat."

Apart from a roll of wide tape, a couple of folding knives, the tool kit beside the safe, and a sachet of white powder, there was nothing in the pockets of the two burglars. The driver's case was different; he had three wallets that contained their names and addresses, together with bankcards and an envelope containing Ricky's name and address.

Removing the driver and one burglar to the small toilet and securing their legs together, they removed the gag from the remaining burglar, warning him to only speak when asked a question and then, in a quiet voice, John said, "This is the gentleman who kicked me on the shins; if he is sensible he will be very cooperative!"

Ricky started the questions.

"How did you open the door?"

"We had lock picks."

"They aren't in the tool bag – where have you hidden them?"

"I don't know, my mate picked the locks."

"*That* is your first lie."

Replacing the gag he pressed on a nerve point, and the burglar collapsed on the floor. Ricky took the gag out of his mouth, and asked him again, "How did you enter my flat?"

"We were given a key."

"Who gave it to you?"

"A lady, she was waiting for us when we arrived. After opening the door, we threw the key out of the corridor window to her."

"Describe the lady."

"She was tall, imposing, severe and had a northern accent... she was in a hurry to get away."

"Who gave you your instructions, what were you paid and what is the assignment in detail?"

"I received my instructions by telephone; we are to be paid a grand at a pub on successful completion. We were told to remove the safe, not to open it unless it could not be removed, and deliver the safe or the contents to a warehouse in the old docks. We're never told the name of our client and payments are always made through a go-between."

"I'm going to release all of you after you have replaced the safe, and tidied up the mess you've made of my apartment. In addition, you'll pay for damaged equipment and professional cleaning of the apartment."

"One of you will be escorted to a cashpoint, where you will draw out the necessary funds and pay me the damages. I shall keep all your bankcards and other relevant information in a bank deposit. Instructions will be given that in the event of any attempt to attack my neighbour or myself by your organisation, all these details will be sent to the CID together with your photographs and those of the safe in the hall."

After the photographs had been taken, the payment for damages assessed and collected, the safe replaced and the apartment tidied up, the unhappy burglars left.

John and Ricky then sat down to relax with a glass of beer.

"John, I must thank you for your sterling work in protecting my apartment. Can I suggest that you join me for a late lunch or early dinner as a small token of my appreciation?"

"I don't wish to intrude on private matters, but everything seems to be happening since you returned from Mexico. Nothing like this has happened in our block before, even the visit of your lady friend suggested something out of the ordinary. Oh yes, your firm have telephoned me three times in the last two days asking me if I could get you to call them back! You are up to something, aren't you? Perhaps you need a minder!"

Ricky laughed. "I've left my job as one of their directors insulted me and for once I was in a position to react, while others in my firm have family responsibilities and are not so fortunate. Yes, I'm in the middle of organising two important archaeological expeditions, based on information that must remain secret and is only in my possession. It's worth a great deal of money to unscrupulous individuals. Others wish to suppress it for political reasons... or alternatively me.

"There have already been two unsuccessful attempts on my life while I was abroad – I promise you this is all solid fact. You'll appreciate I did not wish to discuss the burglary with the police, as the inevitable result would be that the affair would be leaked to the press. Anyway, enough of my problems – let's remove my safe's contents and deposit them in my bank, and after that, we'll go to a top-class establishment and have the sumptuous dinner that you so rightly deserve."

"Do me a favour before we go, telephone your office and speak to the Managing Director, as I'm tired of him telephoning *me* to find out where *you* are!"

Ricky did so and was then asked if he would accept a generous settlement out of court, to save legal fees and the firm getting bad publicity. Ricky asked for the offer to be sent to him in writing and that part of it should be for lost salary and the rest tax-free in a golden handshake. The procedure was agreed subject to an ample settlement.

"There you are, John, all done... and we can proceed with a clear conscience as planned. Frankly, I could eat a horse!"

The evening passed happily, but later that night Ricky reviewed the events of the day and the matter of the key. Was this the spare key he had given to Maria? Or was this the key he had trusted to the cleaners while he was away at work? If it was Maria's, how could it have come into the possession of the senior lecturer, and how could she have afforded the cost of hiring the burglars through an agent? There was also the apartment manager; could *he* have been bribed to provide the key? If that was the case, the price would have been substantial. Ricky realised he could not go on worrying about it. The attempt had been foiled, and those responsible would be unlikely to authorise a second effort.

The next day Ricky requested an interview with the Admiralty Disposals Division and was granted a review of available craft in three days' time.

On the day in question Ricky arrived at Admiralty Disposals and met Captain James Grenavear. Ricky explained his basic requirements for a small vessel that could carry a saturation diving spread. The equipment would require a hoist for either a diving bell or for a Newt Suit atmospheric system. Diving staff would consist of a supervisor, two life-support technicians and two divers in addition to the crew, plus three staff to operate the side-scan sonar. The ship must be suitable for operations along the western coast of Indonesia.

"We have a number of coastal protection vessels for disposal in that area which had been on loan to the Indonesian navy and are no longer required. There are two more at Darwin and they are at present being decommissioned. I can send you details of these within the next fortnight, including an indication of condition. I believe one of these would meet your requirements."

"I appreciate the information, but can you give me a ballpark estimate of cost for this type of vessel? If we can reach an acceptable figure would it be possible to grant permission for two people to visit the ships in the near future? We will, of course, cover our own travelling, hotel and incidental expenses.

"Our present budget figures are between 200K and 500K depending on condition; does this interest you?"

"Yes, we could negotiate on these levels. So when can we visit? We would be available in three weeks' time or one week after receiving the condition report. I would also like details of fuel consumption and engines, either with the condition report or available for us when we arrive to visit the ships."

Captain Grenavear replied, "All this will be set up when you book your first visit to Indonesia. You should allow three days for your inspections before you go on to Darwin. I will work out a proposal giving dates, and this will be forwarded to you with the condition reports. I would appreciate a copy of your findings, as an independent view is always appreciated."

Ricky thanked Captain Grenavear and promised him a copy of their report after their Indonesian visit.

Returning home, Ricky was delighted with the typical efficiency of the Royal Navy, and was now in a position to arrange preliminary appointments to discuss purchase or lease of a Newt Suit atmospheric system, towed side-span sonar, ROV submersibles, decompression tank and full facemasks, with associate equipment for surface diving, to meet all the immediate expedition requirements.

The next day, Kirk Frehier came over with the translation of the first section of text, which was well-prepared with individual interpretations, section by section, with the hieroglyphs alongside.

After admiring the meticulous approach to the translation, Ricky asked, "Kirk, have you made any estimate of cost? The whole text is approximately twenty times longer than this section. After that work has been completed I would require your assessment of the text, but that would be an additional cost, which cannot be determined until you are deeper into the project. There is one other important question to ask you, you seem to me to be highly skilled at this work, yet you look about forty-five so why did you retire early? You don't have to answer this, but it would be helpful for what I have in mind."

"I found my work in a particular department of the organisation both difficult and unrewarding. Team spirit was totally lacking and my associates weren't interested in serious work, other than an unhealthy concentration on backbiting and promotion.

"When I completed a report and it was ready for publishing it was taken from me and the Head of Department or the Senior Fellow published it in his name, with my name as a contributor! Frankly, I got sick of it all. Having been left a little money, I'm not dependent on the salary and took early retirement at fifty. Thank you for the complement of forty-five!

"Regarding the matter of costs, I can already appreciate the importance of this work. Under these circumstances I would be prepared to do the work for nothing providing the complete translation went out under my name."

Ricky replied, "Dealing with the translation and the assessment of those translations, I will give you a written agreement that they go out in your name and if it goes out in book form we share the royalties. I believe the best way to deal with payment is to put twenty thousand pounds in your bank, as a retainer that can be drawn out at the rate of five thousand per annum. If you find from the work involved you require additional funds, we can discuss it at any time and try to reach a solution acceptable to both.

"You will recall our proviso about secrecy? I wish to have a bond established regarding your honesty and commitment by my lawyers. You will possibly have to be interviewed, but it is in my interest that it is established. Please understand that I already believe in your honesty, and if you so desire you can have membership of our two expeditions. If these are, as we hope, successful, it could give you considerable standing in your profession. If you need office equipment and a safe, or other equipment that is essential for your work, I'll have them provided for you on loan as capital cost items, and for all items that are expendable free of cost. Are we in agreement?"

"I never expected such a generous offer, and I fully understand the necessity for secrecy, as there will be a large number of archaeologists who will wish to infiltrate this project and some of them can be completely unprincipled. They will immediately understand the effect of your project and will fight anything that tends to rock the established order of things. In addition, I would be delighted to become a member of your expeditions."

"As soon as the bond is established we will go to any bank you name, and I will deposit the agreed sum. Then you will receive the next section. Until we complete the translation I am unable to provide any details of where the stela is located. Its precise location will never be revealed, but I assure you the text is genuine and the only doubt is the exact date when it was inscribed. Certainly it was before 1500 BC and my personal guess is before 2500 BC, but when we have the complete translation it may be possible to get a better estimate.

"I have given you an accurate translation, but in addition I have reduced it to the essentials so that you can readily understand it. It reads as follows:

Divine Ruler of the Universe,
Whom we call ReRa and whom others call
K'uh Ajaw the Sun God, which is the same.
I am Ptah Sani, true descendant of Isis,
The first Giant to reach these far shores
The last of our race in Egypt and Ethiopia.
In honour of Osiris, Isis and her son Horus
I record a brief history of our society The Giants
For the enlightenment of future generations.
Atlan the Giant's cradle for twelve thousand years
The city and harbour protected by massive walls
The tranquil Emerald Green Sea protected by encircling coral reef
A happy society trading with the known world with all wants satisfied
The city draped in gold and silver to delight the eye of the beholder
Our trading ships the envy of the world, circling the globe.
Constructed from teak and ironwood joined with bronze fittings.
With the imminent arrival of a prophesied cataclysm
Expeditions were sent out to locate new homes near trading posts.
Then the sea inundated Atlan with great loss of life.
The period was 5500 BC, calculated from The Giants' Calendar.

Ricky thanked Kirk for his translation and said, "There are a number of clues here on the location of Atlan, for example, the boats built of teak and ironwood suggest an Asian coastline. The date 5500 BC suggests the cold snap when sea levels increased substantially. Prior to that time, Sumatra, Java and Borneo were connected, but since then the lowlands flooded and are now part of the Continental Shelf. The North Equatorial Current supplies a fast route to Africa, and the counter-current a fast return to Sumatra or Java. Also we're looking for a large feature of a bay, possibly some remnant of a coral reef, and a massive harbour wall. And finally, the Emerald Green Sea suggests a wide, shallow, sandy bay up to the coral reef.

"If the next text reveals the length of the journey to Egypt we may be able to support this assessment of the location of the country of Atlan, and reduce the search area for Atlan, the city."

A few days later Ricky was telling John Goddard of his difficult in finding a suitable engineer who was capable of operating RN coasters, coastal patrol vessels or minelayers. John laughed.

"Clearly you haven't met my old uncle! He has spent most of his life in the navy doing just that – would you like me to arrange a meeting? He was given early retirement as he was shot up badly in a fracas somewhere, but don't worry, he'll tell you all about it! I do know that he's still well regarded in the service and is frequently consulted on matters affecting small ships."

"John, thank you for that. If you can set up an early meeting with him to discuss our project it would be a great help."

The meeting went off well and Ricky found that he would be an excellent companion for his trip to both Indonesia and Darwin.

James White – John's uncle – would make himself available when Captain Grenavear produced the assessments and the proposed programme. Meanwhile White, or Blanco to his friends, would ask around for additional facts about the vessels.

That night Ricky received a threatening telephone call.

"Is that Richard McKay? I have an important message for you. *Back off* your plans for an expedition and turn over the project to the proper authorities. If you fail to do so, every effort will be made to impede your progress. If you get hurt for not heeding our warning, then too bad, it will be your own fault for attempting to damage the reputations of highly qualified archaeologists. Be warned, this is *not* an idle threat." He rang off then.

Ricky frowned, and then, after reflection, realised this was not an unexpected reaction from his detractors. It was clearly an attempt to put the frighteners on him, but to be effective they would have to follow it up with direct action. He would have to afford them as little opportunity as possible, and would fix up a direct alarm system with John Goddard's flat. Intruders entering his flat would be recorded and if John was in residence, suitably confronted.

In the afternoon of the following day he received an urgent and excited telephone call from Maria. She would be flying down to London on business tomorrow and they could have dinner together, but she would have to leave by midday the following day.

She believed Ricky was in great danger from a secret society formed by archaeologists to protect their interests. Apparently it had succeeded in suppressing unwelcome discoveries in the past, but its manner of achieving those successes were, to say the least of it, suspect. She would tell him more about it over dinner.

Next morning, Ricky contacted NASA to obtain space photographs of the coastline of Sumatra. Then off to the City, to purchase the latest navigational charts recording depths over the Continental Shelf.

Maria arrived that afternoon and they sat down to a cup of tea and discussed Maria's anxieties. Putting her arm round Ricky's shoulder and gripping him tightly, she said, "Ricky, I am frightened for your safety! From all I have heard, these people are extremely dangerous.

"Their society has substantial funds and has obtained influence within numerous government offices. Their purpose is to prevent amateurs destroying or looting irreplaceable archaeological sites through either stupidity or greed, or for that matter without qualified archaeological direction.

"Ricky, why risk your life or financial destruction for a project that may well end in failure? Save your money and walk away from it. If you wish to continue, employ a qualified member who is acceptable to the society."

"Maria, I have discussed all this with Yax who is *adamant* that we must continue in the interests of the Maya. The solutions you offer would be to surrender to all those pressures and ignore the attempts on our lives we have already suffered. There is no turning back. Yax is putting in place protection for the project and the society may find it has problems. Now that's settled, let's go out to dinner in a excellent little restaurant down by the river."

Dinner was not a success. Maria was in a bad mood. Ricky had dismissed her warning, and she believed he was more interested in his pet project than pulling back and enjoying a quiet life with her. With all that money they could travel the world! There were so many things she wanted to do and going on expeditions was not one of them.

Maria once again made her feelings known.

Ricky, slightly incensed, retorted, "I have told you before, I have *promised* Yax to persevere with the project, whatever pressures are applied to dilute or abandon it, and to that promise I am totally committed."

Maria stood up.

"I am going to spend the night with a friend; you are impossible and obviously are not prepared to listen to good advice."

"You never intended to spend the night with me, as you came without an overnight bag. It's clear that you came to deliver someone else's message. You should have explained that to me and this situation could have been avoided."

Furious, Maria stood up and walked out of the restaurant.

Ricky, wretched at the manner of their parting, paid the bill and returned home.

A fortnight passed and as promised Captain Grenavear sent the details of the ships, authorisations for their inspection together with a programme, which he required Ricky to confirm as soon as he was able to, in order to book the necessary flights.

Ricky arranged a meeting with Blanco, and they booked the flight details on a mutually acceptable date, confirming the details by an immediate fax to Captain Grenavear.

Ricky, after recalling the threatening telephone calls to disrupt his plans, called Captain Grenavear. He told him about the problems he was having with the opposition, and asked if he could give him a note to say he was engaged on the inspection of Royal Navy ships for disposal. He added that this would help if his identity or the purpose of his visit should be challenged as a means to delay their flight.

Captain Grenavear considered the request unusual, However, from their automatic security, character and financial investigations of Ricky and his family, and taking into account the military record of Ricky's father, he was prepared to issue a suitable statement for inclusion in his passport.

Ricky and Blanco had no problems at Heathrow and soon they were sitting in their air bus heading for Singapore and happily discussing Blanco's experiences at sea that were highly entertaining. While this was going on, the cabin stewardess was called to the telephone and the captain told her that an informant had warned London Head Office that they had a terrorist on board, and the name given was Mr Richard McKay, who they had listed as a passenger in the business class on their flight.

In addition, since they were over Europe, two fighter jets had been scrambled in case the terrorists attempted to take over the aircraft. The flight engineer, who was armed, was authorised to assist the stewardess, who was to discreetly ask to see Mr McKay's passport, then get him to come into the stewards' service area where the flight engineer would be waiting to search him for weapons.

The stewardess came up to Ricky. "Excuse me, sir, are you Mr Richard McKay?"

"Yes I am."

"Apparently London has you booked on another flight. I wonder if I can see your passport to check the details?"

"Of course, here's my passport and a letter from the Royal Navy to explain the reason for my journey."

"Do you mind if I take the letter away with me?"

"I'm sorry, it mustn't leave my possession, but you can take down the details and then inform London who can check with Captain James Grenavear – he provided this letter for just such an occasion. Furthermore, you should determine who initiated whatever this hoax is that you're investigating me for and provide me with the name, and my lawyers will deal with the situation."

"Would you be kind enough to come to my service area as the flight engineer is there and I need to show him your letter?"

"Under protest I will, and I hope you have sufficient reason for this."

Ricky went to the service area where a very nervous flight engineer was waiting with a revolver in his hand!

"Don't be a fool! Put that thing away before you do serious damage!"

The stewardess butted in.

"There seems to have been a serious mistake – his journey is authorised by the Royal Navy and he has shown me the letter of authorisation and said we should refer it to London to get confirmation from Captain James Grenavear at RN Disposals. Could you show the flight engineer your authorisation?"

"Yes, he can read it, but it remains in my possession."

The flight engineer looked uncomfortable. "The captain will want to see it."

"Then he can come out and read it – tell him he should be quite safe – you have your gun, after all!"

"Would you mind if we searched you in case you have a firearm or explosives?"

"You can't be serious! Of course I object, but if you must do it after the detail I have already provided, I shall seek substantial damages from your company and those that carried out the humiliating action."

The flight engineer became extremely nervous, as it appeared that they had made a dreadful mistake.

"I must refer to the captain, please be good enough to wait."

He then returned with the captain, who asked to see the document. Ricky showed it to him.

"Captain, I am not prepared to risk it getting lost so it must stay in my possession and please have its authenticity checked with Captain James Grenavear, who incidentally has run a complete check on my family and myself before providing this letter. I now wish to return to my seat to discuss the situation with my associate who is also Royal Navy retired. Have you any objection?"

"Would you mind if I searched you?"

"I have explained my position on that to the flight engineer. You can demand that humiliation, but if you do I will seek substantial damages from your company! I suggest you pass all this information to London, have it checked and then advise me immediately it has been cleared. As you can imagine I am far from pleased with this personal affront."

"You can go back to your seat while I have the laissez-faire checked."

Ricky returned and explained all that had passed to Blanco, who commented, "Thank God you obtained that letter from Captain Grenavear! Did you see those two Euro Fighters that have been following us? Presumably to shoot us down if we deviate off course!"

The captain came up to their seats.

"The letter and security check have been confirmed; the source of the information was an anonymous telephone call from a phone box. There is little chance of the identity being established.

"Oh, Captain Grenavear said you are right and wished you a safe and rewarding journey."

"So that's it? Well, for me this has not been the pleasant flight it should have been, but compensation will be discussed with my lawyers. Once your staff had read my RN authorisation you could have behaved very differently! Find the name of the perpetrators and everything can be settled amicably. It seems unbelievable that you can accept a personal threat against a passenger from someone who does not provide his name calling from a telephone box."

Arriving at Singapore they passed into transit in time to connect with their scheduled flight to Jakarta which went without incident. On their arrival the Naval Attaché, Commander James Foley, from the embassy, met them and escorted them to their hotel. Then after a welcoming drink, James arranged with them for an early start the following morning, and then offered to escort them during the inspections, a proposal that was gratefully received.

There were four vessels to be inspected. Two of them had clearly passed their sell-by date, but the remaining two Blanco considered worth a detailed inspection.

Blanco and Ricky descended into the engine room, while James had to stay on deck to preserve his uniform. There was a sudden shout from the deck and they saw a large steel plate being tipped over the high-level walkway. They both jumped back and the steel plate crashed onto the floor where they had been standing. There was shouting above and Ricky and Blanco rushed up to the deck to find the attaché and a native fighting on the deck. As soon as they appeared the native sensibly gave up and was quickly secured.

The situation was now a political issue, as the local dockyard police had suddenly disappeared and unless they could be contacted the prisoner would have to be released. James spoke to the ambassador who told him to hold the prisoner for half an hour, while he would report the incident to the chief of the Indonesian police and requested urgent action to collect and charge the individual.

Ten minutes later the ambassador was back on the telephone. The Indonesian police would accept the prisoner, but doubted that he could be charged, as he would probably claim it was an accident and then claim unlawful detention. With feeling running high against the American and British actions in the Middle East, it could be politically dangerous to proceed with the charge. As no damage had been done, the Chief of Police recommended that after questioning, his police should release the prisoner. The ambassador had concurred.

James was far from pleased with the outcome and had to leave immediately to wash and change his uniform, but agreed to return in time for them to lunch together. He would also try to arrange for a local policeman to accompany them when they inspected the last vessel, he said.

When the prisoner was handed over to the police, Ricky and Blanco returned to the engine room for Blanco to complete the inspection of the ship's propulsion equipment. It appeared the hull was sound but was probably foul as the ship had been idle for a year in these warm waters. In Blanco's opinion the vessel was suitable, having adequate space for the expedition equipment.

That afternoon, in the company of James and the policeman, they inspected the last ship; it was also acceptable, but not quite up to the standard of the previous vessel.

After dinner that night they asked James for answers to three questions.

They wanted to know what it would cost to have the ship dry-docked and the hull cleaned and painted with anti-fouling. They also wanted to know, would it be possible to find a crew experienced in this type of vessel and, lastly, where could they purchase or lease weapons to protect the ship from pirates, who they understood still operated in the area?

"Personally, I am unable to provide adequate answers to these questions, but I have an Indonesian friend called Rashid who could offer reliable advice. I will contact him immediately and see if we can all meet up tomorrow after lunch."

He then left to contact his acquaintance. An hour later he telephoned Ricky to confirm that all had been arranged, he had outlined the questions and Rashid had agreed to meet up with them the following day at 2 p.m. in his office.

The meeting turned out to be extremely valuable and all the outstanding questions were now resolved, and in addition Rashid offered to assist them to secure a reliable crew who had previously served on these ships. He also suggested that for a small charge he would apply for a licence to carry weapons on their selected vessel; as the process would normally take two or three months, it was important to apply immediately.

Thanking James for his help, his cheerful company and for saving their lives with his lusty warning, they added that they were counting on his help when they returned with their expedition. After saying their goodbyes, they returned to their hotel, settled their bill and prepared for a very early start to join their flight to Darwin.

The flight was uneventful.

Midday in Darwin was hot and humid and after obtaining an air-conditioned taxi they were rapidly transported to their Marriott Hotel. At the reception desk there was a note from the officer in charge of decommissioning, informing them that he would pick them up next day at 9 a.m. and escort them to the two coastal protection vessels that were being decommissioned.

Next morning, during the journey to the dock, he informed them that unfortunately decommissioning had only just begun, and it was doubtful if their work would be completed in less than three months. This was due to lack of staff and high priorities allocated to essential dockyard work.

Arriving at the dockyard, both vessels looked neglected: one was in dry dock and the hull plating distorted above the waterline, so they decided to see the other one first. The engine room equipment was more modern than those seen in Jakarta and boasted two high-speed gas turbines and diesel auxiliaries to meet the demands of the armament electronics and technicians' living quarters.

While the condition of the vessel seemed excellent to Ricky, Blanco pointed out that the fuel consumption figures were frightening and high speed was not required by the expedition. Worse than that, maintenance of this type of equipment would require a highly qualified crew. The necessary skills would be difficult to find in Indonesia and the wages bill would be prohibitive. Considering these points, Ricky had to agree.

Ricky told the officer in charge of decommissioning that these types of vessels were unsuitable for the expedition work envisaged, so it was unnecessary to go into further detail. Returning to their hotel, they brought forward their return journey to Heathrow to the following morning. While the Darwin visit had been abortive it had satisfactorily resolved the choice of the Indonesian vessel.

The return journey to Heathrow was uneventful and during the journey Ricky thanked Blanco for his valuable contribution and then said, "Would you be prepared to act as captain and go to Jakarta early to prepare the ship for the expedition? I'm presuming that you have the necessary documents and proof of experience to satisfy the local authorities?"

Blanco smiled.

"I was hoping you would make this offer and I am delighted to accept. I have all the necessary papers and have some experience in these waters. Could I also become a member of these expeditions? Accommodation and meals are all I require."

"You are the first person to be appointed other than Yax and myself! Welcome aboard!"

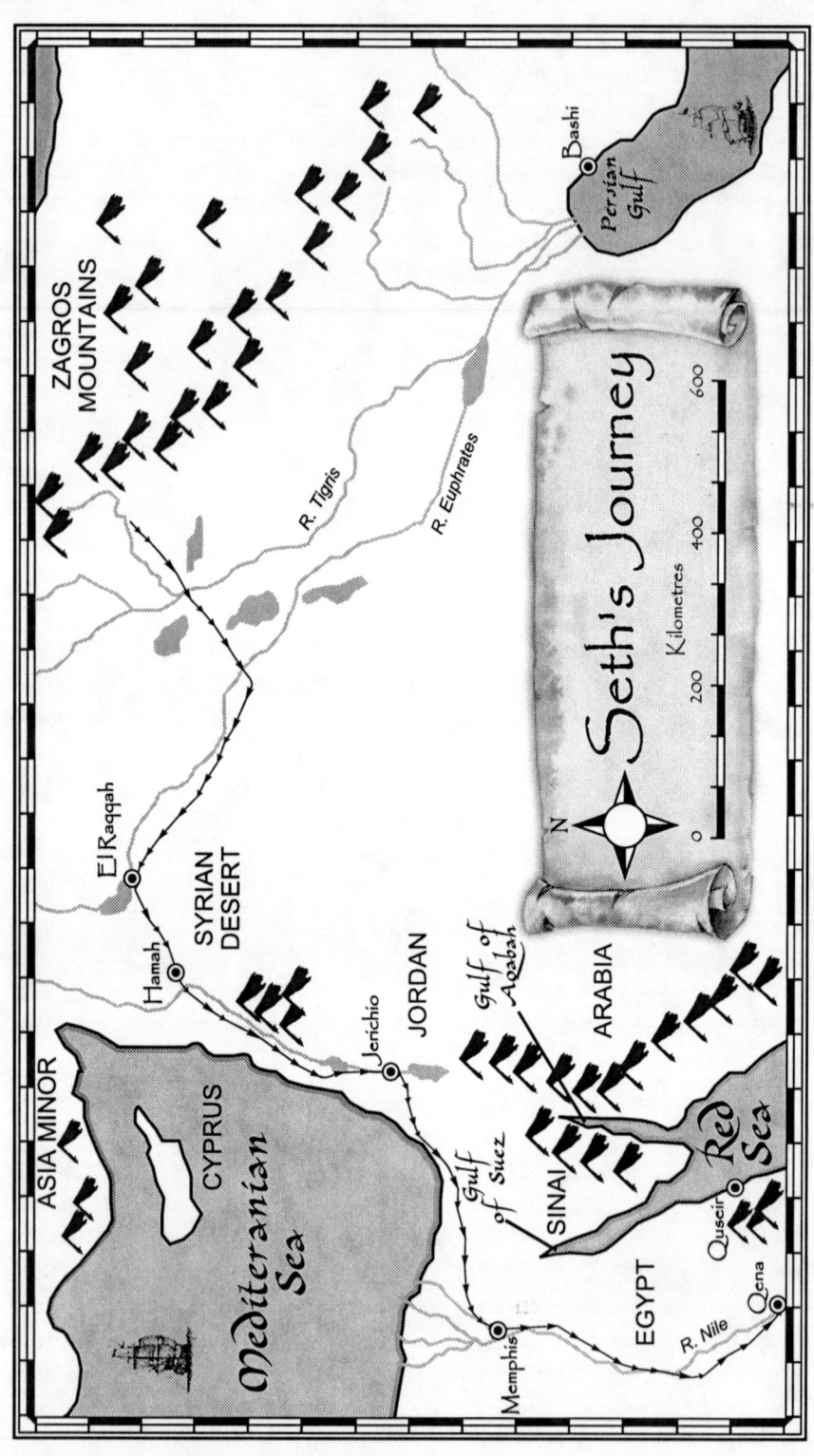

Seth's Journey

5500 BC

In the mountains, the Mesopotamian expedition was just about to experience the same level of storm as that endured by the Egyptian expedition. Unfortunately, their leader, Seth, did not believe in the Prophecy, and did not concern himself with the protection of his group. Having made no provision for their security, he established his own private headquarters in the only deep cave in the area.

The storm struck like a super-heated tornado – suddenly and relentlessly. Half of his team were out in the open and could not reach shelter quickly enough and died.

Nemrod and the rest of the Giants, being close to Seth's cave, forced their way into the shelter it provided. Unfortunately, when the first Giant rushed in, Seth, slightly drunk and in a foul temper, killed him with his kris.

Nemrod and his companions, who followed, overpowered Seth and secured him until the storm died down.

As was well known to all Giants, the basis of their society was that no Giant may kill another Giant. In a case such as this, the miscreant has to be branded on the forehead and cast out.

In the aftermath of the storm, the remaining Giants awarded the leadership of their expedition to Nemrod, and Seth was imprisoned in a small cave, with two armed guards outside, until they could arrange a formal trial on the following day. After the inevitable conviction, he would be branded, and ceremonially cast out as an outlaw.

Seth, fully aware that once he had been branded he would be an outcast to all Giant societies, decided to escape that very night. Calling one of the guards over to him, he pleaded with abject voice, "Tomorrow I expect to be thrown out, and from that time no Giant is permitted to speak to me. I have one last request, would you take a message to my dear friend Enki? I would like to say goodbye to him personally, and ask him to say goodbye on my behalf to Shiva and Heti. I am too ashamed to say goodbye to them in person, but I want them to know I hold them dear in my heart."

To this pathetic plea one of the guards replied, "If Enki will consent to come, I can only permit him to stay with you for a short time, and then he must leave. He must agree to be searched before entering, and again on leaving. I will speak to him and try to persuade him to accept these conditions."

A short time later, he escorted Enki into the cave. Seth kept his head bowed and when Enki came up to him, Seth threw an arm round his shoulder, turning him away from the guard and whispered in his ear.

"Appear sad and distressed at my predicament, but listen carefully. The three of you are bound to me by an oath of loyalty. I must escape tonight; my plan is to travel to Egypt and take command of their expedition.

"I require the three of you to travel with me. We will need water and provisions – hide these somewhere they can be picked up as we leave on the west side of the camp. When you leave me, go with great sorrow and then fetch the others; the guards have to be distracted or killed silently. When I see you approaching them, I will silence one, and you must silence the other. Now leave me with loud lamentations, and I will collapse into a corner and moan. Now!"

Seth lay down to sleep with his head positioned so that he could watch the entrance to the cave and the path leading up to it.

As regards High Lord Seth, it should be recalled that during the Council meeting in Atlan it was emphasised that his father was famous for his prowess in battle. This was said to entice his son to lead the Mesopotamian expedition. However, the truth was that his father was a cruel tyrant, and when, after murdering every man, woman and child in three native villages, he aroused so much hatred in the bordering countryside, the natives raised a large army with the object of attacking Atlan. Before this could happen, by a fortunate chance, Seth was ambushed and killed by a local tribe before he did further damage.

To avoid a disastrous war, Lord Raie had to apologise to the natives on behalf of the Giants, assuring them that his action was not approved by the Council, and to defuse this very difficult situation, he paid them a considerable amount of gold.

Seth was well built, about forty years old, and generally behaved in a similar manner to his father. He had a sardonic facial expression, a cruel mouth and was the embodiment of evil.

His support for the pirates was given in exchange for a large share of their booty; the wealth so obtained was used to strengthen his position of influence in the community. The subsequent and perfidious mass murder of the pirates was, in his view, justified, as their presence was jeopardising both his safety and his immediate plans. He was a typical bully, believing that he was above the law, and killed and cheated to advance his desire for dominance; not a very pleasant character all round.

With small clouds intermittently covering the moon, the guards did not see the three Giants approach until they were suddenly revealed by the moonlight breaking through the clouds. Seth heard their cry of surprise and their subsequent challenge, by which time he was halfway to the cave entrance with a heavy rock in his hand and, swinging round the cave entrance, he smashed the head of the first guard. Hearing the noise, the other guard turned round and was immediately silenced by Shiva.

Picking up the kris from the first guard, Seth then decapitated both guards and, dragging the corpses into the cave, threw them down a crevice at the back.

That part of the plan having been achieved, he turned to his friends, who were in a state of shock.

"We must leave immediately and walk towards the west until we meet the sea, where we will then turn south and head towards Egypt. The remaining Giants will never believe we have chosen this direction as it is difficult terrain, but in rough country there are plenty of hiding places that we may require at any time, until we are sure we have not been followed.

"As you are equally responsible for the deaths of the guards, you have no alternative other than to throw in your lot with me. When I take command of the Egyptian expedition you will be adequately rewarded."

They picked up the water and provisions from the cache and set out south-west down a mountain river to make for the Tigris, one of the two main rivers running through Mesopotamia.

Seth urged the group to go faster, as they had to establish the widest possible gap from any pursuit. The going was difficult as there was only a little light from a partially overcast sky, and scree, boulders, cataracts and rapids all hampered their descent down the mountain.

Seth turned to his three companions.

"It is essential that we maintain this speed of descent for the next two days, with the minimum number of rest periods. To avoid pursuit we must achieve a distance of at least fifteen itru over this period."

Great stands of massive trees lined either side of the ravine down which they were travelling, and the almost vertical ravine walls were covered in lichens and virtually impossible to climb.

By the morning of the third day they believed they had achieved fourteen itru, but as a result they were completely exhausted and they were still in the mountains.

Shiva stopped. "Seth, we cannot continue at this speed down this difficult route until we have had a substantial rest, and in addition, our provisions are running low. Taking these factors into account I suggest that, at the next break in the ravine, we find cover, and then search for habitations and whatever animals we can kill or capture for meat. The other problem we must overcome is that our kris are useful for attack and defence, but virtually useless for hunting; we need hunting bows and arrows."

"I agree and we will adopt that plan immediately."

The group, spurred by the necessary incentive, found the energy to hurry down the ravine, which suddenly widened out, and there, directly in front, was open countryside. The turbulent mountain stream now transformed into a wide placid river, snaking away in the direction of a mountain ridge which they estimated was at least three days' trek away.

They found a secluded place to camp from where they could watch for any pursuit without being observed.

Seth, after a short rest, said, "I will stay here and keep watch. Shiva, you will go south. Enki, you will go north along the edge of the mountain. Heti, go west along the river.

"After one hour you must turn round and make your way back. If you find habitations and people do not approach, keep concealed and return with the information, and in addition all of you must look for animals, and in particular wild ass, goats, gazelles, sheep and donkeys.

"When you all return we will devise a plan of action."

Three hours later, they returned and sat down to discuss their individual discoveries.

Seth invited Heti to speak first.

"To begin with, it is difficult to make progress along the river, but I discovered that in places it is fordable, and on the other side I found numerous tracks, most of which led to fish traps. From the condition of these tracks and traps, I do not believe they have been used since the storm.

"After searching for about an hour I had reached a track that led away from the river, but I decided there was not enough time left to investigate further.

"Enki what did you find?"

"There is one track running along the base of the mountain, but I believe it has not been used for a considerable time, but there is no sign of people or their habitations.

"There is plenty of game, numerous gazelles, and a donkey or wild ass, but they are all nervous and almost impossible to approach. I did make a special effort to approach the donkey that I observed feeding in the deep grass, but it disappeared into thick brush, complaining bitterly at being disturbed – perhaps it was a wild ass, and that would explain its behaviour."

"Shiva, your news… I kept you till last as you exceeded the time limit and I presume it's worth it?"

"Well, to begin with, the general conditions are similar to those recounted by Enki, but just when I considered turning back I noticed a track going back into the mountain. I followed it and it led me into a small canyon. The track finished at a small clearing in which stood two thatched huts. One was empty but the other is still inhabited. I made sure I had not been observed, but I did stay a reasonable time to observe the huts and for that reason it delayed my return. I estimate the distance from the clearing to our location is about one itru."

Seth congratulated them. "It seems you have discovered a great deal about the area. The river is fordable, and there are plentiful fish. There are paths on the north side of the river. There is plentiful game to the north. A habitation has been found about one itru from here.

"So the plan is to arrive at the canyon this evening just before dark, attack, kill any occupants, spend the night there and leave early next morning. We then follow the river, cross over at the ford and visit the fish traps, taking out any fish that have been caught and are still alive. We then continue along the north bank and head for the Tigris that must be two to three days away. For this part of our journey, we must collect sufficient provisions. Are we all agreed?"

This being agreed, they settled down for a three-hour rest, and early that evening set out for the canyon.

The attack went to plan; Shiva and Enki went into the first hut and killed the two occupants, while Seth and Heti entered the second hut, which they found to be empty.

Removing the two bodies they buried them under some debris.

They took what meagre provisions they found in the two huts, but to their delight they found two hunting bows with four quivers full of excellent arrows; in addition, they found skins for carrying water and a good selection of hunting knives.

As soon as the area had been searched, and yielded nothing, they settled down for the night, to make an early start the following morning.

By midday next morning they had reached the fish traps. Seth and Heti searched them for fish, while Shiva and Enki took the bows and arrows and would possibly be away for up to four hours. Should they have a substantial early kill they were to return to the last fish trap, so they could all prepare the meat and fish for drying in the sun, to provide them with an emergency food supply, in case hunting along the route was unsuccessful.

Seth and Heti opened up the fish traps; the majority of fish were dead but they recovered enough to provide them with food for two days. Unfortunately, the traps themselves were in a poor state of repair, and far too heavy to take with them on their trek to the Tigris.

They had settled down to preparing the fish for a meal when Shiva and Enki returned early with two gazelles, and after consuming the fish meal, they all set about cutting up the gazelles and preparing the meat over the fire to package for their journey.

Seth then asked Shiva about the hunt.

"To get away from the river into the open countryside we used the path reported by Heti, and some distance down it we observed a group of gazelles feeding in an area of deep grassland. We managed to get close enough to get effective shots in. Both of us shot simultaneously, but before we could get a second shot in, the majority of the herd were out of range. We did manage to kill the two targets, but we were very lucky to get both!

"The gazelles were far too heavy to carry so we cut away those parts of low food value to make the remainder portable. While this work was being undertaken I detected two natives watching us! In any case, I believe it advisable for us to assume that **had** occurred.

"Normally the Atlan natives are afraid to attack us directly but on occasions will prepare an ambush. Seth, I recommend that we assume these natives will behave in the same way and that we leave here as soon as possible, avoiding those areas that favour an ambush."

"I agree, but we should consider another possibility. We leave everything here and go down the path and kill any natives we contact. The only problem is we have no idea of the size of their community. If it is large, then we might suffer injuries which could jeopardise our plans, so let us put it to the vote."

They all agreed to avoid contact with the natives and set out for the Tigris immediately after packaging the meat into four bundles.

Setting off at a fast pace to put an acceptable distance between themselves and any attempt of pursuit, they were fortunate in finding a new path running not far from the north river bank that avoided its deviations.

Suddenly Seth ordered them to stop, take cover and listen; they then heard the sound of voices and sounds of pursuit – it was clear they were being followed.

As there was no suitable place to set an ambush with any real chance of total success, they set off again, entered the shallow side of the river and, after a reasonable distance, changed over to the south bank, leaving the river and turning eastwards to an area of cover.

At this point Seth stopped and said, "We will make a camp here, while I return to the river bank to watch the pursuit pass and assess its strength."

He did not have to wait long before a party of twenty or thirty natives, well-armed, were trotting past on the north side of the river.

Seth returned quickly to the camp and after revealing the strength of the pursuit, then outlined his plan.

"We must move out to that rock outcrop and take cover overnight; we will take turns in guarding against any attack; in the morning we should be able to observe any movement – with that level of opposition we cannot afford any confrontation. So we will continue our trek, avoiding the natives while, at the same time, being prepared to fight at any moment.

"I do not believe they followed us because Shiva shot a gazelle! It is more likely they know about the two natives we killed in the canyon."

The night passed without incident and after a quick meal they set off again, keeping half an itru away from the south-west side of the river.

The going was difficult to begin with, but gradually changed to ground with sparse growth as they approached the mountain that apparently blocked their path. With clear visibility over the flat country there was small chance of an ambush, so they rejoined the river where it passed through the mountain in a ravine.

When the ravine opened out to flat country it revealed the Tigris river in front of them, and by late afternoon they had reached the river bank, filled their water containers, and then had the problem of crossing a major river with its fast current as there was no apparent place where it could be safely forded. Deciding that a raft was the only solution, and assuming the pursuers were not far behind, they set about cutting down a number of poplars and linking them together with the mardi reeds.

As they were still worried about the natives, they determined to construct the raft before nightfall. Their krises were far from the ideal tool for cutting down trees, but by selecting the smaller trunks they soon had four poplars lying on the ground. Removing the large branches, they carried them down to the water and started to bind them together with the reeds, using the larger branches as posts to stop the raft from drifting off into the main stream. With four of them sitting on the raft they found that it would just support them but with little freeboard.

With sunset only minutes away they emptied their water bags and filled them with air so that if the raft collapsed while crossing the river, they would have sufficient support to reach the river bank.

With the raft complete they spent the first part of the night fashioning poles and paddles for their crossing in the morning. Then, leaving Enki on guard, the others settled down to sleep on the raft. In an emergency they could immediately paddle the raft away from the bank. In addition, sleeping on the raft provided some protection from the vipers and cobras that had made their homes in the river bank thicket.

Just as Enki was about to wake Heti to take over his shift, he noticed a movement in the reeds and caught sight of two natives, presumably scouts sent out to locate them!

If he woke the others it would warn the natives that they had been spotted and give them time to escape, so taking a bow he was about to shoot one, when he realised that, inevitably, the other would escape and the main group would be informed of their location. Considering this, he decided it was far better to wake the others, while he watched their position in case they attempted to attack.

With a careful nudge, Enki put his hand over Heti's mouth and whispered, "Wake up, Heti, we have visitors, wake the others." Enki saw a brief movement in the reeds and the two scouts vanished into the undergrowth.

When they were all awake Enki whispered, "We have been spotted by two of the native scouts – there is no alternative, we must cross the river immediately. The native scouts are very professional and will doubtless recommend an immediate attack as we have our backs to the river in a position that it is almost impossible to defend. I feel sure that the native group will not waste any time in starting an attack on our position."

They all agreed, and pushed the raft off the bank without any further discussion.

Fortunately the night was clear, with occasional cloud cover, so the stars provided a means of maintaining direction. Good visibility was essential as the river was in flood, and the impact of the river currents on the raft confused any attempt to hold direction on a long crossing.

Maintaining direction on the river crossing became extremely difficult and it only seemed a few minutes later that they heard the main party of the natives arriving. Fortunately they were well out into the main river and beyond the reach of bow or spear.

They entered a section of the river where the current was strongest, and the raft started to spin round and it took all their strength to bring it back on course. Fighting the current slowed their progress and the sky was beginning to lighten as they reached the far bank.

Leaving the raft securely attached to the bank, Seth said, "It is essential we move off immediately as the natives might have access to boats or other means to cross the river. Sorry, Enki, that you have lost your sleep but you must do the best you can. I hope after travelling an itru we can find a secure place to hide for a day, as we all need to rest after our efforts yesterday.

"There is a long march for us to the Euphrates river which must be about sixty-five itru from here. Our trek will take at least eighteen days, and even if we are careful, our water supply will only last us ten days. Incidentally, my eighteen days' estimate allows us sufficient time to hunt and gather fruits such as dates, which are abundant in this area."

They set off to the south-west over the rich alluvial plain and by midday had reached a small hill covered with thick undergrowth. Finding an animal track leading upwards towards the crown of the hillock they opened up a path to the top where they cleared a small area, then they rested until the next morning, sharing the guard duty to prevent being surprised by unwelcome visitors.

Fully refreshed, they made an early start and were fortunate to find a number of paths going in the right direction, but they took care to leave the path whenever they came near a habitation. After completing an eight-day trek, they recovered their spirits and were enjoying hunting and gathering the prolific abundance of dates to supplement their food. Meat was plentiful and they had sufficient time to process it properly. Water was becoming a problem as their supplies were exhausted and they considered themselves extremely fortunate when they encountered a small stream crossing their path. Once their water containers had been refilled, they found time for washing and general relaxation.

Before moving on, Seth was concerned with the problem of carrying sufficient provisions through an arid area that they would inevitably encounter.

"To prevent running out of food and water, we require one or two donkeys that can carry sufficient supplies from areas of plenty to those that cross arid lands or sections of desert; these we will doubtless encounter as we leave the Euphrates.

"We have nothing to barter with, and in any event I have no reason to trust the natives. What we need to find are one or two natives travelling with donkeys who can be ambushed, so that we can take possession of the animals and secrete the bodies of the natives to ensure that they will not be discovered. Removing one or two natives to ensure the success of our grand plan is, in my view – and I believe in the view of all of us – totally justified.

"To achieve our aim we must send scouts to see what routes are used by the natives with their donkeys and then select a suitable ambush location.

"First of all I intend to send scouts out from this location for a period of two days, and if we are not successful, we will continue our trek until we find another inhabited area and will search again, and keep up the process until we are successful. Who will volunteer to take on the first scouting mission?"

Instantly Shiva stood up. "I agree with everything you have said on this matter; frankly, as far as I am concerned, a little bit of excitement is overdue. Consequently I am happy to volunteer for this mission and am prepared to leave immediately. Perhaps you can allow me up to two full days to complete my search and agree that if I can obtain a donkey with the minimum of danger to myself, that action can also be acceptable?"

"Shiva, thank you for volunteering and please take one of the bows with you. Regarding your two proposals, the maximum time for the reconnaissance is agreed, the individual action can only be agreed providing there are no witnesses. After our recent experiences we do not want to be followed by an angry band of natives! While you are away we will be hunting and gathering fruits round the camp area, but one of us will always be at our campsite, concealed."

After an exchange of good-natured remarks Shiva left the camp and the others organised a hunt for dates and soft fruits. The time passed quickly and after the two days were up Seth became concerned and then, as they were about to launch a rescue mission, a bedraggled Shiva appeared, leading or perhaps dragging, a very disgruntled donkey.

"Its name is Grunt," said Shiva, "and it is the most contrary and bad-tempered creature I have ever encountered!"

Seth welcomed Shiva and said, "Sit down and relax, have something to eat and drink and then tell us of your adventures."

"The first few hours were tedious – I picked some dates, but they are not ripe enough to eat and I began to feel that there were no native settlements in the area. Then I found a new track which I followed, and it passed through a wooded area. After reaching the edge of the wood I saw that the path led to an enclosure, which was in a hollow and I could see five or six reed-mat huts, and most interesting of all, a fenced area holding six donkeys.

"As it was getting dark I made a den in the woods and rested until early the next morning. There was a lot of movement in the compound and I counted at least twenty-five natives outside their huts at any one time, then I realised they were saying goodbye to a native who was loading a donkey.

"I decided to take a chance that he would be travelling down the path that I had found, so I retraced my steps until, after about one and a half itru, I found the perfect place for an ambush.

"Waiting for action is always an absolute agony and the longer I waited the more convinced I became that I had taken the wrong direction. Then almost ready to give up and return to the native enclosure for one further attempt before returning to you and admitting failure, I heard someone coming down the path, complaining loudly and striking something with a stick. At last it was the native with a very unwilling donkey!

"I remained hidden and when he was almost opposite my position he stopped to relieve himself in the undergrowth – such an opportunity was too good to miss! Being so busy, he did not hear me coming up behind him. One quick slash with my knife and his throat was cut and he collapsed onto the ground. I grabbed one ankle and dragged him into a dense thicket, leaving him there. Then I grabbed the rope bridle and tethered the donkey to a tree.

"Returning to the native I searched his clothes and found two knives and a pocket full of roots, of a type unknown to me, so I thought I would try them first on the donkey!

"Stripping the garments off the body I soaked them in his blood and dropped them off away from the path and hoped that before they were found the hyenas would tear them to bits. The body I dragged to a small ravine and pushed it over.

"Returning to the ambush position I removed any sign of my presence and then carried on down the path for a further itru before turning away, to return to our camp.

"I found the donkey to be a difficult beast, the roots seemed to be a delicacy for him and he could be tempted to move by holding one in front of his head, but after a short distance he would stop and demand another root. Once he had eaten the root he would advance for a short time and then a further root had to be supplied. I got tired of this game and as soon as I got him moving I used the whip mercilessly.

"The journey back to our camp was slow and the donkey must accept the responsibility! I have not examined the contents of the packs on his back and leave the pleasure to one of you!"

With night closing in they took the baggage off the donkey's back, and examining it they found two large water containers, some fishing lines and a piece of netting, and these they kept. The remainder they took away from the camp and buried. They then settled down for the night, taking turns to guard against uninvited visitors, human and animal.

The next morning they set out for the Euphrates, the donkey carrying the main part of their food and water, with Heti and Shiva at either side of the donkey's head and Enki at one side on the rear with a suitable cane. After one or two displays of temperament and loud "he-haws", the donkey decided to behave, and the Giants increased their pace, having reduced loads and having a plentiful supply of water.

After five days' trek they approached a hilly and dry stretch covered in sand with small rocks, no tracks and with very little vegetation, mainly camel thorn and Prosopis. Walking over this terrain was uncomfortable and with a dry wind they were thankful for the additional water carried by the donkey. After a further three days' trek and two very unpleasant nights, they once more descended down into the alluvial plain.

In the distance they could see a large river snaking round in a half circle – the Euphrates. One day later they were down on its west bank, in a sheltered wood of poplars and willows to plan their next trek.

Seth made himself comfortable. "On our way down to the river I noticed a village about one itru south of our present position. We need information on the conditions on both sides of the Euphrates, and also where we can obtain those large animals that we see drinking on the other side of the river before vanishing into the desert. So who thinks he has the facility to attempt to converse with the natives?"

After a long silence, Enki spoke up. "I could converse with the natives in Atlan and that language might form a basis for conversing with the locals, but it could be dangerous to attempt a conversation."

"I would like you to try. I want you to wait until you find a native working outside the village enclosure. Walk up to him without your weapons, just have a bag of dates in your hand and offer to share them with him.

"See what you can find out, do not ask him about his village, just stick to travel information.

"Shiva, you will take a bow and keep Enki within range at all times from a concealed position. Do not shoot unless you get a signal to do so from Enki or you can see he is in real danger. In fact, we must do everything to avoid conflict. I agree with Enki that this is extremely dangerous from our point of view, but the benefits to us of a successful discussion would be considerable. You and Enki must attempt it early tomorrow morning."

As agreed, they left the next morning. Seth and Heti waited, armed and ready in case anything went wrong with their plan. The two returned late in the afternoon and it was obvious that it had been a successful visit. Seth then asked Enki to report on his discussions.

"As I approached the village I saw a native working in a fruit tree plantation and Shiva immediately went into hiding, then I walked over to him eating dates; he greeted me and I was able to comprehend his language. He told me his village was aware of our arrival on the banks of the Euphrates and are frightened by our size. They had spent most of the night strengthening their defences, which he now realises is a waste of time due to our friendly approach. I told him we were passing through on our way to the sea and hoped that our presence would not cause them to have any reason for concern. We would appreciate his advice on the best route to travel and information on those large beasts that we observed walking off into an area of desert.

"He replied that he was not able to provide information on long-distance routes, but he would go into the village and bring the headman who had made that journey and could give the most reliable advice. Off he went and returned with the headman, complete with a young girl carrying a tray of refreshments, and he greeted me in a kindly manner. I explained that the object of our journey was to reach the sea in the west and he said, 'Don't attempt to go directly to the west, as in that direction you will encounter a large and inhospitable desert and, without extensive knowledge of its dangers, you could not possibly survive.

"'I suggest your party follows the river up-stream to the north-west until you reach the village of Raqqah. This will take you between thirty-six to forty days. Do not attempt to cross the river as the west bank is extremely difficult to follow, and the tribes on that side are far from friendly.

"'From Raqqah you follow the river for four days until you reach a lake, then you travel south-west to Hamah across the desert, and this will take at least seventeen days.

"'It would be advisable to buy a camel at Raqqah to carry your supplies across the desert as they can do that distance with very little water, and its feet do not sink into the sand. This is the most dangerous part of your journey so be on your guard every moment you are crossing the desert.'

"I thanked him profusely for his valuable advice and for the manner of his reception and said that we would be leaving in a few days' time and I would visit him to say goodbye before we continued our trek."

"Shiva, have you any observations on this exchange?"

"It all seemed to go incredibly smoothly, and frankly, seeing Enki filled up with refreshments brought out the jealousy in me, and possibly that explains my rather jaundiced view of things. I believe the advice regarding the route is sound, but why did the headman not invite Enki to go into his village? For people knowing of our presence who had been working all night strengthening their defences against an attack by us should provide our emissary with such a greeting is frankly incredible. It is just possible they have heard of our activities and are not prepared to openly oppose us until they can obtain adequate reinforcements, and by their attitude intend to lull us into a false belief in our security within this area.

"In my view, we have the information we require, so let us leave immediately and travel north-west along the river. When we are one itru away and night starts to fall, we move from the track to a place where we can observe the activities of any one on that track who decides to follow us. The sky is clear and there will be a moon tonight so if we are being followed by a number of armed natives, we can be fully aware of their intentions. If they send scouts we can capture one and kill the others if they are armed, and if they are unarmed we let them pass us by and return to their village."

Seth agreed. "We move off at once, and adopt Shiva's plan, in fact the sooner we get to Raqqah the better for our security."

They left immediately and when darkness came they left the track to spend the night on top of a mound that was concealed by a small wood. At about midnight they observed two natives carrying weapons coming up the track, and they stopped at the place where the Giants had turned off and began a stealthy approach up the hill.

"Well done, Shiva, now finish the job. Enki, use the blowpipe; if you miss, Shiva will take out the second scout. Bring the prisoner here and we will question him."

The encounter was resolved silently. Shiva and Enki returned carrying the native who they dropped on the ground, and waited for him to wake up. Shiva dropped their weapons in front of Seth, consisting of two bows and a number of knives.

When the scout regained consciousness they started to question him but apart from establishing that he was part of the native group that had followed them from the Tigris, they were unable to probe deeper, as Enki's knowledge of the language was limited. So they killed him and they hid the two bodies in the cliff side, rolling boulders over them, making it difficult for the natives to remove, if they were ever found.

Seth was relieved when the task had been completed. "The last time we had trouble with these particular scouts the main party was not far behind. So to avoid further harassment we must continue our journey to Raqqah immediately. This will require us trekking from now till morning and then throughout the day with short stops for brief meals, so let us see how many itru we can cover in that time. Will you kindly explain all that to the donkey – or should I say grunt! Each of us will carry a bow and kris from now on in a ready-to-use position. That's all, let's go."

They went down to the track and started their trek to Raqqah. By the evening of the next day they had covered about thirteen itru and, completely exhausted, they found a concealed place off the track, made a quick meal and taking two-hour shifts guarding against being surprised, had a restful night. They set out early the following morning with the intention of covering ten itru before nightfall.

They found this section difficult as the river went through a ravine and the path was uneven, but they made the distance and decided that this would be their target for the next five days. They would keep close to the river so that they could continuously replenish their water supply. They also realised that if the natives were following they would know the obvious shortcuts that were available across the barren plateau.

The five days passed quickly enough and they kept the daily target, and in the evening they were surprised to see a large village ahead of them. They were tempted to ask its name but decided it would be better to avoid native habitations by diverting off the track, then circumventing it by trekking round a small hill with the intention of rejoining the track on the other side.

Seth expressed his delight with the exceptional daily progress.

"Let us continue at this rate, which is double that achieved on our journey between the two rivers, using up our store of food for the next ten days. According to my calculations this should bring us close to Raqqah, then we will move out into the highlands and find a hidden and easily defended place to rest, while hunting and getting acquainted with the countryside. Also think about obtaining some camels, as we were advised that these would be essential for crossing the desert."

The days passed quickly and by keeping a continual watch on the road ahead they were able to divert off the track to avoid contact with native groups. On the tenth day, Shiva went ahead to locate Raqqah, and when he returned he reported to Seth. "There is a extensive native enclosure about two itru ahead, it has a substantial native population and outside their enclosure are large numbers of tethered camels, with groups of natives sitting near them."

"Let us leave the track and, keeping our distance, circumnavigate the town. We must move silently, avoiding any contact with the natives and if possible avoid being seen. We must move at night and this will take us at least three days to reach a point where we can see the river and the path. We must conceal ourselves in a place suitable for our defence and watch for movement on the road. I intend to stay in that location for at least ten days – during that time we must try to determine a plan to obtain camels and a guide. Those of us not watching the road will, during the night hours, replenish water supplies and hunt for food to replace our emergency supplies."

The plan was successfully carried out and by the eighth day they had replenished their supplies of food and water and watched a number of camels loaded with goods pass on the track below them. The four of them sat down to consider their next move.

Seth opened the discussion.

"We need to stop a small party with four or five camels; to do this we require an ambush point where they can be stopped and Heti can ask them to allow him to join their convoy as far as the sea. He can bargain with a piece of gold I keep for emergencies. I believe they will react in one of two ways – if they take the gold then threaten him, we will kill all except the leader who will be made a prisoner and forced to guide us across the desert. If they are well-disposed to him he will inform them he wishes to take some friends with him, then we will consider other possibilities. However, if we have the slightest doubts, we will take over the convoy. Shiva and Enki, you can start to look for the ambush site as soon as you are ready."

The ambush site was selected and a tree at the far end nearly cut through so that when a suitable victim approached it could be dropped across the path to force the caravan to stop. With everything arranged, Seth shifted camp to the ambush site and they sat down to wait, which was tedious but eventually a suitable caravan was sighted. The tree was dropped across the path and Heti stepped out onto the path and waited for the caravan to stop. It did, and a very disgruntled native got off his camel and yelled at his followers to clear the obstruction. While this was going on Heti walked up to the native and greeted him.

"A pleasant day, sir – is this your caravan and are you travelling across the desert?"

"Yes, this is my caravan, my name is Aziz and I am a merchant travelling to Hims. What do you want?"

"I am on a long journey to my relatives who live by the sea. I have to cross the desert to get there and would like to join your caravan. Having no experience of crossing a desert, I can see the advantage of camels, but I am doubtful whether my donkey could make the journey. I have very little to offer you in payment unless you are interested in metals as I have this small bar of gold, which I carry with me for emergencies such as this."

During this discussion, Aziz's three companions came up and stood round Aziz to enjoy the fun.

Aziz said, "Give me the piece so that I can see how much it is worth."

Hati passed the gold bar to Aziz.

"This is all I have but I understand it is quite valuable."

"True, it is gold but of little value, I will keep it as a souvenir. You insult me by offering such a small amount for my services. Be off with you, or we will rough you up a little and then throw you in the river!" Aziz then started to draw out a knife from his kamar-band.

Hati threw himself flat on the ground, Seth, Shiva and Enki immediately shot Aziz's companions then, emerging from their positions, completed the killing.

Seth then put his kris at Aziz's throat who, in a state of absolute terror, collapsed and begged for mercy. Heti, who by now had regained his feet, gave him a couple of kicks for his insults. They then stripped the dead men and carried the bodies to the prepared hiding place, where they concealed them under rocks to prevent wild animals digging them up.

"No time to delay our departure, we can discuss Aziz's position as we travel and give him good advice regarding his behaviour as our guide and prisoner. It has to be emphasised that his freedom depends on ensuring we traverse the desert without undue difficulties. To begin with we will lead the camels, and tonight when we find a suitable location Aziz will show us how to ride a camel and we will reduce the luggage to the essentials."

Without further discussions they set off down the track and after a few riding lessons they were able to mount the camels and endure what, to begin with, was an uncomfortable ride, and fourteen days later they were by the lake on the outskirts of Hims.

With Aziz secured, they sat down to decide his fate. He had been a reasonable guide and prisoner, but there were obvious difficulties with releasing him, and Seth called for Heti's opinion.

"While he has served us well, he cannot be trusted to conceal our activities from the local population, that is a risk we cannot accept. I feel we should retain his services until we reach an area where he has little influence. We should explain this to him and retain his services as camel master until we reach the borders of Egypt."

Seth commented, "If we dispose of him here we will not have his expertise to look after the camels, and we should retain the camels for the journey into Egypt. There is an advantage keeping him with us, as the Egyptian language is very different from his own. By the time he finds someone to listen to his complaints we will be far away, and our destination is unknown to him."

They called Aziz over to them and explained the situation to him.

"I had hoped that you would release me here; however, I understand your concern that I might raise my friends against you, and nothing I can say will change that situation. All I ask is that you supply me with at least one camel and some merchandise to get me home and I will leave without contacting anyone."

The deal was agreed and they set out for Jericho, a journey of twenty-five to thirty days by camel. They took their route through the Bekaa and Hula valleys, Lake Tiberias, and down to Jericho at the head of the great inland lake. Food and water were readily available and they completed the journey in twenty-eight days, the trek raising very little interest among the locals. However, when they arrived near Jericho, the land was flooded and the freshwater lake was now a saltwater lake. Without a fresh water supply they could not stay, so made their way to Ashdod, staying there for two weeks before continuing to Ismailia.

Finally, they arrived at Ismailia and Seth spoke to Aziz.

"You have served me very well and I will let you go, providing we can sell enough of your merchandise to purchase four donkeys in good condition. Only then can you leave with your camels and return home. You will not attempt to cause us any problems in this country; if you do we will have no mercy. Enki will accompany you to the market, while we move to another location."

The exchange was achieved without difficulty; the Giants had four donkeys, all in good condition, and after watching Aziz travelling east into the desert, they set out for Zagazig and then the Nile where they arrived after eleven days.

The Nile in this area was heavily populated, so the Giants continued up river and after trekking for three days found a safe campsite with good visibility in all directions. They then settled down for substantial rest before starting on their long trek to Qena, which would take at least two months.

After their long rest period, with easy hunting and fishing providing ample food to sustain them, and to build up a substantial emergency stock of dried meat, they then set out once more on their long journey to Qena. The conditions were ideal on the east bank of the Nile and after the first month they became casual about maintaining a guard during the night.

One night, Enki was sleeping fitfully when a scraping noise and a whisper caused him to sit up and he noticed a shadowy figure moving among the donkeys. Kris in hand he woke Shiva, put his hand to his mouth and pointed to the donkeys, one of which was being led away. Moments later the native was lying on the ground with a kris at his throat and Shiva standing over him.

Enki then searched for his companion. After searching the area for about an hour and discovering no one, he returned to the camp, where they were all awake, waiting for him, with the native trussed up and their donkey secured and, as usual, complaining.

Heti started to question the native. "What is your name and why were you stealing our donkey?"

"My name is Amar; I only intended to *borrow* the donkey, as mine has just died and I need a donkey to carry both my goods and myself to the north. I have nothing to barter with, so I had no alternative. I have been working on the gold mines in the western desert and have found a valuable gold seam under a heavy rock overburden.

"I am on my way to find friends to join with me to remove the rock and extract the metal. I am sorry for the trouble I have caused, and would be happy if you joined me to share in the substantial profits."

"It is a good story, you say you are a gold miner, yet you also say you have nothing to barter with. Why should we believe you?"

"I have no separate gold, it is true, but I have very rich samples to show my friends that will convince them of the richness of my discovery."

"Where are these samples? You have nothing with you and I have searched the local area and have been unable to find anything!"

"I have concealed them further down the track. I will take you there and you will see for yourself that I have spoken the truth."

"I am very doubtful about all of this, but we will give you the chance to prove it in the morning. Then you will take us to the place where you have concealed your goods. In the meantime you will remain secured, do not attempt to escape, because if we detect any attempt to remove your bonds you will be killed immediately."

Seth took Shiva aside. "You will go with Heti tomorrow morning, and when the samples are retrieved ask Amar to explain them to you – in particular, why are they so valuable? If you are convinced, congratulate him and kill him instantly, get rid of his body by throwing it in the Nile so he can complete his journey up north to his friends. I have an excellent use for those samples!"

The following morning, Seth went up to Amar and called for Heti.

"Release him from his bonds, Heti."

After he was freed, Seth spoke to Amar.

"I have considered your offer and think it might be in our interest to join you on the basis of fair shares for all of us. That is providing the samples support your statement – we can discuss the full details of the arrangement when you return. Remember, I have to convince my companions, so encourage them when they see the samples."

Amar then left with Heti and Shiva, the samples were obtained and Amar explained to Heti the reasons why they were so valuable. As Shiva was congratulating Amar, he killed him and his body was thrown into the Nile.

Heti was very worried and asked Shiva, "Why did you kill him? As you will doubtless remember, Seth wanted to talk over a deal with Amar when he returned to camp."

Shiva laughed. "That was only to obtain information on the samples and at the same time give him an easy death. You were not told, as by this means he was less likely to feel something had gone wrong, while taking us to his hiding place to reveal his cache."

Shiva and Hati returned to camp, and handed the samples to Seth who was delighted with both the samples and the details surrounding the value of them.

"Let's pack our belongings and move out immediately in case our activities have been observed. Five itru to the next stopping place would be a fair precaution."

After a further three weeks' uninterrupted trek they made camp. Seth said to Enki, "Scout ahead for seven itru to locate Qena and the expedition camp and return the next day and do *not* in any circumstances reveal yourself either to the camp or the local natives."

Enki had nothing to report, so the trek continued for a further five itru, after they had made camp, and the process was continued with Enki making a further reconnaissance. Then Seth sent Shiva.

When Shiva returned after three days, he reported to Seth.

"I completed the seven itru in quick time and I thought I saw a building in the far distance so decided to go for a further seven itru. I was not mistaken, as about one itru ahead I observed a large native enclosure, and on the other side of the river, a temple and building works different to native constructions. I thought this was sufficient for the time being, so I hurried back through the night, and now require three or four hours' rest!

"Well done, Shiva, go and have your well-earned rest. We leave for a hide within walking distance of the camp first thing tomorrow."

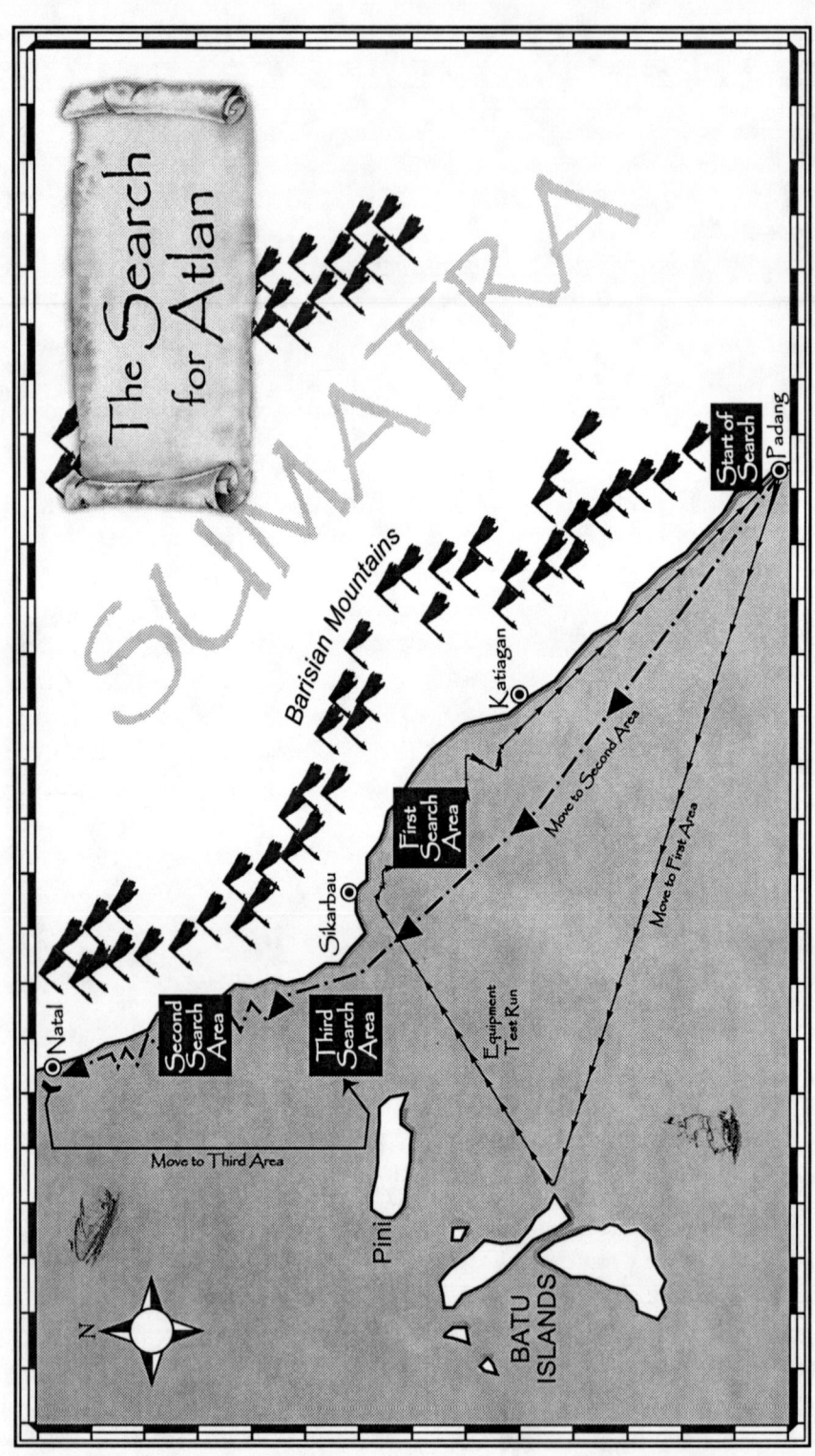

Jakarta, Indonesia

AD 2004

Ricky arrived home by taxi and went up to John Goddard's apartment before entering his own and triggering the alarm. Fortunately, John was in and after parking his luggage in the hall, they sat down for a brief chat.

"Well, John, did you have any problems with my apartment while I was away?"

"Not what I would call trouble, but you had a visitor who appears to have taken up residence! It was your lady friend, Maria; she had a key and let herself in, setting off the alarm. As promised, I trundled around, expecting a rough house, but no luck as it was only your lady, sitting on the bed and looking forlorn. You had warned me she might appear, but seemed doubtful, so I disconnected the alarm on the front door and connected it to an attack button beside her bed, so that if there was any problem she could call me.

"There's been no call, and now you've returned my hopes are dashed! Apart from that incident, everything's been quiet. Now tell me, was your trip as successful as you hoped, and how did you make out with old Blanco?"

"The trip was a success and Blanco's a real treasure; I've appointed him to be captain of our expedition vessel. Erm, John, we must have a serious talk so you can decide whether or not you are prepared to join us – and in what capacity! Can you find me some time tomorrow morning?"

"No problem… shall we say about ten o'clock?"

"Excellent, now I must present myself to the formidable Maria, and once more thank you for looking after my pad."

Ricky returned to a very warm welcome from a repentant and tearful Maria.

"I've been so upset and can't understand why I behaved like that, will you ever forgive me? I have been so distressed that I cancelled all my appointments in order to wait in the apartment for your return."

"Of *course* you are forgiven. It was partially my fault, so let's both forget the whole incident. My visit to Indonesia went well, I have a ship for the expedition subject to finalising the price with RN Disposals. So now there's a massive amount of administrative work to undertake, in particular the appointment of a team, the purchase of equipment, and attempts to obtain financial backing from a selected newspaper in return for exclusive coverage – a grant from the National Lottery would be helpful, and while I now have adequate financial resources to cover our immediate plans for two expeditions, we will require a great deal more money to cover the eventual development supporting and enhancing the Maya Society, as outlined in my discussions with Yax! Anyway, enough of all this... has the lady of the house any food available before I fall into bed to overcome my jet lag?"

"All is available for my returning hero! A light meal and if you stay awake long enough and give me enough space, I can prepare the essentials, then off to bed with you, leaving everything until the morning."

While Maria was preparing the meal, Ricky told her of John Goddard's visit at ten the next morning and asked would she make sure they were awake by eight o'clock in order to prepare for his arrival without rushing.

Next morning, while they were quietly and contentedly having breakfast, Maria broke the silence.

"Ricky, I now know Yax is dead, and that he sleeps with his family. He is in a deep tomb beside a lake – no one will ever disturb him as he has collapsed his end of the cavern. Yax has told me that I must discard all my other commitments and help you complete the Maya project. This information came to me in a dream. To begin with I was terrified, but became calm as I realised who was talking to me. So! Here I am and I hope you will accept my services. I could be useful as secretary and personal assistant, or in any other task at which you consider I'd be capable.

"Perhaps you will understand this revelation when I tell you something that I should have revealed long ago, but was unable to do so... I'm Yax's sister and I have been working for a group set up by him as an agent to gain information from the Far Right. That link was discontinued recently at my request, as they hoped I could work with you. You will appreciate that I cannot return to Mexico for a considerable time, but that's my problem, which only the future can resolve."

"Maria, I know Yax could have sent you that message from my own experience. Thank you for telling me, and if it were not so Yax would have warned me of the deception. All right, you can start work at once! Fetch me another slice of toast, and after that use my address book and call James White and Kirk Frehier and ask them to attend a company formation meeting at ten. Tell Frehier not to bring anything with him, he'll understand."

The meeting started as planned and all managed to attend despite the short notice.

Ricky opened the agenda.

"There are two immediate problems – establishing an unregistered non-profit-making private company, and the appointment of a bonded accountant. Subject to your agreement the company will be named The East/West Archaeology Research Company. At present I have started the company with a capital of eighteen million pounds. Unless we can get additional funds from the lottery or press this must be sufficient for two expeditions, one to Indonesia, and one to Egypt. When members are on expeditions there will be no salaries, but all expenses will be covered including reasonable quantities of alcoholic drinks and a basic weekly allowance for incidentals. Nominations are required for an accountant. A retired but active man, interested in our expeditions, would be ideal. Would everyone please make discreet inquires. Any suggestions will be considered at our next meeting in a week's time.

"I will manage EWARC. Maria Martinez will be Company Secretary and PA and Kirk Frehier will be responsible for hieroglyph translations and the evaluation of those translations and assessments of the search areas. Captain James White will take command of the expeditions search vessel, and employ a suitable native crew. John Goddard... if you decide to join us... you will be responsible for publicity and grants, and later on electronics and search equipment.

"Now, will you all consider how to improve on these provisional arrangements and reveal any special abilities that you have by our next meeting in a week's time? Give me forty-eight hours to deal with my immediate problems, and then you are welcome to telephone me to discuss problems and find means of overcoming them. Now my new PA will provide drinks and refreshments. Then we will adjourn until our next meeting, by which time Maria will try and hire some office space."

Later, while Maria was telephoning agents for short-term office rentals, Ricky telephoned Captain James Grenavear to make an appointment for James White, late of the RN, and Ricky to discuss purchasing or leasing the coastal protection vessel, which they had selected in Jakarta.

James was delighted to hear that Ricky had returned safely and had chosen a suitable ship. He looked forward to meeting them both in his office the next day. A quick telephone to Blanco followed and he agreed to meet Ricky and Maria for a light lunch before they were due to leave for their appointment with James.

Ricky visited John Goddard's apartment and arranged a bulk payment deal that would keep him financially secure while on the expeditions. John was delighted as at present he was still between jobs and had been wondering how he was going to survive.

Meanwhile, Maria had found a suite of six small offices with a conference room and food preparation area. It had been vacant for months so Maria negotiated a satisfactory price, subject to Ricky's inspection and agreement.

That evening Ricky and Maria were relaxing over their evening meal, when they received another extremely threatening telephone call. During the call, Maria pressed the record button and took down the telephone number.

When Ricky put down the receiver, he realised that reporting it to the police would play into the hands of the opposition by bringing their project into the open. Maria suggested calling the number the next day while Ricky was at Disposals. If the caller answered she would cut off the call. If someone else answered she would ask for any name, then, as a distraught secretary, admit she got the names mixed up in her diary, and by this device and a bit of luck, obtain the owner's name. With that information and a copy of his threatening call, they should be able to unmask one of the opposition.

The next day, while Ricky purchased the vessel from Disposals, Maria obtained the name of the person who had sent the threatening message. His address was quickly obtained from the local telephone directory. It turned out that Mr Vernon Drinmead, a well-known archaeologist, had a reputation of being a bully and was mainly known for his extremely bad temper.

It was a simple matter to discover where he lectured, so John and Ricky waylaid him while he was hurrying to a lecture. John grabbed him by the lapels of his coat and lifted him so his feet were only just touching the ground, while Ricky snarled in his ear, "We have a tape that records your threats against my organisation and me. My friends and I are prepared to take severe action against you or any of your colleagues if you are so much as associated with any further harassment. In this case and depending on your behaviour we need not trouble the police. However, for your heart condition and security we suggest a couple of months' holiday overseas would be advisable."

They left him red in the face and apparently on the verge of an epileptic fit.

The next six months were a hive of activity; the ship was transferred to EWARC and insured and the survey equipment, sent out to Jakarta by ship, was to be followed by an expert to install it once the consignment had cleared customs.

Blanco arrived in Jakarta and, with Rashid's assistance, had the vessel dry-docked to clean off the hull and paint it with anti-fouling and then appointed a local crew. All had to be made ready for the expedition start in a month's time. In addition, the firearms licence had been obtained by Rashid from the government – pirates were a worry. Blanco purchased four AK-47 assault rifles, two 8 mm Parabellum Lugers and an MG15 with twin cylinder magazines, modified for hand use, and substantial quantities of ammunition. Blanco was taking no chances!

By this time, the National Lottery had contributed five million rather reluctantly and a national daily had agreed to sponsor the first expedition with two million. Ricky had hoped for more, but without giving too much information away, it had been difficult to press for larger amounts.

Kirk Frehier and Ricky met up in their conference room to discuss the hieroglyphs that he had translated and then prepared an assessment of their value in establishing search areas.

"Kirk, I have read your translation several times and am

impressed. Your separate assessment of the data provided from an archaeologist's point of view is encouraging. You mention the finding of the artefacts – can you expand on that aspect with regards to location?"

"The Giants in their journey from Atlan to Egypt took valuable artefacts with them that belonged to an early Giant civilization that existed some five and a half thousand years before their time. These artefacts they found in a cavern that also contained a massive tomb, which, after clearing the artefacts, left no time to explore in an acceptable manner.

"You will note from rather obscure references in the text that they intended to return to Atlan to open the tomb, but after the cataclysm there were no means available to return and all their efforts were directed to building a copy of Atlan in Egypt. However, the hope remained that someday they would return, so the location was given as thirty-five itru north of Atlan City – approximately eighty kilometres – three mountain peaks mark the general location. The cave is on the south side, high up and that's all there is with regard to the site. When you connect this information with the description of Atlan that we discussed after examining the first text, we should be able to reduce the number of sites we have to survey."

"Kirk, if we assume that the sea level has increased by twenty to twenty-five metres in the last eight thousand years, our area of search for the structures can fall between depths of fifteen and twenty-five metres. South of the Equator there is the earthquake belt. I doubt that a city would have been built there, as it had lasted five and a half thousand years! So it seems reasonable to survey from the Batu islands, Tanahbela and Pini. Eight thousand years ago these islands would have been connected to Sumatra in the Indonesian group.

"To implement this proposal I suggest that you and John hire a light plane in Jakarta, and take it up to Sumatra to survey this area, and if possible, locate a group of mountain peaks that conform to the text description. The information gathered should form a sound basis in the selection of sea search areas, in conjunction with sea depths. That's my general idea but modify it as necessary when you get out there! Are you interested in this proposal? You might get some good photographs for your book!"

"I think it's an excellent idea. When do I start?"

"Anytime from tomorrow, it's totally up to you and John Goddard. Have a word together, it must be understood in the matter of selecting areas yours is the final word, but otherwise work together as equal partners. Tell me how much cash you require to take with you, and I'll also arrange for currency to be available in a Jakarta bank. Good luck! Keep Blanco informed of your intentions so, if you go missing, we'll know where to look."

Ricky put his arm round Maria's neck and said, "Will you risk all and come with us to Indonesia, or would you rather stay and keep David Cartright, our financial wizard, company?"

Maria gave him a hug and said, "Where you go I go – don't worry, I will engage a competent secretary for him, subject to his approval. Mind you, I know if he's given the choice he'd come like a shot."

"Tell him he'll have a place on the Egyptian expedition if he can find someone bonded to stand in while he's away."

Two weeks later, their survey ship the *Yax Nixte* was undergoing its first shake-down cruise and Blanco was happy to report that as no problems had been experienced, it was time for them to leave for Jakarta.

Maria and Ricky were excited and a little apprehensive as they set out for Singapore, faced with the responsibility for the success of the expedition.

When they joined their plane at Heathrow they were surprised to find themselves upgraded from business class to first class, with the complements of the company. In addition they were to be given VIP status on any future flights. Maria's only comment was, "You deserved it!"

Arriving at Jakarta, they were met by Commander James Foley, the Naval Attaché, who escorted them to their hotel. James suggested an early night as the ambassador had arranged a reception at the embassy the next evening. This had been set up to establish firm relations with government officials, who could smooth the way for their project. "Oh yes, the ambassador would appreciate Ricky saying a few words as to the general purpose of your expedition; in addition he suggests you might also add that it would be of considerable assistance if an Indonesian could be nominated by the government to join as a full member of the expedition!"

Ricky replied, "I had already intended to make this offer and this would be an excellent time, and I will emphasise that by this means, their government will, at all times, be fully aware of our activities."

The reception at the embassy was a complete success, and an Indonesian archaeologist would join the ship within two days, and Ricky agreed to delay sailing until he arrived.

Late in the afternoon of the second day, just as it was getting dark and the whole company were getting impatient, the Indonesian team member arrived in a very flustered state. His name was Mohammed Ismail, his English was limited and his appearance did not suggest his interest in archaeology, but he was made welcome.

When Blanco decided that they would sail at first light the next morning. Mohammed was disappointed. "I can assure you that there is no danger leaving the port in the dark, and I am prepared to guide you out!"

Blanco replied, "I'm not prepared to take the risk, minimal as it might be, and we have plenty of time and there is nothing to gain by being impatient."

Ricky agreed, so at first light the next morning they set out for the islands of Batu, Tanahbela and Pini. After that they would start the first and possibly the most difficult of their selected search areas.

Maria walked with Ricky up to the bow, and when they had privacy she turned to him.

"I'm worried about our Indonesian member; I find it difficult to believe he's selected by the Indonesian government for this appointment! I know it sounds crazy but that name doesn't suit his personality. If he's not selected then, there are one or two alternatives – either the official selection has been permanently removed or a junior minister or clerk has been bribed to change the name. In either case his purpose could be sabotage or he's linked with the pirates! In any event, he would know he's in danger of being discovered so if I'm right, he'll make an early attempt to sabotage or destroy the *Yax Nixte*. I favour an attack by pirates as the most probable."

"To begin with, Maria, we have absolutely no evidence; on the other hand there is a strong possibility you are correct. First of all, it's imperative that Mohammed must not know of our suspicions. All our people must be able to collect their weapons quickly when an attack is imminent, but those weapons mustn't be seen by another vessel. I will speak to Blanco so that he's prepared for an attack, sabotage or both.

"Maria, in an hour's time, will you try to join John in a friendly manner, laugh and joke with him and pass on our recommendation? Impress on him that he must make every attempt to avoid Mohammed discovering our preparations. He must warn Kirk, say, an hour after your discussion with him. We must watch Mo but not interfere directly with anything he does, unless it would damage the *Yax Nixte*."

Blanco estimated that it would take about sixty-three hours to reach the Batu island area, a distance of about twelve hundred and sixty kilometres running at the most economic cruising speed. It was about twenty-five hours to the port of Bengkulu and a further sixteen hours to Pedang, both of which had adequate refuelling facilities.

Blanco turned to Mo. "Have you any recommendations?"

"I would recommend Bengkulu as I have an uncle who manages the refuelling station there and I should be able to get a special price. Pedang is all right when it is working, but I personally wouldn't rely on it!"

Blanco, after thanking Mo, announced, "We will arrive in Bengkulu about 11 a.m. tomorrow and set off for Sunda about two hours later, so those going ashore must stay close to the harbour. I will sound the foghorn twice fifteen minutes before departure. John has volunteered to keep me company."

That night Ricky and John took the night watches, not a difficult job with the use of satellite navigation; there were no alarms and by midday they were tied up at the refuelling wharf, and Mo contacted his uncle to negotiate an acceptable price. Two hours later, having refuelled, they set out for the Sunda Islands, with possibly a call at Panang en route.

When they were preparing a watch-keeping rota, Mo stepped forward.

"May I offer to take the early morning watch? As I have always been an early riser it wouldn't be a hardship, and it'd be a pleasure for me to start sharing the tasks with the other members of the expedition."

Blanco thanked him, saying, "I see you are going to be a very useful member of this expedition, and taking advantage of your offer, you now have the early morning shift."

Before settling down for the night Blanco had a quick word with John Goddard.

"I need you to get up at the time of the early morning shift, but keep out of sight. Watch the engine room door – if he attempts to

211

enter he is to be arrested and handcuffed out of sight. Then alert all members to cover both sides of the *Yax Nixte*. The native crew are to be confined to quarters to avoid them being mistaken for pirates.

"Blanco, I think we all appreciate the immediate danger. Don't worry, I will take care of Mo if he tries to sabotage the engines. If he attempts that course, the pirates will be very close and we'll all have to react quickly!"

In the early hours of the morning Mo came up to the bridge and relieved Ricky, who yawned, apologised and told Mo he was looking forward to his bed and went below. Then, waking Maria, they collected their arms and ammunition and waited.

John, hidden from view, watched Mo who kept looking at his watch. After about an hour he took what appeared to be a small torch out of his pocket and pointed it in a northerly direction, then returned it to his pocket. He carried out the same procedure several times until he saw an answering flash on the horizon. Then taking an automatic out of his pocket, he hurried down to the engine room and pointing the weapon at the native duty engineer, ordered him to stop the engines. At that moment John hit him over the head with a marlinspike and Mo fell unconscious on the engine room floor. John handcuffed him to the stair rail and told the engineer to react quickly to any signals received from the bridge.

Returning quickly to the members' accommodation, he passed Blanco, fully dressed, carrying the machine gun and spare magazines to the bridge; everyone was awake and with their equipment were running to their positions. Blanco had the message passed that no one was to fire before he gave the order, and to ensure that their positions remained hidden from the sea. Then he telegraphed engines dead slow, hoping that the pirates would assume Mo had been successful.

There were two small high-speed pirate vessels, and in the half-light they appeared to be packed with natives. As the first vessel arrived and started to close, Blanco called out, "Keep away. We have engine and steerage problems. If you come any closer your vessel might get damaged. What do you want?"

The answer came back in rough English.

"We want your ship. If you are sensible you will surrender and we will land you on shore, except the lady who will be held as a hostage."

On the other side of the ship the second pirates' vessel was closing fast. Ordering full speed ahead, Blanco swung the *Yax Nixte* across the front of the nearest pirate vessel, bringing both of their vessels on one side of his ship and shouted to open fire. He rested the machine gun on the bridge rail and poured seventy-five mixed rounds of ball, armour pierce and tracer into the closest pirate vessel. John spotted a pirate standing up with a flame-thrower, and subjected him to a burst from his AK-47; his equipment caught fire and then he suddenly exploded in a ball of flame – it was napalm and there was no saving their vessel after that.

The second pirates' vessel was trying to pull away, but was caught in a full burst of Blanco's machine gun that wiped out their ship's heavy weapon gun crew. Keeping the pirate vessel under heavy fire, they closed up and then mercilessly shot and killed every pirate that remained alive. Returning to the second vessel they made sure there were no survivors, and then sank both vessels.

With the sharks closing in, Blanco decided it was time to leave the area and while cruising away, the expedition settled down to clean their weapons and clear away the empty cartridge cases.

As soon as the excitement calmed down, John climbed down into the engine room and released Mo, then brought him up to the bridge. Blanco, infuriated with the impostor who had endangered all their lives, picked him up and shook him, then flung him down on the deck.

"You had better explain yourself by telling everything, if you wish to continue living!"

Mo whimpered, "I don't remember very much… I was standing watch and went down to check the engine room, then something hit me and I woke up handcuffed to a rail!"

"Why did you continually signal the pirate ships until you received a reply? And why did you threaten the engineer with your pistol and tell him to stop the engines?"

"I do not wish to reply. I am an Indonesian and you have no right to detain me."

"I am the ship's captain and have full powers to secure you and take you to the nearest port for trial as a pirate."

"If you have a reasonable excuse for your actions I would advise you to tell me. Otherwise you remain in manacles in the chain locker until we are able to hand you over to the proper authorities.

"If you know where the real Mohammed Ismail is held prisoner, you might have your cooperation taken into consideration at your trial.

"Alternatively, if you continue to be stubborn and unhelpful I can arrange for you to fall overboard, and unfortunately the sharks will prevent any possibility of rescue."

"I admit I am *not* Mohammed Ismail, but he *is* safe in a house in Jakarta, and is due to be released as soon as the pirates confirm that your ship has been taken. I was forced to act his part, as a gambling syndicate will clear my debts if I take his place."

"That is all I wanted to know! John, arrange for one of the crew to give him food and water, then put him in the chain locker.

"There is no alternative other than to call in at Pedang and obtain instructions from Jakarta on how to proceed. We can be in the harbour in two hours and as you have observed, I have already changed course."

They arrived in Pedang Harbour two hours later and Blanco and Ricky went to the Harbour Master's office and Ricky telephoned the British Embassy Commercial Attaché. After the introductions Ricky informed him about the attack, assured him that they had not sustained casualties, but that both of the pirate vessels had been lost with all hands.

Ricky continued, "The Mohammed Ismail who joined us in Jakarta is an impostor, and the real gentleman is being held prisoner in a Jakarta house. The impostor clearly knows where Ismail is located, but has not confided that to us. In my view, serious questioning by the authorities in Jakarta might be the best solution, as it might resolve the matter before the pirates learn of the failed attack and decide to eliminate him.

"It is because we were attacked close to Pedang that we have called in here and held him on board until we receive instructions from Jakarta. Would you kindly advise the ambassador and the chief of Jakarta police? We all hope that Mohammed Ismail is unharmed and can be rescued quickly to join our expedition."

Ricky was then instructed to wait in the Harbour Master's office and they would contact him immediately the Jakarta police had been informed and a decision reached.

Two hours later everything started to happen, and they were told to return to the ship and speak to no one. A police escort was now taking off and should reach them in two hours' time. They said they would appreciate it if Ricky could return to Jakarta with them, where

James Foley would meet him at the airport and support him during discussions with the authorities.

Later, the escort arrived, consisting of four policemen and a superintendent to collect the prisoner. He was immediately manacled and shackled and pushed into a military van. Ricky was given a seat in one of the heavily armed escort vehicles and a mad rush was made to the airport. A military transport was waiting on the tarmac ready for take off, and in a matter of minutes they were on their way to Jakarta.

On arrival at the airport, James Foley met Ricky, and after an excited and very friendly greeting, he outlined the arrangements.

"The ambassador has arranged for the Chief of Police and a couple of his senior officers to come to the embassy to be briefed on the impostor and the pirates' attack. The ambassador suggests you give full details of how you detected the impostor, and limited detail on how the pirates were destroyed. As there are no survivors no one can argue and he thinks that this approach will be politically acceptable to the Indonesian authorities.

"In addition to all this there must be no press release! As far as the outside world is concerned there has been no incident. After the conference has been satisfactorily concluded, the ambassador has arranged a small dinner for you, with senior members of his staff, and of course I'm included, and he invites you to stay at his residence during your time in Jakarta."

"Thank the ambassador on my behalf, and confirm that the arrangements will suit me very well. This is certainly the best approach, and I will give the ambassador all the gory details after the reception!"

On arrival at the embassy conference room, he found the room crowded with Indonesian politicians and the Chief of Police with his advisers. After the introductions, Ricky and James were chatting with the Chief of Police when he was called to the telephone. When he returned he announced to the gathering, "I have been informed that the impostor has confessed, and has given us the location where Mohammed Ismail is being detained. A special military assault group has arrived in the area, and is about to move in."

Due to general excitement and heated discussions, the conference had to be delayed until the chief received a further message that the assault had been successful and Mohammed had been released unharmed, although exhausted by his ordeal. The mood of the assembly was joyful and Ricky had no problems in giving a brief report on the action that was accepted without question, and he was congratulated in detaining the impostor and for referring the matter directly to the Jakarta authorities.

"I wish to thank the Indonesian authorities for their rapid response and also to express the hope that Mohammed Ismail will be passed fit enough to join us in a couple of days, so that we can return together to the *Yax Nixte*. Perhaps I could meet him in your offices so that there would be no possibility of a further substitution?"

The final comment produced considerable merriment. Then a senior minister attending their briefing asked if they could provide a navy liaison officer, and if so would there be a cabin for him?

"Yes, we will be delighted to receive him, but that will complete all our available space, so I ask you to understand that we cannot accommodate any further additions. Again, I stress that he would be most welcome."

The dinner in the embassy went well. Ricky gave a detailed report of the action and of the expenditure of ammunition. The guests were shattered with the amount used and the armament they had available. Ricky pointed out that if they had not, by surprise tactics, won the fire fight, the result would have been very different as their actions had prevented the pirates from standing-off and bringing their heavy weapons into action.

When Ricky was able to get James alone he said, "I have a list of ammunition expended and I would appreciate your help to set up a meeting with Rashid tomorrow to obtain replacements, delivered to Pedang in two days' time. I appreciate we cannot tell Indonesian authorities directly, but I have a feeling they already know and not wishing to be involved will permit him to supply our requirements."

"You know I will have to tell the ambassador – I am sure he will understand the necessity to replace the full amount. However, there may be another method to deter pirates. As you may know, these vessels normally fit a multi-purpose Bofors canon for coastal patrol duty, and they will have the original in store in Jakarta. If you're interested we might suggest that they fit it on loan, during the rest of the survey. Doubtless Blanco is fully conversant with its operation. Anyway, we can only ask; if the authorities decline we are no worse off."

The next day, after James had advised the ambassador of the situation, he was then given permission to arrange the ammunition supply with Rashid. Meanwhile, the ambassador would take up the provision of the Bofors with the appropriate minister and would wait for the result.

James and Ricky met Rashid that afternoon and after arranging an extortionate payment, a deal was struck and the consignment would reach Pedang in two days' time.

The following day Ricky was invited to the offices of the Ministry of Culture, where he met Mohammed Ismail, a delightful and highly intelligent gentleman who would be a very real asset to their company. In reply to Ricky's question, he said he would be ready to travel in two days' time and that the ministry would arrange a flight to return them to Pedang.

Two days later they arrived in Pedang with a lieutenant of the Indonesian navy and joined the *Yax Nixte*. Rashid's consignment had already arrived, complete with a present for Ricky, sealed and marked private, which turned out to be a German Panzerfaust anti-tank rocket – a present that they hoped they would never have to use.

With all introductions made, they left the harbour and settled down to the two hundred and sixty kilometre-run to the Sunda group of islands. Arriving just before sunset, they anchored a kilometre off the shoreline east of Tanahbela.

The following day they decided to practise towing the special side-span sonar on their one hundred and twenty-kilometre run to their first selected search area, which started at Sikarbau and extended to Katiagan.

Setting up a pirate watch, the remainder of the expedition and crew retired to their bunks to get as much sleep as possible. Tomorrow would be the start of the first day's run to hunt for the massive harbour walls that, after so many years, would be covered with thick marine growth.

In the morning under the lee of Tanahbela, the sea was calm. So setting their helm at Sikarbau with just enough speed to give steerageway, the towed side-scan sonar array was lowered into the sea. Based on a twenty-metre test depth the array was set to run at nine metres below the surface, with an automatic surfacing command when the water depth was less than ten metres. At this setting the range was one hundred metres when running at twenty-five metres total sea depth.

John Goddard was sitting at the consul watching the scan on the monitor as the seabed changed from golden sand to a mixture of sand

and silt as the depth increased to a hundred metres for the crossing. With the automatic navigation readings, and the depth recordings displayed on a second monitor, it only remained for the captain to order the ship's heading. With the system working satisfactorily, at that depth there was little of interest. Anyway, at the end of the run, if the operator wished, he could pass the stored data through a HP system analyser that would automatically pick up any features above the seabed that had been pre-programmed, and display them with associated coordinates. The side-scan system had made fantastic advances over the last decade.

Having established that the system was working well, they decided to recover the unit and increase speed until the depth sonar recorded the depth decreasing to thirty metres. That evening, approaching Sikarbau, they anchored to prepare for their first run at daybreak.

When dawn broke they weighed anchor, and moved to the start point of their run. They then decreased speed to launch the side-scan sonar. Proceeding at six knots, they commenced a zigzag pattern starting at the landside with the fifteen-metre contour extending to the twenty-metre contour, and then repeated this pattern until they reached Katiagan, a distance of approximately one hundred and thirty kilometres. The time this was going to take depended on the distance between the contours, but the minimum would be four days and then a return to either Pedang or Sibolga to refuel.

By the time they reached Katiagan five days later they were exhausted, with no visible evidence of mounds or lines of uplifted beds that could be interpreted as buildings or harbour walls. So, low in fuel, they decided to go to Pedang.

Before leaving Katiagan, Amin checked with his headquarters and reported their intention to fuel at Pedang. Headquarters suggested that they should reconsider and refuel at Natal where they had their naval emergency refuelling installation. Just before reaching Natal they would find the secluded bay and harbour of Sumur. There, a naval armament section would be waiting to install the Bofors multi-purpose gun with an ample supply of ammunition – the weapon, to be effective and avoid political comment, had to be kept concealed under a canopy when refuelling, or if they visited for supplies.

Blanco told Amin to confirm acceptance immediately and give their estimated time of arrival at Sumur as 1600 hours the next day.

With the new weapon fitted and refuelled, they decided to search the Natal to Batang Toru section, a distance of approximately one hundred and fifteen kilometres.

After five days searching with the side-scan sonar, the results were similar to those of the first search pattern. During their early morning review, Frehier and Ricky were planning to link up the two search areas from Nata to Sikarbau.

Maria interjected: "Last night I had a vivid dream – I was looking down on the area between Labuhanrima and the mainland of Sumatra and in the centre, below the sea, I saw the harbour and a great building of similar massive block construction. In the dream I was being urged to look there first, as for some reason we had limited time, but there is no explanation why that should be. It was all so real and I beg you to change your plan and search that area first."

Ricky pondered and then replied, "Can you show us on the chart where you saw that vision?"

Maria replied immediately. "Yes. There!" She put her finger on the chart.

After a brief discussion, Ricky replied, "We both agree the position indicated is a possible location, but the depth in that area is approaching thirty metres. This is deeper than the current estimates on water-level change in that area between 5500 BC and today, but there may be other factors involved. So we have both agreed to move to your area first. If we find the signs of a harbour, we will go to a state of readiness and service our armaments, to be ready for any trouble that might be linked to the warning in your dream!"

So the *Yax Nixte* moved to the area selected and started their search just after midday. After four hours, a long rise in the seabed was seen on the sonar and this continued for two kilometres. In the centre of this run there was a further rise at right angles, heading towards the shore for at least one and a quarter kilometres.

Using satellite navigation they marked the outline on their chart, and Ricky said, "Maria, will you show me the position of the large building?"

Maria pointed to a position on the chart and said, "There! Yax sent my dream, at least I thought so, but was afraid to speak in case it was only a figment of my imagination! I also know there is more advice to be given, but what about, and when, is all in a mist."

Ricky ordered the side-scan to be retrieved, and replaced by launching the ROV submersible; with Kirk at the controls he started a meticulous examination of the mound, looking for the best place to remove the marine growth in order to examine the construction. With too many onlookers at Kirk's shoulder, Ricky ordered those not occupied to start drawing weapons and preparing them for action. In addition, he asked Amin to practise the previously selected native crew in the operation of the Bofors.

By nightfall Kirk had selected a suitable place for a personal inspection. The depth was thirty metres and by air diving they could have thirty minutes' time at the bottom to expose a block, providing one was there. Kirk and John would put on scuba gear and take a compressed air chisel down to remove the marine growth early the next day when the sun was sufficiently high to illuminate the sea floor.

Blanco, having organised defences, insisted that a watch should be maintained on the radar through the night. Once that was settled, the company departed to their bunks to await the dawn and the excitement they hoped would come with the confirmation of their find.

Next morning with the ROV in place Kirk and John descended to the selected spot and immediately started work. After the specified thirty minutes they returned to the surface and reported they had cleared part of two blocks and were satisfied that these mounds were part of a substantial harbour wall.

Kirk, having removed all his gear, said, "Having established that we have found a harbour wall of massive proportions, there is little point in proceeding further as the finding of any hieroglyphs on that construction is extremely unlikely. As Maria's intuition has proved accurate so far, I propose we use the ROV to record the result of our clearance, then retrieve it and launch the side-scan sonar. Once that is achieved we head towards the area of the building although the chance of both her forecasts being correct is frankly next to impossible!"

Maria, smiling, said, "Kirk, these are not *my* forecasts, they are revealed by something that exists and which I fully appreciate no scientist can accept."

The sonar was launched and the *Yax Nixte* moved slowly to the area indicated by Maria. After crossing it several times they discovered the edge of a substantial mound, and on the west side there seemed to be a large arch. Reverting to the ROV they made a recording of the complete mound, and took satellite positions on all corners. After studying the recordings Kirk said, "The arch is the best possible location for inscriptions, and I propose to make a second dive to attempt to find them."

Ricky replied, "One dive a day for that length of time is enough for anyone. Blanco and I will make the next dive and you can record the result with the ROV after we complete the dive. Depending on what, if anything, is revealed by then, we will agree the appropriate action. While we are diving, you, Amin, will be responsible for the safety of the ship."

Blanco and Ricky quickly put on their scuba gear and descended to the archway; its depth was about twenty metres, so down time could safely be extended to forty minutes. They started work immediately while Kirk, green with envy, watched the work on the ROV monitor. As soon as they returned and the water cleared sufficiently, he could make out the hieroglyphs. There was no longer any doubt about it; the expedition had been an extraordinary success.

As soon as Ricky and Blanco were dressed Kirk approached them. "The amount of inscriptions is insufficient to glean adequate data to establish its meaning, we need to extend the area. Using underwater lighting we can remove more of the marine growth, and if the forecast of limited time is correct, we must proceed immediately to uncover the rest. I'm rested and I expect John will also dive."

Mohammed, who up to this moment had not joined in the discussions on diving, intervened.

"I've done a fair amount of diving and would be happy to volunteer to undertake this dive, but need a partner."

Maria immediately interjected, "You have one… we'll do this together and it will underline the importance of the Indonesian side of this expedition!"

"Then it's settled – we continue with the clearance immediately!"

After forty minutes Mohammed and Maria surfaced with satisfied smiles on their faces, and informed the group around them that they had more than doubled the surface area and they believed the whole of the inscription was now visible. Kirk patiently waited until the sediment had settled and then brought the ROV in close. There it was! The complete inscription! Kirk froze the picture and printed out a perfect copy, and demanded to be left alone for an hour to interpret the hieroglyphs.

Later, after their evening meal, Kirk entered and, with a grand gesture, produced the interpretation:

Atlan
The City of the Third Civilization
This Arch is constructed to honour the memory
Of those who died in the Second Cataclysm.
Also those who survived and, enduring great hardship,
Founded the Third Civilization.

Then the company broke out two bottles of wine, reserved for the operation, and drank a toast to Kirk Frehier, and a second to Yax Nixte, dead but with them in spirit.

Ricky turned to the group. "Let us now try for the gilt on the gingerbread, that is the tomb in the mountains and the artefacts' storeroom, as finding this will help to authenticate the translation made from the Mexican stela."

"Ricky, let us sleep with our weapons and expect some kind of interruption later tonight or early tomorrow morning!"

"Maria, you have been right so far and I accept your advice. Amin, can you sleep by your gun with your gun crew? And Blanco, can you raise anchor and head out slowly, warning the engine room to pay particular attention to the telegraph."

Nothing happened until an hour before dawn, when three weak blips appeared on the radar screen, moving at high speed, clearly on an intercept course with the *Yax Nixte*. Blanco was called to the bridge, and decided to test their intent by increasing speed and making a substantial change in course. Almost immediately the boats adjusted their course to intercept.

Blanco called to Amin. "Can you determine if any of your ships are in this area, if any call for immediate support?"

After a short delay Amin replied, "All our ships are clear of this area, air support will be provided, but cannot reach us for at least one to one and a half hours. They wish us good luck and good hunting! I'm not sure the latter is appropriate!"

Blanco called to Amin. "Clear the bow railings, as you may have to shoot over the bow. I can't believe that the two high-speed launches intend to take on our ship – there must be something else!"

John, who was watching the radar, shouted, "There is another and larger blip on the screen moving directly towards us, not moving as fast as the launches but rapidly closing the distance."

Blanco shouted, "I'm going to close on one of the launches. Amin, fire a magazine when we shorten the range and you can get an effective shot. John, go down to the engine room and ensure that I'm given full speed when I call for it, and that there's no interference by other members of the crew."

Blanco realised that the high-speed launches intended to delay the *Yax Nixte* and in so doing allow the main vessel to close and bring up a heavy weapon to try and force surrender. Calling for maximum speed, Blanco swung the ship to starboard and there was little response from the engine room. Blanco shouted to Ricky, "John is having trouble in the engine room – can you check on him?"

Ricky found John alone in the engine room, with the speed controls locked off to hold the low speed. They both hurried to the crew's mess room and found the crew lying on the floor with one member holding a gun on them. As he started to turn round John shot him in the arm and kicked the gun to Ricky.

They moved them all to the engine room and dragged a now whimpering native to the locks. John put the gun to his head and told him to open them. He made a gesture to indicate he had thrown the keys overboard. John then shot him and stripped the body, found the keys in his shoes and released the locks, before advancing the controls to full speed.

He then ordered two of the crew to throw the body over the side. This having been done, he ordered the crew to stay in the engine room and respond to signals from the bridge, and any failure to perform would receive extreme punishment. They then locked the engine room hatch and returned to advise Blanco of the situation.

After hearing about the cause of the delay in the engine room, Blanco said, "The delay in obtaining full speed made me reconsider my options. Deciding that as there is no point in attempting to ignore evil, it's wiser to go and meet it.

"So I intend to go full speed to meet the pirate ship, holding fire as long as possible, then opening up with all of our armament with the intention of stopping her in the water. If we can achieve that we can play cat and mouse with the speedboats until the air force arrive and eliminate the opposition. Can you go and advise Amin of the situation regarding the natives and explain my immediate plan of action? Also, warn him he may have a traitor in his gun team!"

As soon as everyone had been warned, Blanco turned the ship

around and headed at full speed to directly intercept the pirate ship. They would be in range in two minutes and unless their vessel turned away, the action should reach a conclusion three minutes later. It was now a question of nerve and good seamanship, and Ricky believed Blanco had plenty of both.

The pirate vessel was the first to fire its 75 mm gun, the shell sailing over and to one side of the *Yax Nixte*. The next was again over, but in line. Blanco then swung out to the port and the next shell landed where the ship would have been – a close call!

Turning back on track, Blanco shouted, "Open fire!" The tracers from the Bofors curved gracefully into the pirate ship's bridge, at the same time seventy-five rounds from the MG15 decimated their gun crew.

Swinging the *Yax Nixte* out to port and bringing her round behind the pirate vessel, Blanco yelled to Amin, "Destroy her steering gear!" He needn't have worried as before he had finished his sentence the stern of their ship received substantial damage from the Bofors. Then, as they swept past to port, Amin fired into the hull where the engine room was normally located.

At this point Blanco turned away, keeping the ship out of sight of the bow gun of the pirate vessel in case it had been brought back into action with a new crew, which seemed to be the case as the two speedboats were moving in under the protection of their bow gun.

After all the guns were reloaded, Blanco asked Amin to report the action to his headquarters and ask when the air support would arrive, as they didn't wish to engage in a gun battle with the pirates who had advantages in range and weight of shot.

Amin contacted Jakarta and they informed him that three fighter bombers should be with him in fifteen minutes, adding that he should try to keep out of trouble for that time. In addition, Jakarta required a maximum of three prisoners, the rest to be left to their own devices, and they would appreciate it if Amin would kindly take the responsibility for selecting the three.

As promised, fifteen minutes later, the three fighter bombers swept over from the south and one by one dropped their bombs on the pirate vessel. The speedboats tried to escape but they disappeared in a curtain of cannon fire.

As the pirate vessel slowly rolled over and started to sink, Blanco brought the ship round for Amin to select three prisoners for Jakarta. With the selection completed and those rejected returned to the sea,

Ricky asked Amin, "Could you contact Jakarta and ask if the prisoners could be handed over at Natal? Also ask the navy if it could lend or hire us two jeeps for a couple of weeks or a single cross-country vehicle. Alternatively, is there a supplier in that area who could sell us two 4 x 4 vehicles suitable for rough terrain? These are required to explore a small mountain range north-east of Natal to complete our investigations in Indonesia."

Amin dealt with the matter immediately and two hours later received the reply from Jakarta.

It said to hold the prisoners in custody on board until a police superintendent and escort arrived from Jakarta. They were unable to offer good-condition 4 x 4 cross-country vehicles for that terrain, as local suppliers were unsuitable. Rashid could supply new, or on monthly hire, suitable Japanese vehicles within three days at Natal, subject to agreement on associated costs, and if required camping equipment to be specified could also be provided.

They also suggested that they should contact Rashid immediately they reached Natal. Before closing down, they emphasised that they were extremely concerned for their safety in the area, and proposed they included two Indonesian armed guides from their special ranger company. They assumed they still had personnel weapons and these should be taken.

Ricky then addressed the members of the expedition.

"I believe we have obtained our objective by locating the city and that any further underwater exploration will require a permanent presence for a number of years but this is not part of our present expedition. So we will return to Natal, refuel and hand over the prisoners.

"We will obtain from Rashid three vehicles – the first two will transport the expedition members. The third will carry the two rangers, a cook and camping equipment. Water, provisions and fuel will be equally divided between the vehicles and will be sufficient for fourteen days.

"When this part of the expedition is successfully completed, we will return the *Yax Nixte* to Jakarta and if possible, dispose of our equipment, before returning home.

"The next stage will be to plan the Egyptian expedition; are there any changes required to this plan?"

Mohammed stood up. "If I can get permission, can I join you for the Egyptian expedition?"

"Both you and Amin are members of our expeditions, and are most welcome provided the Indonesian and Egyptian authorities have no objections. You will be kept advised of our plans so that we can all meet up at Cairo, possibly six to nine months after we leave Indonesia."

The following day they arrived at Natal and anchored in the harbour, and Ricky asked Amin to alert Jakarta of their arrival and tell them of their plans and grateful acceptance of the two rangers. Ricky and Blanco crossed the harbour in the inflatable to the Harbour Master's office, where they negotiated a deal with Rashid for three vehicles and camping equipment. As they were about to return to the ship, an American reporter and cameraman approached them.

"Hi there, which one of you is Mr McKay? My name is Mike and I represent International World News Syndicate – will you give us a statement on the success of your expedition for the international press? I heard you had a brush with pirates. That story will get world interest and bolster up the limited interests in an archaeological search for Atlantis!"

Ricky replied, "Your information did not emanate from our expedition members and is incorrect. This is a joint expedition with the Indonesian government, and we have a formal agreement that all press releases will be made through the authorities in Jakarta."

"Well, can we come out and take some pictures of your ship and expedition members?"

"No, I'm afraid we are very busy at present, so we must say goodbye."

"OK, if that's the way of it! But we will follow the expedition you're about to make into the interior of Sumatra. So why not let us join your party?"

Breaking off the discussion, Ricky and Blanco got into the inflatable and returned to the *Yax Nixte*.

Two days later, the prisoners were handed over to the Superintendent of Police, and shortly afterwards Rashid's drivers delivered the three cross-country vehicles, complete with spares and camping equipment. In the meantime, Amin had organised a naval guard for their ship, and with Mohammed, checked out and employed a cook. So wasting no time, they set out for the mountains, Kirk and John leading the way towards the mountain group some eighty kilometres from Atlan.

As they started to climb up the central mountain, Maria shouted, "Stop here! This is our camp!"

They stopped and Ricky asked, "Maria, why here?"

"I just don't know, Ricky, I recognise the spot but... of course I've never *been* here! I can't explain why I said those words, but having done so, I recommend we make our first camp here."

"Maria, there's no water here!"

Maria answered in a vague sort of way. "There's a stream of sweet water just behind those bushes."

Blanco crashed through the undergrowth and shouted back, "There *is* a clean stream coming directly from a spring in the rocks. It's an ideal place to camp."

Ricky gave Maria a strong embrace. "Your insight is amazing, forgive me for doubting your word, or should I say the words from your ancestors!"

The next morning, just before they were about to set out on a reconnaissance, Maria came up to Ricky and said with a sleepy voice, "I know where the cave is located; the cars will not be able to go much further. Just up there on the left is a narrow path leading up the mountain – we follow that to a point just above the cave. Descending to a shelf, the cave entrance will be found behind boulders, we have to take weapons and a sufficient store of torches and spare batteries. I saw all of this in my dreams last night! Kirk and one ranger are to come with us, the rest must stay to protect the camp and our transport. Warn them of a possible attack, they will be safe if they are vigilant, and we will be away most of the day."

Ricky was astounded but in view of Maria's past performance he could not ignore her proposal. Calling the other members together he told them of Maria's advice and asked them if it should be adopted. After a brief discussion, even Kirk approved the proposal, although the thought of supernatural direction was difficult for him to swallow.

So the plan was adopted, and after an exhausting three-hour walk they found themselves standing on a shelf on the edge of a precipice, contemplating a mass of boulders. Maria walked up to the group of tightly packed rocks and pointed.

"The entrance is here! Move them to one side carefully, as they must be replaced in the same order when we leave."

With the four of them working, the boulders were quickly removed and there was the entrance to the cave. Kirk turned round to Maria.

"Who told you? This is far too accurate for any dream!"

"It was all in my dream last night, but now I believe I've always known about it, rather like a lost memory. That is all I can tell you, but I can't remember my real name."

After that statement she walked into the tunnel and when they were all inside, spoke to the ranger. "Guard this entrance and remain concealed!"

"With my life, my lady."

Walking down the cave they came to the perfectly circular tunnel and Maria pointed to the inscriptions on the wall, which Kirk photographed. Then, descending the tunnel, they came to two rooms. Maria turned to Kirk.

"Under your feet is a slab, which has to be removed to access the tomb."

The three of them only just managed to lift one end and slide it clear. This revealed a staircase descending to two rooms. One room was empty except for pieces of timber from which Ricky broke off a sample; the other had a portal with a stone slab door that had been displaced just sufficiently to squeeze past.

The walls and the sarcophagus were covered with hieroglyphs, and as Kirk and Ricky were busy taking photographs, Maria knelt down beside the sarcophagus with tears running down her face.

"As I vowed, my Lord, I have returned. Thoth is already on his way to you. I weep for our people and for my love of you."

Maria got up and, in a distressed state, asked, "Have you completed your photography? We should leave now."

"Can we slide the sarcophagus lid back to see the mummy?"

"There is no mummy, just the remains, which must not be disturbed. I must ask you in kindness to me to leave it undisturbed. I now know my name when I was last here – it is Isis! But that will be forgotten completely when I leave this island. There are no jewels or gold in the coffin; in those days we went out the same way we entered, as goods of this world had no value after death. Let us leave now."

Kirk replied, "We will leave at once since there's nothing to keep us here."

Ricky agreed, and reaching the room at the top of the staircase, they replaced the stone cover and spread the dust over it so that the slab would no longer be visible.

The guard at the entrance of the cave saw them coming towards him with Maria in front, and as he looked at her she appeared to be dressed as Isis, wearing her royal robes, and he sank down on his knees as she passed, but when she stood out on the ledge she was again Maria Martinez. The guard rushed out and knelt down before her, saying, "My lady, do you know who you are?"

Maria smiled down at him and said, "Yes, I was Isis, a High Lord of your country, but I am now Maria Martinez, a Maya from Mexico. This must remain a secret between us."

"Will you first give me your blessing?"

For the last time as Isis in Indonesia, she gave him a blessing in the tongue of the Atlan, and then continued down the path with the others.

As they were approaching camp in the late afternoon, Maria asked them to wait a little time and then turned to the ranger, suggesting he approach the camp silently and without being seen to determine the situation and then return.

After twenty minutes he returned to report the camp had been surprised by a group of armed men who were waiting in ambush for their return. He believed he could rescue the other ranger if they could start coming down the path singing or making a loud noise but not to go further than a tree he pointed to. "Give me ten minutes to get into position and after releasing the other guard I will join you there." He then slipped away into the undergrowth.

After the allotted time to allow the ranger to take up his position, they started singing and moved slowly down the path, making a lot of noise. Reaching the tree, still singing and shouting, they continued the noise until the two rangers appeared. The rangers signalled them to follow as they guided them through the heavy cover away from the track until they reached the rear of the camp.

The rangers then explained their plan. "There are two guards watching the prisoners who are separated. Both of us will try to remove them silently. Immediately that happens you have to release your friends, who must rearm and fall back to this position, then wait. When the ambush party realise they have been discovered, they will move back to camp and we will then be in a strong position and they will either surrender or die. We go now!"

A few minutes later there was a gurgling sound and two natives fell to the ground. The three of them rushed out and released the prisoners, who grabbed their weapons and, with the rangers, waited for the return of the ambush party.

After their treatment, Ricky's party were not interested in allowing them to surrender and as the terrorists entered, they became overexcited and ran over to examine the dead guards. This was an ideal target and Blanco and John immediately expended two magazines from their AK-47 assault rifles; there were no survivors but to be safe, the two rangers searched the area, but as far as they could judge no one had escaped.

The rangers advised that it was unwise to remain in the vicinity and they should load up and return to Natal immediately. There was no argument and they were soon on the road, ready to annihilate any interruption to their return journey.

Reaching the harbour, Ricky stayed in the Harbour Master's office to make arrangements for the cars to be returned to Rashid, and then paid off the cook with the addition of a hardship bonus. He then invited the two rangers to visit the *Yax Nixte* for a drink and a suitable award for their actions in saving the expedition.

By the time they arrived, Blanco had everything running like clockwork and a hot meal was already waiting in the mess room. Amin had advised Jakarta of their return and praised the behaviour of the rangers. So there was nothing left to do other than to thank the naval party for taking care of the ship during their absence.

After disposal of the vehicles, Amin told Ricky that Jakarta had asked them to call in at the Indonesian naval base at Cateureup, where the Bofors could be removed from public scrutiny before they continued their journey to Jakarta.

Privately, Ricky and Kirk had agreed that no mention would be made of the sarcophagus to the other members of the team. Translations of the hieroglyphs would be sent to Mohammed Ismail as soon as Kirk completed the considerable task of making the translations in the UK.

Returning to Jakarta they had a meeting at the embassy to finalise the questions regarding the joint release date of information to the press. This would occur when both interested parties had studied and approved the report on the Indonesian expedition. For political reasons it was agreed that no mention would be made of the pirates and the EWARC report would only concern itself with archaeological matters.

When it came down to the disposal of the *Yax Nixte*, the Indonesian government were interested in purchasing the ship, so Ricky reduced the price of both it and its equipment by assessing the cost he would have incurred if he had hired all of it for one year, and this was accepted.

In addition, he asked the relevant Indonesian authorities to keep them informed on any progress they might make in clearing the city and harbour of Atlan. In return they would keep them up to date on the results of the Egyptian expedition, if Mohammed Ismail was unable to join the team at the start in Cairo. This was all agreed and the members of the expedition headed home to rest, before starting work on the report and preparing for the Egyptian expedition.

First Civilization

5500 BC

Seth set up camp in a concealed location bordering the Nile and outlined his plan to take over command of the Egyptian expedition.

"The most important part of my plan is to ensure that no one knows that I am here. If their expedition came to hear of my presence, they would be warned and my plan would fail.

"This is what we will do – Enki and Heti, you will go to the expedition camp and ask to speak to Osiris, and when he sends for you, greet him with great respect and tell him this story.

"You have come from the Mesopotamian expedition in the mountains; unfortunately, as Lord Seth did not believe the Prophecy, shelters had not been built, and most of our companions were lost in the storm.

"The survivors split into two groups – one group to go and search for food, and anything else they could find that would be of assistance during our return journey to the gulf, and then return to camp, and the other, to stay to bury the dead, and then to start work on re-establishing our temporary base.

"We carried out our responsibilities and waited for the others to return. After a month, we had run out of supplies, and we all agreed that to stay in this location would result in our starving to death. As there was nothing left in this desolate mountainous area, we had no sensible alternative other than to abandon the base.

"Appreciating that the others had gone south and presumably failed to find anything, we decided to walk out to seek food in the west, as we were confident the other party would have returned had they been successful.

"Eventually, half-starved and in a sorry state, we reached the coast where the storm damage was less severe, and food could be collected in the countryside. Turning south, we followed the coast to make for Egypt and to join up with your expedition. Failing to realise that Qena was so close to our present position, we made camp to rest for a

233

while before continuing our journey. It was at this location that we made a surprising discovery.

"We had been clearing a shelter by cutting into the floor of a ravine that had a small stream running through it that flowed into the Nile. It was then we found that the rocks we had to remove were extremely heavy and, on examination, they revealed an occasional metallic glint.

"After cleaning them in the stream, they appeared to be formed by a composite of various rocks that included a considerable number of gold nuggets; the purity of the nuggets was such that they must derive from the mother lode.

"I have two small samples to show you, and that is why we asked to see you alone, as the presence of large quantities of gold might cause difficulties among the expedition members. On the other hand the presence of this mineral wealth in the hands of a dedicated council might facilitate the rapid completion of your city, by attracting peoples from the north to come and work for you and to provide materials not available locally.

"The other solution is to seal the site and access it when the need arises for funds. The answers to these possibilities must rest with you, not only as the leader of this expedition, but also as High Lord.

"At the present there are only three of us with knowledge of this find, which includes the third member of our group who is at present guarding the site.

"I expect Osiris will then ask you a lot of questions about how much of the lode is there and whether there will be difficulties in extraction.

"You will then point out that you have no knowledge of mining processes, but he is welcome to make a private assessment at any time. You will then present the samples we removed from that native gold miner, before he had that rather fatal accident!

"Osiris will want to make a careful examination of the samples, as these are very impressive. Listen to his observations and try to guide him into making a visit, if possible alone, with one of you acting as guide. The other will leave after you depart and take the shorter way back to our camp to warn me of their impending visit."

The subsequent visit by Enki and Heti to the Egyptian expedition was a resounding success, even more so when they revealed that the Mesopotamian expedition has been a disaster, although there was some sadness at the high level of casualties among their friends.

When the excitement had calmed they asked if they could see Osiris; this was granted at once and they told him the fabricated story, which they concluded by presenting him with the samples.

Osiris was intrigued with the story of their nine hundred-itru trek and even more so with the gold samples.

He congratulated them for not revealing the find to the expedition members, as at this moment it would be an unwanted distraction from implementing the plans for the city development.

In addition, revealing the find to the expedition members, before he had decided what policy for the general good should be adopted, might well have caused trouble.

Taking all this into consideration, Osiris turned to Enki.

"Is it possible for me to visit the site?"

"It is a fair walk away, but if we started immediately you could return before dark." Osiris then agreed with Enki's proposal and they set out at once.

Shortly afterwards, Heti slipped out of camp and took the short cut to where Seth was anxiously waiting, before informing him that Osiris was on his way. Having previously selected a good ambush position, Seth got ready with his kris to make a quick kill from behind. The dastardly attack on Osiris was all over in a flash and he died immediately.

Back in the expedition camp, Thoth wanted to speak with Osiris and asked where he had gone. He was informed that Osiris was last seen leaving the camp with one of the new arrivals. After they left, the other new arrival had been observed leaving camp furtively.

Thoth retorted, "I have no information on these new arrivals! Do you know where they came from?"

One of the Giants replied, "From the Mesopotamian expedition that had apparently failed."

Thoth became alarmed and ran at once to Isis.

"If what I fear has happened you must prepare to leave by transporter immediately with your child, as Seth dare not leave you or your child alive, if he is in any way involved. A number of matters require our immediate attention – we have to take immediate action to prevent Seth from accessing the artefacts. Hathor presents a more difficult problem; she must be informed as it might be safer for her to leave with us, but would her husband be willing to accompany her? If Seth believes Hathor knows the artefacts' location she might have a very difficult time, but as a Priestess of the Temple her status should provide limited protection.

"While you are advising Hathor and preparing to leave, I will take a quick flight to find the whereabouts of Seth and his companions."

Thoth then took off immediately, flying silently at just above treetop level; he glimpsed Seth and his three companions hurrying back towards the expedition's camp – there was no sign of Osiris. Tracing their tracks back, he came to a clearing which had obviously been their camp and close by, in the reeds, he found the body of Osiris. He had no time to investigate and returned with all haste to Isis, who was waiting for him.

"Isis! Osiris is dead! With your agreement we must leave at once; we will fly to the tomb of Osiris's ancestor. When we arrive you must make everything ready to receive him, while I go back and recover the body. Then together we will take him down to the tomb.

"Although Seth's party are well on their way to our camp, they still have a considerable distance to travel, that is, if they realise the stupidity of leaving the body in the open, but I can safely recover the body before one of them has sufficient time to return and dispose of the evidence."

Clasping the child Horus to her body, and holding back her misery and tears, Isis replied, "We will leave immediately and all shall be as you have proposed."

They took off in the transporter and after an uneventful flight, they arrived at the top entrance of the cavern, the other entrance being blocked and completely hidden by the substantial landslide, and Isis and child stepped out onto the shelf and entered the tunnel.

Thoth returned to Seth's camp, landed and recovered the body of his friend, before placing it on the transporter and carrying it back to Isis.

The two of them silently carried the body down through the cavern into the tomb and laid the body close to his ancestor.

Isis, with great lamentations and tears, examined the wounds Osiris had suffered, then swore a great oath to ReRa that for every wound suffered by her beloved, she would make Seth and his conspirators suffer twenty times the number while they still lived; their bodies would then be torn to bits and thrown on a dung heap.

After laying his body out in the tomb Thoth led her back to the transporter. Fortunately, all the artefacts and scrolls were already safely stored in the cavern. They decided to seal the only opening to the cavern and tomb, and to achieve this they flew above the ledge and landed close to the top of the cliff where the ground near the edge was unstable due to the heavy earthquake aftershocks.

The two of them pushed boulders over the top, causing the ledge and entrance to the tunnel to break away, when suddenly, with a deep rumble, the ground started to slip. They both jumped back and a large section of the hillside slid down over the entrance; the subsequent mixing of this rubble with the lower landslide made the location unrecognisable, completely changing the appearance of the hillside.

When the dust had settled they boarded their transporter and headed south to find a secure refuge for Isis and her child Horus.

Meanwhile Seth, Enki, Heti and Shiva arrived at the expedition's base and Seth, using his status of High Lord, called a meeting with all the expedition members. Then, standing on a raised platform, he addressed the Giants.

"I have some bad news for all of us! Hoping to achieve a reconciliation with Osiris, I arranged a private meeting with him, as I needed his acceptance before joining you all after the disastrous end of the Mesopotamian expedition.

"The meeting began well but in the end we both realised a reconciliation was impossible. Osiris was upset and said he was returning to his camp and in walking down the wrong path on the edge of the Nile he unfortunately disturbed a large crocodile, which seized him and dragged him down into the waters.

"We heard his shouts and rushed to help, but we were too late and there was nothing we could do to recover the body.

"In view of this sad situation it is necessary to appoint a new leader of your expedition, and it is therefore my duty as a very senior High Lord to take up this vacancy, and in doing so I will try to follow the excellent plans established by the late High Lord Osiris.

"I must now ask you all to continue the work allocated to you, while I familiarise myself with the plans for your city and the best use of the native labour. To do this, I wish to consult High Lord Isis and Councillor and High Priest Thoth. Would they please come forward and join me for further deliberations?"

There was no movement from the shocked assembly of Giants.

Seth, growing red in the face, shouted, "Where are you? I mean you no harm."

There was no reply, and the meeting dispersed.

Seth then spoke quietly to Shiva. "Question all the Giants and find out where they are, or where have they gone and why. There is surely no way they could have known of my presence, or, for that matter, the death of Osiris before this meeting!

"If you have any difficulty in obtaining answers, warn them that any prevarication on their part or any concealment of this affair will result in the application of severe strictures resulting from my displeasure with their behaviour."

After several hours, Shiva returned to Seth.

"I have questioned a large number of Giants who initially were not very cooperative until I gave them your warning.

"It now appears that Thoth spoke with Isis who started to pack clothes and provisions for her child and herself, then Thoth left on a transporter for a short while, returning to Isis who became very upset.

"The three of them then departed on the transporter, and no one knows where they have gone."

Seth then asked, "Are there any additional transporters and if so, where are they stored?"

"I did not ask that question, all I know is that they have made a secret store for the artefacts. But no one is sure of its exact location, as they were taken to it, and returned from it, by air."

"Shiva, you had the job of clearing the camp. What did you do with the body of Osiris?"

"As agreed, I threw it in the Nile but unfortunately it was not carried away by the current, having been trapped in the reeds. At that point the water was out of my depth and I had to leave the body there, but by now the crocodiles must have disposed of it."

"Find Enki and return to the place where you last saw the body; if it is still there destroy it, if it has gone, try and establish if a crocodile had devoured it, or if it had been removed by any other means. Leave at once, it is very important."

Seth, thinking about the disappearance of Thoth the High Priest, wondered who was looking after the temple, and decided to give it a visit.

On entering the temple, Seth encountered Hathor, who he could not recall as being part of the Egyptian expedition.

Intrigued, he asked, "Are you the priest in charge of the temple?"

"Yes I am, the appointment was given to me by Osiris when the temple was dedicated; also I work under the instruction of the High Priest Thoth."

"Where has he gone?"

"I was not informed, but I do know he left with Isis on a long trip, as they took provisions and clothes with them. I am sad, as they left without saying goodbye."

"Was the child with them?"

"I did not see them leave, but I am sure she would never have left without the child."

"What are the artefacts, and where are they kept?"

"The only artefact I have seen and in one case, driven, is the transporter. I have also seen the scrolls that describe the means of operating the artefacts, which as yet I am unable to decipher; but I am receiving instruction from Thoth regarding their interpretation.

"The artefacts and scrolls are stored in a deep cavern in the mountains, but I have never been to the store. Thoth recently brought a few of the scrolls to the temple when he was attempting with some difficulty to teach me the ancient symbols. I do know he is compiling a dictionary to relate them to our modern writings."

"Do you intend to continue as priest of the temple?"

"I believe this is your decision, if you wish me to continue it will give me great comfort to serve ReRa."

Seth told her he confirmed her position and then left.

A little later Shiva returned with Enki and reported to Seth.

"There is no sign of the body or of any crocodile tracks or parts of a body; however, we did find two drag marks in the silty soil from the water's edge to a spot in a clearing where they stop. The ground seemed disturbed but that is all we could find – it is our impression that the body had been removed but have no idea how this could have been achieved."

Seth thanked them and said, "I want the three of you to locate this artefact store and to do so, prepare for a four-week journey. Select two Giants who have worked there and know the general direction to act as guides. Take weapons with you in case you encounter opposition. After two weeks send Heti back to inform me of your location, and also to provide details of the progress you have achieved up to that time. If you encounter Isis and child, kill them, but bring Thoth back for interrogation. Leave by first light tomorrow morning."

The luckless trio left early next morning. The two Giants who were to act as guides had little or no idea of the distance or of the terrain over which they had travelled by air, as they had been incapable of concentrating on the direction or landscape, as during most of the flight they were paralysed with fear. The Giants held out one small hope to the trio that they could recognise the mountain, at least, as it was before the devastation, but they would find that this description would be useless in their search.

Thoth, Isis and her child Horus were heading south on the transporter, having spent the previous night on a rocky outcrop, huddled round a fire to give some protection from wild animals that roamed the savannah.

On the afternoon of the third day they were approaching the Ethiopian highlands when Isis observed a large number of natives hidden in ambush, awaiting the approach of an important-looking procession.

"Land discreetly near that great litter being transported by forty natives, and inform the Great Chief that I request an audience with him."

Thoth landed and the whole column froze with apprehension. Thoth walked slowly towards the litter and as he approached, the curtain was pulled aside and a tall, intelligent-looking young Negro stepped out.

Thoth, after a year's contact with the natives, had achieved a reasonable working knowledge of the native dialect, so he bowed and said, "My lady requests an audience with you, which I am sure will be advantageous to both of you."

The man smiled and replied, "I will be honoured to speak with her."

He then ordered his servants to set up a table and cushions close to the transporter with food and drink, and then, bowing to Isis, he said in the tongue of Atlan, "I know a little of your language which was passed on to me by my family who had contact with your society, so I welcome you and ask what assistance you require of my people."

Isis replied, "I have a request, but first I must warn you that you and your party are marching into danger. An ambush has been set up where the road goes between two small humps covered with undergrowth, and a large number of armed men are hiding on either side of the road.

"If you need confirmation of this you are welcome to send one of your brave young men with my High Priest so that he can see for himself."

The Chief replied, "My name is Sheha and I am the King and Tribal Chief of this vast land. Kindly understand that I believe and trust you, and wish to accept your offer by sending my Commander of the Scorpions. He would require to fly just close enough to the ambush to assess the situation, if possible without drawing their attention to your magic carpet. This will enable our response to be both swift and deadly."

King Sheha called for his commander and then Isis asked Sheha to reassure him that he would be completely safe and on this he had the word of Isis, High Lord of Atlan. The commander looked relieved, then bowed to Isis and thanked her.

Then with Thoth he stepped onto the transporter which took him first to one side of the ambush and then on the other side, keeping the transporter below the level of the scrub, so that if any of the natives had been looking their way they would only have seen their heads, but they were not detected.

Meanwhile Isis, holding back her grief for Osiris, was appreciating the food and refreshing drink provided by Sheha, while they discussed the effect of the storm on his community. The commander returned, bowed to the group and then spoke rapidly to the King and departed, and then the King invited Thoth to sit at their table.

Sheha turned to Isis. "I have sent runners from here to alert two columns of Scorpions who are some one and a half itru behind our procession. As soon as it is dark, my elite troops will silently approach and attack the ambush from both sides. The road will then be open to my mountain stronghold. Now, what assistance do you require from my kingdom?"

"I ask for accommodation and protection for Thoth, my child and myself. My husband was the High Lord responsible for the Atlan expedition to Egypt, and four days ago he was lured away from his camp and brutally murdered.

"Seth, the murderer, had also planned to kill the three of us, as I could challenge him in the future, and my son Horus will inherit by birth a power greater than Seth. Due to the foresight of Thoth, our Chief Priest and Magician, his first attempt on our lives has been foiled and we escaped just in time.

"There is little I can offer in return for your assistance, other than helping to thwart future attacks by use of our transporter.

"When my son, Horus, reaches manhood I intend, with, I hope, your help, to return to Egypt, defeat the tyrant and make Horus king. This will inevitably result in a bond of friendship between our two countries, which will be of mutual benefit to both."

"You will have adequate accommodation close to my rooms, servants and provisions will be provided. You will all have the full prestige of your rank in my country. Horus will be made an honorary member of my elite infantry, the Scorpions, who will teach him the arts of war as soon as he is old enough for training. You are all most welcome in my country and I look forward to a long and lasting friendship."

As promised, the attack on the ambush was both silent and deadly; the enemy were completely annihilated with minimum Scorpion casualties.

With the action complete the King's procession, with a strong escort, made its way past the piles of enemy dead, which were being searched and then cremated on a large fire, with the triumphant Scorpions dancing and cheering to celebrate their victory – a macabre spectacle.

The years passed swiftly by. With the help of Thoth and the magic carpet, the strongest enemies of their country were defeated with heavy losses; no further attempts were made to challenge the boundaries of this kingdom.

Horus was now growing in strength and was enjoying his time with the Scorpions who soon made him a full member as he had become proficient with all the weapons. At eighteen years old, he was a full-grown Giant, taller than all the Scorpions, who themselves were the tallest among their own people.

It was then that Isis decided this would be a suitable time for Horus to return to Egypt and claim his throne, and she told Sheha of her decision.

"I will be sad to see you leave, and fully understand your reasons. However, may I suggest you wait for a year, as during that time Horus must go on intensive training with the Scorpions, including long forced marches over difficult terrain. Then together with my Scorpions and two heavy infantry columns, we will march on Qena. That part of the exercise must be kept a secret, as news travels fast in this country. Even about Goddesses who arrive unannounced!

"While Horus is away on his final training, I will have a small and beautiful temple built to the glory of ReRa and dedicated to the Goddess Isis."

Isis thanked Sheha and accepted his plan without reservation.

Horus then set out on his year's battle training with the Scorpions in the remote parts of the country.

A month later, two Giants, Enki and Shiva, came to the stronghold and requested an audience with King Sheha.

When asked who they represented, Enki replied, "The King of Egypt."

When asked to name their king, Enki replied, "The High Lord Seth."

When Sheha heard this he immediately had them thrown into prison, and informed Isis and Thoth.

Isis asked, "Have you been told the names of the two messengers?"

"Shiva and Enki."

Thoth laughed. "Well, that is very unlucky for them as they were the two Giants I saw leaving the place where Osiris was murdered. They must be severely interrogated to obtain confirmation of their foul deed, also to establish the state of the Egyptian expedition and the whereabouts of the third Giant involved. I presume you have suitable methods to extract the truth, alternatively we can use our method, which is very severe and will end in their very painful deaths."

Sheha replied, "We will use our method first; if that fails we will use your final solution. Thoth, you can ask the questions and I will add any other I think may have been omitted. The questioning will be unpleasant, and it might be advisable for Isis not to watch the proceedings, but to be advised of the results."

Isis laughed. "I thank you for your kind consideration, but I assure you that having to witness numerous Giant interrogations, I would not be disturbed with any methods you may decide to use.

"As I am fully satisfied that the complicity in my husband's murder by these miscreants has been established, it is now essential that the present activities of Seth must be divulged for us to devise his downfall with the minimum of losses to our forces. In essence I wish to attend!

"To condition the two Giants before interrogation, could I suggest they should be held in separate cells? When taken separately for interrogation, could it be arranged for the prisoner to be passed slowly through a room in which there is a large board, of their own height, placed at an angle to the wall, with fresh animal blood running down it onto the floor? This will remind them of the Giants' method of interrogation used for native criminals, but not as yet on Giants."

"This will be done. Let us start after midday by which time all the necessary arrangements can been made. While waiting, I suggest we have a light lunch."

After lunch, they went down to the caves below the rock fortress, entering a large room carved out of the rock face. On one side there was a pleasant-looking alcove cut into the rock wall, with cushions laid out on the matting-covered floor for their comfort, and a servant standing by with refreshments. The main room was a stark contrast – a rock floor, and a large brazier holding lighted charcoal being occasionally brought up to red heat by a slave operating a pair of crude bellows.

Close to the brazier were three muscular Negroes with daunting countenances whose job it was to extract the truth from prisoners committed to their hands. Hanging from the ceiling were chains with manacles attached and on the floor a large wooden platform with shackles for the feet separated by bronze rods. The walls were lined with instruments of torture. Flaming torches cast dancing black shadows on the walls, illuminating the room; the effect was enough to frighten the life out of anyone.

Sheha stood up. "Let the first prisoner be brought in!"

Manacled and shackled, the first prisoner – Enki – was dragged in, naked, terrified and pleading for mercy.

"Enki, you have been brought here to be questioned; if you refuse to answer any question I will have you tortured until you do. Should you be foolish enough to lie, you will be punished immediately, and then will be encouraged to give the correct answer. All your answers will be checked against your companion's replies – if they do not match, the punishment will be severe. If you are totally truthful your case will be reviewed and a decision made as to your possible release. Do you understand?"

Enki sobbed, "Yes," and collapsed onto the floor.

Sheha called to the torturers, "Put him up."

Enki was then manacled up to the ceiling chains and shackled to the floor with his legs held apart. One of the torturers then took a red-hot bar from the furnace and slowly brought it close to the prisoner's body moving it from head to toe, so that he should feel the heat, then returned it to the fire.

Sheha asked Isis to ask the questions, which she proceeded to do.

"Was Seth with you when you left the Mesopotamian camp?"

"Yes."

"Why did he leave when he was in charge of the expedition?"

Enki tried to make up a reply, but the torturer, seeing his hesitation, grabbed the bar from the fire and seeing him approach, Enki blurted out, "He was drunk and killed a Giant."

"He was put under arrest and due to be branded?"

"Yes."

"How did he escape?"

"He killed the guards."

"Did you help?"

"We caused a diversion."

"Why did Osiris leave the expedition's camp and go to the spot where he was killed?"

"He was told we had found gold and then we showed him samples. He was then asked to give us advice on what to do, as we did not wish to cause difficulties in the camp."

"Did he know Seth was there?"

"No."

"Who killed him?"

"Seth, from an ambush."

"Were you present?"

"Yes."

"What was the reason for your visit?"

"That the King of Egypt demands that the King of Ethiopia immediately returns the criminals Isis and Thoth, who he knows are in his custody. If you fail to do so he will lay waste your lands and take them by force!"

"Apart from the Giants, has he raised an army?"

"When I left he was about to do so, but this will be difficult, as the natives do not trust him. However, he will take hostages from their families to ensure they fight for him."

"Where is Heti?"

"He was killed when he gave Seth an unsatisfactory report after returning from the hunt for the artefacts."

"Did they find the artefacts?"

"No."

Isis said she had finished with the questioning.

"I agree we have heard enough. Enki is guilty of assisting in the murder of the guards and that of Osiris. The minimum punishment for that would be to work in the mines as a slave until he dies. To threaten the Kingdom of Ethiopia is automatically punishable by a painful death. Should you wish to apply the minimum punishment I will accept your decision."

"Your decision is perfectly correct and I fully support it, but if possible their deaths should not be made public in view of our proposed return to Egypt. Let it be generally believed that they have been allowed to return, having freely given us all the information required. I also want these criminals to know that I will be witnessing their deaths. When that time is near, can I be informed and attend, as I also intend to witness the very painful death of Seth. All of this being part of my oath I made when I laid my beloved to rest."

The year's exercise passed quickly. Horus had benefited from the physical demands required by the long forced marches, and had developed into full manhood. Now he had the physique of a warrior – thin, muscular – and was a fully trained member of the Scorpions elite. He was impatient to commence the operation that would destroy the forces of the man who had murdered his father, and to bring him to a horrific end.

As soon as the annual Nile inundation had passed, the expedition force set out on the long march to Qena. King Sheha led the army, wishing revenge on the usurper who had threatened his country, and desirous of seeing a friend and strong ally as King of Egypt.

The expedition force consisted of three companies of Scorpions and two regiments of heavy infantry, in all, some three thousand warriors and the associated camp followers. It would take them two months to reach Qena, but there would be no problems with supplies as they intended to keep close to the Nile where there was ample game coming in from the vast savannahs. As they approached Qena, Thoth, with the Scorpion commander, viewed the ground in advance of the army to detect any attempt by the enemy to make a surprise attack.

When they were three days outside Qena, they observed a large concentration of native infantry. The columns were halted and the commanders prepared their formations for a battle.

Isis then spoke to Sheha. "Please wait before launching your attack to allow me sufficient time to appear above them on the magic carpet, as some of them should recognise me, and I might be able to convince them to change their allegiance."

"Isis, I am concerned about your safety, and whether the risk is really worth the outcome if only a few native troops react."

"Many of these troops believe that I am their Goddess and that I can work miracles and punish the wicked by raising my arm. I feel it is my responsibility to take them out of the battle if I can. Another reason is that the loss of these troops will severely weaken Seth's power to resist, in my view that alone justifies the relatively small risk. I ask for your approval."

"I agree, but at the same time I will start my advance, but will not launch my attack unless you are in trouble. If you return successful, then we can decide the next move."

Taking off, with Isis sitting in front of Thoth, who was piloting the transporter, they flew towards the native infantry. When they arrived they reduced height to just above spear and arrow height.

Then Isis stood up and slowly raised one arm towards them.

There was complete stunned silence. Suddenly, some of the natives threw themselves flat on the ground, their example being quickly followed by the majority of the infantry.

Seth's officers tried to regain control but without success.

Then Isis addressed the troops. "March south and join my army where you will be well received. You have nothing to fear and you will all recall that I have given your families my protection."

The natives jumped up to their feet and started walking to the south. A number tried to stop them, but when several of them were killed, the others ran away.

Returning, Isis informed Sheha, "We have been fortunate and I am pleased to tell you that a large number of new recruits will be arriving shortly. Let us advance to close the distance with Seth's encampment, only stopping when my native troops arrive, when I would appreciate your army giving them a warm welcome.

"To ensure their complete loyalty I will address them, demanding their complete loyalty and friendship with the Ethiopian army that has travelled to Egypt in friendship to help me remove them from

Seth's tyranny, and establish my son Horus as king."

When the local troops arrived, Isis tried to speak to them, but they all fell to their knees singing a song to their Goddess, for whom they had prayed in secret to ReRa for her return, as any mention of Isis resulted in severe penalties under Seth's harsh regime.

"Let us now continue our advance. Seth's power is broken, we must give him no time to react when he receives news of his army turning their allegiance to our cause."

Two days later, Thoth and the Scorpion commander flew over the main buildings of the Giants' Egyptian base.

Looking down on the main enclosure it appeared that all the Giants were armed and were having a serious disagreement. When they looked up and observed the transporter it seemed to ignite a fuse, and they separated into two groups and started shouting at each other.

Thoth turned the transporter around and hurried back to report to Sheha and Isis, requesting that two companies of Scorpions should make a forced march to stop the fighting which now seemed inevitable.

Sheha called for the commander of the Scorpions and said, "You are to make an immediate forced march to the enclosure and take whatever steps necessary to stop the fighting. The method adopted should ensure the minimum loss of life for the Scorpions and the saving of as many Giants as possible that are loyal to Isis.

"Whatever plan you adopt, the final solution must result in the overthrow and if possible the capture of Seth and his supporters.

"I invite Horus to lead the attack with my commander of the leading company of Scorpions, as his presence on the battlefield will reinforce his right to be made King of Egypt!"

As the Ethiopian army approached the enclosure, there was a fierce battle raging between the two groups with their native supporters.

The Scorpions spread out and started sounding their battle drums and banging on their shields and singing their battle song as they advanced towards the enemy.

The Scorpion commander called for complete silence.

Horus stepped out from the serried ranks of warriors and shouted, "I am Horus, son of Osiris and Isis, your lawful king. Put down your weapons and submit to me or die!"

The Scorpion commander called, "Attack!"

One group of Giants, on orders from their commander, retired backwards towards the Scorpions, who marched through them and formed up to face Seth's group.

Seth, fighting mad and screaming obscenities, hurled a lance at Horus that landed at his feet – a perfect aim, but short.

Horus lifted his throwing spear and, dancing forward, with a perfect throw, struck Seth in his thigh, pinning him to the ground.

Seth tried to get up but was immediately restrained and bound by a number of Scorpions. As there was no immediate submission by Seth's group, the Scorpions started to advance in battle formation; their purpose was clear and the Giants dropped their weapons and submitted.

With the arrival of the main body of Sheha troops, the Giants and their native supporters were taken to a corner of the enclosure and held under guard.

Isis came up and glared at Seth. "You have murdered Osiris, a High Lord, along with three Giants and possibly another called Heti. For all these crimes you are condemned to death!"

Seth replied, "I ask for a quick death, kill me now."

Isis replied, "This I cannot grant. I watched Enki and Shiva die for assisting you in the murders; it took twelve hours of excruciating pain until they finally succumbed. I told them I would be sending you to Hell to join them. You will be secured with manacles and shackles that I have brought for that purpose, and you will be held by Ethiopian troops until tomorrow morning. When all is arranged you will be brought outside our temple, where you will be tortured, and then revived, for many hours until you eventually succumb. Every moment you live you will be in unbelievable pain.

"Tonight, while you wait for the dawn, you can remember how you robbed my son of a father and I of my High Lord.

"As it is against our law to kill Giants, our friends the Ethiopians, who are skilled in this work, have agreed to undertake the task.

"Do not beg for death, as it will not be granted! Sheha, the King of Ethiopia, whose country you threatened, Horus, the King of Egypt, and I are those who will witness your death. Your body will be cut into little pieces and thrown on a dung heap, so there will be no resting place for you in death. This fate I reserved for you when, with my babe in my arms, I heard of High Lord Osiris's murder, vowing this once more when I buried my husband alongside his famous ancestor, who was also a High Lord of renown thousands of years ago."

The next day a wooden frame was erected outside the temple. The group of Seth's supporters were forced to sit in three ranks facing the frame, and then the three torturers and their slave set up the brazier and started to heat their instruments of torture.

When all was ready Seth was led in; his body hair had been removed and his behind and face painted with red and blue to make him appear like the Egyptian baboon. His wrists were manacled and then secured above his head; his feet were shackled and held apart by a spacer bar.

The sentence was then read to him and the slow painful torture began. This continued for ten hours until he was so close to death there was no purpose in continuing. A red-hot bar was then taken out of the brazier and thrust up his body, and with a terrible scream, he died.

His body was then cut in small pieces, each piece shown to his supporters and then thrown into a midden. The prisoners, suitably impressed, were informed that they would be individually interrogated the next day.

The immediate problem was to collect and bury the dead; two large pits were being dug just outside the enclosure where the Giants and the natives would be buried. The casualties had been heavy and half the Giants of the Egyptian expedition had died or would be dead by the morning.

Sadly the greater numbers of dead were female and this immediately raised a considerable problem that would have to be resolved.

Isis then visited Hathor in her temple, and was overjoyed to find her well. They sat down and discussed all those things that had happened to them after their hasty parting.

When Isis asked if she had had problems with any of Seth's associates after his visit, Hathor replied, "I was very careful to answer all the questions Seth put to me, giving him details that would be of interest, but no help in his search for you and the artefacts.

"After he had confirmed my position in the temple I had few visitors, as the observance of ReRa was discouraged, but at least my position as Priestess saved me from Seth's vicious temperament."

Isis held her in her arms, saying, "Everything will now change, you will be an exalted Priestess in a new temple and we will be as sisters. After our immediate problems are resolved, you should arrange a thanksgiving service to ReRa for the removal of the tyrant, a service to which all Giants will attend without exception.

"This will be followed a few days later with the crowning of Horus as the first King of Egypt. Seth, a murdering usurper, gave himself the title of King – this was not promulgated and therefore will be declared invalid."

The next day, the Giants who had fought against Seth were asked if they had any serious complaints against the prisoners waiting to be interrogated. They replied that there was only Tesh, who seemed to enjoy carrying out the killing of Heti on Seth's orders, and after that he frequently warned Giants that if they did not obey his orders they would suffer the same fate. The rest of the Giants who supported Seth did so in fear, or in return for special favours.

Isis then called for Ethiopian assistance to give Tesh a quick death, as she was fully aware he was both a weak character and a bully, who would only cause trouble if he were to be pardoned. They then took Tesh out into the middle of the compound, made him kneel down and decapitated him.

The Giants, who fought for Seth, were given one year of hard labour in the quarries, after which they could either leave or rejoin the society. The native supporters were given a similar assignment for one year moving the large building blocks from the quarry to the city, after which they could rejoin their fellows and help to build the city or leave the area controlled by the kingdom.

With these matters settled, a small council was selected from the remaining Giants, with two invited native members being selected for their intelligence.

Horus was elected King and his first edict decreed that work on the new temple would start immediately; this was to be constructed below ground level and of sufficient strength to withstand the next cycle of devastation. The temple would be dedicated to the Goddess Isis, so that this link to ReRa would be established for aeons.

A few days before the departure of Sheha, Isis went over to him, and embraced him, saying, "During the many years of our deep friendship I have come to love you with all my heart, and I believe you have the same feelings for me. If we were both of the same origin, we could couple. In our past, after careful consideration of the problems involved, our High Council passed a law that only Giants may couple with Giants. Before this law was passed, coupling between people of different origins had been tried, and the results had been devastating.

"The best we can hope for is to maintain our close relationship, and if ever you or your country need help or assistance from Egypt, it will be provided, and this agreement will be written into our law.

"In addition, we will establish a trading route with you along the Red Sea as soon as we can construct the necessary trading ships and you can establish a safe harbour.

"I have ordered Thoth with Hathor to provide you with daily reconnaissance flights until you reach home safely, in case some of your less friendly neighbours have tried to take advantage of your absence. Needless to say, they are delighted to be of assistance.

"I sadly cannot come, as there is so much to be undertaken if we are to achieve a stable society. As a special favour, would it be possible for a small detachment of, say, ten Scorpions to stay with us for six months? Their duty would be to train a company of selected local natives into a unit that can reflect the high standards achieved by your army. Once this cadre is established we will use it to build an effective defensive force."

King Sheha agreed and the Ethiopians left, accompanied by Thoth and Hathor on the magic carpet.

It proved to be an uneventful and pleasant journey and when they crossed the borders into Ethiopia, at the Scorpion commander's request, Thoth agreed to take him to their stronghold, so that they could prepare a suitable reception for the arrival of their king.

Approaching the mountain stronghold they observed it was under siege by a large army, which had it surrounded and was advancing up the mountain track.

Landing in the stronghold they found the situation critical, but the arrival of the Scorpion commander put new heart into the defenders.

The commander asked Thoth to fly back to the column, taking one of the officers with him to explain the situation to Sheha, and then return, bringing a supply of meat for the defenders. He estimated that with forced marches, the Scorpions should be able to close on the enemy within four days and the main force a day later.

The Scorpions should be able to make selective attacks on vulnerable points selected by the magic carpet, to deflect their forces from the stronghold until the heavy infantry could catch up and take up battle formations.

Thoth set off immediately, returning and reporting to Sheha by midday. Within an hour the Scorpion companies were on the march, followed a little later by the infantry who could not achieve the speed of the Scorpions due to the heavy baggage train.

Thoth and Hathor loaded the transporter with meat and took off for the stronghold, promising to return next morning to collect Sheha and take him up to the leading company of Scorpions.

Three days later they were a day's march away from the enemy, who were closing in on the mountain.

Taking a flight over the attacking force, Hathor noticed a company of the enemy climbing up a ravine at the back of the stronghold. The commander asked to be landed on a ledge above the ravine and asked Thoth to fly in ten reinforcements with spears and bows. Hathor, who as usual had her bow with her, elected to stay with the commander, as a support and an arrangement that would also allow the reinforcements to be brought in, in three flights.

When Thoth returned with the first batch, he found that Hathor, by selective killing, had held up the advance, causing the enemy to seek cover until reinforcements could be brought up.

Hathor was in high spirits and complained she was running out of arrows. Thoth promised to bring an adequate supply when he returned with the second batch.

When Thoth returned, bringing the reinforcements, he gave a substantial supply of arrows to Hathor so that she would have enough to delay the enemy until Thoth brought the third batch of reinforcements, and then she could harass the enemy from the air, while the Scorpions attacked down the ravine. With the reinforcements attacking down the ravine and Hathor picking off their number from the air, the enemy group was now in a state of utter confusion, and as they attempted to escape, the enemy company was completely annihilated.

Picking out and destroying small groups of the enemy proved to be the most effective plan to create confusion and general panic in their army. Consequently, when the heavy infantry arrived the enemy tried to retreat, but were contained and systematically slaughtered without mercy.

During their victory celebrations Hathor was made a full member of the Scorpions, and after a farewell parade, Thoth and Hathor departed for home.

Isis was still extremely concerned about the continuation of their race, as the shortage of partners for the male Giants was already causing friction and there were strong pressures to rescind the law regarding coupling with natives, recalling that in the past this seemed to breed quarrelsome children who enjoyed fighting. As a result, the Council of Atlan had forbidden coupling outside the community.

Isis was faced with the possibility that if she did not repeal this law, the reduced number of Giant females could not sustain the continuation of their society. So at the next Council meeting she had the law repealed, with the provision that the new wives had to be approved by the majority of the Giants.

By setting up trading routes to Lebanon, the Giants made contact with an advanced race living in the north on the shores of the great freshwater inland sea. In particular, their women were comely, gifted and much admired by the Giants.

After many years when most of the main buildings in the city had been completed, the Nile slowly dried up, and the people began to starve. The remaining Giants and their families immigrated to the great inland sea where they found a good living.

Unfortunately, when the salt sea broke in, the majority of the population were drowned and of those Giants and their families that survived, a few returned with Isis to Egypt. The remainder wandered the Known World and became renowned as the Great Men of Old.

Isis and Thoth returned to Egypt, with a few of their old retainers and native staff, to end their days in the deserted city of Atlan. The bountiful Nile was back by then, and crops were re-established by the returning native population. Over the years of their absence the mud, straw and brick accommodation buildings had been demolished by heavy storms and their locations had been concealed by a thick blanket of undergrowth and only the stone-constructed buildings of the temple, palace and administration buildings stood firm, but were sadly neglected.

The years rolled by, and the time came that as a day was drawing to a close, Isis, the Queen Mother of all Egypt, in her temple palace, called Thoth, her Chief Priest and Magician to her side.

"My old friend, in this my seven hundredth year, my body no longer responds to my demands, and your potions no longer dull pain. I am ready to die and require your company on my last journey to the tomb of Osiris, to comfort my passing into the realm of the Sun God.

"I recall those many years ago when the King, my son Horus, before setting out in his last battle with the Libyan raiders, reluctantly accepted my request that when my death approached I would be permitted, without great ceremony, to renew my bond with my beloved Osiris. It is now that time.

"So give me the potion to provide me with the strength to survive the short transporter journey to the tomb and let us leave without delay as my time in this realm is short."

The Chief Priest gently supported her head as he administered the opiate, then, with great compassion and affection, lowered her onto the litter. He called her personal servants to dress Isis in her robes of state before they carried her to the transporter.

When she had been made comfortable, with her two blindfolded attendants she made the short journey to the tomb of Osiris. From the cavern entrance, the attendants carried the litter down to the tomb portal, and then Thoth turned to them.

"Leave us now, go to the cavern entrance and stay there until dawn breaks, when I will return and take you back to the palace."

Thoth, gently cradling this precious burden in his arms, entered the tomb and lay her down on the soft cushions in the sarcophagus and, after making her comfortable, held her hand.

As she settled down, Isis quietly murmured, "Osiris and I will be waiting to welcome you when you leave this life; remember my Ka will always protect you and defend my people wherever they may be."

Then taking the last draught from the small golden chalice, smiling death came softly and released her from her mortal coil. As she departed from him, he felt forlorn, deserted and inconsolable, and then, weeping like a child, he settled down for the night's vigil beside the sarcophagus.

In the mystical silence of the tomb and with the shadows eerily dancing under the dim light of the flickering torches, he drew comfort by remembering how his life had been enhanced by their close partnership. He recalled the time of the Prophecy, those last frantic months at Atlan. As the years rolled back in his mind, he started to relive their companionship when, long ago, they had stood together on the promontory overlooking the bay of Atlan.

Egypt: The Link Established

AD 2004

Home: standing at last at their apartment door Ricky and Maria said goodbye to John Goddard, then, with his arm tightly wrapped around her shoulders, Ricky brought his beloved Maria into the hall. On the floor was a letter from the Metropolitan Police marked "Urgent". Tearing it open, the brief note, dated two days previously, ordered him to contact Inspector Humphries immediately on his return.

Maria, ignoring the stunned silence, declared, "I'm off to make some coffee and toast with, as you will recall, the bread and milk that you so reluctantly purchased at my request before we left the airport."

Ricky telephoned the police station and, after giving his name to the reception, asked to speak to Inspector Humphries; there was a short delay before Humphries answered abruptly.

"Mr McKay, we have received a serious complaint that you and Mr Goddard threatened an important member of our society, and I require that you both come down to the station to receive an official warning."

"First of all, I wish to know the name of the person who made the complaint so I can put this into the hands of my legal adviser. Secondly, I will come down to the station as and when you charge me with some offence. This should not be difficult for you as I presume you have adequate witnesses to verify his statement!

"If you *do* have a written and witnessed statement from that gentleman, I will be happy to hear this evidence in court. Under no circumstances will Mr Goddard or I accept a police warning. Furthermore, I insist on being told immediately the name of my accuser, and a statement from the police outlining the claim and confirming that either the police or the complainant are making a formal charge to be settled in court."

Humphries said, "I am not at liberty to reveal the name – as I have previously stated he is a very important person and to reveal his name could damage his standing in the community."

"Well, I suggest you deal with my legal representative at your police station at 11 a.m. tomorrow."

Humphries, in a more conciliatory voice, said, "Mr McKay, I did not mean an *officially* recorded warning, it was just to advise you of the situation and, subject to it being correct, you must be careful not to reoffend as we have to record his complaint against you."

"You must explain all this to my solicitor tomorrow. Unless your complainant either retracts his statement or initiates a court case, the complaint must be removed or marked up as mischievous. To ensure this action has been taken, I will be requesting a copy of the data you hold against my name on the police computer."

Ricky put down the telephone, then telephoned his legal adviser and asked him to visit the police station and extract the name of the person making the complaint.

Sitting down on the settee with coffee and toast, Ricky started to laugh.

"I wonder what our friend Vernon Drinmead will do now?"

Maria smiled. "I always thought you and John would make an effective pair of villains! Incidentally, you must call John and advise him of the complaint and your reaction before the fuzz get on his trail. Then we go to bed and enjoy the isolation that was unobtainable during our holiday in Indonesia."

Early next morning, a police officer arrived at their door to report that, two days before, their house had been burgled. Fortunately, as the two young burglars left the building, they were apprehended and a large number of letters and documents, stolen from the apartment, were recovered.

When questioned at the police station, they admitted that they had been paid to recover all documents and letters in the house and to leave no trace of their visit. Asked why the theft had been restricted to letters and documents, they replied they had no idea and did not want to know. They received a first payment at a pub to carry out the theft, and the second part of the payment would be forthcoming when they handed over the letters and documents. They did not know the name of the man who paid them and it would have been unwise to ask.

The police officer asked if they wanted the boys charged.

"With the return of the documents it's not in our interest, as frankly we cannot afford the time. Deal with it as you think fit. Has Inspector Humphries been advised about this incident? If not, I insist that he should be informed."

The police officer replied that he would inform the inspector immediately on his return to the station, and after handing over the documents and letters, left.

Ricky turned to Maria. "Would you call a meeting in our offices in three days' time. Starting early morning, say nine thirty, and book us all an excellent lunch after we complete business at twelve thirty. The purpose will be to share out the work covering the Indonesian visit and our preparations for the Egyptian expedition. See how our resident secretary-cum-housekeeper has survived, and decide if she will be an asset in preparing a complex report containing maps and our range of photographs. Presentation, as you know, is everything!"

"All will be done, my lord! But, Ricky, my whole being cries out for us to begin our visit to Egypt. It is almost as if someone is impatiently waiting for me to arrive. It sounds crazy but that's just how I feel."

"I understand, and we'll do our best to bring that about. Meanwhile, I will get fresh provisions sufficient for the next few days, while you visit the office and set up the meeting. After making the arrangements we can settle down and rest for the next two days and you can decide the entertainment!"

On his return later in the day, Ricky went into the darkened bedroom. Maria was standing there waiting for him, clad in a black cheongsam, close-fitting with a high neckline, the skirt split up one side to just above the knee, the outfit completed with black high-heeled boots.

In one hand, she firmly grasped a small silken whip. The light around her was ethereal and tended to obscure her facial features. With a soft and slightly seductive voice, she spoke to Ricky. "By now you know my Ka is with Maria and my presence is required to further the plans of Yax Nixte to revitalise the development of the Maya. You must be prepared to suffer a great sadness in the future, but be comforted, for it is then that I will come to you for a short while. Be assured the project will succeed! Now I will leave you to the tender mercies of your beloved Maria... enjoy every moment of your relationship!"

Three days later, Susan Slade had everything prepared for the meeting in an efficient manner; the places at the board table were laid out with folders and presentation pens and pencils marked with the company logo. On one side was a self-service table with coffee and biscuits and behind Ricky, at the head of the boardroom table, was a small table for the secretary.

After welcoming his friends, Ricky called the meeting to order and asked David to outline the financial situation.

"I will be publishing a financial statement at the end of this month but in general the situation is satisfactory for the work undertaken. The cost of the Indonesian expedition is approximately five million which leaves our capital reduced to twenty million, and there will be interest on our deposits of approximately half a million.

The national press has threatened to recover their investment of two million as they have been informed that the expedition has been a failure and funds have been wasted."

Ricky laughed. "This is the expected move by the opposition! As the Indonesian trip has been a great success, I put it to the meeting that we should reply to the press that as they wish to withdraw their two million we do not object, and that the transfer will be put in hand immediately. The advantage to us is that having removed the element of possible failure, we will be free to offer publishing rights on the worldwide market and obtain a greater return. I now put it to the vote."

All members agreed with the proposal and Ricky asked David to close the deal without commenting on the success or otherwise of the operation.

"Now to allot the workload for each of our members.

"My task will be to obtain permission from the Egyptian authorities for our expedition to operate in Egypt which will involve an early trip to Cairo. From past experience I do not expect approval will be given in less than four or five months.

"Maria, with the help of Susan, will be responsible for assembling the Indonesian report and obtaining additional help from agencies as and when required.

"Kirk cannot take on other work until he has completed his translations, and assessment of their value with regard to establishing possible Egyptian search areas.

"I propose that John, with David's assistance, purchases a two-seater power glider, capable of being dismantled for transport on a small trailer. Also that he immediately starts a course to become proficient with its operation and maintenance. Is that acceptable?"

John was absolutely delighted. "I've done some hand-gliding and always wanted to try my hand on power gliders; it's a wonderful opportunity for me and I am ready to start immediately by making the necessary arrangements."

Ricky laughed. "I must admit I'm a little jealous! Speak to David Cartwright and try to work out a monthly expense account that'll avoid any personal financial hardship to you over the period of this expedition. In addition, when qualified, ask David to take out insurance for you and your passenger for operations in both the UK and Egypt.

"David, as I understand it, you will be coming with us to Egypt. We will all require insurance so please shop around and let us have your recommendations based on a six months' overseas tour, starting within the next six months.

"Well, gentlemen, that's all the immediate business, so let's go to lunch. Susan, I would like you to join us."

The next day, Ricky and Maria went to the office and attempted to contact Mustafa Hassid, the Director of the Egyptian Department of Ancient Archaeology at Zagazig. Eventually his secretary answered and after Ricky had introduced himself, he outlined the reasons for an interview with the director.

"I have just returned from a very successful expedition to Indonesia. Texts obtained during that visit suggest that an expedition to Egypt would be rewarding for both of us. The period of our search is 5500 to 4000 BC. Would the director be prepared to give us a hearing? If so, we can fly out to Cairo at a time to suit him. This discussion is urgent, as the Egyptian aspect of our discoveries will feature in our report that is scheduled for discussion with the Indonesian government within the next two months in preparation for our worldwide release. In conclusion, we have the finance immediately available to mount the Egyptian expedition. Could you kindly fax or telephone a reply if your director is willing to accept a visit."

By the next day, while in the office, Ricky received a fax from Director Hassid that read as follows:

Due to adverse comments on your Indonesian expedition, I contacted a mutual friend at Jakarta, who confirmed that your expedition had been completely successful, but refused to give me details in view of the joint agreement. Taking account of his strong recommendation to both encourage and accept your expedition, I would be delighted to meet you and Maria in my office at 10 a.m. in three days' time.

Mustafa Hassid

Ricky was delighted with the immediate response and Maria was flattered that Hassid should invite her when her name had not been mentioned during the application for the meeting with the director. She emphatically pointed out, "I have achieved international fame it seems!"

Ricky, anxious to maintain his authority, got his own back by asking her to book the flights, the hotel in Cairo and a hire car to meet them on their return flight to Heathrow.

Ricky then turned to Susan.

"Please advise our members of the visit dates. In the meantime, I will arrange for Blanco to review office security on a daily basis, and help you to identify the mass of data accumulated during the Indonesian trip."

He then made a quick call to Blanco outlining the situation, who replied, "I have been intending to ask for a desk in the office and also consider the security precautions totally inadequate! Subject to your agreement, I will come in immediately. I presume you are prepared to authorise spending on both the purchase and installation of additional equipment?"

"I have complete trust in you. Take whatever steps you consider necessary! Inform David on the financial side – if he has any queries, please ask him to get in touch with me immediately, and I will confirm authorisation. As we must process our own photographs, would you also purchase a complete computer set-up to achieve this essential work, with software to secure it from unauthorised intrusion."

Having allocated the immediate tasks, Ricky and Maria left to buy light suits suitable for their formal visit in Cairo.

The flight to Cairo passed without incident, and after leaving their luggage in their hotel, they immediately hired a car to take them down the road to Zagazig and the government offices.

Hassid gave them a very warm welcome, and after settling them down in comfortable seats, had his servant bring in a tray of light refreshments.

Hassid opened the conversation by addressing Maria.

"I have heard strange, if not fantastic, hints about your visit to Indonesia, but generally it is about your intuition or sixth sense, and naturally I am intrigued – is there any truth in it?"

"I'm a member of a great team and all matters are resolved by general consensus, so everything we do has to be blamed on someone, and as the only woman in the team I sometimes receive credit for our successes that are really not deserved. Fortunately, so far, we have had no failures, but that is in great part due to the texts we have been fortunate enough to discover."

Hassid laughed. "That reply is only to be expected; you have carefully avoided a direct answer, but I understand and respect you for it."

Turning to Ricky, he said, "Tell me what you intend to achieve, and how my Department of Ancient Archaeology can be of assistance."

"We are looking for the tomb of your ancestors who died around 5500 BC. We already have a number of sites in mind, but these are not located in the Valley of Kings.

"We have not yet translated the mass of hieroglyphs obtained in Indonesia, but should have sufficient data to be more positive regarding locations in about a month's time. From our current investigations it is extremely doubtful if any treasure will be found in the tombs, and as treasure hunting is outside the interests of our expedition, anything of value discovered will be handed over to you.

"If Egypt can put forward someone from your department to join as a member of our expedition he or she can keep you informed of our activities. For example, in Indonesia, we also had a member of their navy. Perhaps you might also consider nominating a suitable member of your armed forces to join us as well? We will, of course, pay all the costs of our expedition and expenses for your two members.

"And what do you get in return? If all goes well and we succeed, a window into two and a half thousand years of your pre-history. As already stated, we intend to complete our report on Indonesia in two months' time, and as soon as the preliminary draft is agreed we will release a limited statement to the press.

"If you are not satisfied with that report, you can cancel our project in Egypt. However, if you *are* satisfied, you will be given copies of the complete report on a confidential basis."

Hassid replied, "You must give me time to discuss the political implications with the government, but with our direct participation I believe it will be looked on favourably. I have just two questions more. Are the hieroglyphs similar to the Egyptian version? Moreover, whose tomb is it?"

"The hieroglyphs are similar but slightly more complicated. From the first answer, you will appreciate they are your ancestors, and yes, we have tentative names, and they are well known to you, but more I cannot say at this time. Even those two answers are extremely confidential until our press release. I am sure you will understand, as it is imperative that we honour our promises to the Indonesian government, as any accidental leaks might jeopardise our joint project. To close, Maria and I would enjoy the company of you and your wife for dinner tonight at our hotel."

Hassid laughed. "You are too late, we are already preparing a small party for you and Maria at my home in Heliopolis. The guests will be restricted to my family, so dress should be casual. I am afraid there is one drawback – alcohol is not served in my house."

"We accept with great pleasure your kind invitation. I would like to add that my first name is Richard; my friends call me Ricky, and I hope you can accept that name."

That night Ricky and Maria had a wonderful evening with Hassid and his family. Just before their departure, Hassid's wife Horea took Maria out into the garden for a brief stroll in the bright moonlight, while Hassid and Ricky talked on the terrace. As the ladies started walking back towards the terrace, Hassid looked up and saw Maria change into Isis, her dress shimmering with the silver of reflected light. Then, as suddenly as she transformed, she turned back into Maria. Hassid grabbed Ricky's arm and said, "Did you see Maria?"

Ricky, who had seen the transformation, decided not to express surprise. "Yes, she's with your wife. You sound worried – has something happened?"

"No, no nothing, I thought she had slipped on the grass, but she is fine."

Horea then came up and asked them what they were fussing about. Ricky said, "We thought Maria had slipped but it was possibly an effect of the light, and we're relieved to see all is well."

As Ricky was saying goodnight to Horea, Hassid took Maria's hand, kissed it and whispered, "Welcome to Egypt. I did not believe the rumours but I now understand. Your expedition will have our full support and the permits will be issued within two months."

Maria whispered softly, "Let what you have seen remain as a secret between us."

When they returned to their hotel, Maria told Ricky of his promise. Ricky embraced her warmly and said, "You have achieved the impossible! Once again you have proved to be the greatest asset for the realisation of our endeavours."

The journey back to Heathrow was without incident, and first thing the following day Ricky telephoned Kirk and asked him to come into the office as soon as was convenient. Then Ricky and Maria left for the office. On arrival, they found security tightened with entry by touch pad and thumbprint, and a concealed camera recording all visitors. Blanco had been busy!

Kirk arrived shortly afterwards and they settled down to discuss progress in interpreting the hieroglyphs and in particular the route of the first expedition to the Nile. Ricky opened the discussion.

"Kirk, is there any new data on the first journey of the Atlan expedition to Egypt?"

"There is very little data on this subject. Osiris planned his route using their established trade routes to Africa, by following the coast to the entry into the Red Sea and then travelling up the west coast to land at their Quseir trading post, which is the nearest point to the Nile. There is also a note that navigation in the Gulf of Suez was impossible at that time.

"There is mention of the village of Qena on the Nile, which may have been their final destination.

"I am now certain that this expedition set out at least a millennium before the one detailed on the Mexican stela. I also believe we have sufficient evidence to prove this point. I also have no doubt this earlier expedition failed, as there is no evidence from the stela text of any trace of an existing settlement when they arrived at Qena.

"I presume from the northerly position of the Indonesian tomb from Atlan City that their choice of location depended on relatively inaccessible mountains, as direction does not appear to have been an important factor. From the stela inscriptions, they were determined to build their new city with a similar layout to Atlan. These factors can be used to project a circle of sixty kilometres' radius from their base near Qena to select suitable search areas in places where the circle cuts through high mountains."

Ricky thanked Kirk for a valuable contribution and asked for an estimate when the preliminary translations would be ready for inclusion in the report to Mohammed Ismail.

"I estimate one month followed by two months to produce the final version."

"The one-month estimate is ideal, the two-month period will possibly be interrupted. Regrettably, that is practically inevitable, as you are an essential member of the Egypt expedition."

After covering the main subjects, Ricky changed the discussion to security.

"We have heard nothing from the opposition for some time, and frankly I am worried, as they must have heard of your participation in our project. In my view it would be safer for the majority of the hieroglyphs to be retained in our office, with a copy in the bank, and that we should obtain an international copyright in our joint names for all data collated during our expeditions. If there is nothing in your home, I believe you will be safer. If you can accept these working conditions, you can have your own office with special security on the door so no one can enter while you are away, and we will provide you with a first-class computer.

"The other advantage is that you will have typing assistance as and when required, to support you in compiling your book. If you agree, we can immediately make the necessary arrangements."

"I think this is an excellent idea. If we can secure the office and purchase the necessary furniture I could bring my documents and reference books over this evening."

"With luck this can be achieved by tonight, and providing every-thing has been completed to your satisfaction, we will come with transport to escort you from your home to the office."

That evening, after Kirk had been established in his secure office, Ricky telephoned Inspector Humphries.

"Inspector, what was the reaction of the plaintiff to my response?"

"He was upset and withdrew his complaint."

"Have you revealed his name to my solicitor?"

"I'm afraid this gentleman has powerful friends and I have been instructed by my seniors not to reveal his name."

Ricky, far from satisfied, closed the connection.

At home that evening, Maria said, "Ricky, we should warn John Goddard of your apprehensions, he could be in danger and he's very vulnerable in those small planes."

"Well, telephone him now while I finish my bath, also tell him about the precautions we have taken with Kirk."

Maria made the call and explained Ricky's general concern. John sounded troubled and she had the impression that an incident had already occurred. "Anyway, he said that he fully understood your forebodings and he would be dropping by to talk with you."

Early next morning Maria left for the office, while Ricky stayed back prior to keeping an appointment with the local bank. As he left the apartment, a car pulled up beside him; the passenger got out and walked up to him.

"Are you Mr Richard McKay?"

"That is my name."

"A friend of yours, a Mr Blanco White, has had an accident. He's in a serious state in my home, and we have sent for the doctor. He's in considerable pain and asked for you. If you get into our car we will take you to him."

Ricky, alarmed, quickly stepped back from the car – Blanco would never give his name as Blanco White. Carefully he replied, "Give me your address and I'll meet you there after informing my office to cancel some very important appointments."

"I am afraid you have no choice – I'm instructed to take you to him."

Saying this, he produced an automatic and thrust it into Ricky's side, adding in a low hush, "Don't make a fuss or try to draw attention to yourself, or I will finish this off by killing you now."

The man opened the rear door of the car and was trying to bundle Ricky inside, when from down the road John Goddard yelled, "Ricky! Wait!"

Ricky threw himself backwards, falling flat on the pavement. John realised what was happening and sprinted towards him, screaming, "Stop! Police!"

The man panicked and fired a shot at Ricky that missed his head by inches. The assassin's driver decided not to wait and as the car started to move off, the assassin jumped into the rear seat as the car accelerated down the road.

Ricky leapt up, shouting, "They have Blanco!"

John grabbed his arm. "My car's parked over there."

They both ran for it, jumped in and raced off down the road in pursuit. Traffic had delayed the killer's car, but it was already several cars ahead.

Ricky shouted, "Let's keep it in sight but not get too close as they're armed, but we must let them know we're in hot pursuit and maybe they'll make a mistake."

"I heard the shot, are you wounded? There's a trickle of blood on the right side of your face."

Ricky, after examining his face carefully, and much relieved, replied, "It's just a scratch, possibly from a stone splinter or a graze – if it was anything more in that location there would be blood every-where. Anyway, I feel fine, but am worried about Blanco!"

"OK, let's hurry them along, they might even believe that I am an armed policeman and try to escape."

It seemed as if the assassins themselves had come to that conclu-sion as they started to weave in and out of traffic at high speed on the A3. Fortune was not in their favour, and as a result of one of their wild manoeuvres their front tyre blew out and the car vanished down an embankment.

John and Ricky stopped on the hard shoulder and went down to the car, which had impaled itself on a large tree trunk. The driver was dead and the passenger in a bad way.

Ricky, grabbing him, shouted, "Where is Blanco?"

The passenger gasped and with blood running out of his mouth mumbled, "In the bloody boot!" and then passed out.

John opened the boot. Blanco was there, dead.

"There's nothing we can do now. I see the police have just arrived by your car, so let's go back up and explain we witnessed the acci-dent. Then add that we climbed down to see if we could help, but unfortunately we discovered they were all dead."

Ricky and John left their names as witnesses and drove off as the ambulance appeared. They returned to Ricky's apartment and explained everything to Maria who veered between tears for Blanco and relief that Ricky had been saved by John's fortuitous arrival. Then, observing with horror the blood on the side of Ricky's face, she frantically started the essential remedial action.

Predictably, the police would arrive shortly, and Ricky and John sat down to prepare a written statement covering the day's activity, and in it they recorded that Blanco had been a well-loved companion and an important member of their archaeological team. Their description of events concluded with a brief footnote that they had not waited to call the police, as Inspector Humphries had told them that the person who had been causing them trouble was very important and as such was protected by his seniors.

They both signed the statement and Maria witnessed the signatures.

The next morning, two Scotland Yard police officers arrived at the apartment and introduced themselves as Inspector Jobbins and Detective Sergeant Logan. John sat them down and Maria produced some coffee.

Ricky said, "I know why you're here and to save time John Goddard and I have produced a statement covering the death of James White. I'm giving you the original."

The inspector read it aloud, and asked Ricky to confirm that this was their joint statement.

"I confirm that our statement is correct in all detail and that it was jointly prepared with John Goddard."

"You'll be pleased to know the shot fired outside the apartment was witnessed and the police were informed. It seems from the small piece of sticking plaster on your forehead that you had a narrow escape! What I do not understand is your reference to Inspector Humphries – can you please explain the background to this footnote?"

Ricky did so, but he omitted to reveal that he knew one of the persons causing the troubles they had experienced. At the same time, he implied that Inspector Humphries obviously knew more about this dangerous opposition than they did, and doubtless could provide a lead on the murder of James White.

"I had intended to ask you to come to the Yard to make a full statement but at the moment that won't be necessary. Are you asking for police protection?"

"I would appreciate the local police keeping an eye on our office for the next two months, and after that I believe these incidents will stop when we publish our initial findings in the press."

"I will see what can be arranged and will keep you in touch with the investigation as far as Mr White is concerned." With that closing remark, he left with Detective Sergeant Logan.

Ricky telephoned David Cartwright, asking the position regarding the two million. David replied, "I repaid the money and they cancelled the contract. However, they are now keen on reinstating their contribution, saying that the director who decided to cancel had not been authorised to do so by the board. I have refused to reinstate the agreement, and they are now offering an increased payment for the exclusive rights and wish to discuss it with you."

Ricky laughed. "Let them sweat, but they can only discuss the matter with you – providing there is a really firm offer that also allows us to negotiate a deal with the American press, we might then reach some agreement. Tell them the result of our expedition to Indonesia and that subsequent developments have been a tremendous success, and with the risk factor removed, any new agreement must yield a great deal more money.

"Changing the subject, Blanco's murder has been a tragic blow to our organisation, and can I ask you, as a considerable favour, to increase your workload by taking over Blanco's job, providing transport and camping equipment for the Egyptian venture? If you need additional help, bring someone in from a reliable agency for a couple of months, or better still, bring a friend in and pay him on the same basis. If there is any major expense involved, say exceeding a hundred grand, let us know before we are committed. Call a meeting for our members to suggest their requirements for the expedition – this way we will avoid comments on inevitable omissions!"

Days passed quickly until, at last, the preliminary report covering the Indonesian expedition, listing major discoveries but omitting detail, was to be submitted by courier, in a sealed package, direct to the Indonesian Embassy in London. From there it would be sent to Jakarta for the attention of Mohammed Ismail, so he could include any essential omissions or amend data before they jointly set a date for the press release. A separate package was enclosed which included a copyright CD, recording hieroglyphs and their preliminary translations, sonar scans and selected ROV views. Ricky had arranged for the password to access the data to be sent direct to the British Embassy in Jakarta for James Foley to pass to Mohammed Ismail.

All preparations having been completed and with generous Egyptian import permits, the three vehicles and their trailers loaded with heavy equipment were ready to be shipped to Alexandria.

True to Mustafa's promise, the Egyptian government's acceptance of the Egyptian expedition arrived two months after Ricky and Maria's visit. So the order was given to ship the vehicles and associated stores to Alexandria and Ricky started to finalise a departure date for personnel.

Ricky arranged with David to issue the preliminary press release just before they left Heathrow for Cairo. Susan Slade and David's stand-in had to fend off requests for more information and exclusive rights, until the team returned from Egypt.

Mustafa Hassid greeted the group on their arrival at Cairo airport, introducing his nephew Abdel Hassid el Sani, who was studying ancient archaeology in Cairo, and Lieutenant Ashrif Sadar, Egyptian army, who had been nominated by the government as the Egyptian member and military attaché to the expedition.

Hassid, putting his hand on Ricky's shoulder, said, "I have received a message from Mohammed Ismail, who regrets he is unable to join us as he is heading a special government department involved in major engineering works, the object being to expose the harbour wall face and opening up road and port access, to meet the essential services required for tourists.

"We shall all miss him, especially at this time of mourning for Blanco. However, we must look to the future so I suggest that we – and that includes our new members – take up our accommodation in the Marriott Hotel. On behalf of the expedition members, we invite you and your wife to join us as honoured guests for dinner tonight at our hotel. Everything has been arranged! Mustafa, are you and your wife able to accept? No alcohol will be served, and we have reserved a separate dining room."

Hassid accepted and that evening the dinner was a great success, plus the usual antics of the press ensured full coverage in the morning papers.

Early next morning they received the news that the ship had arrived at Alexandria docks and would be discharging cargo in the afternoon. Hiring a minivan, they arrived just in time to witness the unloading of their vehicles and equipment. Due to Hassid's intervention, import duties had been waived; as the complete consignment cleared customs without difficulty, they immediately motored down to Cairo to pick up their baggage from the hotel.

Having loaded luggage and supplies, Ricky said, "It's approximately seven hundred kilometres to Qena. I propose we cover two hundred and fifty kilometres tonight and stop over at El Minya, continuing the remaining four hundred and fifty kilometres tomorrow. With air conditioning, it should a pleasant and very interesting ride."

Ricky then asked Abdel, "When we get to Qena can you select a couple of cooks capable of providing us with both European and Egyptian food? They must be trustworthy; perhaps Ashrif can help you with that task which, from all our points of view, is extremely important. As soon as the camp is established we can start planning the archaeological work."

Arriving in Qena they set about establishing the camp, and with the work underway Ricky asked Ashrif if he could hire a light observation aeroplane with pilot for a couple of days? Ashrif, a member of the Elite Egyptian Parachute Regiment, replied, "No problem, I have a friend with a Cessna who would be delighted to have the job and the cost would be reasonable. I could have him at the Qena strip tomorrow morning."

The following day Ricky, Maria and Kirk, along with special camera equipment, took off and flew down the east bank of the Nile as far as Az Zawa'idah, taking a photographic record of the terrain.

Flying westward for sixty kilometres, they photographed a mountainous area that they listed as Search Area One. After completing that section they then returned to the Nile over Az Zawa'idah, and from there continued thirty kilometres due east until they reached the section where they left the Nile Valley to travel up the sharp escarpment into the western desert. This new location they listed as Search Area Two. After completing their aerial survey, Ricky suggested that they should return to Qena to enjoy a light lunch while arranging to refuel the aeroplane for their afternoon flight.

At Maria's request they flew south down to Ad Dayr ash Sharqi. In a dreamy voice, Maria said, "That was my home," then, pointing in a south-easterly direction, said to the pilot, "We go that way."

The pilot looked across at Ricky, who, guessing what he was about to say, interjected, "The lady has our full confidence, we must follow her directions."

Maria added, "Do not exceed five hundred metres."

Maria continued giving the pilot slight adjustments in direction until they approached the rocky area of Mount Nazzi and then she said, "You can increase to a safe height now, but start to circle this area while we take photographs. This will be designated Search Area Three."

After the photographs had been taken she turned to Ricky.

"We can return to Qena now."

Ashrif was waiting on the airstrip and after greeting him, Ricky called the pilot over to the group.

"I would like you and Ashrif to fly out tomorrow morning at first light, to take infrared photographs along the east bank of the Nile between Qena and Ad Dayr ash Sharqi. Then after returning for breakfast, fly a reconnaissance mission over Sites One and Two. Finally, in the evening, by moonlight, take another set of infrared shots along the east bank of the Nile.

"Ashrif, is that acceptable?"

Ashrif smiled. "I will enjoy a day with my old friend. Breakfast, lunch and dinner on the firm?"

"Of course, it's the least we can do, draw the necessary funds from David."

When they got back to the camp Ricky spoke to Abdel Hassid.

"Please contact Mustafa and ask him to place the area surrounding Mount Nazzi off limits to tourists, press, prospectors and other groups of archaeologists, the restricted area covering a circle fifteen kilometres radius centred ten kilometres due north from the peak of the mountain. Also, please ask him to contact us as soon as the restriction is in force."

As Abdel seemed hesitant, he added, "If you think it safer to contact him personally, you can fly from Qena to Cairo first thing tomorrow and return the next day. It might be advisable to arrange a code word with him, which he can use to advise us that the restriction is in place. Establish a second code word for us to send to him confirming important discovery requiring museum support.

"I strongly recommend that preparatory arrangements for strong support be established immediately but I appreciate this is strictly an Egyptian matter. Before you leave, familiarise yourself with the exact location of Nazzi. When you reach Mustafa, please telephone to confirm arrival. In conclusion, these messages are only for Mustafa!"

Hassid, looking relieved, replied, "I will fly to Cairo first thing tomorrow morning and speak direct with Mustafa."

After the evening meal, Ricky explained their plan for the next day.

"Four of us will take two of our vehicles to Search Area One for any sign of ancient tombs, in addition recording anything we find of archaeological interest.

"John, you will stay behind and assemble your motorised hang glider, you will require enough fuel for sixty kilometres each way. So, first thing the day after tomorrow, I suggest you establish a concealed refuelling point somewhere beyond the cultivated area, towards Site Three. Two jerry cans should be sufficient; they'll weigh less than your passenger on the main flight, which you'll undertake as soon as you return to base and refuel. That is, providing we receive instructions from Mohammed that the site is now a restricted area. If we have to delay, we will make a second visit to Search Area One. After our meal I suggest we study the infrared photographs on our computers and compare differences in ground effects between the two different times the photographs were taken."

The following day they arrived at Search Area One and started a systematic search of the slopes. Ricky called Maria over.

"I'm positive we're being observed; go back to your search area and in ten minutes' time shout that you have found something. As Kirk joins you, tell him to be excited and get him to call to me, I'll rush over. Start taking satellite navigation settings, making a show of recording data. We will then start searching the hillside above, before taking more measurements and returning to our cars and leaving immediately."

The charade was carried out and before they left Ricky decided that, as they had enough time, he proposed to go to Ad Dayr ash Sharqi on the west side of the Nile – the area that Maria had recognised and which had shown some interesting outlines on the infrared photographs.

When they returned to base camp John told them that Abdel had arrived in Zagazig and would be returning tomorrow.

The next day, as Abdel had not yet returned, they decided on a second visit to Site One.

They were not surprised to find a small camp erected on their site. When questioned, the occupants stated that they were part of an archaeological team from London who had been exploring this area for the last month! Ricky appeared to be upset. Therefore, they generously offered to share their exploration with Ricky's group. Ricky replied, "Due to commitments with our sponsor, that kind of agreement is quite impossible, consequently we will have to wait until you clear the area before we can continue at this site."

At that moment, Mike, the American journalist from the International World News Syndicate, who they had seen in Indonesia, came out of one of the tents.

"Hi there, remember me? Mr McKay, you really should combine with this team as it would be financially advantageous to do so. If, by sponsors, you refer to the Egyptian Minister for Ancient Archaeology, then you can rest assured he would support any arrangement you make with them. While their team offices are established in London they are financed by the good old US of A, and any finds they uncover reap very substantial rewards. It will cost you nothing to make the agreement and they are prepared to cover all the costs you have incurred to date – including the Indonesian expedition."

Ricky replied, "Thank you for the generous offer but I'm forced to refuse. My sponsor is a Mr Yax Nixte, a Mexican, and I know he would never agree. So regretfully I must refuse."

Mike replied, "I've been prepared for that response. So how about an exclusive deal with International World News? We know you cleverly returned the two million when the press in London got cold feet, we're also aware that they're desperately trying to renegotiate the deal. Therefore, we're throwing our hat into the ring and offering ten million dollars for the exclusive international rights for both the Indonesian and Egyptian expeditions."

After thanking Mike for the offer, Ricky said, "We'd have to refer this to our sponsor and I suggest you deal with our financial director immediately when we return to London."

After that exchange, they said their goodbyes and returned to the east bank of the Nile to continue their search for the site of the second Atlan expedition's base in Egypt. After a while, they became convinced that they had found it but, unfortunately, the dwellings had, in part, covered the site and the remainder was buried under thousands of yearly inundations of Nile silt.

When they returned to camp, Abdel was waiting for them.

After apologising for being late, he reported, "The Mount Nazzi area has been restricted from tomorrow, and Mustafa has provided the essential government passes for expedition members. In addition, he has sent a radio transmitter which can work directly with his office where they will man their set day and night.

"Ashrif, I have a number of letters, together with a heavy case from army command, only to be opened by you in an emergency."

Ricky said, "That's excellent news. John, have you established the refuelling point?"

"Established indeed, and I await my first customer tomorrow morning!"

"John, your first customer is Maria. I want you to take her to Search Site Three so she can have a close look at the mountains, as she believes that with the information we have been given in the past, she'll be directed to the tomb's location. Find a place close to the selected site where you can land safely, then pinpoint the position with our satellite navigation equipment. Clear a runway and return to us with the information. If Maria wishes to stay, make sure she is safe and has a safe cover before leaving.

"Tomorrow morning we prepare to move camp and must be ready to move out in convoy with all our equipment by eleven, by which time, John, you should have returned."

The next morning all went as planned. John returned with the site coordinates, having left Maria on the mountain.

Ashrif turned to Ricky. "I would like to accompany John on his return flight."

"Subject to John's agreement I have no objection."

John agreed and welcomed the company. After refuelling and collecting a set of climbing equipment, they set off for Site Three, while the expedition's convoy abandoned their temporary location.

As John and Ashrif landed, an excited Maria rushed up to them. "John, have you brought the climbing equipment? Oh, hallo Ashrif, I'm afraid in the excitement of the moment I forgot my manners, but forgive me as I believe I have found a concealed entrance to a cave. It is not far away, let's go. With two strong men we should be able to open it sufficiently before the others arrive."

In an excited mood they approached the top of a high rock face, and as they peered down Maria pointed to a small dark cavity in the face.

"Lower me down so that I can try and open it up sufficiently to look in."

John looked at Ashrif and replied, "No way! One of us will abseil down – we've done it before."

As John started to volunteer, Ashrif interrupted.

"*I* demand the honour, having recently passed an intense army course of abseiling and mountain rescue and claim I am the best qualified – John, do you object?"

"Not at all. I've only tried it once, and didn't relish demonstrating my lack of know-how. Thank you and let's get started."

As soon as they had established an anchor point, John took hold of the safety rope and Ashrif lowered himself down to the cavity. Shining his torch through an opening in the rocks, he could just see a cave floor. He shouted up to Maria and John, who were anxiously peering down from the cliff edge.

"I'm going to come up a metre and swing out and hope the impact of my body weight will dislodge one of the boulders!"

No sooner had he said this, he started to swing out into space using his legs as springs on the return, and when he had built up sufficient swing he crashed in hard and vanished in a cloud of dust.

After a short interval, John's head appeared and he shouted, "Not to worry, I've had worse landings. I'm going to walk in a little way to see how far it penetrates."

Moments passed, and eventually Ashrif's head reappeared, and he hauled himself back up to where Maria and John waited apprehensively.

After Maria had inspected him for damage and had stopped fussing, Ashrif explained. "After breaking through, I landed on a pile of rocks that were extremely uncomfortable; I'm bruised but nothing worse. The cave joined into what appeared to be a black glass cylinder. Approaching the end of the tunnel the floor disappeared and I almost fell down into a deep cavern – my torch was not strong enough to see much more so I returned to report."

Maria was delighted. "This cylindrical construction is identical to that leading into the Indonesian tomb! I feel certain we have found the link with Atlan Indonesia. Our first job will be to establish a safe means of access into the cave and reach the tomb which is a considerable distance down the cavern—"

John interrupted. "How could you possibly know that, Maria?"

Maria replied, "I just do, John, but I'm quite unable to explain. At this moment it's as if I have always known it, but yesterday I didn't – confusing! All I can say is I believe it to be true. So let's sit down and rest until the others arrive, when we can send back for some lumber and bring up the motor generator and lighting system."

By late afternoon the rest of the expedition arrived, and setting up camp was the first priority. By the time the camp had been satisfactorily established, the sun was rapidly sinking below the horizon, and work on the cavern had to be abandoned until first light the next morning.

Early next morning, Abdel set off with David to purchase lumber and other necessities to build the platform. After the rest had unloaded and installed the generating plant, John and Ashrif started fixing temporary lighting along the tunnel walls. With the arrival of the lumber, the rest of the day was dedicated to building the platform and installing the ladders from the cliff top to the platform; Ricky allocated the following day to penetrating the cavern.

John and Ashrif started the descent, fixing safety ropes and lights as they descended towards the cavern floor. The cavern looked menacing until the lighting string reached the lower levels and started to reflect off the stalactites and stalagmites, then with the light penetrating down the cavern it looked more inviting.

Broken stalactites and crushed stalagmites littered the cavern floor. By moving some of the debris, they came across a clearly marked path that appeared to be leading down the centre of the cavern. Calling for assistance they all came down and started to clear the path. After a considerable distance, they came to a junction where additional paths led left and right. Ricky turned towards Maria.

"Which way?"

Maria, as if in a dream, slowly lifted her arm and pointed to the left.

Ricky interpreted. "We clear down the left path."

After some sixty metres, they reached the cavern wall and they encountered a massive archway enclosing a stone portal designed to slide into a recess. Ricky tried the door without success. Eventually, after clearing an accumulation of debris and using their combined strength, they achieved the first small movement, then the portal opened fully with surprisingly little effort to reveal two massive limestone sarcophagi.

Extensive hieroglyphs covered one of the walls, using the similar signs to those inscribed in the Indonesian tomb. Ricky turned to Kirk.

"I appreciate it is impossible to provide an accurate interpretation without intensive study, but can you offer us a rough translation?"

"Give me an hour or so to familiarise myself with the symbols used and I should be able to produce a very rough translation; perhaps the rest of you could use the time to record details of the complete tomb."

Ricky put his hand on Kirk's shoulder. "I promise you will be left in peace! We have plenty to occupy our time, but are, and will be, impatient for your news."

It was almost two hours before Kirk called them round him and he started the translation.

"What I can describe is this:

Before the tomb of my King and Great Lord Osiris, whose Ka has now joined his immortal brothers in the infinite mantel of the universe.

As Chief Priest and Magician of the first Atlan expedition to the Land of the Great River, I place on record that our expedition was formed to ensure the survival of the race of Atlan at the time of the cataclysm, a disaster that eventually enveloped the whole of the southern hemisphere. With great sadness, I record that these great trials ended with the complete annihilation of all but four of our expedition members.

This I note down so that any of our race who have survived the cataclysm may find these records and learn from our misfortunes.

Kirk then turned to Maria and said, "As you can see, he goes into great detail – he mentions the astronomers' prophecy, the destruction of Atlan by fire, earthquakes, great winds and massive waves. Unfortunately, the majority of the Council did not believe the Prophecy! It also records how the High Lord Osiris, at his own cost, assembled an expedition to ensure the continuation of their race. Fortunately, by that time he had just completed two trading ships, the largest in the known world, in which he embarked one hundred expedition members. During their journey to the west, they lost one ship, reducing his expedition members to fifty. When they reached the straits between the Gulf of Aden and the Red Sea, their ship was wrecked and they lost a further fifteen Giants. After further losses, only fifteen reached the Great River.

"By this time there were only sixty days left until the time of the Prophecy, so they sought a safe place in which to shelter. They discovered a small cave that led into the entrance to a great limestone cavern. Then disaster struck once more when a falling stalactite killed Osiris. The remaining Giants worked without rest to build the tomb and the sarcophagus. When this was achieved, ten Giants went out to find food, a major earthquake then occurred and sealed the only entrance to their cave.

"Apparently Thu and his three companions were entombed and after completing this record, and with no hope of rescue, dedicated their lives to ReRa."

Kirk added, "Presumably they all died and we may still find their bodies."

Maria commented, "I'm in no doubt that these Giants are my ancestors and their Baa comforts my soul."

Kirk continued, "Later, I'll make an accurate and detailed translation of the text. I notice on the far wall another set of hieroglyphs. These presumably refer to the second tomb. I'll attempt a quick translation, as this is different from the other set, being closer to the texts of 3000 BC encountered on the Mexican stela.

"As far as I can make out, this is the essence of it:

"To the almighty ReRa, Protector of my people, Isis High Lord of Atlan and your devoted child, surrender my beloved couple Osiris to your care.

"I had this sarcophagus built so that he may lie beside his ancestor from ancient times, knowing that this was the desire he expressed during the cataclysm.

"I record with great sorrow that the Evil Seth murdered him most foully, having lured him away from those who loved and protected him and then usurped the leadership of the great and successful expedition to Egypt.

"Now after many years protected and aided by the army of the King of Ethiopia, I have regained the throne for my son Horus. Your temple has been re-established with great celebration, as during Seth's reign of terror any act of worship was discouraged.

"Seth, the evil tyrant, was tried, found guilty, punished continuously for a day of your reign, and then executed; a sentence carried out by the Ethiopians so that the laws of our society would not be violated.

"Lord ReRa, beloved of my people, grant me that when I depart this life, may my Ka stay close to my descendants to protect them from the followers of Seth throughout all eternity.

As Kirk finished translating, they heard a terrible scream of anguish and there, standing in an aura of shimmering light was Isis, in her full regalia, tears streaming down her cheeks. She collapsed on the tomb of Osiris. Ricky ran towards her and, as he lifted her in his arms, she reverted to Maria and clung desperately to him, sobbing softly.

"My friends, as a kindness, never refer to what you may have seen. We have achieved the object of our expedition – surely that is of sufficient interest? Reporting hallucinations will only result in our being ridiculed which would damage our discoveries. You do not know but I need the Ka of Isis for when I return to the Maya in Chiapas."

Ricky noticed John and Ashrif peering at a great pile of strange devices stacked in an alcove at the far end of the room. He reminded them not to touch it, as it had to be carefully examined in position, and then photographed before removal by the Ministry of Ancient Archaeology.

After Kirk had finished taking photographs of the texts, they removed the access platform to safeguard the site and returned to their new campsite. Abdel Hassid then sent the code word to Mustafa. Then, exhausted, they settled down to a meal under a canopy of stars that seemed to carpet the whole sky. A light wind known as "The Doctor" came up from the east, removing the heat of the day, and apart for the member undertaking the first watch, they all retired, falling into a gentle slumber.

Next morning John and Ashrif took a walk before breakfast and noticed dust trails of three lorries heading towards their camp. Using binoculars, Ashrif said, "They are packed with men. John, I have a bad feeling about this, they will be here in ten minutes. Let's head back to camp and I'll break out the army's emergency stores. Abdel must inform Mustafa immediately."

Hastening back to camp they advised Ricky of the situation. Ricky said, "Move the vehicles under cover of those rocks and disconnect the trailers – we may have to run for it!

Ashrif opened the army command's heavy case – opening was only permitted in an extreme emergency. Inside he found three assault rifles, four machine pistols, a number of blast grenades, together with a quantity of ammunition. In addition, it included a lightweight transceiver with a direct link to army command. He had just issued the weapons when the first lorry rounded the bend in the track. He reflected that if this turned out not to be an emergency he could be in real trouble.

Abdel rushed towards the vehicles and put his hand out, calling them to stop. The armed men climbed down from the lorries, an order was given, then suddenly a shot broke the silence and Abdel tumbled to the ground.

Ashrif shouted, "Do not fire! Take cover."

Then he threw a blast grenade at the front of the first lorry, and a heavy explosion followed and the lorry seemed to tip over and fall on its side in slow motion.

In the following silence, Ashrif used his communicator to call for support from the army and they advised him that an emergency plan had been prepared and would be implemented immediately.

The terrorists had gone to ground, but they could hear them organising an attack.

Abdel's body was still out in the open but Ricky thought he could detect a small sign of life, so he crawled up to Ashrif.

"I will move slowly under cover as far forward as possible. Create a diversion by throwing two blast grenades as far forward as possible. I'll have my ears covered but when I see the flash I'll run forward and drag Abdel back to those rocks.

"If any of the terrorists recover sufficiently to shoot at me, provide covering fire, but do not expend too much ammunition."

They put the plan into effect; the blast grenades produced a period of shock and covering fire was not required. Abdel was swiftly grabbed and dragged back behind the rocks.

"Ricky, we cannot fight them here, we're too exposed and there are far too many of them. In this position we're overlooked from the ridge on our left, so we must fall back up the mountain. There's a good defensive spot near the cave, with an open killing ground on the approach and cliff at our back. Drive our vehicles up the hill, while I stay and give covering fire to delay their advance. When you get there, sound a horn and I will withdraw and join you. There's no time to argue – fall back now."

"We're on our way."

As the vehicles moved off, the terrorists started to follow, but Ashrif dropped three of them with single shots. The terrorists dropped back among the rocks, and Ashrif took advantage of their temporary confusion and moved back to a new sniping position.

Ricky blew the horn and watched as Ashrif darted back, from cover to cover, until he reached the dead ground, zigzagging across the open ground. Ricky, in deep cover, fired just enough ammunition to keep the terrorists' heads down. An exhausted Ashrif dropped down beside Ricky.

They were together again, but there was no place to run. They were short of ammunition and the terrorists had vastly superior numbers; they needed help urgently. Worse still, Abdel needed urgent medical treatment or he would not survive.

Ricky made a snap decision.

"John, take Abdel to your plane, strap him in and fly to Qena airport. Tell the authorities of our position and contact Mustafa. Insist that help can only be effective if it's immediate; there's no time for talk."

John and David carried Abdel to the plane and John managed to take off before the terrorists closed in and started to subject their positions to heavy fire.

Ricky outlined the plan for defending their position.

"Ashrif and I will take up sniping positions on either flank with the assault rifles to harass and hopefully delay preparations for an attack. The rest of you must wait concealed under cover until the terrorists start a frontal attack across the open ground, then wait until they are within one hundred metres of your position, before forcing them back with short bursts from your machine carbines."

The terrorists first tried to advance a small group on either flank under a withering covering fire, but Ricky and Ashrif took out four of them with single shots; the rest fled back to the rocky area. For quite a while, there was an ominous silence, followed by sounds of heavy objects being dragged across the rocky ground. Ricky was just able to see a corner of a metal tray carrying old tyres on which a liquid was being poured, and within minutes flames revealed three separate fires, that soon produced thick pungent clouds which slowly advanced, obscuring the first part of the open area. Using these devices, they kept on advancing the trays at uneven intervals keeping under cover of the smoke, preventing Ricky and Ashrif from finding a target.

Ricky called out, "Be prepared for a mass attack, wait under cover for the order to fire, and then use repeated short bursts."

They had not long to wait before the terrorists came hurtling through the smoke, screaming and firing from the hip. Ricky waited until they reached his one hundred-metre marker before he shouted, "Fire!"

For the front runners it was suicide, and those behind turned and escaped back into the smoke.

Ashrif went round to check ammunition, then returned to Ricky.

"We might have enough to hold back another attack, but it's doubtful. The only thing left is to charge through them in our vehicles firing the last of our ammunition.

Ricky replied, "I agree... wait, listen."

They all heard the familiar sound of jet planes. Seconds later they screamed down across the site, overshooting, then regaining height and banking round to line up on the lorries. Releasing their rockets, the rushing sound reached an unbearable crescendo, until the lorries exploded into balls of flame, almost anticlimactically. The jets then circled the site from a distance, making occasional low-level passes to deter the terrorists mounting any further attacks.

Glinting in the sun's reflected rays in the clear blue sky, the troop carriers appeared in perfect formation and started to disgorge paratroops to encircle the site.

The terrorists attempted to disperse, but without transport and fully exposed on the hillside, they were being engaged in a series of running battles, and against crack paratroops the end was inevitable and only a few prisoners were taken.

A section of paratroops encircled the expedition's position but avoided direct contact except to shout across, asking if they required medical help. Ricky shouted back, "We've been fortunate, no one present has been injured."

Ashrif started to reclaim the weapons and clean them before packing them back in their case, while the rest of the party cleaned the site and the cooks prepared a light meal.

Meanwhile, the paratroops were collecting and enclosing bodies in black bags, and a helicopter landing area was hurriedly being prepared, presumably for the arrival of an important visitor.

An hour and a half later, a large helicopter was guided in, and on landing unloaded a very agitated Mustafa Hassid, accompanied by museum staff and Egyptian guards.

Mustafa rushed over to Maria and gave her a warm hug. "Thank God you are all right, we have been so worried – I came as fast as I could."

He then greeted each of the party warmly, and then, suddenly very concerned, asked, "Where's Abdel?"

"He was severely wounded trying to negotiate with the terrorists; John took him by our observation plane to Qena. I hope they made it as Abdel's life depended on a quick journey. Can you contact Qena airport and hospital?"

Mustafa called over the senior officer of the paratroops, had a quick word, and then turned to Ricky.

"We should get an answer in fifteen minutes. I want to wait until we hear some news. After that we can discuss what must be done to secure this site and protect your party."

Ten minutes later a paratrooper came running up with a message for Mustafa who, after reading it, announced, "They're both in hospital, Abdel is being transferred to Cairo General, and his condition is serious but stable. John was shot in the leg when leaving the site, but he's comfortable and should be released in two or three days."

They all breathed a sigh of relief and Ricky thanked Mustafa for what was great news for both of them.

While the battlefield was being cleaned up by the paras, Mustafa asked Ricky and Maria to take him and his group on a guided tour of the tomb. The platform was quickly replaced and, with Kirk's expertise in translating the hieroglyphs, they spent the rest of the day discussing the texts and outlining the link with Indonesia and Mexico on a strictly confidential basis.

Returning to their camp, now re-established by two very nervous cooks, Mustafa opened the discussion.

"You have achieved everything you promised and I believe you have all the detail needed to establish the link with the Maya in Central America.

"For Egypt this site will become a national shrine and a permanent guard will be established immediately. I understand your reluctance to open the sarcophagi and accept that apart from their occupants they will not contain treasure. The decision on this is a matter for the government but I will vote against them being opened.

"Then there is the question of the artefacts – they have to be removed under armed guard to Cairo. This will be a difficult procedure and without doubt it will take years to clean and separate the individual items. The members of your party will have access during this work, but control of the dissemination of information must remain in the hands of the Cairo museum.

"Now I come to the most difficult part of my review. I believe my government will be worried about the security of your group. You have killed a large number of terrorists and as this information cannot be kept a secret, your lives will be in danger as long as you remain in Egypt.

"Politically and for personal reasons we cannot let anything happen to you. John Goddard already has a twenty-four-hour guard and when you leave here you will have an armed escort. Your cooks will be placed under house arrest until we consider it safe to release them. I can allow you a short time at this site while we establish a permanent base, so will you talk among yourselves and advise me when you are prepared to depart? The Egyptian government is willing to buy your vehicles, provide accommodation and transport to London, as soon as you are ready to make the journey."

Ricky, after consulting the other three members affected, returned to Mustafa.

"We require three more days on site and will then be ready to return to the UK. I suggest that to avoid premature press leaks we send you a copy of our preliminary report through your British Embassy and after including any amendments or additions you wish to make, would you kindly reply and propose a release date. The preliminary report will be mainly technical and will not refer to this terrorist incident, unless by that time it has become common knowledge. After that, our detailed report will be sent to you prior to publication for any amendments. Are we agreed, Mustafa?"

"I agree to all, and I am sad that political circumstances make it impossible for you to stay in Egypt. I am looking forward to your amalgamated reports covering the three countries and hope you will keep us up to date with developments and in addition your translations of our hieroglyphs. For our part, we promise you full cooperation with regards to the development of this find, and access to our joint information will not be granted to countries or archaeologists other than government-sponsored members of my department."

The remainder of the days passed quickly and on their way home John joined them in Cairo with a slight limp but otherwise as good as new. After a select government dinner to which they were invited as honoured guests, they took a flight back to Heathrow with Egypt Air. After arrival at the airport, they agreed to reconvene in their London office in a week's time.

Entering the corridor to their apartments, Ricky turned to John.

"Maria and I would like you to come round tomorrow, say about midday, for a business discussion. Afterwards we will go out together for lunch."

"Until tomorrow, then."

With a cheery wave of his hand, John left for his own apartment.

When the two of them entered their lounge Ricky collapsed in an armchair saying, "What about a cup of tea?"

Maria chuckled. "No way, my hero, I require your services and we are off to the bedroom!"

The next morning, John turned up at midday and after receiving a warm welcome from them both and being comfortably seated, Ricky opened the conversation.

"We both want you to have a private medical examination, including an X-ray of your leg, to ensure it is fully healed and that there's no infection. If you agree, Maria will arrange it for tomorrow or the next day.

"Provided you are pronounced fit, and you agree to undertake a further mission, I want you to visit Ethiopia. Employ someone who speaks good English and studies ancient manuscripts and seek out any historical reference to the Olmec culture. In addition, try to determine if there are any myths concerning expeditions to the west around 2500 to 3000 BC by Ethiopians who never returned.

"John, except for the medical examination, you're not committed in any way. So the question is, are you interested?"

"Ricky, it sounds a *great* idea. Once I have the essential medical clearance I'll make the necessary arrangements."

"Maria, if you can make an appointment for me as soon as possible I'll be ready."

"On your return you'll receive a substantial bonus. If medical opinion is negative then you can claim on your insurance, but your bonus won't be affected. Now, Maria – take us to lunch!"

A week later they all met up in the London office to review progress and determine future activity. When they had all assembled, Ricky asked David Cartwright if he had discussed the financial situation with his stand-in, and if so could he give them some indication of the present position.

"As a ballpark figure our capital is about seventeen million, and there are no debts. I've received a firm offer from International World News for the exclusive international rights for all countries excluding Egypt and Indonesia for the sum of ten million US dollars – about six million seven hundred thousand pounds. The book Kirk is writing is exempt, but their publishing house would appreciate the opportunity to quote, and handle lecture tours in the USA."

"David, get our lawyers to look through it for a fixed price and if there are no serious objections I suggest we close the deal.

"For the immediate future we have to prepare the preliminary press release for the Egyptian expedition, followed by the comprehensive report on the two expeditions, including a brief report on the Mexican find. We will make it clear that further detail will be included in the book being prepared by Kirk. All this is urgent – if we need additional professional help in its preparation then it must be obtained.

"John has agreed to go to Ethiopia to search their archives for myths of ancient expeditions to the west, and any reference to Olmecs. If he finds anything of interest, one of us will go out in support, as and when our paperwork has been completed!

"To achieve the objectives of the foundation, where do we go from here? Maria and I have decided to return to Chiapas, Mexico and give the first public lecture there, or in Guatemala City, subject to Kirk being available. Our end plan is to establish the foundation for the provision of special education facilities for the Maya, and to support their high achievers in obtaining places in overseas universities. This will require a great deal of money, but even after paying bonuses to members, we will have sufficient funds to give a strong start to the Yax Nixte Foundation.

"Letters have already been written to the five 'Ruta Maya' countries of Central America asking for their agreement to allow us to give the first Yax Nixte lecture in the Maya belt of influence. The letters also inform them of our intention to set up a Maya foundation in one of their countries. Initially, it will be directed by us with selected Maya staff, with the understanding that they will eventually take over the operation within the Ruta Maya.

"Well, that's all for the present! Comments are welcome."

Kirk replied immediately. "Your intentions are not altogether unexpected and, having carefully considered my reaction, I volunteer my services to teach in the foundation. Of course I will be there for the first lecture, and if it extends to a lecture tour, to those as well. This is a great challenge to achieve something worthwhile in my lifetime."

John commented, "I have little to offer in the academic field, but if there's a job in this country that suits my abilities then I may stay and try to settle down, otherwise it's up sticks and a landing on your doorstep!"

David sighed and said, "Unfortunately, I have family commitments in this country which prevent me from taking anything more than brief visits overseas. However, if you can accept my help on that basis you have my total support and loyalty to the foundation."

Ricky then closed the meeting and invited them all to a celebration lunch, and by general consensus Maria was given the seat of honour at the head of the table with one seat left unfilled for Blanco.

During the lunch John turned to Ricky.

"Have you any news about Abdel Hassid?"

"Before we left Egypt, I told Mustafa that I fail to understand how the terrorists could have discovered our destination so quickly. Even our cooks were unaware of the new site. After making this comment, I recall suggesting that the prisoners should be interrogated to establish who was responsible.

"Yesterday, Maria telephoned Mustafa and asked if Abdel was still in hospital as we wished to send him a get well present. There was an awkward silence at the other end of the telephone, and then Mustafa sadly admitted that the prisoners had identified Abdel as their informant. It turns out that as he ran over to join them he was accidentally shot. He is still in the Cairo hospital and may not recover. Mustafa then begged Maria to keep the matter confidential, as their families are deeply distressed."

When Maria and Ricky got home that night and had settled down comfortably, Ricky took the opportunity to discuss their future plans for establishing the Maya foundation.

Ricky said, "Returning to Mexico could cause us both considerable difficulties. In your case the Far Right will be seeking revenge, and if *I* return there might be difficulties with the customs in respect of the taxi ride to Ciudad de Guatemala, the explosion and a concussed driver. The British Embassy might be able to intercede providing they're pre-warned. For you there is no protection unless you change your name. You know of my deep love for you, so this is a marvellous opportunity to ask you to marry me. I have no family ties left in this country and I'm quite prepared to settle down in whichever country we decide to establish the foundation."

"Darling Ricky, there are two conflicting messages in your proposal. I know you care for me, and I feel the same way. However, there are other factors to be considered. The essential point is that I must remain Maya if we are to succeed in uniting and strengthening the Maya people to achieve the same status and prosperity as the Spanish Mexicans. The other consideration is that I am host to a second spirit, Isis, who has still to play a vital part in achieving the Yax Nixte project. If her spirit can bring about the re-establishment of the old benign religion, then the way forward will be clear. One thing I can promise, once the foundation has been established I will marry you with the full Maya ritual. That is if you will still have me!"

"Then we must accept the situation and work together until we have achieved setting the foundation on a firm footing. *Then* we can settle down to a happy married life. Our plan must be to fly to Belize and enter Guatemala through Erudad Meichor de Mencos. Yax gave me lists of Maya agents who will help us should we wish to return to Mexico through La Mesilla or Cacahoatan. So tomorrow let's get down to the essential paperwork."

Even with the assistance of three agency secretaries, it took three months to complete the comprehensive reports covering the expeditions, and getting approval from the two governments with regard to their content. This had been achieved and the reports had been passed to the International World News Syndicate, so now there was intense pressure for lecture tours and personal appearances. All these matters Ricky happily passed to the News Syndicate to make the necessary arrangements in conjunction with David, but the lecture tour could only be established immediately after they had completed their first lecture to the Maya.

By this time it was clear that the Mexican authorities had political objections to the lecture being specifically for the Maya. Therefore, they decided to give it outside Ciudad de Guatemala in a large government hall normally used for major political gatherings. The Maya were to be given free entry, with seats being allocated through the Ruta Maya.

All the arrangements having been made, Maria, Ricky and Kirk took a flight to Belize, and after two days in that city, took a flight on to Ciudad de Guatemala.

Word of their visit had reached the airport before their arrival and large crowds of supporters greeted them. During formal messages of welcome, large bouquets of flowers were presented to Maria by Maya dignitaries. Then they were quietly informed that so great had been the demand for tickets that many Maya groups had had to be refused.

It was emphasised that the situation could be satisfactorily resolved if they were prepared to give two lectures, with a day in between, so that they would have time to recover. Ricky was delighted with the strong support and, after being given assurances that press attendance would be strictly limited to representatives of the local papers, agreed.

A noisy and ecstatic escort accompanied their journey to their hotel, and with local bands competing outside their hotel, it was long past midnight before the crowds dispersed and they could get some sleep.

The next day, when they arrived to give the lecture the hall was packed and the atmosphere was charged with excited anticipation. As Ricky mounted the stage and walked to the dais there was a momentary silence, then the audience jumped to their feet and cheered. The stewards, with difficulty, managed to calm the excited uproar sufficiently for Ricky to ask the audience for silence to introduce Maria and Kirk.

Ricky then began his initial discourse, covering the reasons for the expeditions and their proposal to establish the Yax Nixte Foundation in honour of its creator, then briefly outlined the various discoveries. Kirk then followed with details of the hieroglyphs, the translation difficulties and then provided a few selected quotations from the texts.

Then, as Maria entered the bright stage through a darkened doorway, there appeared to be a mist around her, shimmering as it met the light – it seemed to resolve into the tall and exquisitely beautiful Isis. Then, as she walked to the dais, the mist slowly dispersed and Isis reverted into Maria. There was a stunned silence – then the whole audience started excitably talking and shouting; the din was tremendous. After a few moments Maria stretched her arms out to them, and there followed an immediate silence as she declared, "I am a Maya, the sister of Yax Nixte, and I am grateful to have this opportunity to honour our ancestors, who are your ancestors. They were the first Egyptians and the survivors of Atlan who came to our shores in the company of the Olmecs thousands of years ago. Their message to us is to return to the old beliefs of a benign and intelligent society, and to educate yourselves to achieve your intended place in world society. ReRa the Sun God, the Spirit of Life, demands this of you and of your children."

Maria got no further – the audience cheered. It took a considerable time to achieve relative calm. Then she managed to continue with her part of the lecture programme.

The next day, large crowds assembled outside their hotel calling on Maria to appear, and this she did several times during the day, but much as she wished to walk among her people the crush would have made it too dangerous.

The day after that they repeated their lecture and, as Maria appeared in the doorway, the whole area of the auditorium was vibrant with anticipation. Then, walking a few steps forward, she was again Isis until she reached the dais, then once more Maria appeared and Isis dissolved into her body. There was a long hush, then the Maya people started to sing their ancient song of welcome to a returning prince. The air was charged with deep emotion and many of the assembled audience were openly crying, believing the arrival of Maria to herald their deliverance.

Once silence had been established in the hall, Maria repeated her previous address to a spellbound audience. As she completed her lecture the audience in their enthusiasm tried to rush the stage, but Maria slipped away and with a strong escort returned to her hotel.

But even larger crowds than before had assembled outside the hotel, some calling for Maria, others for Isis. Maria went out on the balcony and addressed them.

"I have a premonition that I will not be amongst you much longer as I am going to join my brother. Remember, the Ka of Isis will always be there to protect the Maya; this is her promise to us all. I love our people and am proud to have been born Maya and to take part in this great awakening. I am tired now and must leave you to rest. Tomorrow I go to Belize to arrange matters concerning the Yax Nixte Foundation, but will be back to stay with you all forever in a short while."

Next morning they made their way to the airport, escorted by crowds of happy cheering people. As they approached the entrance, it was lined with people and the path had been strewn with flowers. As Maria stopped to accept a bunch of flowers from a young girl, a man dressed as a priest thrust his way towards her and, producing a revolver, shot her near the heart. He tried to turn the gun on himself, but the crowd prevented him. "Why?" some of them cried. He remained silent. The crowd started to chant, "Kill the bastard!" A group of Maya activists rushed up and took control, dragging the now screaming assassin into a car, to take him away to a remote part of the mountains for interrogation and ultimately to determine the manner of his disposal.

There was no opposition from the police, as this murder was clearly an attack on the Maya people, and their action would relieve the police and government from attempts by the powerful opponents of the Maya to either silence or release the murderer.

While this was happening, Ricky was holding his beloved Maria in his arms as she was slowly dying. She smiled up at him.

"Ricky, I do love you so much, but this is why I could not marry you. Hold me close, I want to rest here, let my people bury me on that hill."

Then, heartbroken, as he cradled her in his arms, whispering tender endearments, he kissed her gently as she slipped away from him.

When the ambulance arrived, Kirk and the distraught Ricky accompanied Maria to the hospital where her body was taken from them and carried to cold storage pending the inquest.

As Ricky returned to the hotel, the Ka of Isis again entered his body and reminded him of her warning, and said that he must continue with the foundation, and undertake the lecture tour to obtain sufficient funds to support its development. When he returned to Guatemala, the tomb would be complete and Maria's body could be transferred to its final resting place. Soon after that, he would find a companion from among the Maya people who also loved Maria and her Ka would support that union. However, Ricky knew in his heart that the memory of their love would never die.

Then Isis told him a senior group of Maya were on their way to his hotel room and that he should trust them to take over the construction of the tomb, giving them an initial fund of one million dollars to cover both the land purchase and construction of it. A further million should be provided for the purchase of land for the foundation within sight of the tomb. The tomb was to be below ground with concealed access and a large plaque on the surface, honouring her as a servant of Isis.

The Foundation

AD 2004

After a hectic six months' lecture tour, Ricky and Kirk, utterly exhausted, returned to Guatemala City to be welcomed at the airport by John Goddard, David Cartwright and Susan Slade, who had arrived a few days earlier. David had secured suitable accommodation for them to attend the memorial service, and the final entombment of Kinuw Nixte – otherwise Maria Martinez.

After arriving at their new home, Ricky and Kirk postponed all business discussions until the following day to provide time to acclimatise.

The next day, after a lazy morning and a light lunch, they all settled down to their first foundation conference. Ricky turned to David.

"Firstly, Kirk and I must thank you all for arranging the excellent accommodation and also for your support at this stressful time. Now, David, for the record, are you able to outline your plans with regard to participating in establishing the foundation?"

"Ricky, I have arranged with my family to stay out here for three months, after that, subject to adjusting my home responsibilities, further visits may be possible throughout the year. A guest house reasonably close to the foundation would be ideal."

"David, that's absolutely marvellous. The guest house is essential and subject to general agreement it should be purchased or built without delay."

"John, what's your position?"

"After the excitement of our overseas operations, I was unable to settle down at home. So, as promised, here I am, and looking forward to joining the foundation."

"John, welcome from us all – as far as we're concerned you have never left the organisation."

"Susan, I'm delighted to see you here, what's your situation?"

"It's all very simple, wherever John goes, I go!"

"If you wish to join the foundation you are most welcome, and include that appointment in your minutes."

"David, as I understand it, the financial situation is strong for the immediate future. Can you give us a general outline?"

"Ricky, before you left the UK, the foundation's capital was approximately twenty-three point seven million. After taking payments for land and tomb construction into account, and income generated by the lecture tours, donations from societies, together with royalties from Kirk's book, our capital has risen to twenty-five million and is steadily increasing."

"This is a useful start, but our effectiveness will depend on maintaining a detailed cash flow, to be examined at a regular monthly meeting. David, can you set up such a system?"

"Possibly, but everything depends on finding local Maya talent. Incidentally, our computer equipment should arrive from the UK this week."

"As we all have a great deal to do, I suggest we close this meeting and reconvene two days after the entombment of Kinuw Nixte."

That night, Isis materialised beside Ricky's bed.

"Ricky, two Maya Elders with two resistance leaders will be visiting you early tomorrow morning, they will ask you if I have any orders for them.

"You are to reply, 'The Maya are to govern Guatemala by a bloodless revolution. Three months after the burial there will be a thanksgiving service for the life of Kinuw, where the multitude will sing joyful Maya songs. During this time, no grieving or bad behaviour will occur until the population starts to disperse, an hour before midnight. Then all exits of police stations and army barracks will be blocked by the people and lorries, and the Maya shall take over government buildings and TV stations.

"'The Ka of Isis will ensure a high level of attendance.

"'All those given details of the plan must swear an oath of secrecy to Isis, and breaking the oath will incur a very painful death sentence.'

"Remember, Ricky, I am with you always."

Then the manifestation faded away.

The next morning, a group of Maya consisting of Wak Tuyue, Popul Yipjay, with two leaders of the Maya Resistance, met with Ricky, Kirk, David and John.

Ricky explained the messages from Isis, then, turning to Wak Tuyue, added, "I've decided to hold an intimate dinner on the last evening of the Thanksgiving holiday for senior government officials and their wives, to celebrate the political link between Guatemala, Egypt and Indonesia.

"This will be held in the Marriott Hotel and will be a lavish affair with music, dancing and prizes, devised to keep them entertained up to the start of the revolution, and for their safety, we'll arrange for them to be detained. Wak, it would be of considerable assistance if you could recommend a list of official guests who should be invited, and include a few Maya officials to dissuade the party from going out on the street."

"Ricky, by the weekend you will have your list, complete with our formal invitation cards. Since Kinuw's lectures and the appearances of Isis, we have spent the last six months preparing for action. Now, by implementing her instructions, we will be assured of complete success. As will be the work of the foundation."

The discussions continued for a short period, then the visitors quietly dispersed at discreet intervals.

That afternoon, representative groups from the five Ruta countries started pouring into the city for the entombment of Kinuw. Since Isis's appearance and her promises, relayed through Kinuw, most of them had, by now, reverted to the benign religion of the ancients and, within the crowds, there was a general undercurrent of suppressed excitement.

The following day the four devoted friends collected the plain white coffin from the city morgue and, followed by government and Maya notables, walked slowly through streets, which were crowded with the Maya singing their ancient song of welcome to a returning prince. Once again, the air was charged with deep emotion, as the coffin was carried to its resting place in the hillside tomb.

Ricky and two Maya dignitaries accompanied the coffin down into the deep tomb where it was lowered into the sarcophagus, and then the heavy marble lid was slowly moved across to seal the opening and protect her Ba. As they climbed up out of the tomb, a massive concrete block was lowered down to close the entrance, then Ricky, heartbroken, placed a single rose on the beautiful rose quartz commemorative plaque.

Wak Tuyue then addressed the vast crowd of the Maya population.

"In three months' time there will be a memorial service to celebrate the life of Kinuw Nixte, and there will be two days' holiday period in the city. The Maya Foundation has given five hundred thousand dollars for the purchase of food during this time, to ensure that visitors to the city will not go hungry. All they ask in return is that the Maya will celebrate with happiness and singing to demonstrate our welcome to the spirit of Isis that has returned at last to our community. During this period there will be no demonstrations or disorder, only friendship to all our people.

"Wishing joy to all of our people in the name of Isis, I ask you, in the name of all the Maya, to prepare for the commencement of the memorial service and the holiday period."

At the end of the week, the foundation group were invited to a garden party with the Maya leaders. When they arrived, a group of Mariachi, playing traditional folk music, escorted them into a substantial tented area, where Wak and senior Maya dignitaries warmly received them. After receiving a welcoming drink, Ricky was introduced to selected academics and leaders of the Maya Resistance. When the introductions had been satisfactorily concluded, Wak took Ricky to one side.

"There are two matters I wish to discuss.

"Firstly, the interrogation of the assassin. It turns out that he was a Catholic fanatic and a member of an extreme right-wing group in Mexico City. They selected him for this task after promising that on his demise the Church would look after his relatives. He had not told them he had a terminal illness, and that he had nothing to live for except his religion. We obtained a signed confession implicating all concerned, and after that, I assure you, he died slowly in an extremely painful manner. Finally, he was cremated and his ashes thrown to the four winds.

"The second matter is on a more cheerful note – there is an

important member of our society, distantly related to the Nixte family, who wishes to be introduced. Her name is Sax Kinuw; she lost most of her family during the troubles in Mexico. When the Kinuws arrived in Guatemala City, I agreed to act as their protector. Can I call her over?"

"Of course, any member of the Nixte family, especially under your guardianship, would be most welcome!"

As Sax Kinuw walked over to join them, Ricky could detect a strong relationship to Maria and was instantly attracted to her. After greeting her guardian, she turned to Ricky.

"I am delighted to meet you, Mr McKay. Firstly to express my appreciation for your dedication to the task of establishing the foundation and also to express my condolences for your tragic loss, which I know is shared by the whole of our community."

"Thank you for those kind words, but my friends call me Ricky, and I hope you will include me as one."

"Of course, if you call me Sax! I have so many questions to ask. Perhaps we could walk a little way from the crowd in the gardens, but we must remain in general view."

"Excellent idea!"

As they walked together, it seemed to Ricky that Isis walked between them for a few moments, holding their hands, then she appeared to merge into Sax. He immediately realised she was the promised partner.

Sax's face had paled, so Ricky, gently taking her hand, asked, "What's happened?"

"I imagined the presence of Isis between us, and she took my hand. I was terrified – what does it mean?"

"Isis promised me that when I returned to the foundation, I would meet someone to replace Kinuw Nixte, and by this action she has given us her blessing. Do not be afraid, she is here for us both. We cannot talk now, let us meet tomorrow, one o'clock at the Marriott Hotel – there is so much to discuss. I will ask Wak for permission, and invite him to stay or provide a discreet chaperone."

"The apparition was truly frightening, but now, having been told about the promise, I am reassured, and delighted to accept your invitation."

The next day, Ricky met Sax with Wak in the hotel foyer, and there he introduced his wife to Ricky, who would act as chaperone. After Wak had withdrawn to his office, Ricky turned to Sax.

"Your command of English is surprising, and your slight accent most attractive. Besides Spanish, can you speak any of the local dialects?"

Surprised at his rather bland question, she replied, "I have a small import/export business in the city, which requires me to be fluent in K'iche, Tz'utujil, and Q'anjobal. I live with my sister in a bungalow outside the city limits and, without these languages, life would be very difficult."

"Sax, you have doubtless heard of my strong love for Kinuw Nixte. You may not know she had agreed to marry me with a full Maya ceremony, but only when the foundation was properly established. I now know this condition was to delay the event, as Isis had told Kinuw that in a short time she would join her brother. You must accept that I shall never forget my love for her. Having explained this to you, I am asking you to marry me, so that together we can successfully establish the Maya Foundation."

"Ricky, as Isis has blessed our union, I joyfully accept. Kinuw was known to me and I promise your love for her will never come between us."

Ricky signalled to the hotel manager who produced the champagne and joined them to drink their health and extend his congratulations to them both.

The following day, Ricky called an urgent conference at the foundation to which Wak and Popul were present. He opened the proceedings, saying, "Thinking about the effect of the revolution on the neighbouring countries, I am convinced we must take immediate action to prepare for the control and defence of our borders. Politically, as a first step after the revolution, we will call for UN acceptance of the new regime, together with the protection of our historic sites, but from past experience the outcome cannot be guaranteed.

"Over the last few days I have been comparing the military strength of Mexico and Guatemala, the findings of which I will read to you, and Susan will provide you with a copy after the meeting:

	Guatemala	Mexico
Population	9,000,000	86,000,000
Total Armed Forces	41,000	250,000
Army	39,000	217,000
Navy	1,100	26,000
Air Force	900	7,000
Aircraft		
Combat Aircraft	20	103
Naval Craft		
Patrol Craft, Inshore	3	
Destroyers and Coastal Patrol		100
Tanks		
Light Tanks	10	40
Battle Tanks		4
Naval Aircraft		11

"There is no possibility of stopping an incursion into our territory by any direct confrontation with our regular army units, but we can make any penetration in depth extremely expensive for the aggressor, by continual hit-and-run tactics by small units that disperse quickly in the mountainous regions. To do this we must obtain substantial quantities of explosives, mainly nitroglycerine-jelled derivatives, already a new and important Guatemalan product.

"From external countries, we require supplies of electric detonators, primers, cortex and high-velocity rifles that can disable soft vehicles and penetrate individual bulletproof jackets. These items should be available from our Russian contact as war surplus, in the form of Boys anti-tank rifles and Russian 14.5 mm A/T self-loading rifles.

"We are now negotiating with a supplier, and I propose to allocate five million sterling for their purchase. Subject to finalising provision of these essential stores, they will be air-freighted immediately on receiving our signal that the airport has been secured. Further supplies are being provisioned to follow when we control the country's finances, and confirm the levels of the existing military hardware.

"John, you are to be responsible for administration and liaison with the senior freedom fighters – Sax Kinuw is your contact with the arms dealer. I am sure we all appreciate that our arrangements must not be discussed outside this room."

"Wak, are these proposals acceptable?"

"Totally. But none of this must be committed to paper, and no interviews given to the press in this period of mourning."

"Right, if there are no objections, we'll take a vote to accept the arrangements as discussed.

"As the proposals are passed unanimously, the minutes are destroyed."

The three months passed swiftly by, and at the Marriott Hotel reception Ricky and Kirk were in conversation with a group of government officials, who were congratulating Ricky on the behaviour of the crowds, as in the past, such a gathering resulted in serious riots.

Ricky laughed. "The foundation can take no responsibility for their behaviour! This is solely due to the calming influence of Isis, as projected through Kinuw Nixte. Like you, we welcome the wonderful atmosphere in your city. But, gentlemen, as the dance floor has been cleared, let us now enjoy the party and organise the prize giving."

With the noise of the band and the brief riotous intermissions for prize giving, 11 p.m. passed unnoticed, until a worried hotel manager rushed up to Ricky.

"A large crowd is gathering around the hotel. At the moment they are too quiet, but anticipating a demonstration we are taking precautions and closing all the entries and exits to our hotel. If any of your guests require accommodation for the night, we can provide it, although it will be a little cramped! I suggest you keep the party going as long as possible until the demonstration, if that is what it is, disperses."

Ricky replied, "I intended to keep the party going to midnight anyway, so will not disturb my guests unless you inform me that the situation has deteriorated. If all remains quiet on the streets... I mean, perhaps they are just waiting quietly to watch the guests as they leave the hotel? In any event, perhaps you can arrange for telephones to be available at the tables?"

"Unfortunately, we have had some kind of breakdown with the hotel telephone exchange – we have tried our mobile telephones, but there seems to be a problem with the network. Although my mobile is in working order, I am unable to dial out!"

"This *is* disturbing! I feel you should be the one to advise our guests of the immediate situation."

The hotel manager hurried over to the band and, using their microphone, repeated the information he had given Ricky. For a moment there was a stunned silence, then there was an explosion of shouting and the manager was bombarded with questions.

Ricky moved swiftly to his side and took the microphone.

"As you are the guests of our foundation, I propose, with your agreement, to go down and speak with the crowd to determine the reason for their presence. Believing I have their sympathy, due to my bereavement, and with the protection of Isis, I have nothing to fear."

The Chief of Police stood up and shouted for silence.

"I have given my special police firm orders to deal with similar demonstrations, and they will, by now, have the situation well in hand. Do not concern yourselves; it will be quickly dispersed! The imminent police intervention outside the hotel makes it unwise for our host to enter the crowd, although I appreciate his offer.

"So, until the streets are cleared, let us continue, and enjoy the party!"

As midnight approached, the hotel manager returned and rushed up to Ricky.

"Wak Tuyue has arrived at the reception desk and is asking for permission to speak to your party. He seems quiet and respectful… in my view, unlikely to cause trouble."

"He may enter under sufferance, but the final decision must rest with our guests. Please leave us now, and wait in the corridor. When agreement has been reached, I will call you immediately!"

As the manager left the room, Ricky informed the company of his message, and asked.

"Are we prepared to receive Wak Tuyue as a guest, or should we refuse to hear him?"

The Chief of Police immediately reacted in a bucolic fashion, but ended up saying, "We might as well hear the beggar; anyway, if he is unpleasant, I will deal with him."

Ricky informed the manager. A short time afterwards, Wak Tuyue appeared and, mounting the bandstand, addressed the guests.

"Ministers, ladies and gentlemen, there has been a popular uprising and, without bloodshed, we have taken over the government of Guatemala. I can promise the safety of all present, but must insist that you remain in the hotel until tomorrow morning to avoid any

303

unpleasant confrontations. In the morning, you can return to your own homes, but for the safety of the state, you must avoid being involved in any political activity.

"In a year's time, when the government is firmly established, there will be a general election, which can be freely represented by all parties."

The Chief of Police jumped up.

"How dare *you*, an ignorant peasant, attempt to take over our government. We have been expecting this uprising for some time and have prepared a very strong reaction with our allies in Mexico. As a start I am arresting you, Wak Tuyue, as an enemy of the state."

Drawing an automatic pistol from a shoulder holster, he pointed it at Wak.

"Chief, look up at the gallery, and you will see a number of rifles pointed at your head. Any attempt to use that pistol will result in your immediate death and, unfortunately, a number of deaths among your colleagues. Providing you comply immediately, your impulsive action will be forgotten."

Realising his impossible position, the Chief of Police slowly returned the pistol to its holster.

"Now that unfortunate situation is resolved, I will return tomorrow morning with escorts to accompany you to your homes to prevent any incidents. In addition, you will be given a list of restrictions, which will apply until such time as we have successfully informed the United Nations that we are now the official government of Guatemala."

Wak waved to the gallery and he, along with his armed escort, left the hotel.

The next morning, Ricky gathered the foundation group to plan their immediate action, when Sax rushed in.

"Wak wanted me to inform you that the airport is firmly in the hands of our freedom fighters, or I should say the Maya army!"

"Sax, contact the arms merchant to despatch the goods immediately."

"Ricky! Last night, after Wak's announcement in the hotel, almost without a will of my own, I rushed to the telephone exchange and sent the message! Wak was very concerned, and thought you would be furious, but I told him you would understand that there are special influences at work. As a result, the consignment is due to arrive at the airport at midday!"

"That's excellent news, but why the extreme urgency? Presumably an attack to secure the airport, so John and I better go up to the airport and assist in preparing for its defence, while the rest of you stay at the office."

They arrived at the airfield just in time to see a well-worn cargo plane on its final approach. At this moment, Wak joined them.

"Ricky, I understand from the army headquarters, now firmly under our orders, that they have a battery of three Gun Howitzers. Purchased after the Second World War, these have only been used occasionally for training purposes.

"However, they could be of use at the border – fortunately the only gun crews are Maya!"

"Wak, get them to the airport at once. They should be concealed near the control tower at the end of the runway and, as soon as the dealer's plane leaves, detain all foreign nationals and airport staff in the airport hotel, under guard, and deny them any form of communication with the outside world. After that, we will have sighting shots up the runway, followed by an airburst! The airport must be closed for incoming flights.

"John, as discussed, after the gun trials, beehive the runways at three intervals and fill with amatol to make cratering charges. Bring the wiring back to slit trenches at one side of the runway. That should keep you busy!"

"Ricky, I'm on my way."

"Popul, can you organise a team to remove preservative from the A/T rifles. Use hot water, then lubricate the mechanism. After cleaning, restrict the issue to trained soldiers. The rifles are to be rested against wooden supports around the control building, ready for use against helicopters. If my guess is right, this is extremely urgent."

By four o'clock all was prepared, the defensive measures concealed and the airport radio restricted only to receiving mode. As a security measure, the air traffic transmitter had been disconnected. They settled down to wait.

About an hour later, they heard the familiar noise of the troop-carrying helicopters approaching. Circling above the tower they called up to request landing permission but received no reply. Presuming the airport abandoned, they came in to land beside the control tower. When they were a few metres above the ground, the anti-tank rifles opened up. Two crashed immediately, the third started to gain height but being a target for four guns, lost both power and control, and crashed on the tarmac, bursting into flames.

The crash tenders were quickly on site and covered the debris with foam. From the other two helicopters, twenty-four dazed survivors emerged. They were given no time to recover, were stripped, and put into workers' overalls to be held in a secure room under armed guard.

After recovering undamaged armaments from the helicopters, the airport tractor quickly dragged the damaged machines into a nearby hanger, concealing the burnt helicopter under a green tarpaulin to make it difficult to identify from the air.

Meanwhile, Wak interrogated the only surviving officer.

"You have entered our air space without permission with specialist troops and sophisticated weapons – what was your purpose?"

"We came at the request of your government to suppress a terrorist attack."

"Presumably your task was to secure the airport?"

"Even that should be obvious to people like you, but I will discuss this with you when we take control!"

"With plenty of armaments but no rations, I assume the main party is about to arrive? Perhaps we can negotiate peace with them? Whatever, we can talk about it tomorrow morning."

"You had better talk to me now, you won't get a chance later!"

"Thank you, our discussion is terminated."

Wak rushed over to Ricky.

"Now it's been confirmed that their main force is on their way!"

"Dress some of your soldiers in the Mexicans' gear, and tell them to go out on the tarmac and wave the air transports in!"

"When the sun goes down, switch on the landing lights. When the first vehicle is committed to landing, switch them off.

"The Gun Howitzers can open fire as the first air transports taxi to within two hundred metres of the control tower. If they make any more attempts to land, or the guns fail, John can fire appropriate demolition charges. At this stage, we must concentrate on inflicting the maximum damage to their force. Prisoners who fall into our hands are an unwelcome liability!"

John, excited and out of breath, rushed up to Ricky.

"Ricky, I have found a massive Mexican flag among the helicopter wrecks. It's far too large to fly from a flagpole and I assume it was designed to be a signal for the main force arriving in their air transports. If it's to denote that the airport has been captured, then we should put it on display, and if in the unlikely event it is used as a warning, they might attempt crash landings or divert to Belize or call off the operation."

"John, brilliant, let's display it on the tarmac beside the control tower and have our Mexican impersonators gather around that area with weapons slung over their shoulders."

"Will do! Wak has asked me to tell you reinforcements are being brought up as reserves; they will be held half a kilometre down the road. In addition, we have found four heavy machine guns in the wrecks in working condition and complete with ammunition. These are being sighted in concealed positions a safe distance from the runway to prevent troops disembarking from the vehicles."

"John, the flag is waiting for you!"

"I'm on my way!"

They did not have long to wait. The first they knew of the main force was a gradually increasing noise of jet engines from the north-west. Looking up into the clear blue sky they could see a formation of four aircraft, and as they approached the airport, it was clear they were large military transporters. Ricky turned to John and Wak.

"Do you recognise these aircraft?"

"From their size I believe they're Lockheed Turbo-prop C130 which I encountered when I was doing my training in the UK. If that's correct then they can each carry approximately four hundred fully equipped troops. So, at worst they have a force of sixteen hundred troops which, if they achieve a landing, could present a serious threat to our revolution!"

"Thank you, John, not a pleasant thought. As the guns are the vital part of our plans, would you go and ensure that they hold their fire to the last moment, and don't let up until those attempting to land are completely destroyed."

Soon the transporters were overhead and circulating the airfield. As they were clearly satisfied that their troops were in charge, they lined up for the final approach.

Standing behind the three Gun Howitzers, John ordered, "Hold your fire until I give the word! Then keep firing until the first two have been destroyed, after that fire air bursts fifteen hundred metres down the runway."

Then everything seemed to happen in slow motion. The first transporter appeared to hover over the runway, and then slowly descended to touchdown. Then everything reverted to real time, the engines screaming as the propeller pitch was altered, and the brakes applied to bring the speed down, then with the vehicle taxing towards the control tower, the second vehicle touched down. Waiting until the first was seen within two hundred metres of the control tower, John yelled, "Fire!"

Three twenty-five-pounder shells drove into the aeroplane, the nose crumpled away and a wing started to drop, followed by a burst of orange light, and then almost immediately the aircraft exploded into a fireball.

"Change target!"

The second aircraft started to swing off the runway to avoid the crash, but firing over open sights it was impossible to miss. As the craft collapsed onto its side, there were screams from the trapped troops, but with the explosion of ammunition in the hull, the transporter burst into flame and there were no survivors. The third transporter just touching down started to attempt a take off. As it was climbing away, one of the airburst shells exploded under the fuselage. It continued to climb and appeared to have suffered no serious damage, and then it rolled over and dropped vertically to the ground where it disintegrated in an appalling explosion.

"Cease fire!"

The fourth transporter aborted the attempt and climbed away to circle the airfield from a safe height.

"Wak, could you bring your reserves onto the airfield to demonstrate a large force. I want to avoid a further attempt on the airfield, either by a crash landing nearby or the use of paratroopers. In addition, I recommend you inform Mexico City that Mexican forces, without any provocation, have attacked our country and that a number of their soldiers have been captured. Subject to their agreement, we are prepared to hand them over to the United Nations for disposal."

"Ricky, I agree, but please stay here and sort out this mess. I will return to the government offices and start the exchange of messages with their President, and at the same time recall our ambassador."

After circling above for half an hour, presumably waiting for instructions, the Mexican troop carrier set off in a north-westerly direction and slowly vanished into the distance.

As Ricky and John were inspecting the crash sites and making arrangements for the bodies to be recovered, Kirk arrived with Sax Kinuw and Susan Slade, who, having heard the explosions from the direction of the airport, bullied Kirk into driving them up to be reunited with their partners.

"Ricky, I'm sorry to disobey your arrangements, but David is holding the fort and the combined demands of Susan and Sax destroyed our resistance!"

"Kirk, I fully understand and would have done the same. However, you've arrived at the right moment to call Popul over for a group discussion."

After reviewing the attack on the airfield, they then sat down to consider what might be the Mexican political and military reaction to their losses.

Sax Kinuw remarked, "As is well known, the Spanish Mexicans are a very proud people and will be ashamed of their failure to take the airfield. By now they and the UN have been informed of the bloodless revolution in Guatemala. Their desire for revenge will make them circumvent any advice or restrictions by the UN. The best way would be to create a situation in Chiapas with the Maya on our border, and follow alleged Maya terrorists into Guatemala. I fear for my people!"

Kirk replied, "I agree with that assessment. Clearly, we, as the foundation, must send an immediate warning to the active Maya groups in Chiapas and Campeche. Ricky, you have the Yax Nixte list of secret groups – select the most important near the border, and perhaps Popul can find a way to pass the information on our situation to them. In addition, we need information on troop movements heading towards the border – perhaps this is already available through the Maya Resistance network."

Popul replied, "We already have some contacts in Chiapas, but the selected Yax Nixte list of major group contacts will be properly protected and destroyed immediately after contact is achieved.

"In these times, those listed would face a death sentence if that information fell into the wrong hands. Regarding troop movements, that's already available, but will now be given special importance for the border areas."

"Popul, thank you for that. I only hold lists of the border groups in Campeche and Chiapas, the complete lists are held in my London bank. After giving you the information I will destroy the discs in my immediate possession."

"Yes Sax, there is something else?"

"Ricky, it is uncanny, suddenly I seem to know where the Mexicans will attack! The main column will be coming down the road from Comitan de Dominguez and will cross the border into Guatemala at La Mesilla. At the same time, their navy will land a light high-speed column of marines at Chulamar near to Puerto Quetzal. The attacks will commence at dawn in fifteen days' time. Our task will be to stop and block both columns for at least three days. Ricky, you will know what to do."

"Thank you, Sax, we have every reason to trust your sudden inspiration, and accept that it comes from a most reliable source! Clearly there is no time to spare if we are to halt and delay these columns. John, contact the Resistance leaders and select four teams of five of their most resourceful men to place explosive charges. You have three days to rehearse them before they start work! Kirk and I, with suitable escorts, will each take one of the routes to select suitable ambush sites.

"Our mission is to avoid direct conflict during the initial contact, by depending on the use of demolition charges to isolate their reconnaissance unit from the main column, and to render the route impassable for their transport in both directions.

"This plan will be executed by installing substantial explosive charges in the piers of the road bridges, wired to concealed firing points. The inspection panels are to be booby trapped, before concealing the opening with reinforced concrete. In certain cases, cutting or overloading charges are to be installed on central bridge spans, and camouflaged on the night before the invasion. Large road-cratering charges are to be installed with magnetic counters, concealed under road culverts. All this work is to be completed at night.

"That's our immediate plan for stage one. Stage two will be based on hit-and-run tactics, aimed at removing their officers from a distance, using our high-velocity rifles.

"Popul, could I suggest that your army commanders prepare for the defence of the city? In addition, small mobile attack units should be set up, ready to support actions outside the city limits. But do not inform them about our immediate plans for the irregular force until the invasion is underway.

"Kirk and I will set out on our reconnaissance at first light tomorrow, so let us return to the foundation and make the necessary arrangements.

The days passed quickly and by the night of the fourteenth day all the preparations had been made. Camped in the mountains at an altitude of two thousand metres, close to their first ambush site, Ricky and his demolition teams had reveille at 5 a.m. and after packing up and consuming a hurried but substantial breakfast, waited for news that the first Mexican columns had crossed the frontier. At 7 a.m. their border watch, using a mobile phone, reported that a column, headed by three light tanks and four armoured personnel carriers with a number of lightly armoured control and wireless trucks, had crossed the frontier. Half an hour later he reported that the main column, headed by four battle tanks, was also crossing the frontier post.

Taking up their positions in the misty morning, they listened with rising excitement for the sound of the reconnaissance party.

The Mexican advance column started up the steep winding road out of the mist-covered lower slopes, and the noise of the engines steadily increased in volume. Now Ricky could see the tank commanders standing up on their turrets, waving to each other and scanning the countryside with their binoculars. Having encountered no resistance to their advance, their exposure was foolhardy but understandable, as they had been lulled into a false feeling of security when passing through villages as the population had run out into the streets to welcome them, on the orders of the Maya Resistance!

At the ambush site, the road changed to a downhill gradient where it had been cut into the side of the mountain, with a sheer drop on the other side. As it swung away around the mountain, the road-safety barrier had been modified to fall when impacted. The last preparation has just been made to cover the road with waste oil on the far side of the curve, out of sight of the advancing tanks with their rubber-padded road tracks.

Ricky watched as the tanks accelerated down the slope to the curve until the first one hit the oil. They tried to steer round the curve but although the tracks responded to the clutch brake system, there was little effect and the tank hit the barrier sideways and tumbled over the side, then, as it rolled down the steep slope the turret broke away, spilling out the occupants. The second tank tried to stop before hitting the oil patch, but ended up half over the edge, with the crew bailing out just before it finally slid over the side to destruction.

Ricky looked over at Auispas, the local Resistance commander, standing impassively, completely fearless, who turned to Ricky and slowly raised his arm to signify all was ready, Then, with a quick glance at the column closing up, Ricky shouted, "Fire the main charges!"

With a muffled roar, a section of the mountain moved outwards, then gathering momentum, engulfed the road. When the dust settled the road had disappeared, and apart from the two tanks in the valley below, the reconnaissance party had vanished.

Auispas called to Ricky.

"There are four of the second tank crew coming round the bend! Do we open fire?"

"They are unarmed and of no threat to us. I doubt if they fully appreciate what has happened. Let them make their way home. However, we must leave this area immediately and join our unit at the main ambush site – if we move quickly, we will be in time to assist!"

Rejoining their transport they headed down the mountain tracks, as in the distance a helicopter came into view, flying up the road and searching for the advance party.

Arriving at the main ambush site, they concealed their transport and joined the Resistance fighters. Alacran, the leader of the group, shouted, "Ricky, what's the news?"

"The reconnaissance party no longer exists!"

"Fantastic! Now we will stop the main column, the battle tanks are slowing down their progress, but they should be visible shortly. Would you and Auispas isolate the tanks, while I close the back door?"

"Agreed, but remember you will have no more than five minutes to target the engines of the unarmoured vehicles, and then we must vanish to our assembly point to determine our next move. There is something else?"

"Yes, John has taken three of our party to close the road, some three kilometres away in the direction of the border by demolishing a bridge, and he should be back shortly."

"That was not in our plan!"

Ricky then ran quickly to the firing position for the two bridges and dropped down into the cover beside two of the demolition team, just in time to see the main force coming into view led by the four battle tanks with an infantry section sitting behind each of the turrets. As they approached the first of the bridges, two sections dismounted and ran onto the bridge to search for demolition charges. Finding nothing, they crossed over to wait for the tanks on the other side. The first tank roared across the bridge and took up a defensive position, and when nothing happened, the second followed, then the last two, with their infantry happily on board, started to cross the bridge. As soon as both had passed the first abutment, Ricky shouted, "Fire!"

The two bridges were enveloped in smoke and debris. When the dust subsided, it was clear that the third tank had reached safety, but its suspension had been damaged and the infantry riding on the back had vanished. The fourth tank was lying partly submerged on its side, in a mass of bridge debris. Until bridging equipment could be brought up, the tanks were now stranded on a small area of rough land bordered by steep slopes.

"Move it! Make for the assembly point, and watch the sky!"

Reaching the assembly point, they were welcomed by their guards. After ten minutes they were joined by the other sections, and a very dirty, but jubilant John and his two companions.

Ricky turned to Alacran. "Have you demolished all the targets and how many soft vehicles were disabled?"

"All our demolitions have been successful, at least ten vehicles are non-runners, but the occupants were busy taking cover so it is difficult to confirm actual numbers. As we had expended all our ammunition, we headed for our assembly point well within the five minutes!"

"John, what in the devil have you been up to?"

"Well, I had a strong feeling that not all the main column would be confined in the trap, so decided to investigate down the road for three or four kilometres. At three kilometres, we encountered a large number of vehicles pulling field artillery, one of the leading vehicles had lost its gun, and that was lying on its side in a ditch. We could not attack, so we travelled a further one or two kilometres, to where the road travelled alongside a tall cliff. Finding a good spot at the top of the cliff, we planted our entire load of explosives that we were carrying, in the hope that enough rubble would drop on the road to delay transport. There was no time to delay and we fired it immediately, there was one hell of a bang and the cliff seemed to split from top to bottom. There is now a deep mound over the road, and it will take weeks for heavy machinery to remove that pile of massive rocks.

"We immediately hightailed it out, as the noise must have been heard by the artillery column. When we were well on our way, two helicopters came down to examine the damage. All in all, we were very lucky and the fall of the rock face was totally unexpected – we had only intended to drop a small piece from the top of the cliff on the road!"

Ricky said, "So far we have successfully achieved our plan without loss, now we must keep on moving as the infantry will be out searching for us with the aid of their air force. Frankly, there is nothing more to do in this area, other than to keep watch on the road to Guatemala City in case they break through our blocks. Alacran, I must leave this to you, but please avoid losing our trained explosive crews, unless an action, risking their lives, can make a substantial difference in preventing further advances by the Mexican army.

"John and I are returning to the foundation to get news of Kirk, and to suggest to Wak that the UN should be advised that Guatemala has not yet utilised its military forces. Supporting this view, we will emphasise that all our actions have been carried out by freedom fighters in defence of their villages.

"At the same time, the military should be deploying their forces to block the approaches to the city."

Ricky and John returned to the foundation to find Susan and Sax provided with their own guard by Popul, and three Maya clerks to maintain a constant liaison with the government.

Much to Ricky's astonishment, news of their activities had reached the foundation before their arrival, even including the lurid details of John's unauthorised adventure. After the excitement of their return had settled down, Ricky explained that John's action had been essential to prevent a bridging company reaching the main column. A timely observation to prevent Susan scolding John for taking unnecessary risks!

As Popul rushed in with two of their army commanders, Ricky shouted, "What news of Kirk?"

"Kirk has fallen back from the beachhead and is preparing demolitions of the mountain roads. He has two of our best freedom fighter commanders with him, in addition to your two demolition teams. The latest report we have received suggests that the Mexican marines are moving up mountains on foot, and this action presents a considerable danger to Kirk's small party.

"There is a garbled report that he has been wounded, but all we know for a fact is that he was able to destroy the majority of their soft vehicles, and demolish a number of bridges. However, the situation is deteriorating as the naval units are now landing field artillery and armoured personnel carriers.

"I have ordered the army to send down a section of six light tanks, with supporting infantry, to establish a defence line overlooking a suitable killing field. Their orders are not to attack unless fired upon, and to provide a safe haven for Kirk and his companions. In addition to all this, the government has released a large sum for Sax Kinuw to purchase combat rifles and grenades for our new recruits, who are turning up at our military barracks in large numbers."

"What about the air force? A surprise attack on the navy unloading equipment seems overdue."

"We're waiting for the UN's reaction, and for the Mexican government to agree a ceasefire and troop withdrawal. Our time limit for holding back our forces expires at midnight. If they withdraw their naval attack, we will hold back our troops. If there is no reply we will assume that Mexico has declared war on Guatemala, and in that case we will defend our country and drive the invaders out into Chiapas."

Sax grabbed hold of Ricky's arm.

"Kirk is in trouble – we must get him out!"

"I don't need convincing. If you agree, John, we'll pick up some explosives, and with a party of resistance fighters reach the defence line, then somehow find Kirk."

"I'm with you, Ricky."

Sax put her arms round them both.

"You'll never find him without me, so I'm coming with you. We may need a lightweight stretcher – no, we *will* need one!"

Popul interjected. "One of our commanders will fix you up with your requirements and escort you to our forward position, then you are on your own. I wish you good luck and bring him home safely."

Saying goodbye to a tearful Susan, they left and were on the road within the hour in a Peep, a larger version of the Jeep, with excellent cross-country performance. Reaching the defence line that was frantically under construction, they dropped off the army commander and continued down the road towards Kirk's last known location.

The weather was clear and as they moved steadily down the road everything seemed to be unnaturally quiet – no animals, no birds – and they experienced a feeling of increased anticipation of an unknown that was waiting for them round every corner. John slowed the vehicle.

"I feel something is wrong, Ricky, can't put my finger on it!"

"I have the same feeling, pull up behind that bank."

Sax shouted from the back, "Don't stop! Turn off to the right, and drive like hell to the valley at the edge of that mountain. You'll find a covered place to hide the car, after that we travel by foot."

"Go for it, John, everyone hold tight, cushion the detonators and pray!"

The ride seemed to take forever, until at last they pulled into the little valley, then Sax yelled and pointed.

"Over there! Park behind that large outcrop of rock."

Ricky jumped out of the truck.

"Each of you take a sixteen kilogram backpack of explosives. Sax, you carry the detonators and stay with me."

"No! I must lead, that way's quicker and safer for us all, and we must hurry!"

Sax set off with her light load and it was difficult for the others to keep up, but twenty minutes later they met one of Kirk's party who took them into a small dimly lit cave, and Ricky rushed over to Kirk who grabbed his hand.

"No time to talk, their marines are climbing up our side of the mountain. I've set two lots of explosives, but not really enough, in the two clefts in the rock on the forward slope. When I got this, the chap carrying the detonators was shot and disappeared down the slope. We're not strong enough to fight them. Can you do something? There's very little time!"

"John, you take one and I will take the other and we'll fire them simultaneously using a twenty second fuse. Kirk, we'll be with you shortly."

"Sax, you must, with the help of his fighters, start getting him down the path now! Do not delay for any reason!"

As they placed the additional explosives they came under accurate fire, but mountain mist brushing across the slope gave them sufficient respite to complete the work. Then, sending their team off to join the others, they cut the fuses and with a shout from Ricky: "Light!" they walked back to join their party descending the mountain, just as Ricky shouted, "Take cover and look up!"

There was a massive explosion and the mountain seemed to shake, followed by a rumble from a landslide slowly growing in intensity. A shower of debris started falling along the path, but fortune was on their side and apart from a few minor cuts and bruises there were no further casualties. Halfway down the mountain they picked up the stretcher, loaded Kirk, and hurried on down the mountain to their vehicle. As they approached, Sax signalled the column to stop.

"Ricky, the Peep is being watched by three marines hidden behind that cover over there. They may have sabotaged the vehicle!"

"Sax, tell the fellow carrying the Boys Rifle to come over, then point out the target, and if anything moves he's to shoot. If they start firing, put two shots low down on the boulder's edge and hope it does some damage, or forces them to keep their heads down. While this is going on, I will examine the vehicle and look for any unpleasant traps left for us! Also explain that if all is well, I will start up and move the truck ready for a quick getaway and the fighters must rush Kirk to the Peep.

"The rest of you break into two parties – one section will run to the vehicle and take firing positions round the Peep, while the second section give covering fire to keep the marines' heads down. Then they will also run in, while the first section give covering fire, until we're all loaded. Then, as we start to move off, we'll commence firing, while the first section jump in and we return to our defence line."

The fighter with the Boys Rifle settled the bipod firmly between two rocks and after forcing the butt hard into his shoulder, watched for movement. Ricky rushed to the Peep, putting the vehicle between him and the marines' position.

Crawling under the Peep, he found pressure-type anti-personnel mines on either side of the road wheels, which he quickly removed. Climbing into the truck, he discovered two phosphorus grenades standing on the floor under the seats, with their leaded tapes removed. Taking them out of the Peep to the safe side, he turned the grenade into the horizontal position, with the base pointing backwards, then, taking his arm back slowly, he hurled it in the direction of the concealed marines. It burst, producing considerable flame and smoke. Repeating the exercise with the second, he started up the engine, then yelled, "Move!"

Within seconds Kirk was bundled into the back and his bearers took up protective positions as covering fire was laid down on the marines' position. The move then went like clockwork and, packed together like sardines, they took off into the open country as Ricky yelled, "Cease fire! Don't waste ammunition. John, check up how much is left."

"Very little. Spare mags are empty. Just a few rounds remain in assault rifle magazines. The Boys Rifle is out of ammunition."

The sun had just sunk below the horizon as they joined the road and picked up speed. Sax spoke quietly to Ricky.

"There's a group of our soldiers on the road in front, waiting for our return with instructions to eliminate us. We must leave the road at the next track on our left and detour round the army's defensive position. For the first two kilometres we travel at walking pace with no lights, after that we can continue with sidelights only, until we enter the city from the north, then return as normal to the foundation."

"Will do."

Following Sax's intuition, they arrived safely at the foundation and a doctor was quickly obtained for Kirk, who was weak from loss of blood and was immediately transferred to hospital for an operation to save the leg. Hearing of their return, Popul made a quick visit to congratulate them on their success in recovering Kirk, and his diminished group. After thanking him for his visit, Ricky replied, "Due to Sax's intuition we had to divert before reaching your defensive line, as we wished to avoid a small unit sent forward from that line with, we believe, the intention to eliminate our group. The reason for this action must be speedily determined. Who ordered them forward? In addition, what of the identity of the soldiers taking part?"

"We have no proof of their intention, but I must insist that they be returned to headquarters for questioning."

"Ricky, I assure you Wak and I have no knowledge of this. I'll go to the commanders with a suitable escort and bring them back to the city."

"Popul, the delay may have caused Kirk to lose his leg, and I insist on being present with Sax when they are questioned. I strongly recommend that your escort and the commanders consulted are Maya. In my view, your political opposition and Mexican right wing may have planned this attempted murder. Please take every precaution during your visit, and warn Wak before you leave. Firm friends are hard to come by!"

As Popul left, Sax, Ricky and John subsided onto the floor and, utterly exhausted, fell into a deep sleep.

Early next morning they were awakened by one of their foundation clerks.

"Wak Tuyuc is downstairs and wishes to speak to you urgently."

"If he can accept us as we are, ask him to come up."

"Good to see you all. Dishevelled but unbowed! Popul obtained the name of the commander who tried to escape, but was shot dead by one of his escort. The section officer has been arrested, but was so badly beaten he will need two or three days before he can be questioned. His section was not informed about the true purpose of their patrol, as they were ordered to destroy an enemy patrol probing their defensive position! However, they've been arrested for questioning.

"Now the good news. The enemy has agreed to a ceasefire, all units will remain in their present position until we can agree terms for their safe withdrawal. The conference will be in Belize in two days' time, chaired by the UN. Except for Sax, who will be our assistant, we would like you to advise our deputation, but to remain out of sight. Alacran and two of his men will guard you both day and night. Kirk already has a guard outside his hospital room, and is receiving the very best attention. I'm assured his leg will be saved, but I regret to tell you he will be left with a limp."

"Thank you for that, Wak, it's good news, apart from the leg, but I know he'll accept that without complaint. Regarding Sax, I believe she could become a target, if they hear of her activities. She must be specially protected and kept away from crowds, especially when travelling from the conference centre to the hotel."

"Ricky, remember she is a member of my family! I will do all that, and whatever else it takes, to ensure her safety. Anyway, I look forward to producing her for your Maya wedding!"

At the meeting in Belize City, Wak Tuyue, as President of Guatemala, was permitted to open the discussion.

"The establishment of the new government is fully supported by the Maya people who make up sixty-five per cent of the country's population.

"The change in government has been achieved by a bloodless revolution, the previous government was detained during that period, and the situation fully explained to them before they were released and sent home. It was after this that members of the ousted government called on Mexico to come to their aid, well knowing they no longer had any influence in Guatemala.

"We presume that the Mexican authorities had not been made aware of the actual situation and unfortunately did not believe the information sent to the UN and their government, prior to the release of the old government officials.

"To avoid escalating the extremely serious situation, we withheld our armed forces from engaging, while we negotiated a ceasefire to advise the Mexican authorities of the real situation. The independent and heroic action of a few, not more than one hundred village defence police, fortunately delayed the advancing invasion forces, thus providing sufficient time to establish the ceasefire.

"Two immediate problems have to be agreed – the withdrawal of the Mexican forces from our territory, and the establishment of good relations with the Mexican government to include a political treaty through the UN to guarantee the security of our joint frontiers.

"Regarding the removal of forces, due to landslides and destroyed bridges, it is impossible to recover the majority of vehicles. It will be difficult to provide food, so we offer your soldiers safe passage to march back to the border with their personal arms.

"Until the roads are cleared, we will protect the military equipment and the dead, in and under the landslides, from acts of vandalism.

"Subject to the conditions of withdrawal being agreed, we will raise no claims for compensation, providing the Mexican authorities disclose the names of the dismissed officials who made the fraudulent call to the Mexican authorities."

The Mexican delegation asked for an adjournment until the following day, to study the proposals. This was agreed and the delegates returned to their hotels.

Ricky was standing on the hotel balcony above the main entrance with Alacran when the cars bringing the delegates started to arrive.

"I have a foreboding that Sax is in danger. Go down to the entrance and defend her with your life! Don't worry about me! Go!"

Ricky looked round for something to cause a diversion to allow Alacran that extra moment. There were a few small pots containing cacti, and so, selecting one, he balanced it on the balcony rail and waited.

Wak stepped out of the limousine first, and held the door for Sax. The crowd started to surge forward against the police cordon to get a better view. As they started to walk to the hotel entrance, two men broke through the cordon, drawing revolvers. Ricky hurled down his plant pot, striking the shoulder of one of the assassins. The other, startled, glanced to one side, and as Alacran hurtled towards him, there was a flash of a knife, and the assassin dropped to the ground with his throat cut from ear to ear. The second assassin recovered sufficiently to fire at Sax but Wak stepped in front of her and took the shot in his chest. As the assassin was forced to the ground, Ricky yelled to Alacran, "Don't let them kill him, we want him alive!" Alacran moved in and, with difficulty, prevented the heavily damaged assassin from being torn to bits, at the same time shouting to the Belize police, "Papers will be presented demanding his immediate extradition to Guatemala for interrogation!"

A tearful Sax was bending over Wak, but Wak, seeing Alacran, yelled, "Don't just stand there, come over and help me into the hotel!"

As Alacran reached him, Ricky rushed out of the hotel, and between them they supported him into the hotel reception office, removing his bulletproof vest, and after admiring his heavy bruise, took him up to his room and sent Alacran to find a reliable Maya physician, much against Wak's wishes, but to mollify a very determined Sax.

The following day, under close police protection, Wak and Sax were escorted to the conference hall. After receiving a warm welcome by all the delegates, Wak took his place to hear the reply from the Mexican delegation.

Senor Miguel Lopez, the Minister for Defence and Internal Security, stood up and, after making the appropriate pleasantries, addressed the delegates.

"When we sent our forces to the aid of the previous government we were not convinced that there had been a popular uprising, and that this had been achieved by a bloodless revolution. The persons calling for our assistance described a very different situation, and, for political reasons, we do not wish to name them, as they have been firm friends of our country. Our latest intelligence confirms that no intervention is at present required. Orders have already been issued for the army to retire to our mutual border, and for our naval expeditionary force to fall back to their ships and return to our naval base.

"To resolve problems already mentioned regarding the recovery of wheeled and tracked vehicles, we offer the assistance of our heavy road construction equipment, which is at present operating close to the border.

"At this time we are not convinced that it would be sensible to undertake the treaty proposed, but after the promised general election, we are prepared to negotiate a non-aggression pact with Guatemala through the UN.

"We make no apologies for our reaction under the treaty negotiated with the previous administration, but it does emphasise the danger of making treaties with countries that have still to establish a substantial period of political stability.

Wak replied, "In friendship we accept the comments made by their minister, and express our regret that so many of your young men have been killed due to the existence of this private treaty. We were unaware of its existence until the Chief of Police referred to it during his brief detention in the Marriott Hotel. Apparently, our copy has been mislaid!

"The small number of your assault force that survived the attempted landing at the city airport will be handed over to the UN representative in Guatemala City, who will arrange for their return home."

The UN representative then adjourned the meeting for the agreement to be drawn up and signed by both parties.

With the agreement signed, the delegates returned to their countries.

David had already left to rejoin his family in the UK and John was undertaking the unpleasant task of clearing the airport of unexploded cratering charges, and the ammunition and rockets spread about the site by the crashed transporters.

A week later, Wak, Sax and Ricky set off for the Maya wedding to be held in Dos Pilas at the El Duende Temple and the bat cave complex.

Sax was dressed in a long blouse and a wraparound skirt. Her neckline was enhanced with a jade necklace, in similar form to the necklaces worn by Egyptian princesses in 2500 BC. Interspersed with pearls and symbolic precious stones, and with rods of black obsidian, it was held together with a network of gold wires.

Hanging between her breasts was an emerald green jadeite with the K'uh Ajaw hieroglyph, and from her waistband, suspended by braided silver ropes, was a small obsidian-bladed knife with a gold and silver composite handle.

Ricky had been persuaded to abandon his European dress for the occasion and was dressed as a Maya warrior, before the conquest, with a prince's headpiece.

They were attended by several hundred Maya dignitaries standing on the plaza, which was vibrating with the rush and roar of the waters racing through the underground network of caves after the recent rains. The atmosphere was magical as they moved to the temple at the top of El Duende Pyramid for the secret coupling ceremony. With the formalities complete, they returned to the plaza for the celebration feast.

Returning the next day to the foundation, they took a much-needed day's rest and reverting to their normal dress, attended the official reception in the Marriott Hotel.

Their honeymoon had to be deferred as the government had asked the foundation members to attend an important meeting in two days' time.

That night Isis appeared to Ricky in a dream.

"Ricky, I have told Sax about your agreement with Kinuw Nixte and she is also of the same mind. My Ka finds this behaviour agreeable as I know you do!

"It is now most important to construct a strong security fence around the foundation site, and to complete the site sufficiently to house your staff and guards."

"Plans are being prepared in Mexico by the right wing, in collusion with some members of the previous government, to infiltrate a commando unit into Guatemala City. They will be given orders to remove and then destroy utterly the body of Kinuw Nixte on Mexican territory. They are also authorised to kill all members of the foundation when encountered, except Richard McKay, who is to be captured and taken to Mexico. There, after treatment with drugs, they intend to hold a public trial, and ridicule you, before committing you to prison for life!

"To ensure the effective continuation of the foundation and the

Maya people, it is imperative you annihilate the whole of the force after obtaining the names of the supporters in Guatemala, who must be quietly removed from their houses at night and liquidated with the exception of young children who are to be brought up in an orphanage. These are drastic measures, but if similar attacks are to be avoided there is no alternative, as the loss of a few fanatics will help to secure the existence of the Maya nation."

Having said this, Isis took Ricky in her arms, held him close and said softly, "I do envy Sax," and she dissolved into the night.

After a blissful two days, Ricky and Sax joined Kirk (with his limp), John and Susan and attended the government conference. After Wak confirmed government appointments, he informed the meeting about the successful removal of foreign troops from Guatemala, and the steps being taken with the UN to obtain grants to repair or replace damaged bridges. He then called on Ricky to outline the position of the foundation and to put forward requests for any help from the government.

"Clearly we have to press on with construction work, in particular with site security. I have just received intelligence that plans to infiltrate a commando-type unit in our city are being prepared by a right-wing group in Mexico, in collaboration with some members of our previous government. It is reported that the object is to steal and destroy the body of Kinuw Nixte, and to kill members of the foundation!

"To annihilate the attacking force we require the assistance of the resistance leaders Alacran and Auispas with their teams that were so effective in halting the Mexican invasion. Government assistance is also required to facilitate the completion of the strong security fence around the foundation complex, by the provision of additional labour from the armed forces. At this stage, it would be unwise to bring in members of the previous government for questioning, as it might forewarn the plotters that we are aware of their plans. In conclusion, for obvious reasons this information, and details of our preparations, must not be discussed outside this room.

"Ricky, be assured you will have the full cooperation of our government, and we will establish suitable cover stories to conceal these preparations, for example using the re-establishment of the tourist trade. Any action you or your assistants take to destroy the perpetrators will not be subject to legal procedures, and will be fully supported by our government. The meeting is now closed – it will be reconvened when those responsible are utterly destroyed, as a lesson to those who might consider undertaking a similar venture."

Preparations to protect the foundation proceeded day and night. Ricky and his party established themselves within the temporary accommodation set up by the army for both them, the Resistance leaders and their sections, now designated the Royal Maya Guard.

In the afternoon, Ricky was talking with Sax when her conversation suddenly started to drift away, and Ricky saw her features change and meld into an apparition of Isis.

"Ricky, the commando unit is on its way, and will attack tomorrow night. They are trained killers and any wounded must be killed immediately. The commando with the yellow band round his arm must be taken prisoner, securely bound, and interrogated severely to obtain the names of his supporters. Understand I am always here to protect you and Sax!"

Isis faded away and Sax's features reappeared.

"Ricky, I seemed to have dozed off! Was it Isis?"

"Don't be alarmed, it was Isis, warning us to be prepared for an attack tomorrow night, and I must leave at once to advise the others. I think for your safety you should go to your sister outside the city until this is over."

"No! I stay here with you! No Maya wife would leave her man under these conditions! Anyway, Isis might have a message for you!"

At that moment, Susan and John entered the room, and before Ricky and John could say anything, an indignant Susan turned on Ricky.

"If what I thought I heard is true, what Sax has said goes for me too – I stay with John! It's not for further discussion, my mind is made up."

"Well, if that's the position, take assault rifles, and change into something more suitable, but remember – it's shoot to kill and make sure your target is dead! Are you still certain you can participate to that extent?"

"That is the agreed policy with the government. We both discussed the implications, and have accepted them!"

"There's nothing more to say. Get plenty of sleep, we must be prepared for twenty-four hours without sleep. I have some tablets from our doctor, which will help if necessary. John, from that Mexican ammunition dump issue two phosphorus grenades to each of us, for use if they break through our defences.

"I should have mentioned this before, but I have made an arrangement with Popul, our Minister of Defence, to order a military exercise tomorrow night. On my signal, they will fire flares high above our enclosure to illuminate the attackers, and enable us to engage, at an early stage, with our high-velocity guns."

The hours passed quickly and with the final preparations completed, and as the evening closed in, they settled down to wait."

As midnight approached, Alacran sent one of his men to search for any unusual activity; it was not long before he returned.

"A group of twenty to thirty men are assembling in the north, about a kilometre away. I used my night vision binoculars but was immediately detected, so I switched them off and ran back under cover."

Ricky turned to John and Auispas.

"Take grenades, tins and wire! Then trap the path at intervals! Return after six minutes, whether or not you have completed the task."

As John left, Sax grabbed Ricky by the arm.

"They're splitting into two sections, one will follow the path, the other attack will come from the east!"

"Alacran, take your sections and defend the approach from the east. "Sax, warn Popul in dialect that we will require illumination in the next few minutes, and to be ready for our signal."

"Susan! Where are you going?"

"To the path to give covering fire to protect his return!"

"Up to the security fence only! And don't fire unless *they* are under fire! It's too easy to make a mistake in the dark."

A few minutes later John returned.

"We only managed to put two traps out within the time, but it should be sufficient to signal their approach, and with luck cause one or two casualties!"

It was not long before there was a shout of "Grenade!" This was followed by two sharp explosions. Ricky yelled, "Sax! Illuminate!"

"Acknowledged, Ricky!"

In the distance they heard the cough of mortar fire, seconds later the whole site was illuminated with parachute flares. Ricky screamed, "Fire the Boys!"

Three of the raiders were killed outright when Ricky screamed, "Hit that rocket projector!"

Just in time they got a direct hit and there was a massive explosion. The flares died out and dropped to earth and darkness enveloped the site.

"Sax, tell Popul to wait for one minute, then illuminate!"

"Fire the heavy machine guns on our fixed line traverse!"

Then the parachute flares were re-established, and a rocket projector was fired into the security fence; there was a massive explosion and a section of the fence disintegrated. A section of commandos, screaming and firing from the hip, rushed for the opening through the machine guns' crossfire, and four survived through the fence. The firing was intense. One headed for Ricky, who picked up a phosphorus grenade and hurled it at the charging commando. Ricky's leg collapsed under him as the attacker was enveloped in flame.

Sax, in a fury, standing over Ricky, emptied her assault rifle clip into the commando, reloaded and calmly walked up and shot him in the head! Ricky yelled from the ground, "Auispas! Finish off the wounded now!"

Sax was on the ground beside Ricky, examining his leg. The bone had been damaged but the bullet had passed through. Bandaging the wound tightly, she laughed in relief.

"This will keep you out of mischief for a few weeks! You can now keep Kirk company and limp together!"

In the light of new flares now being replaced by searchlights, the regular troops were forming a ring around the foundation."

Alacran, followed by Kirk, making good progress with his crutch, came over to Ricky.

"Kirk refused to stay in bed and joined me. We made an excellent team and have killed all the commandos on our side, apart from one survivor with a red armband, who is suitably wrapped up for delivery. I've lost two of my men and three have light injuries."

"Auispas, what's our situation?"

"One dead and three injured, including you!"

"Alacran, we have got to obtain information from the commando leader. I don't care how you do it, but take extreme measures to obtain the names, within the next two hours, of the Guatemalan traitors. When you are able to inform me that you have extracted the truth, he is to be executed. This extreme measure is fully justified as, having a truce with Mexico, makes these the terrorists! Releasing survivors could be an excuse for the renewal of hostilities. As far as Mexico is concerned we regard this as an internal affair."

"I fully agree, but it's not much time… we'll try the magic mushroom, then further measures if required!"

Ten minutes later, Popul turned up with his commanders. After congratulating them on the defence of the foundation, and lamenting Ricky's wound, he informed them that, when clearing the area, they had encountered three commandos attempting to escape but, unfortunately, they were shot while resisting arrest. The cordon would be left in place until the morning, when the situation would be renewed in the light of day.

"In fact, you can all go to bed, and I have already arranged transport to take the wounded and our dead to hospital!

"The cremation of the enemy dead will start immediately."

Ricky insisted on waiting with Popul for Alacran's report on the interrogation, and two hours later Alacran returned.

"Our commando is now singing like a canary. I have made a rough list of the previous government members, which includes the Police Chief and the Minister for Defence, apparently. There was no written agreement with Mexico and the treaty was an agreement between friends!"

"Alacran, can you arrange with the RMG to raid their houses immediately, remove the families to the mountains, and dispose of the bodies, leaving no evidence. Try to finish the job within the next two days."

"Ricky, they'll be seized and transported before morning – all arrangements were made a week ago!"

Popul, Alacran and Sax took Ricky to hospital where the surgeons had just completed treating the injured and were waiting impatiently to operate on his leg. Before leaving Ricky, Popul commented, "It is proposed to continue our conference in two weeks' time, and if you're unable to walk, Kirk has volunteered to push your wheelchair!"

Turning to Sax, he said, "That should speed up his recovery!"

The days raced past, and the foundation members attended the reconvened government meeting, with Ricky and Kirk limping into the chamber together, and obtaining a standing ovation, followed by some ribald comments.

Then Wak, as President of the Republic, called the assembly to order.

"The purpose of this and subsequent meetings is to initiate long-term plans for a number of problems. The three most important for today's discussion are the security of the Republic, the Maya Prophecy, and the foundation development, with direct government participation.

"I know Richard McKay is concerned with all of these matters and we would value his comments."

Ricky stood. "In my view, all these items are directly linked – you have long borders to protect with a force that is a tenth of that available to Mexico. To combat intrusion we have the highlands and their defensive facility has to be enhanced.

"To provide for the possibility that the Prophecy will be fulfilled, we must encourage the population to develop shelters. If those shelters are linked into a defensive network and provisioned for defence, we will have a system that would deter any attempted invasion. With strategically located armouries, weapons can be drawn out by local volunteer forces, as and when required.

"Your immediate action should be to design and construct a number of defensive positions and encourage the locals to build shelters as satellites, as this would provide them with a national communication centre. Once the first installation has been developed to your satisfaction, the layout can be replicated throughout the highlands. This is a substantial task for all members of the Maya community, but we have six years to complete our installations and, providing we start immediately, we may be able to save the majority of the Maya population.

"Other countries in the world are apparently ignoring the Prophecy, but at the same time are intercepting asteroids. Guatemala cannot afford to join in with these exercises, but as shelters have protected people from these cataclysms in the past, it is the only protective measure within our reach. Even if Nemesis fails to appear, we will not have wasted our time, as we will have constructed a first-class defensive system.

"We have only six years to educate gifted youngsters, from the ages of ten to sixteen, and this work must begin immediately, either within the foundation or else in European schools. Eighteen-year-old students, who are already capable of taking the necessary entrance exams in science or medical subjects, must be offered subsidised university courses, providing they agree in return to utilise their skills for the development of the Maya."

"Richard, your proposals seem to have full support from the government and will be put in hand immediately to ensure the continued existence of the Maya."

Printed in the United States
111200LV00001B/114/A